ACCLAIM FOR
SPRING FOR SUSANNAH

"This is the kind of character-driven book many first novelists hope to write and few achieve. Richmond leaves the reader begging to know what happens next to her protagonists. More, please!"

—*Historical Novel Reviews, starred review*

"Richmond arrives on the inspirational fiction scene with a moving debut novel . . . The backstory of the emotions of a mail-order bride—a favorite among historical-romance readers—deepens Richmond's tale, and readers will be filled with hope that Susannah will learn the true meaning of love. Highly recommended where inspiring, romantic historical fiction is in demand."

—*Booklist*

". . . charming inspirational story about a man's extreme faith, a woman's bravery, and God's amazing grace. Catherine Richmond has penned a treasure in her debut novel, *Spring for Susannah*. She gives realistic details of life in the 1870s, works in a good measure of inspiration, and just the right amount of romance. This is truly a must read!"

—*FreshFiction.com*

"*Spring for Susannah* follows one woman's journey to the Dakota territory where she learns not only to survive the elements, but to also trust that God has a plan for her. I loved watching Susannah transform from a shy and timid woman who feels unworthy to a strong, independent pioneer in this new world. Filled with history and well researched, *Spring for Susannah* kept me cheering for these well developed characters until the very last page. Fans of this genre will welcome this refreshing read from debut author Catherine Richmond."

—*Beth Wiseman, best-selling author of*
Seek Me with All Your Heart

"Upon rare occasion, one discovers a book that sweeps you into its world so completely, you never want to leave. Catherine Richmond's *Spring for Susannah* is such a book, transfixing the reader with a tale of an unlikely love that whispers and sways across the pages like the grasses across the prairie, ripening into a heart's desire that touches the very soul. A stunning debut that will capture your heart and never let go . . ."

—*Julie Lessman, best-selling author of* A Hope Undaunted

"I can't remember being drawn in so hard by a debut novel. Cathy Richmond wrote an absolutely beautiful, sweet, funny, exciting romance. I fell completely in love with the hero and heroine. The shy, sweet Susannah who's been trained that a woman doesn't spout opinions or show emotions, and poor lonely Jesse who is dying for someone who will talk to him. It's full of passion and danger and humor and charm."

—*Mary Connealy, author of* Montana Rose

"*Spring for Susannah* is a captivating debut! Susannah's plight captured me from the beginning, and I didn't want the book to end. Catherine Richmond wove beautiful details throughout this novel, and I savored her wonderful description along with her story."

—*Melanie Dobson, author of* Love Finds You
in Homestead, Iowa *and* The Silent Order

"*Spring for Susannah* is a tender, realistic story full of memorable characters. This vivid portrait of life in the Dakota Territory will transport you into the life of a brave woman who must take the ultimate risk as she awakens to love in body and spirit. By capturing the earthly beauty of a good marriage, Cathy Richmond puts the 'inspiration' in inspirational romance."

—*Rosslyn Elliott, author of* Fairer than Morning

"Brimming with fascinating details and endearing characters, *Spring for Susannah* is as refreshing as a cool Dakota breeze. An accomplished debut!"

—*Dorothy Love, author of* Beyond All Measure

THROUGH
RUSHING WATER

ALSO BY
CATHERINE RICHMOND

SPRING FOR SUSANNAH

THROUGH RUSHING WATER

❦

CATHERINE RICHMOND

THOMAS NELSON
Since 1798

NASHVILLE   DALLAS   MEXICO CITY   RIO DE JANEIRO

LAKE COUNTY PUBLIC LIBRARY

3 3113 03078 7545

© 2012 by Catherine Richmond

All rights reserved. No portion of this book may be reproduced, stored in a retrieval system, or transmitted in any form or by any means— electronic, mechanical, photocopy, recording, scanning, or other—except for brief quotations in critical reviews or articles, without the prior written permission of the publisher.

Published in Nashville, Tennessee, by Thomas Nelson. Thomas Nelson is a registered trademark of Thomas Nelson, Inc.

Thomas Nelson, Inc., titles may be purchased in bulk for educational, business, fund-raising, or sales promotional use. For information, please e-mail SpecialMarkets@ThomasNelson.com.

Publisher's Note: This novel is a work of fiction. Names, characters, places, and incidents are either products of the author's imagination or used fictitiously.

Library of Congress Cataloging-in-Publication Data

Richmond, Catherine, 1957-
  Through rushing water / Catherine Richmond.
     p. cm.
  ISBN 978-1-59554-925-9 (pbk.)
1. Women missionaries--Fiction. 2. Ponca Indians--Fiction. 3. Dakota Territory--Fiction. I. Title.
  PS3618.I349T48 2012
  813'.6--dc23

                                2012010650

Printed in the United States of America

12 13 14 15 16 17 QG 6 5 4 3 2 1

*To those who went out to change
the world for Christ and returned
with a changed heart.*

"When thou passest through the waters, I will be with thee; and through the rivers, they shall not overflow thee."

—*Isaiah 43:2*

"Everone thinks of changing the world, but no one thinks of changing himself."

—*Leo Nikolaevich Tolstoy*

CHAPTER ONE

S ophia Makinoff had the perfect job.

Her students were brilliant, conscientious, and far too well bred to consider cheating on an examination. Sophia could, without impunity, allow her attention to drift. She opened the window with a gentle push. A breath of air, damp with a hint of this morning's rain and spiced with blooming lilacs, relieved the chalk-dust stuffiness of the classroom. Two flights below, a brisk *clip-clip* indicated a gardener neatening a hedge. From a distant music room came the strains of a Mozart sonata.

Behind Sophia, a student sighed.

The view was dominated by the east wing of the College, with its basement laundry, first-floor dining hall, and second-floor chapel, providing cleanliness, sustenance, and godliness. Across the lawn, a gasometer fueled lights throughout the College. To the southeast stood the gymnasium where Sophia had practiced calisthenics and learned the pastime of bowling, a game similar to the nine pins her father played at the garrison. She had walked the paths, attended lectures and concerts, visited the art gallery. But she had not left campus since Christmas.

Behind her, a petticoat rustled.

Above the trees the cupola of Montgomery Hill glowed, a light to the world. On days like this Sophia would serve tea on the veranda for diplomats and captains of industry, addressing topics from immigration to workers' rights. In the front parlor she would hold a salon as lively as any in Paris, discussing justice, reform, and an end to corruption in government.

Since the election of Rexford Montgomery to Congress, Sophia had made a regular practice of reading the newspapers. She could converse intelligently on subjects as varied as the Boss Tweed and William Belknap scandals, or the Grange Movement and Civil Rights.

Now if only New York's youngest congressman would—

"Mademoiselle?"

Sophia bumped her head against the window frame. "*Oui,* Elizabeth?"

"Oh, I'm so sorry. Are you all right?"

"But of course. With this much hair I am immune to injury." She patted her chignon. "How may I assist you?"

"*J'ai finie.*" The student handed over her examination, then leaned toward the window. "Was there something outside?"

Something? Only a world in need of saving. Sophia cited the College's doctor: "Fresh air strengthens the constitution."

The bell rang. The rest of the students turned in their tests and hurried off. They were all involved in planning a celebration of the US centennial. Sophia, however, was making other plans.

Rexford had been hinting all month. Last week he had mentioned the importance of spiritual compatibility to the marital partnership. She took the reference as a positive sign; they were members of the same church.

"Miss Makinoff?"

The geography teacher blocked the doorway with his corpulence and tweed. "Guest speaker in chapel tonight. From the Board of Foreign Missions. Interested?"

"Unfortunately I have another obligation this evening."

"Blasted Montgomery." His lower lip returned to its bulldog position and he let her slip by. His attempts at courting would cease once her engagement was announced. In the meantime it took all Sophia's restraint to keep from shouting from the rooftops: "I am to be the wife of a congressman!"

She hurried to the suite she shared with one of the English teachers. The parlor was empty. In the bedroom, chemises and camisoles hung from Annabelle's open drawers. Ribbons, lace, and jewelry lay scattered across the bureau. A stocking was draped like a silk bookmark over the open dictionary.

If the matron saw this, she would undoubtedly launch into her favorite lecture: the importance of housekeeping, setting an example for the students, doing one's best in this grand experiment in female education.

Whimpering and sniffling would ensue. Annabelle was easily undone.

Where was she? Surely she couldn't have forgotten they were dining with Rexford Montgomery.

Sophia exchanged her violet muslin polonaise for a satin dinner dress in sapphire that played up her eyes. The square neckline and Marie-Antoinette sleeves framed her gold necklace and bracelet, family heirlooms from her mother's side. The removal of a hairpin allowed a curl to corkscrew down her back.

The riding instructor awaited her in the corridor. He bowed. "Mademoiselle." The baron fancied them two of a kind, even though her father's title had been awarded, not inherited.

"Good evening, Baron."

"It is a beautiful evening for a ride, is it not? I could saddle Schatze for you."

"Regrettably I am otherwise occupied. You are too kind." And too persistent. Could he not see she was dressed for an entirely different activity than riding? "Please excuse me."

"That Montgomery gent again?"

Such questions did not merit a response. He and the entire College would know soon enough.

Sophia hurried to the south wing, to the apartment of Professor Montgomery, and knocked. Her intended would answer the door with an armful of roses, then drop to one knee. No, he could not take her hand if his were full of flowers. The roses would be in a vase on the table. He would speak poetically and she would say yes.

But first he had to open the door.

Sophia listened for footsteps on the carpet. Silence. She rapped with a trifle more authority, but no one answered.

Perhaps he had been detained and left a message. She would inquire at the clerk's office on the first floor.

She headed for the main stairs, where she found her way blocked by a milling crowd of students and faculty. Sophia leaned over the balcony rail. Below, in the entrance vestibule, Congressman Montgomery addressed an assembly of faculty and students.

". . . since you welcomed me within the bosom of this institution of female education . . ."

Sophia winced at his unfortunate juxtaposition of the words "bosom" and "female."

". . . the most worthiest of women . . ."

Oh dear. She must take up the task of polishing his speeches, lest his orations sink under the weight of florid sentimentality and improper grammar.

"Shouldn't you go down?" the Latin teacher whispered.

Yes, it would be wise to put the man out of his misery.

". . . whose grace and wit thoroughly enchanted me . . ."

The biology teacher glimpsed her pushing through and directed the students to clear a path. With a swish of petticoats and urgent whispers, the way opened.

"*Félicitations*, Mademoiselle Makinoff," someone murmured. "I'm so happy for you."

Sophia arrived at the base of the steps as the congressman reached the end of his address.

"May I introduce the woman destined to become Mrs. Rexford Montgomery—"

Sophia took a deep breath, pasted a smile on her face, and stepped forward into the vast, empty space around Congressman Montgomery.

"Miss Annabelle Bedlington Smith."

Too late. At that exact moment his fiancée stepped from the reception room into his waiting arms.

Gasps, murmurs, and giggles echoed around the hall.

In that weighted fraction of a second, as the blood rushed to her face, Sophia considered her options: retreat through the pitying crowd, stand and be the object of more pity, or move forward with all the poise expected of a graduate of St. Petersburg's Smolny Institute for Noble Maidens.

Momentum propelled her across the floor. Decorum and a tight corset kept her upright. "Let me be the first to congratulate you."

"Dearest!" Annabelle embraced her in an eye-watering cloud of perfume. "You'll never believe what happened! Rex proposed!"

Annabelle was right: Sophia did not believe it.

Annabelle Bedlington Smith did not meet a single one of Rexford Montgomery's requirements for a wife. She had no interest in government, spoke no foreign languages, hated travel. She never read the Bible, rarely attended church, and, in fact, dabbled in phrenology. And she was far too careless to run a house the size of Montgomery Hill.

Montgomery Hill. Sophia's breath caught. No carriage rides ending in the porte cochère. No arranging flowers on the sideboard. No receiving the movers and shakers of this world.

Sophia pressed her fist to her lips and glanced over her room-mate's head. The man knew better than to meet her eye. He looked down at Annabelle and his chin disappeared into his neck.

A weak jaw. *Quelle horreur.* How had she missed that?

"Oh, you're speechless! He surprised me too." Were those diamonds swirling around Annabelle's finger, or was Sophia dizzy? "Let's go to supper, dearest. We have so much to talk about."

Like engagement dinners and wedding dates. Trousseaux and bouquets. Receptions and honeymoon trips. Chaos in Annabelle's inept hands.

"I am sorry. I was coming to tell you, we have a speaker in the chapel and I must . . . my presence is required."

"I hope they don't need you to interpret, dearest. You know what a headache that gives you."

"I never get headaches." Until now. "Please excuse me."

But Annabelle would not release her. "Wait, dearest. I'm going to need a bridesmaid. Would you do me the honor?"

Exile to Siberia would be preferable. "Perhaps you should consult your sisters."

"Oh, of course! How could I forget!" She turned to Rexford. "I have three sisters."

Sophia made her escape. She moved rapidly up two flights to the chapel. Her hand pressed her heart, finding it bruised but not broken.

Rexford had made his choice. The suffering was his.

The geography professor cheered—or was it jeered?—when he spotted her. "Montgomery jilted you, did he?"

As the news of Annabelle's engagement made its way through the College, she was in for weeks of hand-patting, tepid tea, and *quel dommage.* Sophia lifted her chin and turned to the lady principal. "How may I assist you?"

The principal assigned her to serve refreshments. The rhythm of pouring and passing offered a certain kind of solace. Just before the hour, students filed into the pews. Sophia perched on the back row, awaiting an opportunity to slip away.

The speaker, an elderly woman dressed head-to-toe in gray, had served as a missionary to the heathens in China. Spiritual and physical poverty beset the land. The men were bedeviled with opium. The women had their feet bound.

Annabelle's feet were no bigger than those of a child. So much about her was childlike . . . or more accurately, childish. How would she manage, with her flights of fancy, to conduct a dinner party for twelve? She would never command the respect necessary to manage a household staff the size of Montgomery Hill.

"'Study to show thyself approved unto God,'" the missionary quoted. "My daughters, students of the College, have you studied to be approved?" She stared right at Sophia.

No, she had not. She had studied to please Rexford Montgomery, had studied to be mistress of Montgomery Hill. And all along he had thought of her not as a prospective bride, but merely as a convenient chaperone for Annabelle.

How foolish to look to a man for approval.

"How will they know lest we tell them?" the missionary went on. "Someone must share the Good News. Someone must speak the truth."

The truth. *Pravda.* Sophia's father always spoke the truth. His military advice had earned him a place close to the tsar. Alexander had even listened to Father's advice on freeing the serfs. But when the tsar took Sophia's classmate as his mistress, the truth endangered her father's life.

The missionary continued. "How many Chinese will be consumed by hell's fire, because you would not leave your hearth fire? How many Chinese will die in ignorance and darkness because you were too afraid of the unknown? What will you give, out of your comfortable life, so that another may live?"

Sophia was the daughter of Constantin Ilia Makinoff, Master of the Horse Guards and Speaker of Truth, may he rest in peace. She was not afraid. She would speak the truth.

Her back straightened, resisting the lure of repose. Perhaps her work would not be so earthshaking as her father's, but it might be more meaningful than teaching wealthy young women to better themselves with French.

And might she accomplish more as a missionary than as a congressman's wife?

"Who among you," the speaker continued, "is ready to go where the Lord sends? Who is willing to give up her life of ease for the rigors of mission work?"

China bordered Russia. Sophia could serve out her term, then return home. Surely the tsar would have forgotten her father's denouncement by then. Surely he did not blame Sophia. He was nearly her father's age; he, too, might die.

Besides, what other choice did she have? Stay and watch Annabelle take her place at Montgomery Hill? Unthinkable.

The speaker raised her arms and her voice. "Who will go?"

For the second time that day, Sophia stepped forward.

Chapter Two

The steam engine banged to life. Chains rattled and the stern-wheeler creaked ominously. The boat jerked, throwing Sophia off the bunk. Muttering imprecations that would discredit her both as a missionary and as a lady, she opened her eyes. Dim light from the window announced the sun had begun its rise. Further attempts at sleep would be futile.

Sophia pushed upright. Her valise and Catharine Beecher's *Educational Reminiscences and Suggestions* were still wedged against the door with its broken bolt. She pried her hairbrush, a poor substitute for a weapon, from her clenched fist. At the College, she had never locked her door. And now on this boat full of crude and dangerous men— Enough. Better a hundred sleepless nights than one more word from Annabelle about her wedding.

She peered through the curtain. A haze of humidity blanketed a mud-choked river. Misshapen trees, like those securing the boat last night, stippled eroded riverbanks.

Did her prayer book have a confession for impetuousness and rash decisions?

If she had been patient, or tolerant, or even deaf to Annabelle's constant babbling, Sophia might have waited for the Mission Board to send her to China. Instead she had accepted their first assignment, and now, less than a week later, here she was in the Dakota Territory.

The frontier would offer no opportunity to be a woman of influence. Perhaps God was disciplining her for her ambition to marry a congressman.

Very well then, she had learned her lesson. God could recall her from the Wild West and send her to China anytime.

At the tiny washstand Sophia poured water from an ironstone pitcher onto a cloth too thin to be called a towel, and washed the unclothed parts of her bruised and insect-bitten body. Considering the heat and humidity, the effort was woefully inadequate. She pinned a sachet to her neckline and consoled herself with the thought that she was not the worst-smelling person on the *Benton IV*. Unfortunately there was plenty of competition.

She gave herself a shake. *"Think on whatsoever things are lovely . . ."* or however that verse went. She must work harder for God's approval or she'd never be called as a missionary to China. Morning prayers would be appropriate.

In the name of the Father, and of the Son, and of the Holy Spirit. Amen.

What came next? Unfortunately she had packed her prayer book. How could she forget the prayer that began every morning of her twenty-eight years?

Sophia retied her corset, buttoned her skirt, and attempted to smooth out the wrinkles. She had altered her navy dress, turning the bustle into a pleat so that it would fit the confines of a rail car and stateroom. But she never imagined herself sleeping in it.

With a sigh of frustration, Sophia swept her hair into a knot and tied on a straw hat. Armed with Miss Beecher's book, she made a foray into the thankfully deserted dining salon. She managed to consume most of her biscuit and tea and read three pages before her peace was invaded.

An officer, whose mustache would do a Cossack proud, clomped in on mud-caked cavalry boots. "How do, ma'am?"

Sophia gave a pointed stare at the black felt flopping on his head. He snatched it off, revealing matted blond waves. Could this be the famous General Custer?

Sophia extended her hand. "Miss Makinoff."

"Lieutenant George Higgins, at your service." He piled a plate with ham, biscuits, and gravy, and poured coffee into a chipped mug. "So where you hail from?"

Sophia never knew how to answer the question. Russia? France? "Lately, New York."

He tilted his head, studying her as if she were an exotic species in a museum. "New York, eh? You one of those society ladies taking tea with Mrs. Astor?"

"Hardly." Sophia suppressed a laugh. "I am not Dutch or English, nor do I live on inherited wealth."

"So what brings you out this aways?"

"I am to be the missionary teacher at the Ponca Agency."

He raised his eyebrows and mug in a toast. "I'll be your neighbor, up the river at Fort Randall."

Hopefully not close enough to become a regular nuisance. "How far away is the fort?"

"Twenty-five, thirty miles or so." He refilled her tea. "Lucky for you the Dakota Southern laid tracks Sioux City to Yankton, else you'd be steaming twice as long."

His evaluation of improved travel conditions in Dakota Territory did little to encourage her. Sophia had embarked from the railhead with the hope of arriving within hours. Now she wondered if they would reach the Agency before Christmas.

The officer gestured with his utensils, leaving a spatter of gravy on his dark-blue uniform shirt. "Good thing you came out when the river's high, or this would be a real slow journey. My first trip out west just after the War, I rode the Missouri all the way up from St. Louis. Took seventy-five—"

The boat lurched to a halt. Again. Sophia slid a ribbon into her book and stepped outside. Lieutenant Higgins followed.

The fog had dispersed, revealing grass-covered hills running parallel to the river. The Missouri carried a thick load of mud and tree parts, but smelled cleaner than the Hudson. A battalion of swallows fought a losing battle with a cloud of insects. Several dozen men, most in red shirts and canvas pants, clustered around the paddle wheel.

"You miserable, empty-headed sons of—"

Sophia opened her fan with a snap.

The mate noticed her and changed his tune. "Lady."

Lady. The word raced through the crew.

Was this her calling as salt and light, a city on a hill, to dampen swearing? No, it would take more than a snap of her fan to please God.

Without profanity the crew resorted to work, leaving only blackbirds to squawk about the proceedings. Apparently one of the many stumps hiding in the Missouri's mud had entangled itself in the paddle wheel.

"If you'll excuse me." The officer returned his hat to his head. "I'll see if I can be of assistance."

Sophia doubted anyone could save the *Benton IV.* But an extended session of grunting, muttering, and whacking with a variety of tools led to a victory shout. The boat escaped the evil clutches of the submerged tree and resumed its noisy progress upstream.

At the bow two sailors took soundings and called the depths to the pilot. They entered a maze of sandy islands that changed shape as she watched.

Back at the College, Sophia had gone for boat rides on the Hudson—sedate afternoons gliding past mansions with manicured lawns. Wooden filigree-work touched with gilding decorated every surface of the boat. Uniformed waiters delivered cold lemonade on silver trays to guests seated in Windsor armchairs.

Completely unlike this precarious journey.

The boat jerked backward. Sophia took hold of the nearest support.

"Easy there, girly. Don't want to have to haul you out of the river." A thin man who reeked like decaying meat grabbed her elbow.

"Thank you, sir." Sophia lifted her chin, freezing him with a look that would do the tsar proud. He withdrew his hand.

"Be glad to fish her ladyship outta the drink," volunteered a thicker cad.

"I trust that will not be necessary."

"I'll hang on to you." A soldier swept off his hat, showing greasy ropes of hair. His wrinkled and patched uniform gave no indication of rank or unit. Grimy toes poked from one brogan. Was there no soap west of Chicago?

Her father would have had him flogged, but perhaps he was the best this young country could muster or afford.

Most of the ship's occupants milled about the deck and engaged in a deafening debate about the cause of their delay and several possible cures. Unfortunately Sophia's trio of admirers were more interested in her, the only woman aboard.

But she was a missionary now, she reminded herself. She should see Christ in every man.

She shifted her position, wondering briefly if Christ ever maneuvered himself to stay upwind from the unwashed. "Where are you men headed?"

"Gold fields," the civilians replied. "Custer found gold up in them Black Hills and we aim to get us some."

"Will the Indians object to your mining enterprise?"

"Well, if'n they do, we'll just bore 'em full of lead."

"Them Injuns just sitting on that gold. Not doing nothing."

"So, you out here visiting?" The soldier had a freshly blackened eye.

"No, sir. I am a missionary to the Poncas."

"Well then. God be taking care of you."

"And you, sir?" she asked the soldier.

"I'll be over to the fort, protecting you from the Brulé."

Surely he was incapable if he couldn't hold his own in fisticuffs.

Then the word registered, and Sophia's breath caught. *Brulé* meant "burned" in French. Did they burn as well as scalp? "The Brulé?"

"Fierce band of Sioux warriors. Ancient enemies of the Poncas. The Brulé swore death to them for signing a treaty with the Great White Father. They scalped a Ponca buck last week, out working in his cornfield." His eyes gleamed like the villain in a melodrama. "A few winters ago Brulé caught a family between here and the Omaha Agency downriver, killed 'em all. Only a little boy survived, ran across the ice naked, to tell the story."

One of the prospectors objected. "Hey, I hear tell it were soldiers done it. Raped the sq—"

The other slapped his bony hand over his companion's flapping beard. "Can't talk that way front of a lady."

"Nothing was ever proved." The soldier glared. "Them was from Iowa, anyhow."

Lieutenant Higgins charged up the companionway, halting the argument before it progressed to fisticuffs or knifings. "Hey, take that fight down to the deck," he said. "Maskell, you show your ugly mug up here again and I'll throw you overboard."

The *Benton IV* made a brief stop at the Santee Agency, munity with a church, hospital, and school. Indians neatly dress in citizens' clothes engaged in productive labor: tending gardens, planting fields, and carrying deliveries from the boat to their warehouse. Perhaps this assignment would not be so onerous after all.

Upstream tall, plumed stalks and an occasional tree grew on the sandbars. A lively river burbled into the Missouri from the south. White birds stood in the shallows.

"The Niobrara River and its town, nearest outpost of civilization to the Ponca Agency, where you get mail and such." Lieutenant Higgins pointed to the southeast bank where a cluster of two-story wooden structures lined a muddy street. Nearby fields showed signs of cultivation. "Some of the Poncas live across the river in Point Village." He pointed at the western bank, a buff and white cliff devoid of any sign of habitation.

He folded his gauntlets into his belt and clasped Sophia's gloved hands. His mustache trembled with earnestness. "Miss Makinoff. Any day I expect the Brulé to unleash their anger against the white race. Take care."

"Where might I buy a pistol?"

He laughed so hard his hat fell off. He retrieved it before it blew away. "Oh, Miss Makinoff. Never fear. One of the duties of Fort Randall is for me and the US Army to guard you."

At the present rate of travel, it would take two days for the fort to learn of and respond to any attack on the Agency. "Is there a telegraph line? Or do you use heliography?"

"He-le-og?" He blinked.

"Signaling with mirrors." *Apparently not.* "I am asking how you know when the Indians are on the warpath."

He shrugged. "Sometimes we see smoke."

So, communication depended on the vagaries of the wind. "May God keep us both safe, then."

The boat lurched to a halt at a broad opening in the first ridge. A roustabout splashed to shore and tied the boat to a stump. The deckhands swung the landing stage to the levee.

"Pardon me," Sophia called to a deckhand. "That is my trunk."

"Yup. And this is where you be getting off."

Lt. Higgins nodded. "The Ponca Agency."

This was nothing like the Santee Agency. No one met the boat. Two dozen frail structures, more likely to be victims of weather than protection from it, were scattered along a footpath. Weeds choked sparse gardens. A building with a bell might be a church or school.

Her second trunk joined the first onshore. Sophia searched out the captain. "Pardon me, sir. How long will you be staying?"

"Just long enough to unload. Got to make Fort Randall before dark."

Sophia hoped her face did not show her fear. "Well then. Thank you for safely conducting me to my destination."

"Hope you won't be cursing me for it." He seemed to recall her profession. "I mean, God bless you, and all that."

Sophia retrieved her valise from her stateroom.

"Hey, lady," yelled a roustabout. "Your turn."

He did not know he dealt with a seasoned traveler. Sophia brandished her bill of lading. "No. I have three more crates, another trunk, and two large barrels."

The mate spit into the river. "This here's more'n enough."

Thanks to Sophia's continuous vigilance, her luggage had made the journey by wagon to the depot in Poughkeepsie, across the country by train to the railhead at Yankton, by hired dray to the docks, then onto this steamboat. Most of it was destined for her students and for the mission.

She planted her feet on the deck. "I am certain you will find every item."

With considerable muttering, her shipment was finally located and unloaded.

"Come along, now. Can't be waiting for the tomahawks." The mate handed her down to the shore. Before she could thank him, he vaulted back onto the boat and swung the landing stage forward. The boat steamed into the current and headed northwest.

CHAPTER THREE

Will pushed the wheelbarrow filled with shingles and planks toward the house of Fast Little Runner.

Brown Eagle followed with the ladder and toolbox. "My sister is visiting."

"That's good." *That's bad.* "Your wives need the help."

"My sister does not have a husband."

Will grunted as the wheel bumped through a hole. "She'll find one soon."

"She likes you."

"She can do better than me."

Will knew it would never work between him and Brown Eagle's sister. The strongest joints came from similar timbers with matched cuts on each end. If he ever got married, that's the way he wanted it to be. Not the way it was in most marriages.

Will had seen how his brother carried the load in his marriage. Harrison bore most of the responsibility, while his wife, Tilly, entertained herself with shopping and fashion and teas. With the Indians it was just the opposite—the women seemed to do more than their share.

What Will wanted was a partnership. A joining of equals. Not much chance out here at the Ponca Agency of finding a woman who'd splice her life to Will's with any sort of balance.

"My brother says business is picking up in Omaha. I'll have to go back soon."

Brown Eagle shook his head. "Omaha. The city took an Indian name, but won't take an Indian."

Brown Eagle had the right of it. Back in Omaha his sister would be given the cold shoulder and her children shunned. Even if he were so inclined, courting now would lead to hurting later.

Fast Little Runner greeted them, then showed them a spot across the room. "The floor is soft."

No surprise, given the poor shingles the government had sent. They ought to issue buckets with every hundred.

Will crossed the floor, each squeaking step reminding him the wood hadn't had time to season before it was put to use. He knelt and probed the floor with his awl. The plank gave easier than a rotten potato. It was a wonder no one had fallen through.

Will handed the tool to Brown Eagle to mark where the bad boards had to be cut out, then headed out to fix the roof. As he propped the ladder, a loud thump echoed from the house. Will hurried back in as Eloise, Fast Little Runner's wife, dashed out with her grandbaby.

The ax head was lodged in the wall where it had flown off. Brown Eagle studied the end of the handle. Thank the Lord no one got hurt.

"Lousy allotment junk," Will said. "Throw it away." He handed the toolbox to his friend. "Use a drill and a saw."

"Boat!" Eloise called.

Will pulled the spyglass from his toolbox. A stern-wheeler. A new one from the looks of it, though with the wild Missouri, none of them lasted to old age. The letters on the side spelled out *Benton*.

And a female passenger. One foolish enough to come upriver. Too well dressed to be following a gold miner. Wife of one of the officers at Fort Randall maybe. The roustabout unloaded an assortment of trunks, barrels, and crates, staggering under the weight.

It couldn't be the allotment. Those boxes arrived empty.

Dear Lord Almighty, the lady got off the boat. She carried herself like the Queen, although weighing a few stones less. The boat pulled away, leaving Her Royal Highness standing, hands crossed as if waiting for communion. And the agent nowhere to be found.

Will would have to go try to make some sense of it. He left his tools with Fast Little Runner and loped to shore.

Sophia set her valise on a trunk out of the mud, then surveyed the village. The huts were reminiscent of the slums of the Lower East Side of New York City but lacked their stench. The air smelled of vegetation growing and decomposing, a whiff of woodsmoke, but no hint of bread baking or meat cooking. A shabby fence enclosed a stable and a pile of hay, but no animals.

She turned her head to listen. The low *cluck-cluck* of chickens punctuated the rustling of the wind across the prairie. No voices spoke, no one sang, no one called or cried. Villages destroyed during the Crimean War had more life than this.

What possible good could she do in the face of such grim poverty? Certainly God would not waste her talents by keeping her here, would He? She glanced back at the river, but no boat came to her rescue. She was stranded.

The sole two-story structure seemed to be in better repair than the others. It boasted a fence and the beginning of an orchard. Perhaps it was the agency house. Where were the agent and his staff? Had they been killed? Surely the steamboat captain would not have left her here if there was any danger.

A pair of children darted between houses. They peeked at her, then dashed closer, using other houses as cover. The black-haired one wore a tattered pair of pants. The one with a reddish tint to his hair had a cloth tied around his waist. What sort of game were they playing? And why, midafternoon on a weekday, were they not in school?

Oh yes. School. That was why she was here. Well, she would do her best to teach them until the Mission Board could send a suitable replacement.

An elderly man with a white tuft of a beard and a turban exited the nearest hut and shuffled toward her. A woman with an infant on her back emerged from the cottage behind the two-story house. More children joined the first two. A tall man with a long wave of dark hair ambled down from a large building.

Their round heads, broad faces, and dark coloring reminded her of the Mongol people. In contrast to the Santee tribe, the Poncas wore rags and scraps of blankets. The newspapers might call them "blood-thirsty savages," but they looked more like starved Russian peasants during the Time of Troubles.

The Indians formed a circle around Sophia and her luggage. Was this how it felt to be outnumbered, a minority? Sophia glimpsed the inch of skin, white skin, between her glove and sleeve, and felt the weight of coins in the drawstring bag at her waist.

No. She could never fully understand.

She held out her hand to the oldest male, supposing he might be the chief. "Good afternoon. I am Sophia Makinoff. The new teacher. I am pleased to make your acquaintance."

The chief and his people shrank away, whispering. Sophia heard a few guttural sounds similar to German. Most of the vowels seemed to be "ah."

"Does anyone speak English?"

No one answered.

"Sprechen Sie Deutsch?"

No response.

She tried again. *"Parlez-vous français?"*

Silence.

The Smolny Institute for Noble Maidens had trained her in appropriate forms of address for the myriad ranks of nobility. But nothing in her education had prepared her for this moment.

After three, almost four years with the Poncas, this white woman looked funny to Will. Pale as new-cut pine. Her cheeks were round, not all sunken in like people who'd been without food. And she wore a complete set of clothes, from shoes all the way up to a silly flower-covered hat too small to shade her face.

She conversed with old Lone Chief, who didn't know English, in . . . French?

Was she a Papist? The reverend would fly off the handle faster than that allotment ax head.

Her Highness stepped forward again, reaching out, trying to look them in the eye. The people drew back. Will looked over Little Chief's shoulder.

"Your gloves."

The woman blinked up at him, looked directly into his face with eyes as blue as the sky. The force of her gaze hit him and he, too, stepped back.

She spoke, and after a long moment, Will's brain deciphered her words. She said, "Oh, you speak English."

Yeah, he and half the people on this beach. But not with such a pretty accent. He cleared his throat and nodded at her gloves. "Yes'm. Uh, shiny blue hands don't look real to them."

Instead of quoting some rule of etiquette, Her Highness pulled them off. "But of course. There now, I am honored to make your acquaintance. *Enchanté.*"

Lone Chief made a study of it, keeping his hands tucked into his blanket. They would wait, for hours if necessary. Will had never seen such patient people as the Poncas.

The woman stood with her arm in the air. From the corner of his eye, Will saw the reverend finally emerge from his house.

Scurvy dog. He'd have to end this standoff. Will reached between Little Chief and Lone Chief and took the woman's hand in his big mitt. Soft. Smooth. Cool.

After a moment his manners overcame the shock of her touch. "Good day, miss. I'm Willoughby Dunn, the Agency carpenter."

"Pleased to meet you. I am Sophia Makinoff, the teacher."

"Teacher?" The rev had sent off for a teacher three months ago, when the last one up and bolted. Will hadn't figured on a another coming so soon, especially a woman, what with the trouble and all.

"Perhaps you could assist me. I need to arrange transport for my baggage. Is there a wagon for hire?"

Will had stopped listening to her words, hearing only the music of her voice. Seeing only the flutter of her eyelashes and the way her lips shaped the words.

"Reverend Henry Granville." The preacher, all fancied up, elbowed aside Standing Buffalo Bull. "My mother is at the house. Come, I'll introduce you."

The teacher said her name again. Will listened this time. Sophia? He'd never met a Sophia before. Below her hat, a knot of hair shone the color of oiled maple.

"Let's get you settled in. You must be tired." The rev tried to take her arm.

She stepped back. Her upturned wrist included the Poncas. "Perhaps I might meet the people I will be ministering to."

"Uh, well, they're not all here, the children, your students." All Poncas looked the same to Henry.

Will raised his hand. It's what you did around teachers. "I'd be glad to introduce you." He started to his right. "You've met Lone Chief."

Miss Makinoff slipped her hand into the old man's and dropped the first curtsy seen this far up the Missouri. They resumed their conversation in French.

Henry tugged on her sleeve. "Mother's putting supper on the table," he said. Will had never known him to miss a meal. "You boys—" Granville pointed to Black Eagle, White Swan, Standing Buffalo Bull, and Black Crow, all older than he. "Bring the teacher's luggage up to the house."

"Is there no wagon? The containers are heavy."

Standing Bear directed the young men, assigning two to each trunk. Will grabbed a barrel.

"Don't want to be left out, my friend?" Yellow Horse asked with a sly grin. "Impress the teacher with your muscles."

"What else do I have?" Will grinned back.

A tall man finally came out of the house, took off his hat, and bowed like a dandy. "Welcome. James Lawrence, the agent, at your service, ma'am."

Will barely recognized his boss. He must have spent the last few minutes oiling his hair, donning his coat and vest, and knotting his bow tie.

James directed the stacking of the baggage on the porch. "No traveling light for you, eh?"

"These are my personal effects." Miss Makinoff indicated the trunks. "The rest are school supplies."

"The government finally decided to honor their own treaty?" Will asked, earning a scowl from the agent.

"They are not from the government. These are gifts from my

former place of employment and the churches in New York." The teacher shook Yellow Horse's hand. "Thank you ever so much. And you are?"

"Miss Makinoff, you'll be wanting to wash up, I'm sure." Henry herded his prize inside.

Yellow Horse turned his palms up next to Will's hand. "He's worried my red will stain her white."

"Maybe you'll turn pink."

"Didn't work with you and me."

"My hide's too tough." They clasped arms. "Tomorrow," Will promised, "soon as we finish at Fast Little Runner's, we will put a roof on your house."

Chapter Four

A rotund woman raced out of the kitchen, her apron flying, her smile as wide as the river. "We are blessed!" She pulled Sophia into her embrace. "I'm so glad to have another woman around the house!"

"I am pleased to meet you, Mrs.—"

"Granville, Henry's mother. Call me Nettie. First names, please. We don't stand on ceremony here. Supper's ready." Nettie steered her through the kitchen to the back porch.

As quickly as possible, Sophia washed and dried her hands, then turned toward the kitchen. Behind her the agent and the minister scowled at each other, got into a battle of elbows, and managed to knock over the bucket.

Men! Sophia thought as the two maneuvered for position. She had been so long, too long, in the company of only women and academics.

"Boys!" Nettie dismissed them with a toss of her gray curls, then waved Sophia back to the room with the large stove and long table. The fragrance of chicken filled the room.

"Take a seat. I do all the cooking." Nettie paused, then continued with a certain amount of reluctance. "You're welcome to join me . . ."

"As teaching duties permit, I would be glad to serve as your *sous chef.*" At the woman's expression of incomprehension, Sophia corrected herself. "Your assistant. But I must warn you, I have little experience in the kitchen. For the health of the staff, close supervision is required."

The plank table had been set with white ironstone plates and steel cutlery. The red-and-white checked napkins matched the curtains. Sophia chose a seat by the window, giving her a good view of the action.

Coats and hats removed, the reverend and the agent attempted to barge through the doorway at the same time. When they realized Sophia was watching them, they paused.

"After you."

"No, no. Go ahead."

"Thank you." The reverend—Henry—the one with the thick beard, entered. He proceeded directly to the chair next to Sophia at the end of the table.

The agent, the tall one, James, considered his move with all the care of a grand chess master, then sat at the opposite end from the minister. Secular balancing spiritual.

Will, the carpenter, arrived next, taking the seat beside Sophia. Nettie sat opposite.

The reverend recited grace with thanks for the safe arrival of the teacher. Sophia crossed herself before the others opened their eyes, too travel-weary for a theological discussion.

Everyone at the table ate the chicken with their fingers. Feeling quite primitive, Sophia dispensed with utensils and did the same.

"Makinoff." Nettie passed the asparagus. "Could that be Russian?"

"You are correct. I lived in Russia until I was sixteen."

Henry choked. "You're Russian? What was the Mission Board thinking?"

"I wondered that myself," Sophia said. "Perhaps my experience learning English and a new culture will be of benefit to the students."

"Russian? Aren't they . . ." The reverend traced the shape with his fingers. "What are those onion-domes?"

"Cupolas. It is a style of building. The equivalent of a steeple."

Henry's scowl deepened. "You're Christian, right? The Mission Board wouldn't send us a—"

"Yes, of course. I grew up in the Orthodox Church, which is the keeper of the true faith since Rome broke away and Constantinople was seized."

This revelation earned her more frowns than friends.

"I have attended Episcopalian services since arriving in this country." And God had been with her all along, a detail of little interest to these men.

"Keeper of the true faith?" The reverend bristled.

"You speak good English." The agent interrupted with rusty flattery. "Been in America long?"

Sophia responded to the easier question. "Since 1870. We lived in Paris a few years, traveled a bit, then landed in New York."

James leaned back and studied her through narrowed eyes. "Wandering like a gypsy."

"I am most certainly not a gypsy." She straightened. He had never seen a Romani if he mistook her for one. "I enjoy discovering new places."

"I went to New York once," the agent said. "They were having a riot about the draft."

"Fortunately we arrived after the end of the war."

"You and—"

"My father. He has since departed this earth."

"I'm so sorry," Nettie said.

A thump under the table indicated she kicked her son, who choked out, "My condolences."

"Have you done any teaching?" James asked.

"Yes. Most recently at a women's college in New York."

"There's a college for women?" Henry asked. "What for?"

"Our graduates occupy a variety of jobs: physician, principal, author, lecturer, bookkeeper, settlement worker, chemist, editor."

Worry lines creased Nettie's forehead. "With a background like yours, you're probably used to fancy food."

"Not at all. The College believes simple meals are best." Sophia indicated her empty plate with a turn of her wrist. "Everything was delicious."

"Well then." Straightening her shoulders, Nettie brought out a custard pie and sliced it into pieces.

Perhaps having to share the food with one more person generated tension within the staff. Or perhaps the addition of an available female transformed them into rutting stallions.

Certainly she would do her best to turn their opinion around, in whatever brief time she might have to stay here. She turned to the agent. "And the students? They are all from here?"

"Pretty much." James rested his large head on extended fingers. "The villages shifted a bit over the years, but they've always lived near where the Niobrara meets the Missouri. The Ponca tribe today consists of 730 peaceable, well-behaved Indians."

"And how many poorly behaved ones?" Sophia could not resist the jest. The agent's face flushed, and she hastened to soothe him. "Perhaps I will have a few mischievous children in school."

"You will," Henry said. "Indian parents rarely exercise control over their children, believing they develop best if left to themselves."

James straightened, attempting to tower over her without standing. "I taught a class of seventeen girls and thirty-three boys in '71. We had no discipline problems."

"Coffee?" Nettie waved the pot like a truce flag.

"Is there tea?" Sophia asked before she thought better of it. The question earned indignant scowls from the men at the table. "Coffee will be fine."

Reverend Granville grabbed control of the conversation. "Our mission here at the Ponca Agency is to turn these Indians into Christian American farmers, prepared to assume their place in society as productive members of our great land."

He paused for a breath. "American?" Sophia asked. "Are they not American by virtue of residency on this continent?"

Out of the corner of her eye, she thought she saw the carpenter smile. James shook his head. "He means citizens of the United States."

"They are not?"

"No. Each tribe was a separate nation. But now, after the treaty, they are wards of the government."

"You must speak to them in English only," the reverend said. "Not French. And do not attempt to learn their language." He glared at Will, who stacked the plates and took them to the dishpan without responding.

"My teaching materials are all in English."

Sophia had more questions, but fatigue was rapidly overtaking her. The brief acquaintance with these men told her another opportunity would present itself soon enough.

The teacher stood. "If you will excuse me, please," she said. "It has been a difficult journey, and if I am to teach tomorrow, what I really need is to sleep."

"Seasick?" Will asked.

She shook her head, loosening a few curls from her hairpins. "I traveled the North Atlantic with ease. But this steamship . . . there was no way to lock the stateroom door."

At least she got a stateroom. Will had slept on a bag of flour, between stacks of lumber that threatened to crash down on him when the boat lurched. The guy in the next bedroll was on the run from the law in Indiana. The fellow on the other side had been jailed in Missouri for public intoxication and busied himself continuing the practice.

The staterooms had been filled with cardsharps and land speculators and no end of trouble. For the teacher to have arrived in one piece, she must have sat up all night praying.

Nettie put her hand on the younger woman's forehead, then nodded. "A good night's rest will set you right."

Grunting and groaning, James and the rev hauled one trunk upstairs. Will followed with the second. The room had a narrow bed, table and chair, and closet, but no chest of drawers. He'd done his best, but he couldn't fix where the planks didn't match, where the boards had warped out of plumb.

When they returned downstairs, Miss Makinoff excused herself and went to her room. The men settled on the porch.

James tipped his chair back. "New teacher's a beauty."

Henry grunted. "I wonder why she left that college."

Why, indeed? From what Will had read, Vassar had been built with every sort of advantage, all the latest innovations.

"Did you hear her ask Nettie if we had a water closet or bathing room?" James raised his whiskey-laced coffee. "Two bits says she's gone before Christmas."

"Before first snow." The rev snorted, then realized his mother could hear from the kitchen. "Sorry, clergy don't bet."

"By first frost," the agent said. "No, the next time the Brulé raid."

Will worked his knife through a chunk of wood, carving out a limberjack for Frank. Since he'd arrived in '73, three so-called teachers had tried the job. The longest lasted four months.

Usually Will didn't part with his money so easily, and it might have been wishful thinking on his part, but mixed with the fear in her eyes, he saw a spark of determination. "You're on."

CHAPTER FIVE

Smoke. Wood burning.

Sophia sat up in bed. Why was it so dark? And where was she?

The Ponca Agency.

She rolled off the prickly mattress, crossed the bare floor, and pulled aside the muslin curtain that had failed to bar the mosquitoes.

No fire this direction. No light at all. Merely darkness, and darker shadows from moonset. A rhythmic chorus of insects and amphibians echoed from all directions.

The distinctive smell of burning wood tainted the air.

Could that other tribe—the Brulé, the Burning—have set fire to the house? Sophia's hand gripped the wood frame of the window. No fireproof brick here. No iron doors or attic water-tanks. No night watchman.

Sophia exchanged her nightgown for one of her navy dresses and slippers, then stepped into the hall. Nettie's door was closed. Should she knock, report the fire? An unnecessary alarm would disturb the dear woman's sleep. And she certainly did not want to rouse the men.

The one with the thick brown beard, Reverend Henry Granville, might unleash a sermon on her. And the tall one, the agent, James Lawrence, also showed the inclination to lecture. Had the fine art of civil discourse escaped this place?

On the other end of the spectrum, the carpenter—Will Durham, Donne?—barely met her gaze, and spoke to her only indirectly. Yet he conversed easily with the Indians.

They all seemed to have a touch of ill humor, even Nettie. What manner of mess had Sophia gotten into? And how quickly could she extricate herself?

The smoke persisted.

Sophia's boxes formed a hulking tower in the parlor. She worked her way past them to the front window. No fire to the east, nor out the kitchen window. The stove was cool, its coals banked. The exterior doors were barred, and it seemed prudent to leave them so. Tenor and bass snoring echoed from the interior chambers.

Sophia returned to her room.

Now what should she do? The noise of unpacking would wake the others. If she had a lantern or candle, she could write to the Mission Board, request her reassignment to China.

A pang of homesickness rolled over her, but it was the convenience of gaslights she missed, not the College as a whole. Especially not Annabelle and Rexford. Off on their honeymoon to Niagara Falls, undoubtedly boring each other to tears.

Outside her window, dogs barked a wild anthem, starting all at once without obvious prompt. Sophia moved the chair to the window and sat with her forearms on the sill to keep from scratching her collection of insect bites. Still dark, no movement.

After several minutes the dogs stopped, again for no apparent reason, and the chickens started. Roosters, actually, several of them in a hoarse chorale. No sunrise yet. And no more smoke smell.

Imperceptibly the darkness began to fade. Sophia could make out a long ridge to the south and a bluff looming over the village to the west. A stooped elder, possibly the Lone Chief who met the steamboat yesterday, climbed to the top. He faced the sun and raised his arms.

He appeared to be praying.

She hoped he said one for her. Without her icon and prayer book, she certainly needed it. After a few minutes he lowered his arms and began a cautious descent back to the village.

Sunrise lit the roofs of houses, all of them at a uniform pitch like a factory town. Next to each stood an elevated framework reminiscent of the pergolas of Italy. But instead of grapes, these were draped with drying plants or laundry. A yellow dog trotted between the nearest houses, nose down, followed by a rolling trio of puppies. Farther away a child emerged, bucket in hand, and raced off toward a cow.

Where were the horses?

Morning's light revealed the monastic simplicity of her room: plastered walls, a painted floor, a narrow bed cobbled together with a few boards. Nothing like the carpeting and wallpaper of the College, or the tall windows opening to her balcony in Paris, or the gold-trimmed walls and inlaid floors of St. Petersburg. Even on military campaigns, her father had more luxurious quarters than this.

Most of all Sophia missed plumbing. Chamber pots were a nuisance, and washing up from a pitcher and bowl was woefully ineffective. How long would she have to endure such conditions?

A fragment of a Bible verse floated to the surface of her mind—something about learning to be content in plenty and in want. She should have paid more attention. A missionary ought to know these things. With a sigh of resignation, Sophia attended to hygiene, then went downstairs.

In the kitchen James and Henry, in shirtsleeves, served themselves from the stove.

"Good morning, Sophia! How are you feeling?" Nettie bustled about, apron fluttering over her poplin dress.

"Fully restored, thank you." She must not let these men see her as weak. "I smelled smoke earlier."

"One of our lost sheep," the reverend said.

Sheep? She had not seen any sheep. She frowned.

"Lost sheep," Henry repeated. "Like in the Bible. He sets fires for no particular reason, but doesn't burn anything down."

"He's insane," added the agent, apparently referring to the Ponca fire-starter, not the reverend. "But asylums don't take Indians."

"Chilly mornings he may need the warmth," Nettie said. She directed Sophia to the stove. "There's coffee, oatmeal, sausage, bread. And hot water for—"

"My tea." Sophia held up her tea ball, primed with her morning infusion. "How kind of you."

Henry blessed the food. In the middle of the prayer, the carpenter came in, set two buckets of water on the stove, then slipped into his seat.

"Mr. Dunn is chronically tardy, even to church," the reverend noted. "As the schoolteacher you may take corrective action."

It hardly seemed fair to reprimand the man for working. "May I also correct your grasp on your fork?" Sophia asked.

Nettie hooted. "I've been fussing on that since he was a wee pup."

The minister lifted his eyes to heaven in supplication, then rotated his wrist into the proper position. "After breakfast Will can hitch up the wagon to haul your boxes to the school. It's a half mile south. James will show you around."

Sophia nodded. "When does the school session start?"

James refilled his coffee. "Since you're here, today."

"Oh dear." There would be no time to unpack or prepare lessons. She consulted her pocket watch. "At what time?"

"The Indians don't have clocks, so when you're ready, ring the bell. Slow means school. Fast means Brulé."

Sophia started to help wash the dishes, but Nettie shooed her off. "Go along now. You've plenty to do setting the school in order and I've got Moon Hawk, er, Rosalie Nichols, coming to help this morning. Bring down your clothes and we'll wash while you're gone."

Back in her room the bed had not been made and the chamber pot had not been emptied. No lights. No plumbing. No servants.

For a moment she considered changing into a better dress, but with the Indians' dearth of clothing, she might seem to be flaunting wealth. And certainly she did not need to add to Nettie's workload. In view of the lack of sidewalks, though, she exchanged her slippers for boots.

The bed crunched when she sat. She unbuttoned the mattress. Straw? No, prairie grass. Considering the green hills surrounding the village, they had plenty to spare.

Her mind raced forward. What would she need for school? A true missionary would no doubt begin her morning with prayer, but Sophia had yet to unpack her prayer book and icon.

Below her window she heard a heavy *clip-clop*, accompanied by the rattle of harnesses and the creak of wooden wheels. She hurried downstairs to meet the dray.

Will loaded her baggage and his toolbox in the wagon's box, then hopped up beside them. James arrived after the work was done, in time to hand her up to the seat. He shook the reins and they bumped across the grass.

"Were you the first teacher here, James?"

"No, the year before, they had a lady, Mrs. Reed, for a few months."

"Then you taught until your promotion to agent?"

"I was sent elsewhere until my appointment this year. Others came here, but none stayed long."

Guilt threatened to choke her; she did not plan to stay either. "So the students have not had the benefit of regular schooling?"

"It's been hit or miss."

"Mostly miss," Will said.

James shot an angry look at the carpenter. "Even when we have a teacher, the Indians are not in the habit of following the calendar."

Will rested his arm on his bent knee. "Likely they're hungry or sick. Can't come in winter without coats and boots."

"I found the Ponca students excel at writing, speaking, and memorizing, but not comprehension," James said. "They are suspicious of strangers—"

"Smart of them," Will muttered.

"—but teachable."

"What would you say is the current rate of literacy among the Poncas?" When the answer was not forthcoming, Sophia rephrased her question. "How many can read and write?"

James muttered, then nodded east. "Miss Makinoff, your schoolhouse."

It was the same size as most of the houses, about twenty by forty feet, and painted white. A bell topped the roof. A pair of cows trimmed the lawn.

"It is new," Sophia said.

"The previous one was uninhabitable." James unlocked the door, then handed her the key.

Another change. No one locked doors at the College. A rush of hot musty air blew past.

"When was the schoolhouse in use most recently?"

"We had a teacher here in February and March."

"Three months ago? Surely children cannot learn in such

sporadic sessions." Sophia wondered, with a surge of panic, how long it would take for the Mission Board to send her successor.

"Government's breaking the treaty." Will pulled a rag from his back pocket and cleared the cobwebs, working his way around the partition forming the anteroom.

"With your experience," Sophia asked James, "could you not keep the school open?"

"My duties as agent fill the day." His expression hardened, a clear message that his assistance—and interference—would be limited. That was something to be thankful for.

"There's room for fifty students, but you probably won't see that many."

Instead of desks, the schoolhouse was furnished with long tables and benches in gradually decreasing height. The teacher had a kitchen chair and a desk made of packing crates.

Sophia closed her eyes for a moment, seeing her classroom at the College: her walnut desk and matching chair, shelves stocked with Pylodet's *Littérature Contemporaine* and Otto's *Grammar*, the wall map of France.

"Where are the maps? How can you teach geography?"

"I hope you brought your own." James pressed his finger to the space between his eyebrows.

"I did. Where are the bookcases?"

"No books." He rubbed his forehead with his knuckle.

"No books? None at all? No bookcase?" What would Catharine Beecher say?

"Tell me what size and I'll build one," Will said.

Sophia turned to Will. "About waist high, to fit under the— Is there not a chalkboard?"

Will pointed. "I can paint the wall black."

Sophia nodded and ventured a smile in his direction. This handyman was quite handy indeed. And innovative.

Sophia examined the packing crate desk and found it empty. "Where are the enrollment lists, attendance records, and grade reports?"

The agent shrugged. "Aren't any."

How was she to teach in these conditions?

At least she would have fresh air. Sophia attempted to raise the nearest window, but it did not move, not even a fraction of an inch. Was it painted shut? She made a fist. A strong hand caught hers before she could slam it into the frame.

"Locked." Will removed a long nail from the sash. The window slid up easily, then as swift as a guillotine, swooped back down to slice off her fingers. Will pulled her hand out of the way in time. He propped the window open with a stick. "Careful."

"Thank you," Sophia whispered. Perhaps her heart would return to its normal rate sometime today.

She managed to unlock, open, and prop the other five without incident. Then her morning tea made another need known. She walked around the building. "Where are the latrines?"

"There aren't any." James reddened. "The boys use the bushes and the girls use the ditches."

"Other way around," Will said. "I'll build you an outhouse. We'll unload while you . . ." He tipped his head toward the brush.

"If you will excuse me, I believe a bit of mushroom hunting is in order." Miss Beecher had not warned of this either.

Sophia availed herself of the opportunity. Her father's soldiers had built latrines wherever they stopped. Failure to do so was unsanitary, an invitation to illness. How could any education occur in the absence of the most basic of necessities?

When she returned, James had left with the wagon. In the yard Will reconfigured one of the crates to form a bookcase. He worked with swift, sure motions, at one with his tools. Sophia applauded. "Bravo!"

Still no smile. He lifted his chin. "Your students."

Three urchins of uncertain age and gender stood at the edge of the schoolyard. Is this what they wore to school, scraps? No shoes? Did they not know better, or was this all they had? At least their faces were clean and their hair braided.

"But I have not rung the bell. And this place needs a good scrubbing." Apparently also her responsibility. Heedless of her objections, Will continued his carpentry. So. Planning time had ended and teaching begun.

Sophia called to the children. "Good morning, students."

The trio shuffled backward a few steps. The smallest put a finger in his or her mouth.

"Come along." Sophia motioned to them. "Come to school."

They stared at the ground.

Sophia took three steps toward them, hand extended. "I am your teacher, Miss Makinoff. What are your names?"

They dashed behind a tree stump. Now what should she do?

Behind her a deep voice spoke in their language.

"Do they speak English?" she whispered.

"Some."

Some? Is that how he answered questions? Sophia turned to glare at him. One eyebrow gave a you-are-the-teacher twitch. What would it take for this man to smile? Perhaps if she stuck out her tongue—

"Did the Mission Board tell you anything about the people, about the Poncas?"

"Only that my job would be to teach reading, writing, the use of money, the Christian faith, sewing—"

"The Poncas don't look each other full in the face. It's not polite."

"They stared at me yesterday." Now that she thought about it, they had glanced away when she smiled at them. "Ah. But not my face."

"Put your hands down by your side. And wait. Quietly."

Sophia straightened her arms. After a moment a small hand—hopefully one that had not been in a mouth recently—slipped into hers. "Good morning," she said again, glimpsing the child from the corner of her eye. "My name is Miss Makinoff. Please tell me your name."

After a moment the carpenter said another Ponca word.

The child whispered, "Marguerite."

"Rosalie," murmured one behind her.

"Susette." Another hand slipped into hers.

Très bien. She smiled and, wonder of wonders, Will smiled back. Or perhaps it was another twitch, so quickly was it over.

"Have you attended school before?" she asked the girls.

No answer.

"We must prepare our school." She stepped into the building, the girls in tow. How could she tell them apart if she was not to look at them? She handed the bucket to the tallest, whom she guessed to be eleven or twelve years old.

"Marguerite," she said tentatively, earning a nod. "If you would be so kind as to collect some water."

To the next, perhaps eight years of age, she handed the broom. "And, Rosalie—no, Susette—if you would sweep."

And the rag to the littlest, estimated five years. "And, Rosalie, if you would dust."

Perhaps an unconventional start, but surely necessary. And housekeeping skills were considered part of their training. Marguerite walked away, swinging the bucket.

"Is it far, the pump?"

"It's a spring." Will handed her a tin pail covered by a red-and-white checked napkin. "Your lunch."

"Thank you." Sophia nearly dropped it. "It is quite heavy."

"For sharing."

"Ah, yes. The girls did not bring lunch pails. They do not return home to eat?"

"No." He started out the door.

"And you?" If he left he would not see her fail. But if he left she would have no one to answer her questions.

"Building your outhouse."

Will Dunn was a man of few words apparently. And for her, the bare minimum. Well, she was not here to win his approval, but to show herself approved of God. She had come for the children, who were busily stirring up a dust storm.

She guided Susette—no, Rosalie—in brushing off the tables and benches. And Susette in sweeping the floor front to back. All three girls had round faces, brown skin, and black hair. How would she keep them straight when she had more than three to remember? She would learn—immediately, it seemed, since Marguerite had returned with a full bucket and two other children about her age. The newcomers' hair had been cut ear-level, perhaps an attempt at shingling gone wrong.

"I'm Frank. He is Joseph." Frank's shirt and pants sported matching patches. Joseph's clothes seemed newer, but several sizes too large for his thin frame. Neither had shoes. "We go to school here. In May."

"May? I thought Mr. Lawrence said March."

The boy watched Rosalie wipe. "Yes. March. The month of sore eyes."

"Sore eyes?"

Now he stared at Susette. "From the snow."

"Ah, from the sunlight. I understand. Yesterday I had sore eyes from the sun on the river." Sophia shook the rag out. "If you boys will help Marguerite wash the windows, our school will be ready."

Sophia distributed the supplies from the first box. The ledger went on her desk, the slates on the tables, and the McGuffey

Readers went on the new shelf. She must take attendance as soon as she found a pencil. Perhaps in the other box.

"Books!" Susette let the broom clatter to the floor.

The four older children raced to the shelf, chose a reader, and flipped the pages. They chattered over the simple drawings like a flock of birds feeding on scattered bread crumbs.

Rosalie dropped the rag. Her eyes widened and her mouth formed a little circle. Slow steps brought her to the front of the room. Her hand stretched toward one of the readers on the shelf and stroked the cover. Then she brought the book to her face, breathed in its smell, and rubbed it against her cheek. With a glance at the others, she opened it. "Oooh!"

The library at the College contained over ten thousand volumes. Texts and reference books stocked each classroom. Shelves of favorite books graced every parlor. Yet none of those generated a fraction of the reverence received by a simple reader in the Ponca Agency school.

Ressaisis-toi, mon Dieu! Succumbing to tears would undermine her authority.

The chattering continued. "English, please," Sophia said. "Frank and Joseph, you are to help Marguerite."

The boys looked at each other then the floor. Finally Frank informed her, "Women's work."

An argument used by men the world over. Sophia shook her head. "Schoolwork. Marguerite, give the bucket to Frank. The next window is his. And the last is Joseph's. Rosalie, please return the book to the shelf and take a seat at the first table."

Whether from lack of English proficiency or defiance, none of the children did as she asked. Sophia took the bucket from Marguerite and passed it to Frank. Guiding his hands, she helped the boy squeeze out the rag, wipe off the first pane, and rinse. "Now finish the rest, then hand it to Joseph."

"I am Joseph."

Sophia bit her lip and narrowed her eyes. She looked him up and down. The patches. "You told me your name is Frank."

The boy nodded. "Teacher smart."

"The last teacher didn't bother to learn their names," Will said from the doorway.

Sophia jumped. The open-door policy, necessary in the summer heat, would require some adjustment. "I can see how that would take a certain amount of discernment."

He frowned at Joseph, engrossed in the sounds a wet rag made on glass. "Ponca men don't do housework."

"I have been so informed. Fortunately, this is schoolwork. May I help you with anything else?"

"Where do you want your outhouse?"

"At least twenty paces downwind. Unless . . . I am sorry, I do not know the geologic term. Will you dig into water?"

"Not likely." He returned to the yard. Out of the corner of her eye—the part that would get the most use apparently—she saw him pace off and mark a spot with the heel of his boot. A man with waist-length black hair began shoveling.

Now, she must be about her own work. The children had smeared the dirt on the windows, leaving dark streaks running down the wall to puddle on the floor. They should wash their hands before handling books.

Rosalie tugged on Sophia's skirt. "Water? Drink?"

"Certainly." Sophia looked around. Had she used the drinking water bucket for chores? It should be washed. Thoroughly.

She clapped her hands twice. "Students. Form a line. We will walk to the spring."

The line looked more like a pile, with the boys elbowing each other and bumping into the girls. Sophia set them in order, then directed Marguerite to lead the way.

"Leaving already?" Will asked from his work site. Besides the man shoveling, two others sawed planks.

"To the spring." In that brief moment while she was distracted, the line fell apart. The boys raced ahead. Little Rosalie lagged behind. Sophia opened her mouth to reprimand the children but reconsidered. Was order necessary to become an American or a Christian?

Well, church members lined up for communion. Men lined up to vote. All right, then, she would teach them to form a line. As soon as she caught them.

The path passed by a house. It had been built the same size as the others, then a newer addition set perpendicular had almost doubled it. Several rags, laundry perhaps, fluttered in the wind on the pergola. Yellow puppies scampered out from beneath the steps to greet the children.

"Whose house is this?"

No one answered.

"Who lives here?"

Five voices said, "Me."

Ah! They looked alike because they were related. "So you are brothers and sisters?"

No one responded.

"You are family? With the same mother and father?"

"No," Susette said. "Yes. Uncle."

All these children lived in one house with just an uncle to supervise them? No wonder they were so poorly dressed. Perhaps the clothing the church ladies sent could be put to use.

The spring burbled from the bluff behind the house. Marguerite scoured the bucket with gravel, then rinsed three times. The children all drank from the spring, which seemed a good idea until Sophia drenched her skirt.

"Frank. Joseph," she called to the boys. "Do not leave Marguerite to do all the work."

"Women's work."

Apparently their only sentence in English. She raised an eyebrow. "Perhaps you are not as strong as Marguerite. Your arms cannot lift the bucket, even if two of you carry it."

They rose to the challenge, growling and snatching the handle. Half the water splashed out and the lesson on walking in line was postponed yet again.

Will's dark eyes lifted from his hammering to watch her return. Would his expression change if he hit his thumb?

"All right, students. Please take your seats." She guided Rosalie to the first bench. The older girls sat in the next row and the boys took the last. The teacher she had spoken with in New York—had it been only last month?—recommended starting with the youngest for recitations. But what could this little one know? "Frank, we will start with you. Stand up and—"

Rosalie tugged her skirt. "Hungry."

Sophia consulted her pocket watch. "Yes, it is lunchtime. Did anyone bring food? Is anyone going home to eat?"

The students stared at the pail. Once again the carpenter was right.

"Since it is a beautiful day, let us eat outside. Form a line." This they did with a minimum of wiggling, testimony to the motivating power of food. Sophia led them to a shady spot on the opposite side from the latrine project. She swept her boots through the grass. "Are there any snakes out here?"

Will called, "No poisonous ones."

Remarkably good hearing. Quite annoying.

Sophia distributed the bread and cheese, then hesitated. Should she not say grace? She had heard prayers before every meal at the College, but never had to say one.

Perhaps she could ask one of the children to say thanks. But no, they were nearly finished.

Oh dear. What sort of missionary forgot to say grace?

Chapter Six

There is a spark of God in everyone.

Will believed that. And he believed God wanted His people to look for that spark in others. But he hadn't really expected to find it in Miss Sophia Makinoff, an obvious member of the upper crust.

Yes, she was pretty, with her pink cheeks and all. Like gingerbread trim on a house—fancy but of no real use.

Still, she hadn't quit at first sight of the village. And she hadn't pulled away when the children touched her. Then finally, this afternoon, as he built her outhouse, he found the spark. He paused in his hammering to listen. She had a voice. She could sing.

The Poncas sang—with enthusiasm. Although, over the past three years he'd been living here, most of what he'd heard was mourning songs. But the teacher . . .

She stopped singing to point out a drawing of a lamb in the McGuffey Reader, then the picture in the front of the room of Jesus carrying a sheep. Since the people didn't have sheep, she had a bit of explaining to do. Which she did with her pretty way of speaking, with pauses as she searched for the right word and different ways of saying her vowels.

Henry worried the children might pick up some foreign language. To Will's mind Russian would be a far sight better than what they'd heard from the previous schoolmaster. He had turned the air blue with his cursing, never used polite words, and—

Yellow Spotted Buffalo passed him a plank. His coworker didn't say a word, just raised his right eyebrow a sixteenth of an inch and let the end of the board thump into Will's palm, meaning "Get back to work."

"Please sing!" Rosalie asked. Good girl.

Miss Makinoff started in again with the children this time. Then she stopped. After a bit, he heard the *plink, plink* of a stringed instrument. Yellow Spotted Buffalo looked at Will, then at Brown Eagle and Long Runner. In a flash all four men dashed over to the windows.

The teacher looked up, surprised but showing no fear. Long Runner still had his scalp lock, which scared most white women.

"I am so sorry. You must have thought I was tormenting a cat. It is only a Russian instrument called a *gusli*. Similar to a harp or a zither."

She brought the thing to the window and handed it to Long Runner. It was a wing-shaped piece of wood about a foot and a half long, with a dozen strings—as she said, rather like a lap harp. Long Runner gave it a good looking-over, plucked each string, then passed it to Yellow Spotted Buffalo.

"Do you sing to your children? Do the mothers sing? Music helps with learning, especially mathematics, and diaphragmatic breathing—" She stopped. "Oh, I am so sorry. You have work to do, and I ask too many questions."

How gently she got them back to work on her outhouse, Will thought. Like a lady. That's what was wrong—this place wasn't a good fit for her. They needed someone more . . .

More what? More crude? No, they had plenty of scum with no manners, no morals, no aim other than lining their own pockets. Maybe God had sent them the right person. Well, none of his concern either way.

She sang again, teaching the children "Mary Had a Little Lamb." Will found himself keeping time with his hammer. If she didn't know he was listening before, she would now.

Maybe she could bring the thing—gosling?—back to the house at night, sing some more. Henry would want hymns, of course, but perhaps the rest could persuade her to try a little "Oh! Susanna."

"What songs do you know?" she asked the children. Frank started their warrior song. The other children joined in, their feet shaking the floorboards. The work crew added their voices, keeping time with their hammers. They sang with pride, the way people back in the States sang "The Star-Spangled Banner."

The teacher finished the music lesson and moved on to a less distracting subject. The crew finished the outhouse and anchored it over the hole.

Brown Eagle wiped down the tools. "So, tomorrow we roof Yellow Horse's house?"

Will slapped his forehead. "I forgot." So much for being the only white person to keep his promises.

"Pretty girl changes the weather in your head." Yellow Spotted Buffalo plucked the saw, making a *woo-woo* sound, and grinned.

Will felt himself flush. Yellow Spotted Buffalo was right: thinking about the teacher had him in a fog. He'd best keep his distance.

Brown Eagle loaded up the wheelbarrow. "Do not worry. Bear Shield told him you work here today."

"You are done already?" Miss Makinoff stepped outside. "Excellent workmanship, and such speed!"

Brown Eagle's children ran over to check out their new outhouse. Will called out to the boys.

"What did you say?"

"Aim like an arrow."

"Thank you."

Will was impressed. Most ladies would faint at the mention of a normal body function, but this one nodded and smiled. She turned to the children. "Does anyone have an extra bucket at home? We need water for washing hands. Perhaps since we have five students and five days of the week—"

"No. No extra buckets."

The flood of words stopped. Bright blue eyes focused on him.

"There's one at the agency house." He'd paint "School" on it tonight, try to keep it from being stolen.

"And a dipper? The children have been scooping with their hands. Quite unsanitary. Perhaps they could each have a cup. And I would like one too. My throat is rather dry." But it didn't stop her from talking.

Will nodded. Maybe he could put to use the empty tin cans he'd been saving, if he could find some without sharp edges.

"Well then. Class dismissed. I shall see you tomorrow." The children headed home with Brown Eagle. Sophia started to walk back to the house.

"Lock up. And bring your lunch pail." Was it too much to ask that she bring her gosling?

"But I am planning to return this evening, to finish unpacking and clean up from our cleanup."

"Your stuff will grow legs and walk away."

"The Indians steal from their own school?"

"No. Crooks come out west, running from the law back in the States. And regular fellows move here, realize there is no law, and take advantage. If they're caught, the courts side with whites against the Indians, no matter who's right or wrong."

She rolled her lips together, then pointed to the back wall of the schoolroom. "I can understand that the criminal mind would not see value in the prints of George Washington, Abraham Lincoln, or Jesus with the lost sheep. But I am surprised the furniture did not disappear."

"Too long to get out in one piece."

"You, Mr. Dunn, are clever. And a useful person to know." She locked the windows and door.

And you, Miss Makinoff . . . He didn't know what she was, but she sure sidetracked him today.

CHAPTER SEVEN

T his is lovely, walking to and from work." Sophia swung the lunch pail. A breeze off the river kept the air fresh. A scattering of puffy clouds decorated the sky. Perhaps she might stay for a while—at least through the summer. "Wonderful exercise. I shall enjoy this very much."

Will pushed a wheelbarrow full of tools. "Not by yourself."

She was no schoolgirl, needing a chaperone. Not to mention the fact that neither Will nor anyone else within several hundred miles might qualify as an appropriate escort. "You said the Poncas are civilized."

"Don't leave the agency house alone."

Had she exchanged the confines of the College for another cloister? "Are you concerned about this person who set the fire this morning? He is dangerous?"

"Buffalo Track? No. Nettie's right. He's just trying to get warm. His wife will take him back before first frost, or he'll go visit his brother at the Omaha Agency." Will shook his head. "Outlaws don't stop at theft."

"Well then. I would like a pistol."

"Yeah, you and everyone else around here." Brown eyes flashed from beneath his wide-brimmed hat. "You survived your first day."

Dare she confide in this man? As taciturn as he was, he would not share her confession with the others. "I thought teaching a few Indian children would be easier than college-level instruction of the pinnacle of American womanhood. I was wrong."

"Don't imagine it pays as well either." He cleared his throat. "Brick building almost as large as the Capitol. Steam heat, gaslights, piped water, electric bells to wake you. Makes me wonder why you're here."

"You are quite well informed on the College."

He shrugged. "I read. And my brother and I build houses in Omaha."

"He can spare you?"

"It's been slow since the Panic of '73."

"So you have been a missionary for three years?" A long time to endure the hardships of this assignment.

He shook his head. "I'm not a missionary. I'm paid by the Indian Office."

The path turned at the first house. Under the pergola, a young woman in a faded dress tended a baby. Will introduced Julia, then conversed with her in Ponca. Her son, Timothy, had no difficulty focusing his bright onyx eyes on Sophia's face. Perhaps the youngest members of the tribe could lead the way.

Sophia knelt next to him, covered her face with her hands, and said, "Ku-ku, I see you!" She opened her fingers and the baby laughed.

Will said, "I thought it was peek-a-boo."

Oh dear. Had she made another mistake?

A yellow dog crawled from beneath the porch, followed by three puppies, all enthusiastically wagging their tails.

"Zlata and her troika!" Sophia petted them, then caught Will's frown. "In English, it would be 'Goldie.'"

"Don't name them."

Was he no fun at all? Or had she violated some Ponca custom? Apparently she had more to learn than she had to teach.

"Hello, fine lady, gentleman," called a middle-aged man. His skin was darker than hers, but lighter than the tribe members'. Tufts of kinked hair stuck to his head and chin. He held up a long stick with the word *Missouri* carved into it, misspelled. "Isn't this bountiful? I can make one for you. And what might your name be?"

"Don't tell him," Will murmured.

Sophia ignored him. "Ekaterina Mikailovna Dolgorukova," she said. Her old classmate would no doubt be surprised to be remembered on the American frontier. She was probably busy with her duties as the tsar's mistress. One moment—was the penalty for lying worse for missionaries? "Thank you kindly, but I have no need of a walking stick."

"What about tomorrow?" The peddler followed them. "What about your friends back home? Wouldn't they be proud to own this memory of you?"

Did he mean "memento"?

"My friends' memories are intact, thank you."

Will picked up his pace. Sophia trotted along behind, not wanting to be left with the salesman.

"Wouldn't your father look extinguished carrying this?"

Did he mean "distinguished"? Whoever taught him English should be reported. "Thank you, but my father is already quite extinguished. In heaven, walking sticks are not necessary."

"Reynaud." The carpenter evidently had heard enough of the man's spiel. He raised his hand, palm out, and said one Ponca word. The man nodded and loped off in the other direction.

"Mr. Dunn, you are quite proficient in the native language for only living here three years. You are a quick learner. Children pick up languages easily, but adults have a more difficult time of it. Did you take classes?"

"Aren't any."

"So you learned by hearing and using it. Do the Poncas have a written language?"

He shrugged. "One of the earlier reverends was working on it."

"Perhaps the women would be so kind as to teach me."

Will stopped and stared at her.

"People can learn more than one language. I know Russian, French, a little German, and English. My Ukrainian is a bit rusty."

"You've already figured out there's a difference between how men and women say things." He blinked and shook his head. "I was here two years before I noticed that."

"Once you learn one language—"

The earth vibrated with thundering hooves. Will grabbed her elbow and maneuvered her to the side of the path. A dark blur of a horse passed, then another. Both were ridden by soldiers.

Sophia coughed and waved away the dust. "Is there an emergency? A skirmish?"

"A race."

"A race? Right through the village? But the children! Where is their commanding officer? I will lodge a complaint."

"The commanding officer was the second fellow."

Sophia was furious, and her father was no longer here to discipline these louts. She uttered a word missionaries were forbidden to say. But perhaps it did not count since her escort did not know Russian.

Well, she would simply have to pray about the soldiers. What else could she do? Unless . . .

"Is there a livery nearby?"

"We have the team that pulled the wagon this morning. The saddles are locked in the stable."

"Perhaps something more . . . agile."

"I'll check with Long Runner," Will said. "If the Brulé haven't run off his herd, he might have one you could borrow."

They turned the corner to the agency building. Two dozen Ponca men filled the space between the fence and the porch.

"Uh-oh." Will took off at a run.

So much for always being escorted.

"The teacher!" The group turned toward her, faces set in anger, arms crossed.

James separated from the crowd and marched to meet her. His hair stood on end. "Miss Makinoff."

What faux pas had she committed now? "Yes, Mr. Lawrence?"

"You did not ring the bell."

For whatever reason, this seemed to be a serious offense. Sophia opened her mouth to apologize, but Will intervened. "The school didn't officially open. Brown Eagle's children helped Miss Makinoff get ready." He repeated the statement in Ponca.

"I am so sorry for whatever offense I may have caused." Sophia addressed the Poncas. "Please forgive me. School will begin tomorrow morning. Please send your children when the bell rings." She extended a hand to the nearest, hoping she was not violating protocol, and tried to smile without looking him in the face. "Good evening, sir. I am the teacher, Miss Makinoff."

He had seen enough white interaction to pump her arm and utter a long string of syllables.

"Cries for War," Will said in an undertone, then guided her to the next.

"It is a pleasure to meet you, Mr. War."

"Buffalo Chip."

"Enchanted, Mr. Chip."

"White Swan." This man's hair waved as if it had been crimped.

"I am honored to make your acquaintance, Mr. Swan."

Will's conduct was worthy of a diplomatic interpreter of any embassy. Within minutes he restored peace and cleared the yard. Sophia's tongue passed from dry to parched. She hurried inside, searching for water.

"Miss Makinoff." James followed. "Do not ever do that again."

She found a pitcher on the table, poured herself a glass, and drank. She turned to the agent. "Perhaps you could provide an explanation—"

Nettie sent them to wash up.

James guided her out to the porch. "The previous agent withheld rations if the Indians didn't send their children to school."

"How horrible. No wonder they were upset." Where was the soap? And the towel? She shook her hands dry. "I hope you have discontinued his policy."

"Of course."

"If all those men are fathers of students, my class will have more than fifty."

Henry joined the hand-washing line. "They've nothing better to do than raise a fuss."

"They're all related one way or another to your students." Will held the door open for her. "They know the future of the tribe depends on schooling."

The future of the tribe? Perhaps this position held more import than she had first estimated. "Nettie, may I help?"

The woman bustled between the table and the stove. "No, dear, it's all ready. After teaching, I imagine you're done in."

Done in, but her mind still raced with questions.

The men took seats and Henry began his prayer. Sophia paid attention, thinking she would memorize it and teach it to the students, but as the minutes ticked by and the prayer showed no sign of ending, she abandoned the idea.

"Amen," he finally said, and Nettie served roast and potatoes.

The reverend continued in his pulpit voice. "The duty of missionaries at this Agency is to allay discontent and encourage the spirit of goodwill, hope, and faith in the government, and obedience to its wishes. We must provide true light to their darkness."

The others concentrated on their food; apparently this was another familiar sermon.

Sophia took advantage of his pause for coffee. "My students today were Frank, Joseph, Marguerite, Susette, and Rosalie. They live in the house near the spring. Do they have parents? What is their last name?"

James looked to Will. Did the agent not know?

"Frank is the son of Brown Eagle and Mary." The carpenter tapped the table, drawing out the family tree. He had not rolled down his sleeves. Muscles rippled beneath his skin. "Mary's sister-in-law, Joseph and Marguerite's mother, died of cholera. Their father, Fork, was killed by the Yanktons, returning from their Agency last year."

Frightfully complex. Or perhaps Sophia had been distracted by the man's physique. She directed her attention back to Brown Eagle's genealogy.

"The Yanktons claimed Fork was intoxicated." James's black look indicated he did not think much of their excuse.

"Susette is the daughter of Elisabeth and Stands Dark, who drowned when the Missouri flooded a few years back. Elisabeth is Mary's sister. And Rosalie is the daughter of Elisabeth and Brown Eagle."

"Two wives." Nettie shook her head.

"If not for Brown Eagle, Elisabeth would starve." Will's voice was quiet, but his clenched fist betrayed his feelings.

"So," Sophia said, "Brown Eagle taking in Elisabeth is charity, as in the Bible, where a man marries his brother's widow?"

"It's like those Mormons." Henry thumped the table so hard the butter dish rattled. "They came through here a few years after the Catholic priest. Muddied the waters."

Nettie held out a fragrant offering with a lattice crust. "Pie?"

Hostilities ceased immediately.

A lesson for military commanders around the world.

CHAPTER EIGHT

Will figured after teaching all day, Sophia wouldn't have much to say at night. He was wrong. After untangling Brown Eagle's family tree, she asked the biggest question of all.

"Why are the Poncas so poor?" Sophia set her fork on her empty plate. "The Indians at the Santee Agency are dressed in clothes, not rags. Their buildings are in good repair, their fields are cultivated."

"We're doing the best with what we've got." The agent pressed his knuckle to his forehead, ready for his evening dose of medicinal whiskey. "They're ready and willing to work, but ignorant of proper ways and need constant supervision. The farmer quit in April and I had to fire the blacksmith last winter, so they've been short of guidance."

"Ready and willing to work?" Henry turned up his lip in a sneer. "Not likely. Sloth is a common vice among the Poncas. They're supposed to learn to be white men, farmers. But they hide inside all day."

As if he ever left the house.

"Smart, what with the threat from the Brulé," Will said. "The Poncas have been under attack since the treaty of '68, when the government messed up and gave their land to the Sioux."

"Why do they not correct the treaty?" Sophia asked.

"It's more complicated than correcting a student's essay." James braced his head on his fingertips. "The Poncas have had horrible luck: drought, floods, hailstorms. Some years they've had to beg food from Fort Randall, the Omahas, the Pawnees."

"And horrible staff," the rev added. "One pocketed their annuity. Another brought Indian women into the house every night." He shot his fiery glare down the table. "So the government sent the church to the Agency to provide salt and light."

"Unfortunately the church hasn't been able to do anything about the allotments," Nettie said. Worry lines creased her round face.

"That's probably one of your most important jobs," James told Sophia. "Teach them about money. The Indians didn't use it before, so the whole idea is new."

"You won't make friends with those in town who've become rich on the Indians' ignorance." Will smiled in Nettie's direction. Her spats with the merchants had gotten her banned from most stores in Niobrara.

"Finance is hardly your most important subject." The rev reached for his Bible. "What good is it if a man gains the whole world, but loses his soul?"

"These people are closer to starving to death than gaining the world." Sophia stood. "I appreciate your advice, all of you. With so much to teach, a good sleep is in order."

"Sophia, wait." Henry put up a hand. "If the rest will excuse us, I have something to discuss with you."

What sermon would he drop on her now? Whatever it was had Nettie pondering the grain of the table. James lingered in the front room, delaying his imbibing ritual to read a March issue of the Yankton *Dakotaian*. Will went to his room, but left his door open.

"May I take the opportunity to clarify the protocol here?" The teacher sounded not the least bit cowed. "The use of first names is acceptable. And the escorting of an unmarried woman?"

"Is necessary for your safety," Nettie said. "Conduct yourself as if someone is always watching, because the Poncas do watch us. And we must show them good Christian behavior."

"Sophia." Henry used his voice of doom. "Mother discovered an idol in your room. On the wall over your bed."

"It is not an idol," Sophia said in her teacher's voice. "It is an icon. Common for Orthodox Christians in eastern Europe."

"Idol worship is a grievous sin."

"I agree. But icons are not worshipped. They are used during prayers, to help focus."

A chair scraped. "I'll have to report you to the bishop."

Will grinned. Icon, idol? He didn't know which was what. But the mile-wide gap between the bishop and the rev, he had witnessed with his own eyes.

Sophia would be staying.

On her second morning at the Ponca Agency, Sophia slept until the dogs barked. After inspecting her mosquito bites, more every day, she peeked outside. Fog swirled a sheer curtain around the house. The humid air carried no hint of smoke; perhaps the moisture prevented the setting of a fire this morning.

Sophia lit the candle she had brought upstairs and opened her prayer book. She flipped through the pages. Ah, here it was: a prayer before mealtime.

She translated the words from Russian. *O God, our Creator and Sustainer, Thou nourishest our souls . . .*

Dreadfully complex. Perhaps something simple: *O God who made us, thank You for food that fills us, keeps us healthy, and gives us strength. Amen.* It might be easier to memorize if it rhymed, but Sophia had never been adept at composing poetry in English.

The roosters started their raucous chorus, her signal to proceed to morning prayers.

In the name of the Father—

A puff of damp air blew out the flame. How inconvenient. She had no more matches. In her next job, she must insist on gas lighting.

And of the Son, and of the Holy Spirit. Amen. Sophia leaned out the window, trying to determine how soon the sun might provide enough light to continue the morning reading.

Lone Chief emerged from the mists, climbed to the top of the bluffs, and raised his arms to the rising sun. He did not have a prayer book. Perhaps he had memorized prayers. Or perhaps he simply spoke what was in his heart.

Which is what she should do.

Sophia bowed her head. *Dear Lord, I regret to inform You, through grievous error, I have been sent to the Ponca Agency. Here my skills are of little use. I can accomplish nothing for You. Please rectify the situation by sending another teacher, someone more suited to the rigors of this assignment, so I might continue on to China. Or perhaps it might be best to send me home to Russia. Amen.*

CHAPTER NINE

Sophia unlocked the school and gasped. "A chalkboard!"

A large black rectangle stretched across the front wall of the classroom. The odor of fresh paint filled the air. She hurried to prop open the windows. The latrine had been whitewashed too. Will must have returned last night. The windows were polished. The puddles the students made had been cleaned up. Why had he not asked her to accompany him?

This morning Will had gone to help someone named Yellow Horse, so the dispute between James and Henry over who would accompany Sophia to the school ended in a draw. They both did. While neither could build a bookshelf, she would put them to work in other ways.

"This barrel contains clothing collected by my church in New York."

Henry held up an elaborate dress. "Do they think we're running a fashion parade?"

James shook out a double-breasted chesterfield, complete with a velvet collar. "Easterners have no idea."

"The fabric is good. Perhaps Nettie can find a way to adapt it. Although Frank would look rather distinguished in the top hat." Sophia glanced at her watch. "It is eight o'clock already. If one of you men would kindly ring the school bell."

After tense negotiations, James elected to haul the barrel back to the house and Henry rang the bell. He greeted the students as they came and sent them to Sophia's desk to be entered in her ledger.

Frank, Joseph, Marguerite, Susette, and Rosalie arrived first, being the closest to school. Sophia was pleased with herself for matching names and faces. The girls were easily differentiated by size. Frank's round face resembled her cousin Yevgeny, and Joseph's pointed chin reminded her of Uncle Ivan. "Last name? Brown Eagle? Or simply Eagle? Or wait . . . tell me your fathers' names."

"Pick a surname," Henry said. "A white name."

Sophia lifted an eyebrow. Perhaps she should name them all *Romanov*. If it was good enough for the Russian royal family, it should be good enough for Henry. "Should not their parents be consulted?"

"If they had an idea, they'd have made their choice by now."

What name would fit? "What name would you like?"

Henry made an ugly noise in the back of his throat. "Washington. They were first, so they'll have the first president's name."

A lot of letters to remember, but distinguished. Sophia entered it in the ledger. In the next group, four boys needed first and last names. Did they live in the same house? Were they siblings? A round of questions between them and the newly anointed Washington children did not resolve the issue. "How about Nicholas, Alexander, Vladmir, and Alexi Alexandrovich?" Names good enough for the tsar.

Henry scowled and pointed at each child. "Last name Adams. Matthew, Mark, Luke, and John."

Sophia hoped the children would remember.

The reverend took the boys outside. They returned in tears, their hair shorn. The Washington children circled to console them.

"Reverend Granville," Sophia hissed. "Was that necessary?"

"Our mission—"

Before he could launch into another sermon, Sophia turned to face the portraits over the chalkboard. Jesus' hair hung to His shoulders. George Washington's curled to the lower lobe of his ears. Even Abraham Lincoln had his neck covered.

"Miss Makinoff, how dare you!" Henry stormed off.

Good riddance. Er . . . Thank You, Lord.

Fortunately the next group already had English names: Emily Knudsen, Logan LeClair, Hannah Howe, and Jim and Francis Roy.

The classroom filled with children. Twenty-seven wiggly, noisy students. How did James manage fifty? How would Catharine Beecher handle this situation?

Perspiration dampened Sophia's brow. "May I have the fifth graders up front for recitation, please."

Unfortunately no one could identify himself as a fifth grader. John Adams started a fistfight with Thomas Jefferson. *Dear Lord*, Sophia thought, and then realized she had hit on the answer.

"Let us pray." The children had attended enough church to recognize the words. They bowed their heads and clasped their hands. "Thank You, Jesus, for all Your wonderful students. God bless our school day. Amen." And before they could take a breath, Sophia dove into assigning seating.

Traveling with her father, Sophia had met innumerable ethnic groups, from Finns to Tatars to Turks. Each group had customs to ensure its continued existence.

The Ponca rule against looking another in the face, however, would impede survival in a world run by Europeans. Will might disapprove, but the students' lives would go easier if they could learn to look others in the eye.

She had an idea. She directed the older boys in moving the tables and benches in a U shape, so they could watch each other. Beginning with Joseph, Sophia said "Good morning," shook his hand, and held it.

"Good morning," the boy said. And then for a fraction of a second, he returned her glance.

⌒⌒

Will sat on the roof of Yellow Horse's house and paused for a drink from his canteen. He wiped the sweat out of his eyes. If this heat kept up . . .

Just past the cornfield a movement caught his eye. He grabbed up his spyglass. Several dozen well-armed warriors on horseback splashed across the river.

The school! *Dear Jesus!*

The Sioux didn't have to be sneaky. They knew the Poncas had no way to defend themselves.

Will clicked his tongue to catch Yellow Horse's attention, then swung down from the rafters. They'd better not set this house on fire. He'd just about finished it.

He sent Yellow Horse to the church and took off at a run for the school. If only he had a rifle—no, a horse. He changed direction, only to find Long Runner's yard empty. Will hoped the herd was well hidden.

Behind him the church bell sounded the alarm. To the south Black Elk's wife snatched up their baby in her cradleboard and raced from their garden to the house. The yellow dog herded her puppies under her steps. Little Chief broke into a run, heading for his cabin. If Will wasn't in a hurry, he'd stop to watch. It wasn't every day you saw an elder run like a deer.

By the time he reached the school, Will's lungs burned and his legs wobbled. The children weren't outside. And they weren't wandering to and from the spring. Good. He leaped to the stoop and yanked on the door. Locked.

"It's Will . . . uh, Mr. Dunn."

Sophia pulled him inside and barred the door behind him. "Did you bring any firearms?" The children sat on the floor in a tight circle, solemn as saints, but none crying. Tough bunch, these Poncas. The windows were closed and locked. The air steamed with sweat.

Sophia sat on the floor in a puddle of skirts. She flipped through the first part of the Bible. "I was just about to tell the story of David . . ."

David was Will's middle name, so he'd made a point of studying the Old Testament king. Most of his life seemed to be a warning: be careful around women.

Sophia closed the Bible. ". . . David and Goliath."

He raised an eyebrow. "Fitting. Mind if I join you?"

Rifle fire echoed off the bluffs.

"Not at all." A beam of sunshine caught in her hair. If the Brulé looked in they might see her, but the children were hidden behind the half-wall.

He took up a post in front of the door. They'd have to get through him. And once they did, the children would all be goners. He couldn't think what they'd do to Sophia. Or the possibility they'd set the school on fire.

She began in a whispered voice: "Now, David was a shepherd boy. His job was guarding the sheep." She looked at Will. "Has the tribe considered raising sheep?"

Will nodded, but someone higher up than he and the agency farmer had decided on cattle and hogs. He told the children, "David guarded the sheep like Hairy Bear herds the cows, like Walking Together watches the horses." The men were out in the fields now, with no place to hide. Will sent up another prayer for God to keep them safe.

Sophia resumed her story. "When lions— Do lions live here?"

"Coyotes."

"When coyotes tried to eat the calves, David used his sling to throw rocks at them." Sophia acted out the throwing motion, looking more like a dancer than a warrior. "He became skilled at throwing rocks. He could kill a coyote with one rock."

The children were impressed.

"One day David's father called him. 'Please take this lunch pail to your brothers. They are fighting a war.' David was a boy, about the age of Thomas Jefferson, here."

Thomas Jefferson? How had White Knife become—?

Oh yeah, the rev had walked Sophia to school this morning. No doubt he was to blame for the haircuts too.

"Not old enough to be a warrior," Will explained.

Back in the village a woman wailed. Will gestured for the story to continue.

"When David got to the field where they were fighting, he found his brothers were afraid. A big enemy walked up and down the field, saying he was ready to kill David's family. His name was Goliath."

"Bigger than Mr. Dunn?" asked Marguerite.

"Bigger than Big Snake." The tallest man of the tribe.

Sophia nodded. "As big as Mr. Dunn, Reverend Granville, Mr. Lawrence, Big Snake, and Brown Eagle, all put together."

"Oooh."

"David asked his brothers why they were not fighting Goliath."

"Because he's Brulé," Joseph whispered. "He's got guns."

"No, I cannot remember what tribe he belonged to, but he was not Brulé and he did not have a gun. But he was too big for the brothers. Little David said he would fight Goliath. His brothers could not talk him out of it, so they gave him their armor." She glanced up at Will for a substitute.

"Shield."

"But the shield was too big for David, so he—"

"If Goliath was so big, where did he sleep?" Frank asked.

Will said, "In a big tepee. His feet stuck out the door. Now, let Miss Makinoff tell you what happened."

More women took up the cry in the village.

"David gave the shield back to his brother. He found a good stone in the creek. Then he returned to the battlefield. At first Goliath did not see him . . . David was so little."

Sophia moved as much as a Ponca storyteller, but with prettier motions. Had she studied that fancy dance, ballet?

She squinted and held her hand over her eyes. "Goliath said, 'Is that a mouse? Is it a bird? No, it is a boy.' Goliath taunted him, called David bad names. Then David put the stone in his sling. He swung and threw it as hard as he could. It hit Goliath and killed him!"

"I want to kill Brulé," said Rosalie from her hiding spot deep in Marguerite's lap.

"Me too," said the rest of the children.

Sophia widened her eyes at Will.

"Can you kill a coyote with one stone?" he said. "No? Then God hasn't trained you to be a warrior. But He's teaching you a lot here in school."

The floor shook as someone walked up to the school. Will put his finger over his mouth.

"They are gone," Brown Eagle called. "You can come out now."

Will opened the door and gulped fresh air. The village echoed with wailing. Brown Eagle pulled his children close. The other students ran for home.

"Good afternoon, Mr. Eagle." Sophia struggled to her feet. Her fingers shook as she raised her pocket watch. "Oh dear. It is only three—"

"No one will fault you for letting school out early."

"Class dismissed. I will see you tomorrow," Sophia called to their retreating backs, then whispered, "God keep you."

"Well?" Will asked his friend.

"Walking Together. Thirty of our best buffalo runners. Two cows." Brown Eagle swallowed hard. He put Rosalie on his back and they headed for home.

Will shook his head and looked down.

"Pardon me?"

"They killed the young man who guards the horses."

"This is an outrage. I want a rifle! How am I to keep my students safe?" Amazing how many shades of red a white woman could turn. "Could you make shutters, please? And an escape hatch in the floor. Where are the soldiers who are supposed to protect us?"

"Fort Randall might send someone over in the next day or so. If they can find anyone not on sick call." Will took a gulp of water from her bucket, then dumped the rest on his head. "The locals object to arming Indians."

"But the Brulé were shooting. I heard them."

"Between buying from smugglers, stealing from settlers, and negotiating a better treaty, they've managed to stockpile quite an arsenal." He nodded toward the river. "Those steamboats heading upriver are full of breech-loading rifles for the Sioux. The entire Ponca tribe owns one musket, a few shotguns, couple pistols, bows and arrows. No ammunition."

"Well, it is wrong. Unjust. The situation must be rectified." Sophia swiped the blackboard. "I have never been so frightened."

"You hid it well."

Her back straight, chin high, she punctuated her words with angry swings of her arms. If her students could see her now, they'd run away and never come back. "My father, Constantin Ilia Makinoff, was never afraid. Even when the tsar threatened him with exile to Siberia."

"Not that you know of."

"Huh." She snorted, not letting up on herself.

"You kept your wits yesterday surrounded by angry Poncas, even with Long Runner."

"Russian officers travel with their families. So I have seen Cossacks, Mongols, and countless others who wear their hair differently, dress differently, look and act differently. It is not a reason for fear." She studied him, her head tilted, as if puzzling him out.

Well, he'd been doing his own puzzling, and she'd just given him a big piece: she hadn't grown up in a palace.

She turned with a swirl of her skirts. "Thank you for completing my Bible story. It is more difficult to teach than one would think, the Bible."

Will nodded. "And even more difficult to live."

Chapter Ten

From the wails echoing around her, Sophia could almost imagine she attended a Russian funeral. At home she would have been looking at a gold-ornamented iconostasis at the front of the sanctuary, filled with images of Jesus, the apostles, the saints, and other holy icons. Here, the Church of the Merciful Father was plain.

A wooden cross hung on the wall. A linen cloth covered the altar table. The pulpit had been constructed from a packing box, like the school's furniture. Instead of stained glass, clear windows were propped open with sticks. Instead of gold-brocaded vestments, Reverend Granville wore an unadorned black cassock. Instead of singing, he droned through the Episcopalian funeral service.

Henry really should remove the benches so they could worship like Russians—standing, chanting, prostrating themselves. Finally he said the "Amen," then pumped out a dirge on the melodeon. The pallbearers left with the coffin. The rest of the tribe shuffled about, making no attempt to be orderly. A son of the tribe had been cut down in his youth. Forming a line would not ease their pain.

Sophia followed Brown Eagle's family. Little Rosalie had fallen asleep during the long service. Her pregnant mother, Elisabeth, struggled to carry her as Mary guided the other four children. Sophia reached for the girl.

"No." Henry caught her arm.

"But—"

Will must have sensed her thoughts. He turned back, eased Rosalie onto his shoulder without waking her, then followed Brown Eagle up the bluff. Sophia could not have managed the climb while holding the little one, but Will's long legs conquered the slope without difficulty.

"You do not continue to the graveside?" she asked Henry.

"To the burial ground?" He followed her gaze and shook his head. "We need to set a good example for the tribe. Show them that our funeral service is sufficient. There's no need for barbaric dancing, wailing, cutting themselves."

Cutting themselves? Sophia allowed Henry to turn her toward the house.

His grasp tightened as if holding her prisoner. "They used to bury a brave with his horse, food, and possessions for the journey to the happy hunting ground."

"And now they are too poor to follow their tradition."

"Thank God."

Thank God? Sophia pulled away. Did he ascribe the tribe's suffering to a loving God?

"As we gain access for the truth into the hearts of the people, their superstitious prejudices and heathen rites are melting away. They have given up their dumb idols, magic, taboos, cults. They no longer send their boys out for days, without food, in search of a vision."

"Orthodox monks fast for illumination."

"Hallucinations brought on by hunger." Henry enjoyed eating too much to consider dispensing with meals in search of spiritual enlightenment. "I've seen their shamans draw a stick or worm from a patient using sleight of hand."

There was no sense battering against this fortification. She changed tactics and launched from a different direction. "Have you ever considered simplifying the service?"

Henry's horrified glare spoke volumes. "The Book of Common Prayer was developed by the finest minds of the Church. I would not dare to change one jot or tittle."

"Few who speak English as their first language understand 'disquieteth' or 'howbeit,' 'celestial' or 'terrestrial.' The concept of grass growing and withering is universally understood, but couched in such archaic terms it is incomprehensible. I do not suggest changing the intent or content, but merely paraphrasing for clarity."

He sputtered, then retreated to the comfort of his favorite sermon. "Our mission here is to—"

"I understand the mission. But how much better Christians would they be if they comprehended your teaching?"

Henry's scowl deepened.

"Well then, if you are not inclined to simplify the text, perhaps you might share it with me ahead of time. I will teach my students the King's English, so they might explain it to their families."

"The king? This is America. We won't have a king!" Henry stomped off toward the house.

"Better than a boxing match." James chuckled behind her, then matched his stride to her short steps. "Do you do that deliberately?"

"Do what?"

"Annoy Henry."

"Certainly not." She ought to be ashamed. And she was, at least a little. Still, it would be easier to behave in a Christlike manner if Henry was not such a—what would her students at the College call him? A ninny.

The agent grinned. "Sophia, you're a most entertaining addition to our staff."

Chapter Eleven

Sophia arrived last for breakfast the next day.

"Ah, I see you don't follow 'early to bed, early to rise,'" James said.

"Hmm?" Sophia said. "Oh yes. Benjamin Franklin. But it is Saturday, after all." She poured her tea, then picked out a muffin. She took the seat across from Will. "I wrote letters until late in the night. When is the mail picked up?"

"I'll take them to town if a steamboat doesn't stop by in the next few days," James told her. "You're writing home, telling your friends of your adventures in the Wild West?"

"I am writing a New York congressman about the conditions here. It is a disgrace."

"Sophia, you've got to understand." The agent straightened to his full height. "Best estimate, we've got three hundred thousand Indians in this country. At any time a good portion of them are ready to slit our throats. The problems of seven hundred docile Poncas are of no interest to anyone in Washington."

"Then we must make them so."

"I've sent plenty of letters." He pinched his forehead as if he might be suffering from a headache. "You'd better let me see what you're writing. Don't want to make the situation worse."

"Certainly," she said, with no intention whatsoever of honoring that request.

Henry wandered in with ink-stained fingers and hair standing on end. Laboring over tomorrow's sermon, no doubt. He spotted Sophia and pushed his hair down. "Mother's been awake for hours, doing laundry."

"Is that one of my duties?" Sophia asked with a raised eyebrow.

"She's managing," he muttered.

"I heard that." Nettie waltzed into the kitchen and waggled her finger at her son. "It's not as if you ever spell Will from hauling water. Laundry's done, except for your bed linens, Sophia."

"I shall—" Sophia started to stand.

Nettie waved her back into the chair and poured herself a cup of coffee. "Finish your breakfast. I plan to sit a spell. And then I'm thinking we could dive into that barrel of clothing from your college friends, see if we can make any sow's ears out of the silk purses they sent."

⁓

"Silk, velvet, lace. Why ever would they give away such fancy dresses?"

"The Founders Day committee wore them when they had their photograph taken two years ago," Sophia said. "It would never do to wear a dress everyone recognized."

"Vanity is such a waste," Nettie huffed. "Look at these dresses. Flimsy, gauzy, not a bit useful out here on the plains."

"Like me," Sophia said. "Useless."

Nettie chuckled. "Don't you believe it. God's going to use you in amazing ways."

"The problems here are enormous, overwhelming." Sophia sighed. "The men are convinced I am hopeless."

"They ought to know better. Especially Henry. He went to seminary. God uses all sorts of people. A murderer rescued Israel out of Egypt. A fisherman led the early church. A peasant girl became Jesus' mother. You can count on God to put you to use."

Nettie sorted through the dresses and went on talking in her brisk, no-nonsense tone. "No one here has a bustle, so let's remove the trains and hand them out as they are. This one would be perfect for Julia, raise her spirits after Walking Together's death."

"Julia? In the house near the school?" Sophia took up a pair of scissors and began to snip away at the fabric. "Her husband was the one killed in the battle? How awful to lose a spouse so young, with an infant to raise. Will she be accepting callers? Will she be home?"

"Where else would she be?" Nettie finished removing the train and held the dress up. "Let's take it to her now."

"Julia's a gem," Nettie said as she and Sophia walked to the nearby house. "I'm supposed to be training the women of the tribe in housekeeping, but Julia teaches them things I'd never even consider, such as not peeking into the windows and knocking before you enter. And she always has a lesson for me, like what plants are good medicine."

"All the women of the tribe? You have many students, then."

"Somehow Julia organizes them. Every morning she sends a different woman to help. On laundry day, she'll send one of the strong girls. On bread day, someone who's running short on food. On sewing day, someone whose husband needs a new shirt."

They stopped at the house where yellow flowers bloomed beside the steps. Nettie knocked and called the woman's name.

The door opened and dark eyes peeked out. Julia wore a loose dress of uncertain color and vintage. Her hair was neatly braided and hung down her back to her waist. Nettie pointed to the ball gown draped across Sophia's arms. "We've brought a dress for you."

Julia's eyes grew wide. She stepped back to let her guests in. The interior had been divided into two rooms. The front contained only a cookstove. Pouches tacked to the wall held cooking implements.

The back room held a pile of pelts. In the middle lay Timothy, the new baby. How practical, Sophia thought. The mother did not have to worry about the baby falling out of bed, although it could not be easy to clean. Julia knelt next to him, covered her face, and said, "Ku-ku, I see you!"

The baby kicked and giggled.

"You taught her that?" Nettie asked Sophia. "God's already using you."

Nettie unwrapped the sheet from the dress, a basque with embroidered velvet down the front and a skirt with five rows of fringe and a ruffle. "Now, this is awful fancy for everyday, but you can wear it to church and for the Independence Day doings Tuesday. Let's see it on you. I brought my sewing kit, in case you need alterations."

Both windows were bare. One had cracked glass and the other had a gap between the frame and the wall. Sophia stood in front of the one within view of the neighbors. "Perhaps we should make the trains into curtains."

"Good idea." Nettie helped Julia remove her dress.

The woman wore not a stitch of undergarments—no chemise, no corset, no vest. Of course not. Julia had been forced to rely on gift barrels from eastern churches. People never donated undergarments. Even nightclothes were worn until ready for the ragbag.

Sophia's temper rose. If the government was going to insist that the Poncas dress and act like white people, shouldn't they be provided with the basic necessities of life? Should it not be guaranteed in America to have at least a pair of drawers? The Bill of Rights did not address the issue, but then, it had been written by men.

Sophia helped Julia into her new basque and skirt. Her experience of entering in this country through Castle Gardens and the Lower East Side of New York City had led her to equate poverty with strong body odors. But Julia smelled clean. Not rank like the poor of Manhattan or overly perfumed like some Europeans, but like someone who gave careful attention to hygiene.

The ruby red silk complemented Julia's coloring, whereas the intense shade had overwhelmed its previous pale owner. And the dress fell just at her ankles. Perfect.

"The bodice is a little loose." Nettie made a few stitches, bringing the neckline into the realm of modesty.

"Oh!" Julia spotted herself in the pocket mirror hanging on the opposite wall. She spun around, making the skirt bell out, then studied herself again. "Oh!"

Her fingers tore the thread off the ends of her braids, then unraveled her hair into a dark sheet of satin. She patted Sophia's coil. "Teach. Please."

Sophia pulled out her hairpins and undid the knot. "Twist forward and wrap around your hand, then push the end through with the other hand. Pull tight, then wrap the ends and pin."

Julia did not have any hairpins, so Sophia donated hers. The woman was a quick learner, and the effect was charming. The perfect oval of her face, her smooth complexion, and her wide, dark eyes—why, she would be the talk of any ball in St. Petersburg or Paris. "You remind me of Russia's most beautiful queen, the Empress Elizabeth." Sophia curtsied. "Magnificent."

"Thank you." Julia returned the gesture, then caught Sophia's wrist. "Oh."

"Mosquito bites." Sophia pulled her sleeve down over the welts. Nettie shook her head. "Fresh blood is their dessert."

"I make." Julia opened a round tin and dabbed ointment on the bites.

The itching stopped. "Ah. How wonderful." Sophia sniffed the medicine. "What is in it?"

Nettie put her nose to the question. "I'm guessing some plants."

"Plants. Yes." Julia handed Sophia the tin. "You keep."

Sophia thanked her. They helped her out of the dress and said their good-byes.

"What a great way to introduce the new teacher," Nettie said as she closed the door behind her. "Let's go see how Little Flower looks in that green dress."

"But, Nettie . . ." Sophia rolled her lips together, unable to find the words.

The older woman linked arms with her. "I know—Julia has so many needs. But did you see the look on her face?"

Smoke Maker's cow had scratched her back against his house, pulling off the corners and splintering half a dozen clapboards. Will pried off the damaged pieces, then measured and sawed a patch.

Smoke Maker squinted at the end of the board, then waved his hand over the diagonal cut. "Why is it like this?"

"Straight cuts open up."

"This will stay?"

"Until the next time your cow has an itch."

Smoke Maker nodded and nailed the board into place. As they worked, Will watched Sophia and Nettie shuttle between the agency house and others in the village, carrying bundles of clothing. It reminded him of how his sister used to dress up her doll in handkerchiefs and scraps.

Girls. They might grow up, but they still—

Whoa. Sophia had her hair down.

Will's hammer slid from his grasp and thudded to the ground, missing his foot by an inch.

Smoke Maker grinned and lifted his chin toward the women. "Girls playing. Gives boys something to watch."

CHAPTER TWELVE

James sprawled in his seat, his elbows on the table and his head propped up with one hand. His skin appeared yellow in the lantern's glow. "Well, Teacher, any spelling errors? Misplaced commas?"

"Your handwriting is beautiful. Perhaps you could teach penmanship to my students." Sophia read from a ledger sheet, at the top of which he had noted *No Funds*. "Padlocks, lime, linseed oil. What is 'bail of oakum'?"

"Caulking. Oakum is made out of rope fibers, hemp. It's used to seal the linings of ships, but it also is useful to stop up gaps in the walls, of which we have many."

Sophia hoped the oakum was substantial. Her room was rife with gaps. "'Tar paper, pump, ponies, sulky, reaper, rope, sash—glazed.' So what did you receive?"

"Ax handles."

Each of the agent's letters began, "I have the honor to report . . ." even when the news was grim. She closed his file. "You write a thorough, factual account. All requests are well justified. But, as no action has been taken, I shall cast a wider net. Appeal to the public, to men of influence. Speak out for justice and mercy. Speak the truth."

"Tap into their vein of sentimentality."

"It is necessary."

Footsteps echoed in the front room. Sophia watched the carpenter exit, bound down the steps, and stride off on his long legs into the evening. Where was he going this late? The village lacked any of the usual entertainments distracting men on a Saturday night. She curbed an odd impulse to call him back. Will was not in a position of authority, did not know those who were, and showed no inclination to eloquence.

"Miss Makinoff." James leaned toward her, exuding a cloud of whiskey fumes. His hand shook as it reached toward hers. "I perceive you are quite independent."

"And I perceive you are a bit *dependent*." She studied his reddened eyes, his pallor. He had been a handsome man once. She gentled her tone. "Are you not concerned about the example you set?"

"I never imbibe outside the house."

Which, Sophia suspected, did not disguise his problem from anyone in possession of a working nose. "Do you not care about your health?"

"None of us is here for our health." He grimaced and withdrew his hand. He lowered his eyelids and dismissed her with an indulgent smile. "We'll see how long you tilt at windmills before you realize no one cares one straw if these children learn. Maybe you'll turn to drink too." He pushed to his feet and staggered off to his room.

Fool, Will thought. He was seven kinds of fool. Just because he'd found her first. The picture of Sophia and James in the pool of lamplight burned behind his eyes. Sure, they'd be a good match. Both with a bent toward being in charge, using fancy words, speaking out. They'd do well together.

But with James filling her head with the Indian Office's schemes, who would tell her the truth about the Poncas?

Will climbed to the top of the bluff and surveyed the surrounding territory. No Brulé, no prairie fires, no storm clouds. Wind rippled through the tall grass. A red-tailed hawk stretched his wings high overhead. The sun headed for the horizon, turning the sky red and the hills purple. Sophia probably knew fancy names for all these colors.

He plopped down on the grass. *Dear Lord, help me . . .*

But what did he want help with? Letting go of Sophia? She had never been his, anywhere other than his foolish imagination. Still, he repeated the prayer: *Lord, help me—*

A white head appeared at the edge of the bluff. Lone Chief. The elderly man turned slowly, moving as if he searched for something. Lone Chief, Will knew, was near to blind.

Will stood. "Are you looking for me, Grandfather?"

The man nodded and said, in English, "Let us pray." He raised his arms toward the sunset.

Will waited, not wanting to disturb Lone Chief. No words, no thoughts, came to him. No prayer beyond the plea for help. The colors in the sky deepened. Rays of light shot upward. A cool wind rippled the grass. Will's heart filled and the tension in his shoulders eased.

"Amen." Lone Chief took Will's hand and placed it on his shoulder. The chief's old bones creaked and ground as they walked.

"You do not come here every day at this time, Grandfather."

The elderly man chuckled. "No. Only in the morning. Unless someone wanders up here and needs help getting down."

Oh yeah. Lone Chief was right. He would never have found the path without a lantern. He'd have been waiting until sunrise, shivering without a blanket, hoping no storms popped up to shoot him with lightning. Either that, or risk falling a hundred feet straight down.

Without hesitation, Lone Chief led him to the edge of the bluff, to a narrow trail hidden in the tall grass.

"How did you find this? They told me you cannot see."

"My eyes no longer work, but my heart knows the path."

Lone Chief had lived here all his life, however many years that might be. No doubt he knew every pebble, every blade of grass.

When they reached the village, the elder squeezed Will's hands. "With your eyes on the beauty, you lost your path." Then he shuffled toward his house.

So the whole village knew Will was moonstruck over Sophia.

CHAPTER THIRTEEN

O h my word." The rev scowled out the window, fists on his hips. "I knew that teacher was nothing but trouble." Will looked over Henry's shoulder. Out of the Sunday morning fog came five women in fancy dresses. They flocked in front of the church, holding their skirts out of the mud from last night's storm. Lone Chief's black-and-brown dog guarded them. "Don't blame Sophia. This was your mother's idea."

James stepped out onto the porch for a better view. "Besides, Sophia didn't choose what her college friends sent."

Nettie sailed into the kitchen, a satisfied smile on her face. "Aren't they beautiful?"

"Vanity. Vanity," Henry muttered.

"You'll notice Crescent Moon and Buffalo Woman are present this morning. They've never attended church before."

"So we've lowered ourselves to bribery now?"

"No, we're making straight a road in the wilderness." Nettie frowned at her son. "I should have had a sister for you. Then you'd understand."

Will's sister had nearly burned off her fingers using the curling iron on her hair Sunday mornings. "They look . . . fine."

Sophia hurried down the stairs, wearing another dark-blue dress, smoothing gloves over her fingers. Her Bible slipped from her elbow. Will retrieved it for her. She nodded her thanks, lowering her eyelids and smiling at the same time. He got all hot inside and had to look away.

The rev gave her a head-to-toe scowl. "No ball gown?"

"I am woefully underdressed." And not the least bit intimidated. She nodded over Henry's shoulder. "Although, to be precise, none of those is appropriate evening wear. Julia's crimson silk faille is a visiting dress, formerly worn by the teacher of Mineralogy. The violet foulard is a walking suit belonging to the teacher of English Rhetoric. The mauve piqué is a reception dress, Elementary Drawing and Perspective. The rose percale is a watering-place costume, Musical Theory. The green cretonne is a carriage dress, Ancient History."

Will clamped his hand over his mouth to hold in a laugh. Henry muttered something about keeping their minds on heaven.

Nettie took her son's arm and they led the way across the yard to the church. Henry motioned for Sound of the Water to ring the bell.

After a rousing rendition of "O Worship the King," the reverend read Psalm 30. It was the lectionary text, and he used the "weeping at night, joy in the morning" in his sermon of consolation for the latest raid. Will wasn't one to tell another his business, but he figured the message would go down a mite easier if Henry would smile once in a while.

The psalm had a verse about putting off sackcloth to be clothed with joy. Nettie and Sophia beamed at each other. Henry shot them a cranky look, the kind of expression Will's sister warned would freeze on his face if he wasn't careful.

So was it wrong to get dressed up for church? Ma always said the Saturday night bath and Sunday-best clothes honored God. No telling what the Ponca women thought.

The reverend wrapped it up, announced the doings for Tuesday's Fourth of July celebration, and gave the blessing. The five women clustered around Nettie and Sophia, thanking them for their dresses. They wore their best moccasins, the ones decorated with beads and quills.

Walks in the Mud's wife sent her daughter to tug on Sophia's skirt. "Teacher?"

Sophia shook her student's hand. "Good morning, Martha Jefferson."

"Good morning, Miss Makinoff." The little girl tipped her head up and, for a moment, looked in her teacher's face. Then her gaze cut to her mother, who hid at the corner of the building. She wore a loose sack of faded calico Will recognized—the fabric had come up the river with him. "Mama wants a dress too."

Sophia glided over to the woman and took her hands. "I am so sorry. I want nothing more than to give you a beautiful dress, but only five were in the barrel and I have given them all away. But I promise you, I will write to the churches in New York and ask for a dress for you. For you and the other ladies in the tribe. Next time. I promise."

Walks in the Mud's wife wasn't getting any of this. Will figured he'd better step in, lest the poor woman drown in Sophia's flood of words. In a low tone, so Henry wouldn't hear, Will explained as best he could. He didn't make any promises. The Poncas, having been disappointed so many times, didn't expect much.

"I am so very, very sorry."

The woman accepted the news without tears. Given all the other tragedies in her life—losing her house to the river last spring, most of her family dying the winter before, and that German farmer stealing her cow—the loss of a dress was just another day at the Ponca reservation.

Prairie Flower, Bending Willow, Mariette Primeau, and Angelique Gayton circled, wanting—no surprise—new dresses.

Will relayed all the requests, then tipped his head toward the agency house. "You don't want to miss lunch."

Sophia waved over her shoulder. "Is there a dressmaker in Niobrara or Yankton? I could—"

"Don't."

"But I have money."

"Enough to outfit seven hundred people? You saw how riled up people got when they thought you were favoring Brown Eagle's children at the school. When I first got here, I tried helping out some." Will shook his head. It was a wonder any of the Poncas called him friend after that mess. "Stirred up a hornet's nest."

"I fear Nettie and I have fanned the coals of covetousness."

Maybe they'd done something of the sort. Or maybe they'd just brought a little color to a few gray lives. It wasn't his place to judge. Besides, he was busy trying to figure how Sophia's hand had come to rest on his arm and wondering what to do about it. Maybe they could take a stroll around the village. Who needed lunch anyway?

"Thank you kindly for your assistance," Sophia said, leaving him with a smile as she let him go. How had they gotten back to the house so soon? And how could he get her promenading with him again?

Chapter Fourteen

I am surprised the Indians celebrate Independence Day," Sophia said as they sat down to a dinner of cold chicken. "I would think the birth of the United States might be more of an occasion for mourning for them."

"You're Russian." Henry salted his food before tasting. "Of course you wouldn't understand."

A thump echoed beneath the table. Henry grunted and glared at his mother, who serenely buttered her roll. Had Nettie kicked him? Good for her.

James passed the greens. "It's part of becoming American."

Nettie set down her knife. "I don't know Russian history. Do you have an independence day?"

"Russia was never a colony, so no. We were occupied by the Mongols in medieval times, but saved through God's intervention. That event is a religious holiday."

"Didn't Napoleon invade Russia?" James said.

Of course Americans would focus on another country's humiliation. "We had to burn down Moscow to get rid of him, so it is not a fond memory."

"And what will your students be presenting Tuesday?" Henry asked.

Sophia choked on her tea. "Presenting?"

Henry threw down the gauntlet. "In my school, students read the Declaration of Independence and sang 'The Star-Spangled Banner.'"

Sophia had thought memorizing her students' names was a sufficient accomplishment. She set her cup on the table gently, so it would not crack. "You have rather high expectations for a teacher who has only been here a week."

❦

Lightning flashed and thunder echoed off the bluff. The curtains flapped. Henry dashed in from the outhouse, rain sheeting off his fancy slicker. A door slammed.

"Whose window is open?" Nettie asked.

James pushed away from the table with a groan. "Oh no. Papers all over the place," he grumbled from his office.

Will closed the kitchen windows, then watched as debris blew across the yard. He made out a pail, an empty peach can, and a bunch of cottonwood leaves.

Sophia joined him and muttered in Russian.

"Weather usually blows through here pretty quick," Nettie said. Another bolt flashed overhead. Rain fell so hard, even the closest houses disappeared. "When the sun comes out, we'll have our Independence Day party."

"Little Chief said it would storm all day," Will said.

The next boom came right on the heels of a flash, rattling the windows. The wind shifted, coming more from the east. Hail battered the roof . . . and the crops.

"I suppose there are no lightning rods on this house." Sophia used her teacher voice over the roar of the storm.

"We have to trust God for our safety." Nettie set a bucket under the leak in the front room.

"What can we do? The students worked so hard on their performance. Would they all fit in the school or the church?"

"All seven hundred? No. We'll just have it tomorrow." James topped off his coffee.

Sophia paced to the front window, as if the weather might look better on the north side. "Will it be difficult to reschedule? Should we send someone to the other villages to notify them?"

"Schedule?" Henry snorted.

"Instead of expecting the weather to change for them," Will explained, "the Poncas change for the weather. They get up at daybreak, go to bed with the sun. If it storms, they stay inside." It was one of their many strengths.

"Well then. I found a dress for Martha Jefferson's mother." Sophia hurried upstairs and returned in a moment with an armful of green fabric.

"The pompadour waist and flowing sleeves are outdated," Sophia said, as if trying to excuse her good deed. Instead of the greediness Will expected from a wealthy woman, he found Sophia to be the soul of generosity. "I am sure Mrs. Jefferson will treasure it more than I ever did."

"She's a bit shorter than you. Let's see. If we—" The women went into the front room to talk hems, flounces, and whatnot. The rain eased to a steady downpour.

"Foolish woman," Henry muttered. "Bringing such an ostentatious dress out here."

James pressed his hand to his heart, leaned back in his chair, and stared at the ceiling. "Yes, but what I wouldn't give to see her in it."

And for once Will agreed with the agent.

CHAPTER FIFTEEN

Little Chief had been right about the weather: the Fourth of July had been stormy all day, but the fifth was sunny enough to bake the paths dry.

Sophia fanned herself with the lyrics. Her students ran to the windows and called greetings to friends walking by. All morning people from the other two villages had passed, headed to the Agency and the Independence Day celebration.

The door opened and another little one entered. How could anyone teach with these constant interruptions? She must mail off her resignation letter without delay.

Martha Jefferson gave him a hug. "My little brother."

Thomas Jefferson joined her. "My little brother."

"Welcome," Sophia said. She tried to shake his hand, but he ducked under the table.

"No white woman before," Frank explained.

And probably no school before, small as he was. Well, there was no time to complete the registration and naming process. Hopefully the newcomers would follow along with the others. She glanced at her pocket watch. "Let us pray before we go. Dear Jesus, please help us follow our teacher's instructions. Amen."

Frank carried the flag. The soldiers at Fort Randall had donated an outdated one, short two stars, and Will had fashioned a pole for it. The students lined up, smallest to largest, giving the newcomers plenty of guidance.

"All right. Let me look at you." Sophia went down the line, smoothing hair, tucking shirts. The students had dressed in their Sunday clothes today, but still no one had shoes. Many wore around their necks a braid of gray-green grass that gave off a pleasant fragrance. The girls wore flowers in their hair like Ukrainians.

"What a beautiful class! Remember to sing loudly. All right, Frank, lead the way."

Rosalie had to use the latrine. Marguerite volunteered to stay with her and help her catch up so the rest would not be late. How Russian these students were, Sophia thought, always considering the good of the group. Perhaps it was because they were all related, all family. *But are we not all the family of God? Should we not always look out for each other?*

The line stretched the distance of a city block. Sophia counted forty-eight children and six dogs. If the Brulé chose today to wage war, where would she hide them all?

This week she had discovered her students were gifted at memorization. They had learned the lyrics to "America" in an hour. Singing in front of seven hundred family members was another matter. Sophia had asked if the church's melodeon could be rolled outside to serve as accompaniment, but Henry had informed her it was bolted to the floor to prevent theft. When they arrived at the church, she found Will had moved the pews outside. The students lined up in front of the room. Their families sat on the floor inside or stood outside around the open windows. How Russian, she thought again.

Henry placed his hands on the keyboard.

"'America,'" Sophia told him.

"'My Country 'Tis of Thee'?" he whispered. "I thought you were singing 'Yankee Doodle.'"

"The students asked me what it meant and I could not explain it to them. 'Doodle' sounds very much like the German word for simpleton. Not good. And 'With the girls be handy'? Is that a sentiment you want in church?"

Henry grunted, as close as he would come to agreeing with her, then turned to the hymn. He gave the opening chord and the students came to attention.

"My country 'tis of thee . . ." They started tentatively. And as well they might. Was it really their country?

"Sweet land of liberty . . ." In their short lives, the tribe had lost considerable liberty.

"Land where my fathers died . . ." At least that line applied.

"Land of the pilgrims' pride . . ." How did they feel about the pilgrims, those early invaders?

"From every mountainside, let freedom ring!"

Would freedom be possible for the Poncas? What would freedom look like for them?

The second verse spoke of love for their native country with its hills and woods. The students' voices gave their best to this verse.

Henry launched into the third verse, then realized the children had finished, and sounded a belated final chord. The parents applauded and the children dispersed to their families.

"Thank you for accompanying us."

"That song has four verses," Henry snapped.

Nettie stepped between them to hug Sophia. "And your students learned half of them. In only a day. Well done! Few Americans know that much by heart."

The congregation exited the church.

"Teacher." John Adams tugged on her elbow. "This is my aunt. She wants a dress like her sister, Julia."

"I am so sorry." Sophia clasped the woman's hands and tried to remember the words Will used. "The dresses were all given out. I have written letters to friends in New York, requesting more." And fabric for more practical garments, such as underclothes.

Soon she was surrounded by women from Point Village and Hubdon, asking, she assumed, about dresses. They would not look her in the eye, but had no reservations about lifting her skirt to examine her shoes, fingering the trim on her sleeve, and touching her hair. Sophia had pared down her wardrobe to modest, simple designs and sober colors, befitting a missionary. But for those who had so little, it must seem an abundance of wealth.

A middle-aged woman towed a tall boy into the group. "Hello, Teacher. I am Bear Shield."

"Pleased to meet you, Mr. Shield." Sophia was delighted to meet anyone capable of interpreting.

The boy put in requests on behalf of the women, who then hurried to the pit where Will carved slices of beef that James served with biscuits.

Bear Shield, however, stayed fixed in place. He looked down at his toes and scuffed a foot in the dirt. "Do you have any books?"

Sophia blinked, then smiled. "You like to read?"

Bear Shield knew words to warm a teacher's heart. "Yes, but I might forget if I do not practice."

"I would be glad to have you attend school."

He shook his head. "I must help my father farm."

She nodded. A head taller than her oldest student, he would not fit in. "What reader did you complete?"

"I do not remember. I read the story of Jesus and the blind man."

"The fourth reader. Excellent. Yes, I will find a book for you. Could you stop by the agency house this evening?"

Bear Shield agreed, then galloped off to eat.

Nettie linked arms with Sophia. "When I'm surrounded by people all asking for one thing or another, I remember how the crowds followed Jesus during His time on earth. No wonder He went away alone sometimes."

"Yes, it is fatiguing." Sophia paused to catch her breath. "Will warned me not to show favoritism."

"I wish I'd heeded his warning. Put your money toward one small problem and you've soon got a hundred big problems on your hands." Nettie's shoulders slumped as if the entire weight of the tribe rested on her. "Take your moment, then come eat."

Below them the entire tribe assembled in one large picnic. Families sat on the grass to eat and visit. Young children raced between groups. Julia and the other elegantly dressed women fluttered, showing off their finery. Zlata and her puppies circled, watching for anyone who did not have a good grip on his sandwich. The sun shone over all, as American as any picnic. All they lacked was a baseball game.

Perhaps the New York teams might donate their old uniforms and equipment. Perhaps baseball fans could donate clothing to the tribe. Why should she limit her requests for help to churches?

But none of this would happen if she went to China.

A steamboat sounded upriver. Sophia hurried into the house for her letters.

James reached the river's edge first. "Something's wrong," he said in an undertone.

Soldiers with rifles lined the boat's decks. The man in the pilothouse, whose job it was to watch the river for sawyers and sand-bars, was flanked by more riflemen studying the bluffs through spyglasses.

The landing stage extended, and the captain met them half-way. He leaned close, face grim. "Indians on the warpath. Custer got wiped out, scalped, him and the whole entire Seventh Cavalry. I'd advise you and the missus"—he nodded at Sophia—"and any other Americans, to evacuate."

Sophia chilled. Her hand, of its own volition, touched the nape of her neck.

"What the—" James sputtered.

"How far away is the battlefield?" Sophia asked. "Were there wounded?"

"No, ma'am. Not a one left. It was a massacre. Way up off the Yellowstone River, in Montana, thousand miles or so." The captain jerked his thumb over his shoulder.

For the third time today Sophia was reminded of Russia: here, too, the rivers crossed extraordinary distances.

The captain wiped his brow with an embroidered handkerchief. "Go round up the rest, get packing. I'll wait half an hour. No more. Want to get as far downriver as I can before nightfall."

Were they in that much danger that they should leave immediately? Did the warpath lead here?

White Swan and several other men brought out drums and began pounding out a four-beat rhythm. Were they signaling other tribes, making plans to continue the slaughter?

Perhaps she could do more good for them by going east to collect the supplies they needed. She could speak to the government officials she had met at Montgomery Hill, travel to Washington City even. She could bathe in a proper tub and catch up on her newspaper reading.

"I'll tell the others," James said.

Sophia turned to follow. A colorful flash caught her eye—Julia in her new dress. Rosalie crowned Moon Hawk's baby girl with a circlet of yellow flowers. Frank and Joseph ran a three-legged race against the Adams brothers. Lone Chief and Little Chief stood by the church, arms raised in prayer.

Sophia put her letter to the Mission Board in her pocket, then handed the rest of her correspondence and a dime to the captain. "I will be staying. If you would please post these, I would be ever so grateful. And now, if you will excuse me."

"Hey, lady," yelled a private. "You want to be scalped like Custer?"

She supposed she should make some missionary comment about God's will, but she was not in the mood. She was no stranger to death. She had seen battlefields in Crimea and Caucasia. Fathers, brothers, sons. Bodies destroyed by cannon fire, scattered across fields, stacked like hay. Blood running in the trenches. The wounded crying for release. And the smell—

Sophia hurried toward the latrine. Too late. The side of the house was as far as her feet managed before her stomach rebelled at the nightmare memories.

"Sophia?" Will touched her shoulder. She shook her head and tried to wave him away, but he did not leave.

"Here." He held out a dipper of fresh water. "You're staying?"

She took the water, rinsed her mouth, and nodded. "Yes. I find I have fallen in love."

He froze with his hand reaching out toward the dipper. "With James?"

"Perish the thought." She placed the dipper in his hand. "With the Poncas. With little Rosalie and her siblings, Moon Hawk and her daughter, Julia and baby Timothy, Lone Chief."

Will's eyes locked on her face. One eyebrow rose, and he nodded. Had she finally met with his approval?

"Perhaps I cannot accomplish anything as grand as my father's freeing the serfs, but I will do my best. And you? Are you staying?"

"Yes." He studied the bluffs. "Lone Chief says it was the Cheyenne and the Lakota, relatives of the Brulé. The Poncas won't be siding with the likes of them."

"He knew?" Her stomach settled.

Will nodded but did not elaborate. "If you're all right, I'll go see what Henry and Nettie have decided."

She pushed off the wall. "I shall come with you."

The church bell rang. Faces grim, the villagers hurried to the building.

Henry sat with his head bowed, fists clenched between his knees until James thumped his shoulder. The reverend dragged himself to the pulpit. He opened the Book of Common Prayer, then with a slow shake of his head, set it aside. "Dear brothers and sisters in Christ." He scanned the congregation, tears in his eyes. "Sad news has reached us this morning of a horrible battle upriver. Let us join together in prayer."

He bowed his head. "Heavenly Father, we lift up to You the souls of those lost in this violence, that You would conduct them to Your heavenly gates with due dispatch . . . er, quickly. We pray for those who were injured, that they will find relief from pain. We pray for the families of those lost in this battle, that You would comfort them. And we pray for the government in Washington City, that they will make wise decisions in the face of this tragedy. Help us labor together for peace. In Your name, amen." He led them in singing "Jesus, Lover of My Soul."

A fool, Sophia thought. *But a holy fool.*

Families took their children in hand and started the long walk home. The joyful noise of this morning had ebbed into silence. The women did not keen, the children did not talk. Once again, no one would meet Sophia's gaze.

James ran back to the steamboat and waved it on downriver. The whistle sounded three low notes, then their lifeline to civilization disappeared around the bend.

An isolated cloud rolled over the village, blotting out the sun. One bolt of lightning with its attendant thunder shook loose a drenching downpour. The spaces between buildings turned to mud.

Sophia hurried into the house and up the stairs. A waterfall spouted from a drooping spot in the ceiling. The rain was drenching her bed and her books. Ruined! All ruined! Unreadable by Bear Shield or anyone else.

Those in English she would replace at her next bookstore visit.

The French she could reorder. But the Russian—no, not her father's copy of *Fathers and Sons*, signed by Ivan Sergeyevich Turgenev himself!

The day's accumulation of tears breached her defenses, her loss of control adding to her misery. She flung the books into the hall, wrestled the window closed, dragged the bed across the floor, and positioned the washbasin under the rivulet.

Such a waste. This whole teaching experience was a waste. She should be on the steamboat out of here, out of this wretched land with its ravenous mosquitoes and bottomless poverty and—

"Sophia?" Will called from the foot of the stairs. "What was that noise?"

"I am rearranging the furniture. To accommodate a waterfall."

"You decent? I'm coming up."

Decent? A glance in the mirror showed a bedraggled rat, hair hanging in Medusa-like snakes around her face, dress splotched and limp. Sophia found a handkerchief that had somehow escaped the deluge and dried her eyes.

Will paused in the doorway and looked up at the ceiling. "Those shingles would have to be twice as good to be second rate."

Sophia dared a glance at him. His hair had responded to the rain by curling into ringlets. He sat on his heels and picked up the nearest book. "I'm sorry."

"You did not make it rain." She bent to assist him. Her Russian poetry might dry. Several volumes of the lives of saints were not as damaged as she had first thought.

"I built this house."

Will was responsible for this loosely connected pile of lumber? Yet he handled her books with reverence, easing the pages apart and setting them on end. "Hey, Catharine Beecher autographed this to you."

"You know who she is?"

"My sister's a teacher." He squinted up at her as if she were a puzzle. "What's a pearl like you doing with us swine?"

"I am hardly—" A glance out the window showed the Agency's resemblance to an animal pen. "I am trying to serve God."

He made a sound in the back of his throat, then nodded at her bed. "Best get you another."

The addition of water to the old mattress added an unwelcome effluvium to the air.

"What is it about this place?" Sophia removed the sheets.

Will rolled up the dripping mess, then paused, waiting until she met his gaze. His eyes warmed. "You mean one moment you're thinking you're right where God wants you to be, and the next you're wishing you were long gone?"

He understood. Her tension drained and she managed a smile. "Exactly."

CHAPTER SIXTEEN

Any news?" Sophia asked James on Monday afternoon. The school building was far enough from the riverfront that she might have missed hearing a small boat.

"No. It's been quiet." He helped her close the windows. He had dispensed with his vest and wore only a muslin shirt. In this heat, fashion and propriety surrendered to practicality. "I thought perhaps we would have more students now that the parents have seen the school is open. But instead many were missing." Sophia poured the last few drops from the water bucket onto her wrists, trying to cool off from the oven-like heat. Unfortunately, discarding a few layers was not an option for women. Julia's ointment had cured her mosquito bites' hot itching, but the rest of her skin threatened to erupt in a heat rash any moment. "Have the Poncas gone on a hunt?"

"Not without permission. Or horses."

He did not volunteer any theories, leaving Sophia to carry the conversation as they walked. "Well, I took advantage of the small class. Marguerite, Frank, and Joseph have been promoted to the second reader. Rosalie can now say the alphabet and Susette can write it as well. All can count to one hundred, write their numbers, and recognize coins."

Zlata and her puppies emerged from a cool hole under a bush. "Sit," Sophia said, holding up a bit of leftover sandwich. Four furry bottoms hit the dirt.

"All that, and you've taught the dogs English as well."

He gave her a sidelong glance, and Sophia couldn't tell if he was praising her or mocking her. She handed out the treats to the dogs, who then joined their parade.

The agent fell silent again as they walked, staring straight ahead.

"James, what worries you?"

"We haven't seen anyone from Fort Randall. After the news, I expected them to step up their patrols."

Considering her experience with the soldiers at the fort, Sophia imagined them to be cowering under their beds or drowning their sorrows. "Perhaps they await orders."

"No. They have standing orders to protect us. And the settlers. Ah, that's it. Bet they're playing host to a bevy of homesteaders."

"You did not consider joining them?"

He cocked a skeptical eyebrow at her. "You've met a few of their soldiers."

"Perhaps we should pray for them." There, now she sounded like a missionary.

He rubbed the back of his neck. "After this battle with the Sioux, I expect there will be more talk about closing the Agency and moving the Poncas to Indian Territory."

"Close the Agency? But . . . this is their homeland." How many decades had Lone Chief and his predecessors prayed over this land? Will said their burial ground was on the bluff. "Where is this 'Indian Territory'?"

"Six hundred miles south of here."

"A significant change in climate and vegetation."

James shrugged. "The Poncas have talked about leaving, maybe going to live with the Omaha tribe—they're cousins of a sort. But Nebraskans are calling for all Indians to leave the state."

"Why? You said the Poncas are considered well on their way to becoming civilized."

"More civilized than some whites, but most don't recognize that. This land is in demand for homesteading."

They emerged from the copse to a refreshing breeze off the river.

Sophia waved at the surrounding green hills. "So much open space here. Should there not be room enough for all?"

He swabbed his forehead with a dingy handkerchief. "In Indian Territory they'll combine the Poncas with the other tribes already there. Save some tax dollars." A muscle in James's cheek twitched. "Congress voted to move the tribe."

"But the Indian Office just built a new school. It would not make any sense for them to close the Agency."

Will spotted them and waved, yelling about a problem at the mill. James loped off, yelling over his shoulder, "Next I suppose you'll tell me the Russian government is always logical and efficient."

In the shade of the porch, Nettie shelled a large bowl of peas while Henry read the newspaper.

"What is the news?" Sophia asked.

"Our troops were massacred," Henry muttered from behind the Yankton paper. "Five companies. Custer, his two brothers, nephew, and brother-in-law, all gone. The battlefield was a slaughter pen."

"They're calling the Indians savages, saying it's time to settle their barbaric roaming." Nettie flung a pod into her bucket. She nodded at their neighbors' pergola, where Black Elk played with White Buffalo Girl, lifting her over his head, blowing kisses on the baby's belly until she giggled. "What worries me," she said as another pod struck with a ping, "is that most white people can't tell a Ponca from a potato."

✦

Will hefted the dishpan and carried it outside to dump. A flicker on the bluff caught his attention. A prairie fire? He dropped the pan and dashed inside for his spyglass.

"What is it?" James followed.

"Bonfire." He passed the glass.

"May I see?" Sophia asked. She'd gone upstairs earlier and come down with a copy of *Gulliver's Travels* for Bear Shield. "Oh, the Poncas seem to be having a party."

Henry took the spyglass from her. "Not their usual sun-worshipping."

Will yanked on his boots. He thought he was wise to the Poncas' doings, that they'd taken him into their confidence, that they trusted him. But he hadn't heard one word about a bonfire tonight.

"May I come with you? I would like to see the top of the bluff."

"It's not safe," James and Henry said in unison.

"Not much of a trail," Will said. "And it'll be night on the way back."

"I shall bring a lantern and my pistol."

"What?" all three men chorused.

"Where did you get a pistol?" The agent loomed over her, as if his height might intimidate Sophia.

"Monsieur LeGrand, the drummer."

"He's a charlatan of the first degree. Probably took your money and left you a theater prop."

Sophia straightened. "I should say not. The pistol is accurate at fifty feet. And Monsieur LeGrand was quite fair in his negotiations."

"Accurate? That was you this morning?" Will asked.

The rev growled. "Lucky you didn't shoot your foot off."

"My father, Constantin Ilia Makinoff, instructed me in marksmanship."

"How much?" James asked. "What'd you pay him?"

Before their eyes, Sophia transformed into Queen Victoria.

She managed to look down at the agent, giving him a royal how-dare-you, even though James was a foot taller. "Exactly where did you grow up, Mr. Lawrence? I should like to know where it is considered acceptable behavior to make such inquiries."

"Fiendish dancing." The rev returned the spyglass to Will, then marched off for the bluff. James took a few leaping steps, trying to escape Sophia and use his long legs to be first up the narrow path.

"I love dancing." Sophia took the lantern off the back porch and followed.

Will joined the parade. "Only the men dance."

"I shall watch, then."

"They didn't ask us to come." Silly woman, sticking her nose in where it didn't belong. At the least he hoped she'd slow the rev down, but unfortunately she kept up, even on the steep scramble to the top.

A skeeter-scatterer, as Will's sister-in-law called the wind, blew off the heat of the day and cooled his sweat. The yellow dogs greeted them with wagging tails.

"Zlata and her troika! Are you enjoying the party?" Sophia petted them, then stretched her arms out as if embracing the prairie. "It is beautiful. Like the Russian steppes."

"You Russians put steps in your hills?" the rev asked between huffing and puffing. He grabbed Thomas Jefferson as he darted by. "What is the meaning of this fracas?"

"Treaty." The child squirmed away. "Hi, Teacher!"

"What treaty?" James gave up on his official pose to brace his hands on his knees and gasp for breath. "I didn't sign"—he heaved again—"any treaty."

Will scanned the horizon. Sophia was right. It was beautiful. Evening's sun turned the Missouri's mud to gold and the sky to deep blue. Ponca Creek sparkled in from the south. Up here the reservation seemed peaceful. Up here the fallow fields, pastures emptied by the Brulé, and houses built of scrap didn't show. "Stay with me," he told Sophia, but he'd already lost her.

"C'mon, Dunn. I need an interpreter." The rev marched to the bonfire. God ought to blister Henry's butt for failing to learn the language. But no, English-only was the policy until something needed to be said. Will wove his way through the dancers, keeping an eye out for the fearless, foolish teacher.

The Poncas' song sounded like the one Will had heard once before, when they'd brought home a buffalo. Five men sat around the big drum, keeping time. The rest circled the bonfire clockwise, doing their fancy footwork, shaking gourd rattles. They wore their traditional clothes, deerskin decorated with beads, feathered head-dresses, breastplates of bone hair pipe, red face paint. Several had sleigh bells around their arms and legs. The women stood around the outside of the circle, holding children or clapping and stamping their feet. Everyone sang, raising their voices to the sky, thanking God for His care.

The rev dragged Will into the circle, where he grabbed Lone Chief's arm. If his plan was to block the dancers, it failed. The circle widened to accommodate the obstruction. The chief kept moving, towing Henry along.

"What is the meaning of this heathen display?" the rev yelled. "I demand you stop! Immediately!"

Will said in Ponca, "He wants you to stop."

Lone Chief removed the cedar whistle he'd been blowing and grinned. "So I guessed."

"What did he say?" The firelight and setting sun made the rev's face look as red as the devil's.

"He knows you're not happy." The beat was contagious. Will's feet moved in time.

The rev waved his fists as if he'd like to grab the elder and give him a shaking. "Then why is he doing this?"

Because your happiness is not his goal, Will thought. He turned to Lone Chief, wondering how to fit his carpenter's vocabulary to the question. "Why?" He made a sweeping motion, encompassing the fire, the drummers, and the dancers.

"We made a treaty with the Brulé. We bury the past to survive the future."

Will relayed that message.

Henry whipped his head back and forth hard enough to make his hat fall off. He stabbed the air with his finger. "You can't make a treaty without the government, without the Great White Father! Where is this treaty? Did you even write it down? Who witnessed it? You didn't have permission to leave the Agency and the Brulé didn't have permission to come here, so you're all in violation."

Will boiled the tirade down. "He has many questions."

"Yes, he does." Lone Chief nodded. "But now is the time to celebrate, to thank God for the end of the war."

"He said they're thanking God the war's over."

"He said the name of his God, not ours. This is a heathen ritual. It must stop. If they want to thank the one true God, they must come to church." The rev pointed to the building at the base of the bluff.

"Too small," Lone Chief said in English. He shook off the rev and moved back into the flow of the dancers. Will made his escape. Henry made a "stop" motion at the drummers, who grinned and picked up the pace. He tried again with a cluster of dancers who waved back. Finally he stormed off. Sunday would bring a blistering sermon.

Will had ventured an opinion once, that the Indian's God and the white man's God was the same, just that their name for Him was different and they worshipped differently. After all, Sunday mornings with the Baptists didn't look the same as the Methodist song-fest or Episcopal hullabaloo.

The rev had just about tarred and feathered Will, ranting that other denominations were on the ragged edge of salvation, hanging on to heaven by their fingernails. Will had better not be weakening the gospel message with any heresy. After all, he hadn't been to seminary. What did a carpenter know anyway?

The rev had been dispensed with, and James was watching the festivities with crossed arms. Will figured he'd best rescue Sophia from whatever trouble she'd gotten herself into—if he could find her in this crowd. The only people moving were the dancers, so Will stepped into the circle.

"Welcome, brother!" Brown Eagle clapped him on the back. Will hadn't recognized him under his headdress. "You do not dance?"

"Not well." Will tried to keep up with his friend's footwork. "I look for the teacher."

"She is with my daughters."

Well then, he might as well dance. Will went around the circle twice until his feet stung. How did these men stomp in their moccasins? He waved to Brown Eagle and stepped out. Sophia had been on her feet all day. She might be ready to go too.

A flickering outside the firelight caught his eye. Sophia's hair had fallen out of its knot to form a gold cape down her back. She led a circle of girls, hands linked at shoulder height. They wheeled around, stepping and stomping. As the tempo changed, she showed them more moves, little kicks, stepping into the circle while making a bow over one arm, clapping overhead, spinning. Even though she danced beyond the light of the bonfire, beyond the lantern's weak flame, her face glowed. She spotted Will and waved.

"The beat is a little slow," she said breathlessly, "but it is perfect for teaching."

"Shouldn't the children be learning from their parents?"

"But they do not have a dance for the girls." She stopped and pressed her hands to her cheeks. "Have I violated some cultural taboo? Or a religious rule? Episcopalians dance, do they not? But then, I suppose learning a Ukrainian dance will not help them become American." She sighed. "Being a missionary is complicated."

Like the Poncas' dance.

During his growing-up years, Will's older brother had coached him on how to behave at a dance, trying to break him of his bashfulness. He'd learned how to invite girls to dances, ask them to partner with him for the next set, and escort them home. Did any of those lessons apply here?

Didn't matter. He couldn't recall a bit of what Harrison had said anyway.

"So, we have settled our curiosity about the bonfire, attended a party without an invitation, and congratulated the tribe on successfully ending warfare with the Brulé. I suppose we should leave them to their celebration and return to the house before full dark." Sophia wished the girls a good night. "Should we collect James and Henry?"

"Already went down." Will raised his chin toward the house where the men stood. Then he grabbed the lantern and led her to the path. "Aren't you tired? You've been standing all day."

"I sit frequently."

"Only for a moment. Like a chickadee." *A chickadee?* He sounded like a fool.

"Will. How poetic. I keep thinking, if I were a better teacher, I could run the classroom from my desk, the way a pilot runs the steamboat."

"The pilot steers the steamboat from on high. But he's got the leadsmen on the bow checking the river's depth, the engineer watching the boilers, the fireman feeding the fuel. The school only has one person. You."

Sophia smiled at him. "So. I steer the classroom, but must also check the depth of knowledge, watch for snags of frustration, feed new material to the students. Brilliant analogy, Will. How many years did you attend school?"

"A few. Here and there." *What's an analogy?*

"A self-educated man. You must read a lot."

"The Bible mostly." He reached a steep part in the trail and turned to help her. Her hand slipped easily into his. It was less easy to let go. "Other books when I get a chance."

"Thanks to your help, my library has recovered from the deluge. Please feel free to borrow whatever you like."

Now, that was a grand offer. When Will had asked the rev, he'd been turned down flat, probably out of fear he might get sawdust on the pages. "Thank you kindly. I'd be glad to take up your offer this winter, when I've more time."

Sophia nodded at the house, where sunset glinted off the peak of the roof. "Speaking of my books," she said, "I am curious about what you used to patch the hole."

"Ran out of shingles but we had plenty of empty cans. I flattened them out. Let me know if you have more leaks."

They reached the bottomlands and could walk side by side. Her hand slid up to rest on his elbow. The wind blew her hair across his forearm. He wanted to run his hands through it, from her scalp down to the curls at the ends. It might be worth getting slapped, but it wouldn't be worth losing Sophia's kind regard.

"James said Congress voted to move the tribe. But now that the Brulé are no longer a threat, the tribe will not have to leave."

Will stifled his frustration. Just when he thought he was making progress, Sophia took to quoting the agent. "Hope you're right. Most often money disappears before it makes it all the way out here."

"So you are not worried."

"Plenty to pray about."

"What do you think of this treaty?"

"Henry says it's not worth the paper it's not written on."

"As the Russians say, written with a pitchfork on water."

James and Henry stood on the porch, looking as grim as parents whose daughter has been brought home late. "Where have you been?" the rev demanded, as if he had no idea.

Sophia spun in a circle, arms out. "At the dance. What a blessing to be relieved of the constant threat of raids! And to see my students are safe and planning to return to school. How American of them to take the initiative and make their own treaty!"

Will didn't have to say a word.

CHAPTER SEVENTEEN

B last, it's time to fetch Sophia." James stepped into the kitchen. "Will. Good. Solomon Draper's visiting, you know, from the Niobrara newspaper."

Will didn't know Mr. Draper, but he did know a bit about Sophia. If no one arrived to escort her back to the house, she might take it into her head to walk back alone. He took off at a run as fast as the July heat allowed. Besides, he enjoyed watching her teach. She got as excited as the children about learning. And maybe she'd play that gosling.

Will wasn't the only one visiting the school today. Bear Shield was just leaving, having exchanged *Gulliver's Travels* for Jules Verne's *Journey to the Center of the Earth*. Then Lone Chief and Little Chief made their entrance, accompanied by Lone Chief's black-and-brown dog.

Sophia looked up from helping Rosalie with her numbers. Her gaze took in the elderly men, then shifted to Will with a questioning arch of her eyebrows. She greeted the chiefs in French, gave the dog a pat, and shook Will's hand. "Good afternoon, Mr. Dunn."

Why was she being so formal? Oh. She was teaching, setting an example. "Good afternoon, Miss Makinoff."

In Ponca the chiefs told her they had come to see the ball of the earth.

The what? Will started to interpret, but Sophia raised a regal finger in his direction—*wait*—and nodded at Joseph.

"They have come to see your round map of the world," said the boy.

She nodded. "You may show it to them."

Will peered between the chiefs' shoulders. He'd heard of globes and seen one in a store window once, but his schoolhouse had only a flat map. Both old men were losing their eyesight, so the boy moved their fingers to show the men where the Poncas lived, where Washington City was, and the many places their teacher had lived. They asked about Belgium, where the Catholic priest Black Gown had been born, and had Sophia recite the Lord's Prayer in Russian.

Sophia unrolled a map of the United States. Frank showed the chiefs the locations of their friends, the Omaha tribe, and their old enemies, the Brulé. And they showed her the Ponca hunting grounds, from the Black Hills to the Rockies down to Kansas.

Then Joseph held the globe, one hand on each pole, in the sunbeam and showed how the earth rotated for night and day.

"Whose hands hold up our earth?" Lone Chief asked.

"God's," Little Chief answered. The two elders and the dog headed out.

Sophia thanked Joseph for interpreting, then dismissed the class. Eyes sparkling, she turned to Will. "Shall I count that as a science or Bible lesson?"

"Both, I figure." He smiled back. She was smart, beautiful, had a sense of humor. Compassionate, dedicated to God, hard-working. What was wrong with the men in the rest of the world that they hadn't asked her to marry?

Will put the globe in its stand. "Speaking of lessons, I've got one for you. If you don't mind."

Her hands stilled on the window. For several long seconds, he figured she did mind. What could a carpenter from a one-room schoolhouse tell a teacher from a fancy New York college? Then she turned and smiled like a lantern had lit up inside her.

"Will." Her voice had a surprised note to it. "Yes, I would appreciate knowing all you would like to teach me. Please. Go ahead." She perched on the middle bench, motioned him toward the teacher's desk with a fancy turn of her wrist, then folded her hands in front of her.

Will looked down at the scuffed toes of his boots. "It's nothing big. About the names. Of the people. They're all one word. No first and last names. Like, Standing Bear is *Ma-chú-nu-zhe*. White Eagle is *Ke-tha-ska*. Buffalo Chip is *Ta-zha-but*. All one word."

She closed her eyes, put her fingertips to her mouth, and shook her head. "Oh, Will. Names are so important. I have been saying, 'Mr. Eagle,' when it ought to be 'Mr. Brown Eagle'?"

He nodded. "Mission Board should have told you."

"I have erred with all I have met." She winced. "Are they terribly offended?"

Offended? After smallpox and broken treaties, bungling a person's name didn't make the list. Yesterday, he'd heard Yellow Horse and Long Runner joking about coming up with a Ponca name for the new teacher.

"Maybe if you wrote a note of apology, had the butler take it around . . ."

He glanced up, wondering if he'd gone too far.

He hadn't. Sophia burst into a hearty laugh, giving him an "ahh" feeling, like when he measured a trim piece and it fit perfectly, without a gap.

"So." She locked the school. "The butler, not the footman?" Her smile faded, replaced by a sad, longing look. "No. A stable boy towing a three-year-old thoroughbred."

Back to wishing they could solve the tribe's problems. "If wishes were horses . . ."

⤫

Such good memories, these children. Sophia held out a handful of coins. "Which is the penny?" she asked Martha Jefferson.

The little girl pointed to the small copper coin. A murmur of approval rippled through the students.

"Correct. The three-cent piece? The two-cent piece? The nickel? Good. The half-dime and the dime?" She held her breath. The students called these tricksters, but they did not fool Martha. The little finger touched each coin. Sophia stood, stretching the ache in her back from bending over her small students. "Bravo! After only a month of school everyone in our class knows the coins! Let us celebrate with a song!"

All smiles, the class stood and sang what Will had told her was their warrior song. Sophia added the simple accompaniment she had worked out on her gusli.

Halfway through the third stanza, Henry barged in. "Stop!" He marched to the front of the room. "They must speak English. No other language."

Wide-eyed, the children cowered on the benches. The little ones, Martha and Rosalie, hid behind their older siblings. How dare he interrupt her class and frighten her students! Sophia stepped in front of him. She would keep them from harm.

"Students, let us show Reverend Granville what we have learned. All together." She held up a coin. "This is a—"

Matthew and Frank gathered their courage. "Half-dollar."

"Very good. Everyone, please. This is a—"

Most of the class said penny. They correctly identified the nickel, dime, and half-dime too. What was Henry here for anyway?

Sophia glanced at her watch. Four o'clock already? "Reverend Granville, do you have a closing song for us?"

His frown had her students hiding their faces again. "No. Class dismissed."

The children escaped. Sophia crossed her arms and glared at Henry. He propped his hands on his hips and scowled like Ivan the Terrible. "Miss Makinoff, I was perfectly clear. The children must speak English and only English during the school day. They have plenty of time at home for Indian gibberish."

"But—"

"Authorities at high levels in the Department of Interior are questioning the entire concept of Indian education." Henry went into fire-and-brimstone mode, complete with pacing, pointing, and pontificating. "If the children do not learn in day schools, the Commissioner of Indian Affairs may require boarding schools. The children would be taken away from their parents and sent hundreds of miles away. Maybe you didn't mind boarding school, but these parents dote on their children. Do you want that on your head, that because of you, these children could not grow up in their homeland?"

"Certainly not! Catharine Beecher disapproves of boarding schools."

"The inspector can visit at any time. And he expects to hear children speaking, reading, writing, and, yes, singing English. Do I make myself clear?"

Sophia clenched her fists. She refused to cry in front of this man. "You have no right to interrupt my class."

"I have every right. I am your supervisor."

"Is that what you want to teach the children?" she asked. "The one who has the loud voice wins?"

"I wasn't through talking. You interrupted me."

Will walked into the classroom carrying a plank and hammer. "Ah, Christian harmony."

Henry snorted. "If the Board had sent an American teacher, he'd be teaching American songs." He stomped out.

Sophia's jaw ached with suppressed words. Taking as deep a breath as her corset allowed, she forced her fingers to straighten.

With a few quick bangs of his hammer, Will attached the piece under the chalkboard.

"A chalk tray. Thank you." She locked the windows, collected the slates, and righted the books on the shelf. "Students at the College sang 'My Grandfather's Clock.' But timepieces are scarce in this community."

He wiggled the wood. It held. "I'll teach you some American songs, if you bring your gosling back to the house."

"My gosling? Oh, the gusli. That would be so kind." Sophia wrapped the instrument in its cloth bag. Her mind pictured Julia wrapping baby Timothy in his blanket, Black Elk hugging White Buffalo Girl, Brown Eagle pulling his children close. "Is it true, that the government might take the children away?"

"You're asking me what the Indian Commissioner's planning?" Will set the wiping rag and chalk on the tray.

"Does this inspector visit often? Are we notified of upcoming visits? Should I prepare a program?" Sophia collected the lunch pails and walked out with Will, pausing to lock the door. "Does he inspect you? Is he quite strict?"

Will waved his hammer at the bluffs where wildflowers bloomed in abundance. "Lilies of the field."

"Ah, yes. Do not worry. Besides, compared to the many worries besetting the tribe . . ."

The yellow dog and her puppies dashed to the edge of the path and sat in a row, watching her with eager brown eyes and wagging tails.

"Ah, Zlata, if everyone was so happy to see me . . ." She divided the remains of her sandwich among them, then continued along the path with Will. "I have some ideas."

With an easy swing of his arm, Will tossed his hammer in the air. It circled twice. He caught it by the handle. "I bet you do."

❧

"Will kindly offered to teach me American children's songs," Sophia announced to the others around the table at supper. "If any of you would care to join us."

So much for having Sophia to himself. Will set his plate in the dishpan. Well, he couldn't expect a lady to sit alone with the likes of him.

Nettie clapped her hands under her chin just like little Rosalie. "That sounds like fun. Let's meet on the front porch, where it's cooler."

"I have a sermon to write." The rev stomped off to the office, earning a glare from his mother.

"Be glad to help." The agent didn't pass up a chance to impress Sophia.

While Nettie washed up and James tanked up, Sophia unwrapped her gusli. Since it was Will's idea, he took the seat next to her. A brisk wind off the river kept the mosquitoes away. Far to the north lightning lit up a line of clouds.

"What is that?" Sophia nodded at the pieces of wood in his hand.

"It's a limberjack, to help keep time." Will showed her the dancing doll attached to a stick. "Let's try 'Pop Goes the Weasel.' I'll show you how it works." He put the thin board under his leg and held the limberjack over it. The loose-limbed man at the end danced on the board, keeping a smart pace. At the 'pop,' he jumped with a loud snap.

Sophia laughed. "A percussion instrument. How delightful. Could you bring it to school?"

"Sure. I made one for Frank, if you can get him to play it." He motioned for Sophia to join him on the gusli. She turned out to be as good at playing by ear as she was at everything else. "Do you know 'Camptown Races'?" he asked.

She frowned and whispered, "Yes, but are you certain singing 'do-dah' is permitted for missionaries?"

"Sure. My mom sang it." They had made it through "Turkey in the Straw" when Nettie and James joined them.

"You've been talking to your students about sheep for 'Mary Had a Little Lamb.' Do you know 'Baa, Baa, Black Sheep'?" Will sang it.

Sophia joined in. "But of course! It is a French melody. Mozart used it for his piano variations."

When they finished, James put in his two cents. "Same tune works for 'Twinkle, Twinkle, Little Star.'"

"And 'The Alphabet Song,'" Nettie added. "That'll help your students."

They sang those three.

"One melody for three songs. How efficient."

James wasn't finished trying to impress. "The tune for 'Mary Had a Little Lamb' goes to 'London Bridge' also."

"We should teach you the game that goes with it." Nettie collected Henry from inside.

"London? As in England? This is considered an American song?"

"Sure." Will grabbed the opportunity before James could. He led Sophia down the steps to the grass in front of the house and took her soft hands in his. The sun set straight down the Missouri, making her hair shine like gold. "We'll be the bridge."

The others crept under their linked hands until "my fair lady," when they caught James.

"My students will love this." Sophia's eyes glowed.

"I'm getting a crick in my back." James traded places with the teacher, leaving Will with the much less satisfying job of holding the man's sweaty hands. They sang through the verses and caught each other.

"And that's the last," Will said after "Give him a pipe to smoke all night." He let go and dried his hands on his pants.

The agent knew better. "No, there's a verse or two about a dog."

From the shadows came a chorus of giggles and snickers. The entire village had gathered to watch their antics.

The rev muttered about dignity and ordered the staff inside. Only James followed.

"Guess we're a pretty funny bunch." Nettie joined in the laughter.

Will rocked back on his heels and chuckled. "About time we gave them something to smile about."

Sophia grabbed Little Chief, who was about as short as she was, and formed a bridge. Will started the song. Nettie bent and wiggled under, then the rest of the people and Sophia's yellow dogs followed. The bridge captured Little Rosalie on the first verse, Good Provisions on the second, and Moon Hawk with baby White Buffalo Girl on the third. Then Big Snake, at close to seven feet the tallest man in the tribe, got caught. Sophia's hearty laugh echoed against the bluffs, joined by hoots and howls from the people.

Only God would know that a Russian French teacher was just the right person for the Poncas.

CHAPTER EIGHTEEN

For the first time in weeks Sophia could breathe. They had all decided, given the blistering heat, to take the day and go to the waterfall. A magnificent cataract cascaded into a large pool, then flowed into the creek. The moving water cooled the air, and the lush vegetation around the pool made the place feel like Paradise itself.

Sophia's bathing costume consisted of a blue flannel suit trimmed with white braid. The trousers were gathered at the ankle and covered by a calf-length overdress. Modest by any standard, but when she removed her long bathing mantle, jaws dropped. Henry turned purple and seemed ready to burst into a sermon. James and Will were speechless.

Brown Eagle chuckled and tapped their chins. "Going to eat flies."

"Sophia, what an adorable outfit!" Nettie pulled the back of her skirt between her legs and tucked it into her belt. "Much more convenient than this nonsense. Well, I'm ready."

Paying no attention to all this adult drama, the children plunged into the pool, accompanied by Zlata and her lively puppies. "C'mon, Teacher," Rosalie called.

"Miss Makinoff!" waved Frank.

Sophia stepped into the cool water. "Heavenly!" She glanced at Henry, wondering if he might consider that blasphemous, and amended it to, "We are blessed."

"God has provided." He rolled up the legs of a worn pair of pants and led the way up.

Sophia watched as Will began to climb, the water sluicing down his well-muscled calves. He reminded her of the Samson statue at Peter the Great's palace. Would the rest of him be as well formed? She tried to rein the thought back in but failed. What a pitiful excuse for a missionary she was.

Sophia bent over and dangled her hands until they cooled, then splashed water on her neck and let the drips run down her back.

Every day in August had dawned hotter than the last. The school turned into a furnace, inhabitable only by flies. Will had built her a pergola, which he called a brush arbor, allowing Sophia to conduct classes outdoors in the shade. Even so, it was too hot to concentrate, so she sent the children home soon after lunch.

These deviations from the norm earned her a good measure of disapproval from Henry. She might remind him that most American schools closed for the summer, but it would be a futile argument when her students had so much catching up to do.

"C'mon, Teacher," Frank called.

Sophia would be quite content to stay with Nettie at the pool. But Mary and Elisabeth, Brown Eagle's wives, linked hands, then reached for Nettie. Sophia held her breath, wondering if the older woman would make any comment about the evils of polygamy. Henry certainly would have, had he not been otherwise occupied. But Nettie just smiled, grabbed on, and started up the waterfall. "Save some watermelon for me," she called.

Julia joined the chain and clasped Sophia's hand; she had

little choice but to follow. The Ponca women were as sure-footed as mountain goats, even though Elisabeth was *enceinte*, and Julia carried baby Timothy on her back.

For the first few steps, through the pool at the base, Sophia had no problem finding footholds. But the slope quickly steepened and the water churned. Trees along the bank formed a green tunnel overhead. The shade mottled the surface and further obscured the view of the creek bottom.

Nettie yelled and pointed. Sophia could not hear her words over the roar of the water. She put her foot where the woman indicated and plunged into a hole.

"Ooh!" Blessedly cold water swirled up to her waist. The women giggled, and Sophia hoped Nettie would point out a neck-deep hole the next time.

Will showed Joseph and Frank how to squirt water between their palms. His large hands shot a higher stream than the boys'. Marguerite and Susette splashed back. Rosalie squealed and hid behind her father.

Sophia paused to look behind her but could not see the bottom. She hoped they did not have to descend it. What if someone—herself, for instance—broke a leg? Or twisted an ankle?

Brown Eagle ran down the waterfall, leaping like a deer, and yelled to the women, "This way."

"Halfway to the top." Long-legged Will bounded behind him and called, "Ignore the rushing water."

Sophia laughed. Ignore the rushing water? How could she? It was everywhere! She grasped an overhanging branch and felt for the next foothold. It was here somewhere. Ah, solid rock.

At last she arrived at the top. The children and dogs romped in a quiet pool while the adults dried off and the sun lowered enough to make cooling shadows.

Brown Eagle's Mary handed her a chunk of watermelon. What

a treasure. The family had been carrying water to their garden twice a day all month.

"Thank you." Sophia sat on the bank beside Rosalie and enjoyed the sweet flavor. "This is the most perfect watermelon ever. Magnificent."

Julia dangled her son in the shallows. The boy kicked, spraying himself in the face. His eyes opened wide, then he chuckled and did it again.

"Give me that little man." Will pulled Timothy through the water, splashing the older kids. The man's wide grin showed even, white teeth. He was so good with children. Was he thinking of marrying Julia? He would make a fine husband.

The few who had shoes put them back on. Escorted by yellow and orange butterflies, they walked the long way around, down a gentle slope past newly mown hay fields. Brown Eagle and his family headed south to their home. Julia and her son continued on to hers.

Nettie fanned herself with her hat. "I hope they don't move to Indian Territory. I can't imagine living in a place hotter than here."

Henry said, "Last winter you said you couldn't imagine a place colder than here."

"True. Winter was wicked. Won't be any better this year, with the grasshoppers eating the corn, the sun burning up the wheat, no one having shoes." Nettie tied her hat on. "Sure would be handy to have horses again. And our own boat, so we wouldn't have to wait for a ride to town."

"If we had the money," James said.

If we had the money, Sophia thought as she prepared for bed that night. *If* the tribe did not move to Indian Territory. *If* the grasshoppers didn't return. *If* the annuity payments came on time. *If* the government sent cash instead of trinkets. So many worries.

Will's words came back to her: *Ignore the rushing water.*

CHAPTER NINETEEN

Sophia should have been listening to the oldest students recite, and watching the younger ones write their alphabet and the middle group work their sums, but her mind kept wandering.

The funds allocated for the Poncas' removal could just as readily be used to purchase food and clothing for this winter. Could she write to Congressman Rexford Montgomery? Why did no one seem to care? Without help, her students would sicken and starve. And why had the Board of Foreign Missions not sent the fabric and shoes she requested?

Ignore the rushing water.

Ignore the rush of thoughts and focus on the students.

Sophia smiled at Marguerite. "Perfect. Go trade in your second reader for the third. And the next section . . ."

Halfway through dinner, a low whistle and a plume of smoke announced the arrival of a steamboat.

Please, let it be clothing, fabric, shoes, Sophia prayed. Mail. Barbed wire. Food. Money. What did they not need?

The steamboat tied up to the trees and unloaded several barrels and large boxes. The captain handed Henry a packet of newspapers and mail, including a letter from the Mission Board to Sophia.

"What?" She scanned the page. "They want to know what size shoes and what color fabric to send. Seven hundred seventy-one people will freeze because the Mission Board is afraid of making a fashion error."

James pried open the first barrel. "They'll starve to death first."

Nettie gasped.

"It moves." Sophia stepped back. She was going to lose her dinner.

Will poked his screwdriver into the gray mess. "Pork. Infested with maggots."

Henry groaned. "This shipment was for us too."

Lone Chief's black-and-brown dog sniffed the box, yelped, then ran away.

The next barrel held fifty pounds of mealy flour. Nettie grimaced. "Bring the flour to the kitchen. I'll put a bay leaf in it."

Will hammered the lid back into place and rolled the flour to the house.

Sophia's stomach churned. Had they been eating food made with infested flour all this time?

"I'll send samples to the Commissioner of Indian Affairs," James said. "See if he'll eat it."

The third contained hundreds of pairs of baby booties, thirty andirons, and one palm-sized porcelain doll.

"A Frozen Charlotte," Nettie explained to Sophia. "It's from a ballad about a foolish girl who refused to wrap up warmly for a sleigh ride and froze to death."

"Now the entire tribe is in danger of becoming Frozen Charlottes through the government's foolishness."

Henry held up an andiron. "Useless. All our people have stoves."

"I'll see what I can make out of them." Will took it from him. "Least they didn't send mirrors, combs, and ax handles this time."

"Perhaps these might be useful." Sophia studied the booties. "They might fit Julia's Timothy and Moon Hawk's White Buffalo Girl."

"Two thousand of each for a tribe of seven hundred?" James ran his hand over his face.

Grass waved gold and burgundy on the bluffs. Cottonwood trees fluttered yellow. Winter approached at a gallop.

Nettie found a loose thread and pulled, unraveling the bootie. "Know how to knit?"

"Unfortunately, no. I misspent my youth learning useless embroidery stitches." A brisk northwest wind sliced through her shawl. "As Peter the Great said, 'Delay is death.' I should like to know what curse word I am permitted to use."

Henry's scowl threatened to knock her feet out from beneath her. James fled before the oncoming sermon, and Nettie hurried back to her kitchen.

"One of the drawbacks of growing up around soldiers is a rather extensive education in inappropriate language," Sophia said by way of apology. "I shall endeavor to discipline my speech."

The reverend closed his eyes and released a long breath. Sophia braced for a lecture on guarding her words, bridling her tongue, and speaking always with grace. She had heard it before, in several languages. Instead he surprised her with a murmured, "Thank you."

"Pardon me?"

He speared her with a narrow gaze. "You barge in here with all your vigor and cheer . . . making me feel even more drained and ineffectual than ever. But if you've taken up swearing—"

"Resumed," she corrected.

"Resumed swearing . . . well then." His beard twitched with a fleeting smile. "Guess I'd better pray for you."

Sophia bowed her head, shamed by her own deficiency. She and Henry were on the same side, God's side. They both cared about this mission. But instead of working with him, she waved the battle flag at every opportunity.

"Only if you allow me to pray for you," she whispered.

In mid-September the school filled with new students. The first arrived shortly after lunch. A family walked up the path from the other villages, opened the school door, and deposited their son. Thomas Jefferson slid over to accommodate the boy.

Ah, yes, Sophia remembered him from the Fourth of July celebration. The brother who resembled Louis-Charles, Marie-Antoinette's son. Two minutes later, another child arrived. Then three more. Was it another Ponca celebration? No, they always included their children.

"Welcome, visitors. We hope you will join us every day."

"Teacher. Miss Makinoff." Frank finally remembered to raise his hand. "They're here for the annuity."

The annuity had come? A steamboat had whistled midmorning, a common occurrence. How had the families from Hubdon and Point Village known it contained the annuity? Had the Mission Board sent her requested supplies? And what should she do—

Ignore the rushing water.

Five more children wandered in.

"All right, students. Let us divide into teams." Chaos broke out and Sophia had to resort to prayer. "Heavenly Father, please help us learn what we need to know about money. Amen."

Authority restored, Sophia mixed the visitors among the regulars. When Catharine Beecher had emphasized the importance of pupils instructing each other, Sophia had not imagined how essential her advice would be. She distributed her coins. "Today we shall learn about money. Everyone in your group must know how to count, know the names and value of money, and know how to add it up. Recitations begin in five minutes."

While the students worked, Sophia set up a store in the front. What could she use for stock? She looked around the room. Every student needed shoes. Sophia took hers off. Henry was too busy with the annuity to come and check on her. She set them on the desk.

Sophia briefed Frank and Marguerite for their upcoming debut in "The Perils of Shopping." From their accurate memories and dramatic storytelling, the Poncas had a well-developed oral tradition. Using drama to reinforce lessons was a natural choice.

When even the youngest could say the names of the coins, Sophia directed the students to sit on the floor.

Marguerite played the storekeeper. "What do you want, you mangy dog?"

Sophia had not told Marguerite to be rude. Did she speak from experience?

Frank held out a few coins. "Please, sir—"

"Ma'am," Sophia whispered.

"Please, ma'am. I need shoes. But this is all I have."

Marguerite grabbed all the coins and shoved the shoes into his hands. "Good-bye."

Sophia applauded. "All right, students, what went wrong?"

Everyone had an opinion, but not everyone spoke English. "He showed how much he had." "He did not ask how much the shoes were." "She took all of the money." "He should slit her throat for name-calling."

"Yes, name-calling is wrong. But responding in anger, hurting people, is wrong too. Frank might end up in jail, or the storekeeper might shoot him. Let us try again." Sophia put the shoes back on the desk.

"Good morning," Frank said.

"No Indians! Get your dirty carcass out of here." Marguerite waved like she was shooing chickens.

Oh dear. Were the shopkeepers in town so evil?

Frank stood his ground. "I am a Christian like you. I have money and I need to buy shoes for my family."

"Money? How much?"

Frank picked up a shoe. "How much are your shoes?"

"One dollar."

"This one is worn. I would like new."

Marguerite put an invisible pair on the desk. "You're mighty particular for an Indian," she drawled, then pretended to spit on the floor.

"The Great White Father says I must learn to live like a white man." Frank pretended to try on the new shoes. "These are too small."

"Okay." Another invisible pair appeared and this time they fit. "That'll be two dollars."

"You said one dollar."

"For the worn-out shoes. New ones are two."

"Hmm, maybe I don't need them so bad. How about one dollar and one dime?"

"You're killing me." The storekeeper crossed her arms. "One dollar and two quarters."

"One dollar and one quarter."

"Sold!"

The class applauded. Large hands clapped at the window, and Sophia turned to see Will standing outside. Why was he here? He winked and jogged back toward the village, not giving her time to ask questions. She hoped he would not tell Henry he had caught her with her shoes off.

The students had a lively discussion, then Joseph and Susette tackled the complicated issue of credit.

"No fair!" the students cried when the drama finished. "The shoes will be worn out before Joseph pays for them."

"Right. So what should he do?"

"Don't buy on credit."

"But he needs shoes. Winter's coming."

"Wear moccasins."

"If he had moccasins, dog, he wouldn't be buying shoes."

"No name-calling." Sophia squeezed between the two boys. "He needs to have it written down, one for him and one for the store." After a string of broken treaties, no wonder the Poncas had no faith in written promises. "The paper should say Joseph will pay a little more, not the cost of six shoes."

"That's why we learn to read," said Marguerite.

Thomas Jefferson and John Adams gave a final drama.

"Hey, Injun," John whispered from behind the desk as Thomas strolled by. "Got something for you. You're going to love it."

"What?"

John popped up and handed him the dipper. "Fire water."

"Oh yeah!" Thomas handed him a quarter, drank, staggered around, then fell flat on his back.

John crept out, emptied Thomas's pockets of his imaginary money, gave him a kick, then ran back to his hiding place.

"Students?"

"He wake up and hit his woman and his children."

"And he will smell bad. And be sick."

Sophia asked, "So what should he do?"

"No buy. No drink."

"And tell the agent. It is against the law to sell liquor on Indian land."

Sophia glanced at her watch, then hurried into her shoes. "Please line up—we shall march to the agency to find your families." And hope the students had learned enough to help their parents.

Will watched the line of children march to the agency village. At the end, Sophia held Rosalie's hand and carried someone's baby. Will would have Brown Eagle put the word out: don't send children to school until they're five years old.

The yellow puppies did their sitting trick, like some sort of circus act. Sophia told them, "I am sorry. I had many extra mouths to feed today. All the food is gone."

The students spotted their parents, broke ranks, and ran to them. Sophia saw him. "Do you know whose baby this is?"

"No, I—"

A woman from Hubdon approached. The baby grinned and reached for her. Sophia handed the infant over. "There are more than a thousand people here. Who are they?"

"Mixed breeds, white squaw-men," Will said. "That's what takes so long, deciding who's in the tribe and who's not. Although seven dollars seems hardly worth fighting over."

"Pardon me?" Sophia's eyes widened. "Please tell me more is coming. They cannot survive the winter on seven dollars."

An officer spotted Sophia, trotted his gray over, and dismounted. "Miss Makinoff. I hear the annuity arrived. We've come to maintain order."

"Lt. Higgins, this is Mr. Dunn, the man who built this village. I met Lt. Higgins on the journey here from Yankton."

"Agency carpenter," Will corrected. As rickety as the buildings were, he didn't want blame. "Pleased to meet you." No wonder Sophia wasn't interested in James or Henry—she had an officer on her hook. Military life probably seemed a good fit, what with her father being in the cavalry and her wandering nature.

"Lt. Higgins, the Brulé purloined all the Ponca horses. If you happen to come across any extras in your line of work, I would appreciate if you would send them our way."

The officer brayed like a donkey, all open mouth and big teeth. "Oh, Miss Makinoff. You are a delight. Horses are near as scarce as ladies around here."

"Well, I know you are frightfully busy, so I shall let you go."

Will suppressed a grin. She'd just sent him off with a polite boot in the butt, and he didn't even know it. Sophia turned toward the river where a half dozen men had pulled up boats and laid out stuff to sell on blankets. "Who might those be?" she asked Will.

"From the town."

"Perhaps I can be of some use."

"A verse in Proverbs warns about meddling."

"The Bible warns against usury, admonishes us to look out for widows and orphans, and to work for justice."

"This is a small tribe. We don't get many traders through here. They have to make a living too."

"If you had heard the children—"

"I did. And I know the traders turn into Indian skinners when we aren't looking."

She headed for the riverfront, a full head of steam ready to blow.

Will hurried to keep up with her. If she drove the Niobrara merchants off, James would have a hard time convincing the farther-away Yankton storekeepers to fill their place. They were busy with the Sioux; they didn't need the Poncas' trade. Besides, the Poncas were angry enough without Sophia setting off this powder keg.

"Lady and gentleman." Reynaud tried to block her way. This time he'd misspelled "Dakota" on a walking stick.

Sophia ignored him and marched up to the first merchant, from the general store in town. "Good afternoon, sir."

He spit, then stepped forward to shake her hand. "Well, what do we got here? Such a pretty girl in this ugly place."

She stepped back. "I am Miss Makinoff, teacher at the Ponca Agency school." She seemed to grow taller as she spoke, managing to look down her nose at a man who towered over her by a foot.

"Well, how de do? I'm Mercer. Supposing you got paid today. How much they give you to learn them Injuns?"

"What do you have in the way of dry goods?"

"Here's a pretty bit of ribbon for a pretty girl. Or maybe you like some beads. Shiny beads."

"Do you have any wool, denim, canvas?"

He pointed east. "Over to my store, sure. Or I could bring it to you tomorrow. What color?"

Sophia narrowed her gaze. "Thank you, but quality is more important than color, Mr. Mercer."

The man was too dense to realize he'd been insulted.

Sophia turned her attention to the next boat. "Good afternoon. What is in your jug?"

The beanpole looked for rescue. Will shook his head. The shifty eyes went back to Sophia. "Molasses."

She reached out. "May I?" It was a command, not a request.

"Well, I'd . . . You see . . ."

Over her shoulder, Sophia said, "Please signal the lieutenant. I believe we have found a candidate for his penitentiary."

"What?" The man paled and backed up.

"No jail for him. Selling whiskey to Indians is a hanging offense." Will hadn't read the law, but figured to scare the guy.

"I best be getting home." The moonshiner pushed his boat into the current.

"Wait! Where you going, Zeb?" Another white guy ran out from behind the church, carrying two jugs. "They're just starting to hand out the money!"

"Got the gallows ready." Will rocked back on his heels. "It's not much more trouble to hang two."

The accomplice double-timed it to the boat, threw the jugs in, then they rowed away.

Sophia shook her head. "He will set up shop at one of the other villages."

"Probably."

"So has anyone ever been convicted of selling liquor to the Indians?"

"Not that I know of."

Sophia muttered in one of her many languages, then marched off to her soldier.

CHAPTER TWENTY

The school day had finally ended without any additions to the enrollment. Joseph was busy washing the blackboard. Marguerite swept the floor, and Rosalie checked the windows. Sophia exhaled a sigh of relief. All ready for tomorrow. When her helpers were finished, Sophia gathered the lunch pails, locked the school, and waved good-bye. "See you Monday!"

James had walked her to school, but he had not shown up this afternoon. Had there been a mention of who was to escort her back to the house? Perhaps with the threat of the Brulé gone, she might walk by herself. She set out at a brisk pace through a shower of bright-yellow cottonwood leaves. The day was unusually quiet, without so much as the sound of insects or birdsong.

Two white men stepped out of the brush—the liquor runners from yesterday. "We don't take kindly to anyone poking her nose into our business."

"No, we don't," said the second, brandishing an oar.

Sophia chilled. The school was too far behind her, and the men stood between her and the village. She could not outrun them. She pressed her hand to her empty pocket. Why had she left her pistol in her room? "And I do not think much of those who tempt Indians with spirits. These people do not have enough money for necessities. They cannot afford to waste it on whiskey."

The skinny one unraveled a whip and snapped it. "And what right do you have to tell them whether they can or can't? Who are you to say what's right and wrong?"

A phrase surfaced from her morning prayers: *Defend me from assaults.* Or was it last night's evening prayer? Whichever it was, she needed it answered now.

"Who am I?" she said. "I am the teacher with a classroom full of students who go barefoot and hungry because you took their money."

"We didn't take it." The liquor dealer snapped the whip. "We provide a service. So they won't have to cross the river."

"'Sides that," the second one said, "Injuns don't never wear shoes." He slapped the oar against his palm.

Sophia remembered: she had a knife in one of the lunch pails, used for dividing apples. If she could just keep them talking, she might have a chance to find it. "Indians must wear shoes," she said. "Since the emigrants arrived, there is no longer any game to hunt—for food or moccasins."

"Well, they'll just have to get off their lazy butts, stop waiting for the government to feed them, and work like the rest of us."

"Work?" She slid her hand into the first pail. Empty. "Your heinous misdeeds cannot be legitimized nor glorified by calling them work."

"You some kind of Indian lover? Maybe you need some loving from your own kind." He reached for the buttons on his pants.

The second pail was empty as well. "I see none of my kind around here. Merely two examples of vermin who must have crawled out from beneath rocks. Certainly not anyone who was raised in a loving family by a Christian mother—"

"Don't you go talking against my ma!" The one with the oar tightened his grip on his weapon.

Sophia searched the third pail. "What would she say about your behavior, about your descent into crime?"

"Hey, a man's got to make a living."

The well-exercised corner of her eye searched for a stick or a rock but found neither. "You have made my point. If you were a man, you would be making a living instead of taking it from others." Was someone coming along the path?

"Oh yeah?" The whip snapped. "Well, our preacher don't think we're doing wrong. He stops by for a nip now and again."

"He know you're threatening a missionary?" Will asked from behind them. "Don't turn around. Drop your weapons and put your hands on your head. Quick, or your preacher will be conducting your funerals."

"Can't take two of us." They swung around but met fists from Will and Brown Eagle. The skinny one crumpled onto his back and the oar-wielder hit his knees. Brown Eagle used the whip to tie their hands behind them.

Will poked them with the oar. "Stand up. I'm not wasting my strength carrying you two back to the Agency."

"You broke my nose." The oar-wielder sniffed. Blood ran down the front of his shirt. "You going to hang us?"

"Yes, but first you're going to have a good long listen to Reverend Granville. It doesn't sound like your preacher does his job real well."

He turned to Sophia. "You all right?"

"Of course," Sophia whispered. She was having a bit of difficulty getting a full breath of air. "And you are not going to hang them, because I intend to shoot them first. Along with whomever was supposed to be my escort."

"That would be James. He was detained at Point Village." Will scowled. "I didn't realize until I got back to the house. I'm sorry."

Will and Brown Eagle marched the scoundrels to the Agency, aided by Zlata, who growled and snapped at their heels. They shackled the lawbreakers to empty stalls in the stable.

Sophia staggered into the agency house.

"You poor dear." Nettie hugged Sophia. "You must have been out of your mind with fear."

"Out of my mind, yes." Legs shaking, she sank into the nearest chair. Now that the threat was behind her, she returned to her senses. "What kind of Christian calls someone a vermin and threatens to shoot him?"

⌒≈⌒

Will stopped at the spring and dunked his head into the water. He didn't know who to be mad at first. Those two skunks for attacking Sophia. The government for not keeping them locked away when they were caught peddling whiskey last summer. James for being late. Sophia for thinking a gun would have saved her.

Or, most of all, himself.

He'd been trying to avoid Sophia to keep his heart safe. So he hadn't obeyed God's prompting to check on her earlier.

Brown Eagle yanked him up by his shoulders. "If you drown, the water will taste bad."

Will gasped a breath. Then he'd have another reason to be mad.

Brown Eagle looked him up and down. "God is big. Big to love. Big to forgive."

Forgive the whiskey sellers? Forgive himself? Will resisted the idea. But God forgave those who crucified Him.

All right, he'd forgive. Someday. Meanwhile, he'd keep guarding Sophia and trust God to guard his heart.

Chapter Twenty-One

Sophia glanced outside. Will sat on the stump, wrists resting on his bent knees, as he had every afternoon since she had been accosted. She consulted her watch: ten minutes to four. Right on time.

The scoundrels who attacked her had been delivered to Fort Randall; her safety was no longer in doubt. And while she appreciated Will's company, she sensed a new reserve in him. She did not blame him for withdrawing. She had behaved despicably. He could not be more upset with her than she was with herself.

The children finished their lessons and duties, then Sophia dismissed them. Will called each child by name. He knew them all, what their Indian parents called them as well as the name Henry had assigned to them.

Sophia locked the door. "Good afternoon, Will."

He nodded. "The school needs a vestibule."

An uncommon word, although perhaps carpenters were more familiar with terms having to do with parts of buildings. "Yes, a vestibule would help keep the snow and cold out. And give us a place to keep firewood." She pulled her shawl over her head. The wind rippled through the tawny grass. A formation of geese flew high above them, headed south. Every northbound steamboat might be the last.

"Need to cut some wood."

"The students bring sticks, but it will not be enough." She pointed to the bluffs. "All these stumps, but no stacks of wood. Was it used to construct houses?"

"Trees were cut for firewood and sold to the steamboats. Most were cottonwood, which warps too much to be any use in building." He nodded at the bluffs. "The tribe used the money to buy the farming equipment the government was supposed to provide: reapers, mowers, hay rakes, plows."

"A worthy purchase, but what will they use to heat with?"

"Now that the Brulé are no longer a threat, we can cut timber farther away from the Agency."

"Using only those cart horses and the wagon?"

"They'll make a raft and float it down. In winter, a sled."

Zlata and her puppies greeted them at the edge of the village. Baby Timothy lay on a blanket and shook a noisy bean pod, while Julia dug potatoes in her garden. Moon Hawk ground corn as White Buffalo Girl pulled herself to standing on the pergola's post. Both women waved.

"I am trying to follow your advice."

Will shook his head. "What advice? I don't generally give advice to anyone, especially you."

"You told me to ignore the rushing water."

"How's that?"

"The day we climbed the waterfall, you told me to ignore the rushing water. Ignore everything that tries to pull you under or knock your feet out, or obscures your view. Plant your feet on solid rock. I try to do so with my students. Ignore all the other problems and focus on them."

"You keep talking like that, my head will swell." He scuffed through a pile of yellow leaves.

"It is a wise lesson, the only one I have learned here that makes any sense. Thank you."

His jaw moved as if chewing his words into order. Then his brown eyes focused on her. "Sophia, this is a dangerous place. To body and soul. Seems like we're all battling demons of one sort or another." He studied the hills, making her wonder what demons he battled. "It's good to have someone praying for you. Maybe your church back in New York?"

With her abrupt departure, she had not had time to request prayers. "I do not know. Perhaps . . . the Mission Board?" Surely it was their obligation to pray for her.

"I'll ask my home church." Will opened the door for her.

The staff stood around a new crate. "Newspapers came." James pointed to the stack on the table.

"Excellent. I can keep my students apprised of the events of the day." Sophia flipped through them. The Niobrara *Pioneer*, Yankton *Dakotaian*, and Sioux City *Journal*. None from New York or even Chicago. Enlightenment would be delayed once again.

Will opened the crate with a few easy pops of his crowbar. The contents included three bolts of coarse wool and two dozen pairs of brogans in a large size.

"This is all?" Sophia asked. "For seven hundred people?"

"Seven hundred seventy." James propped his arm over the window and stared out.

Sophia lifted the wool and held it in front of the lantern. "As coarse as burlap and nearly as itchy. We need muslin and flannel." Hot anger flashed through her. "It is wrong that these people should have so little. Wealthy women in New York City change clothes five times a day: a morning gown, a visiting dress, a carriage dress, a walking dress, an evening gown. Sixteen to twenty yards of fabric for each, not counting petticoats, balayeuses, paletots, pelisses. And each piece covered in embroidery, lace, pearls—"

In spite of her best effort, the tears welled up. New York's wealthy did not care about the poor on their own doorstep, in the tenements of the Lower East Side. How could Sophia make them care about people they had never seen, people more than a thousand miles away?

"I recognize this bolt." Nettie cut a corner off. "Normally with loose-woven fabric, I wash it in hot water to felt it. Ends up fewer yards, but it's tightened into something useful. But with this . . ." She poured an inch of water from the kettle into a pie pan, then added the scrap. The fabric dissolved and turned the water cloudy.

"Useless." Black dye streaked Sophia's hands. "Worse than useless."

"The rest seem higher quality." The other scraps passed Nettie's test. She held up a length to her round body. "None of the Ponca women has any extra padding. With straight skirts, no gathers or pleats, six yards might make a dress."

"If they had blouses, we could make *sarafans* . . . What is the English word? Pinafore? Jumper?"

"That's a good idea." Nettie folded the fabric. "Cover their legs. Use a shawl or blanket for their arms."

"I estimate they have only six weeks' provisions." James frowned at the neighbors' gardens. A few weeks ago a cow had broken through Eloise's willow fence and trampled her crop of squash. "They're slaughtering their livestock and eating next year's seed."

"Perhaps the Mission Board should have sent a farmer instead of a teacher."

The agent shook his head. "The agency farmer was supposed to teach modern techniques, like using a plow instead of a buffalo scapula. Unfortunately the Indian Office never sent the plows."

Sophia strode past the stove. "Can more food be purchased?"

"I suppose you have enough money." The agent drummed his fingers.

"Could the merchants extend credit?" She paced to the door.

"The government is six years behind on payments." Will glared at James, as if he blamed the agent for all their problems. "You'll have to ask Fort Randall for emergency rations again."

"I'll send soup with you, Sophia," Nettie said. "At least the children will have a warm meal on school days."

Her feet took her to the locked door of their poorly stocked pantry. "Mary and Elisabeth were digging by the spring for some sort of turnip." They had prayed before digging, but Sophia would not mention that. The Ponca version of "Give us this day our daily bread" would look like a pagan ritual to Henry.

Will crossed his arms. "With so many bad harvests, they've pretty much stripped the hills bare."

"What about all these migrating waterfowl?"

"The government won't give the Indians guns. Makes the whites nervous," the agent said. "And we're out of ammunition."

"What about fish?"

James's voice grew heavy with fatigue. "The allotment one year included fish hooks, but they weren't the right kind."

"Could they seine?"

"The Seine's a river in France."

Sophia paused. "Henry, you made a joke. Mark this day on the calendar." She resumed pacing. How could they feed and clothe these people? "Do they have any fishing nets or anything they could make them from?"

Shrugs and shakes all around.

"We have already had our first frost." She picked up one of the shoes. "How will we decide who goes barefoot?"

Will leaned on the crate. "Henry, how about a prayer, loaves and fishes style?"

The reverend started to argue but caught a stern look from his mother. He bent his head and did his duty.

Sophia added her own plea. *Oh Lord, I will do my best. I will write everyone I know and even people I do not. My students must have shoes.*

Before Henry could make his way to the amen, a harsh voice yelled outside. A stubby man with thin yellow hair held a rifle on a tall Ponca man Sophia did not recognize. They both stated their case with vehemence. Neither spoke English.

"Quiet!" James waved his arms, then addressed the blond man. "Put down your gun. Who are you?"

"I am Schumacher. Just south of the river, I farm. I work hard. He beg and steal." The man pointed at the Ponca with his rifle.

The noise drew a crowd of villagers who gathered in a circle around them. Little Rosalie squirmed from her sisters' grasp with a delighted shout, raced to the Ponca man, and caught him around the knees in an embrace. Directly in the line of fire.

The farmer shifted his feet and swung the muzzle around the circle. He was clearly outnumbered now. His eyes bulged and beads of sweat broke out on his forehead.

He let go of the trigger to wipe his face, and Sophia took the opportunity.

"*Guten Tag, Herr* Schumacher. So pleased to make your acquaintance. Allow me to hold on to this for you. *Danke.*" She dazzled him with a smile, swept the rifle from his grasp, then glided out of reach.

He blinked. His mouth dropped open. "Johann," he said. "You may call me John."

"I think not."

Will coughed. "This is Blunt Tail from the Point Village." He interpreted with all the authority and composure of an ambassador's senior assistant. "He has no food for his family. He has no money. His wife is sick. His children are hungry. He went to this man. He asked to work. But this man yelled and pointed a gun. He forced him into the boat."

Will tipped his head toward the riverbank. A second blond man waited at the oars.

With both hands free, the farmer pointed and pounded his chest with abandon. "Government gives money to Indians. I must work for mine!"

"That's payment for their land," Will told the farmer. "And it's not enough to raise a family on."

Blunt Tail picked up Rosalie and repeated his request for work.

"Perhaps *Herr* Schumacher needs some assistance on his farm."

"The Poncas are not allowed to leave the reservation." James crossed his arms. "He'll have to look elsewhere. Not allowed."

Zlata and her puppies wandered over and inspected the farmer's shoes.

"*Hund?* I need dog. So. Take?" He pulled a coin from his pocket. "Buy?"

"*Nein.*" Sophia shook her head. Anyone who treated a man this poorly was surely unworthy of Zlata's puppies.

"We're sorry for the misunderstanding." James retrieved the rifle from Sophia. He escorted the farmer to the rowboat, returned his gun, and waved him off.

Blunt Tail made a concluding statement, raised his chin toward Sophia, then returned Rosalie to Brown Eagle.

"He thanks you for your courage." Will wiped his forehead with a kerchief.

"I hope he thanked you for your skill in interpretation."

"Foolish woman!" Henry scowled down at her from the porch. "Why can't you stay in the house where it's safe?"

"If I wanted safety, I would have stayed at the College."

Nettie gathered her in an embrace. "God is using you here."

Sophia's vision blurred with tears. "Mr. Blunt Tail is not the only one looking for work. What happens the next time if the farmer is quick to shoot?"

⌖

"No, Susette!" Sophia pointed. "First base!"

The girl stopped running and turned when she reached third. "But Matthew is there and he has the ball."

"The rule says you must go to first."

Susette shrugged and marched to first, where Matthew tagged her out.

From the pitching mound, Luke tried to console her. "When you bat better, you will hit it over his head."

Susette's face brightened. "Mr. Dunn!"

The carpenter emerged from the woods, carrying a canvas bag over his shoulder like a sailor.

"Good afternoon, Mr. Dunn." The tension in Sophia's shoulders eased. Will brought a sense of peace with him, a certainty that, with his assistance, she could handle any crisis.

But— Sophia checked her watch. He was an hour early.

"Students," she said, "let us thank Mr. Dunn for building the new vestibule for our school." She clapped and the children cheered.

"You're welcome." He glanced at the schoolhouse. "Be careful the ball doesn't break any windows. I'm clean out of glass."

"Martha hit it over our heads." Matthew gestured toward the Missouri with his chin. "The river swallowed the ball."

"Mr. Brown Eagle gave us another." Sophia handed it to him. "The exterior appears to be some sort of animal bladder. I am uncertain of the interior."

"It does not hurt when you catch it." Rosalie held up her palms.

"But it does not go far when you hit it." Susette pouted.

"Keeps the windows safe." Will returned it to her, then handed her an envelope. "You need to read the letter first. It's about what's in the bag."

The letter was from one of her students at the College. The young woman's uncle owned a shoe factory in upstate New York and had kindly made a donation—

Will emptied the bag onto the ground. New shoes. Sturdy, with leather soles and uppers.

"Shoes!" The students squealed and dove into the pile.

"Students, form a line by size of feet. Rosalie at one end, Frank at the other. Oh dear. Mr. Dunn, perhaps we should have done this a different way." *With less anarchy.* "Some children will be disappointed."

The children tumbled over each other like puppies. He grinned. "Miss Makinoff, we prayed about this." He bent to help John Adams tie his laces.

Marguerite helped her sisters find shoes that fit, then make their bows. When she finished, the pile was gone and all the other students had shoes. Her smile drooped. She blinked away tears.

"This is what I mean, Mr. Dunn," Sophia said in an undertone. Perhaps they could find the girl a pair in Niobrara.

"Everyone stand up." Will waved his arms. "Do all the shoes have feet in them?"

"No." Thomas Jefferson pointed to a pair he had been sitting on.

"Trying to hatch them like a chicken?" Will picked up the shoes and handed them to Marguerite.

If they were too big, she might stuff them with grass or newspaper. Too small, perhaps she could trade with another.

Will winked at Sophia. "What are you holding your breath for?"

Marguerite slid her feet in, tied the laces, and jumped up. "They fit!"

They fit! Will had prayed and God answered with a miracle. Impulsively, Sophia wrapped her arms around him.

He felt solid and warm. She inhaled his scent, very male, with a touch of sawdust. His eyes widened and he patted her shoulder.

Sophia let go and stepped away quickly, then hugged each child, each well-shod student. Tears filled her eyes. They all had shoes! Before it snowed!

"Everyone, sit, so I can tell you how to take care of your shoes." The students formed a circle. "Shoes should be brushed nightly and polished with blacking every Saturday." Sophia looked at Will. "Oh dear. Does anyone have a shoe brush?"

"I'll bring mine tomorrow. And some waterproofing." Will grabbed a twig and took over the lesson. "When you get home, scrape the mud off the bottoms on the edge of your step. Then use a little stick to clean the mud off the uppers." He took off his shoe. "Each night open them up to dry out the inside. But don't put them on the stove. The leather will crack."

"My brother eats everything on the stove." Thomas Jefferson giggled.

"All right. Your teacher will lead us in a prayer thanking God for providing shoes."

Her prayer book had St. Ambrose's Prayer of Thanksgiving, but not a word could she remember. Sophia closed her eyes, lifted her hands, and said, "Thank You!"

Will added, "And please send socks. Amen."

Henry finally concluded his lesson on Thanksgiving.

Sophia turned her back to him and asked her class, "Does anyone have a question for Reverend Granville?" The minister had spent most of his lesson on the bountiful harvest and subsequent feast, a foreign concept to these starving children.

"Why do you say Columbus discovered America?" Matthew asked. "Indians were already here."

"Yes, well, I'm referring to Europeans."

Joseph raised his hand. "Does God love white people or Indians more?"

Henry scowled. "God loves everyone the same."

"Then why do white people take our land and God does not punish them?"

Henry started to perspire in spite of the drafty schoolhouse. "The government bought your land. The white people came to Christianize and civilize you."

"But white people bring disease and whiskey. And take the buffalo." Joseph hammered his point.

"Look at the time," Henry said. "Class dismissed."

Sophia glanced at her pocket watch. The parents would be surprised to have their students home so early. She supervised the closing chores, then headed down the path with Henry.

He wiped his brow again. "I didn't realize Joseph's father was so . . . militant."

"I do not know that he is. Joseph is bright. He studies an issue and comes to his own conclusions."

"He bears watching."

"Perhaps some individual tutoring, the loan of some of your history books . . ."

Henry shuddered. Will had told her that the reverend did not let anyone touch his books.

"He would be a good lawyer. I could see him in the legislature, like Patrick Henry, 'Give me liberty or give me death.'"

"Sophia, don't fill his head with foolish thoughts. No college will accept an Indian student."

"He could read the law like Abraham Lincoln."

"And no lawyer would take an Indian student."

"But is it not our goal to help them become like white people?"

"To become farmers, yes." Henry scratched his beard.

"If I had a class of twenty-five white students, I would not expect all to become farmers. Not every Ponca is suited for farming." Most were not, she suspected, but Americans seemed blind to allowing Indians any other path.

"But that is our job, to prepare each family to farm his own plot."

"Another quandary, the division of the land. The Poncas are used to communal living. Being forced to move to individual plots—"

"But that's how Americans live."

"We do not. The agency house is occupied by a group of adults, not a family."

"Well, that's an exception, for the circumstances."

"And at the College, the teachers and students lived together."

"We're talking about farming, each on his own land."

"Russian peasants farm communally. It allows for specialization, sharing skills and tools."

"Sophia. Could you—" He shook his head. "I would think you'd be tired after teaching all day."

She took the hint and continued the walk in silence. Why was he so angry? But asking the question would only exacerbate his temper.

Ahead, three black shapes moved through the underbrush beside the river.

"Turkeys," Henry whispered. "I wish I'd brought—"

Sophia pulled out her pistol, sighted, and squeezed off a round. Two birds took flight. The third flopped to the ground. She pocketed her pistol and walked over to inspect it.

"How—what—?" He turned whiter than usual. "Madam, you are armed!"

She lifted the carcass by its feet, estimating its weight at around fifteen pounds, and handed it to him. "Happy Thanksgiving."

Will dashed out of the woods carrying a box. Zlata and her troika followed him. "I heard a shot. You're all right?"

Henry held the bird away from the dogs. "We have a sharp-shooter among us."

"Sophia!" Will whistled.

"My father taught me." She nodded at Will's box, eager to move the attention away from herself. "Another allotment?"

"No. My sister, Charlotte, collected socks from her students." Will pulled out a pair. One was gray with white and red on the cuff, the other solid blue. "You know how sometimes you lose one? Or you might have enough yarn for half a sock? They're matched for size and thickness, but not color. About a hundred pairs in here."

"Enough for each student and their families." Sophia grinned. Only Henry's presence kept her from embracing Will again. "We have so much to be thankful for."

CHAPTER TWENTY-TWO

Will could listen to Sophia talk forever. Finishing a story about her students, she used a Ponca word to make a pun. She glanced up to see if he caught the joke.

Will grinned and kicked the leaves in the path. "You're picking up on the language."

Her lips pressed together. "I trust you will not mention it to Henry."

"'Course not."

"I have been wondering." She did a lot of that. "Should there not be more animals here? Even in the cities, I have seen squirrels and raccoons."

"Used to be deer, beaver, muskrats, weasels, but they've been hunted out. Still a few prairie dogs up on the bluff, but they're about as fit for eating as rats."

"And another concern. My first morning here I smelled smoke. Someone had set a fire. But I have not smelled it since."

Will nodded. "Buffalo Track. His wife took him back in. He wouldn't hurt you."

"Given the enormous changes the Poncas have suffered, the uncertainty of their future, the changing roles, especially of the men, I would expect madness to be more prevalent. Do you think—"

Sophia broke off as her army officer came trotting down the hill on his large gray, leading a saddled chestnut mare. "Howdy, ma'am."

"Good afternoon, Lt. Higgins." She had eyes only for the horses. Sophia stretched her hand out and cooed, "Who have we here? What is your name?"

The lieutenant stuck out his chest, as if hoping Sophia would pin a big medal on it, and introduced the mare. "This is Pumpkin. Only on loan for today, I'm afraid. Couldn't find any for you to keep. She's a gentle, steady mount. Good for a lady like yourself."

The horse looked equally in love with Sophia, twitching her ears to every word. She lowered her head for a scratch, let Sophia lift each leg for a check of her shoes, and allowed her girth to be cinched.

Sophia hurried inside to change clothes while the officer watered his mounts. Will grabbed a mug of coffee and a spot on the porch. She returned quicker than he'd imagined any woman could undress and dress, not that he'd spent much time imagining such.

She wore a top hat, a dark-green riding dress with gold braid, and shiny black boots. She'd brought a stub end of carrot for each of the horses, and she fed them with more murmured words of encouragement.

Then, without waiting for the soldier to put his grubby hands on her, she sprang into the saddle and rode off like a princess on her way to a fox hunt.

What was that dirge about the old gray mare? Sophia tried to remember as this nag's gait threatened to jar her eyeballs from her head. The mare's teeth were worn to a nub; her hooves needed filing and shoes replacing. She had not been curried this decade.

And keeping her from wandering off to snatch a bite of vegetation required a firm hand.

The saddle, a rawhide Mexican-style model, had been worn paper-thin, with stitching coming loose and stirrups threatening to break with the slightest weight.

But ah, the joy of riding again!

The lieutenant led her upriver. James and Henry would lecture about her leaving the Agency without permission. Will would not say much, but disapproval would exude from him in the set of his shoulders, the tension in his jaw. The man's body talked for him.

A mile from the Agency all evidence of human occupation vanished. Perhaps now that the Brulé were gone, the Poncas could spread out, make the best use of their land. And what a beautiful country it was! The Missouri, bordered with white chalk bluffs, rolled peacefully to their right. A gray line wavered high over the river. As it came closer, it resolved into migrating waterfowl. "Hurry, hurry," the geese honked to each other.

Sophia pointed at a smudge underlined by red on the horizon. "What is that?"

"Prairie fire."

Unbroken dry grass burned with frightening speed. "What ignites it?"

"Dunno. Lightning, Indians. We see them a couple times a week hereabouts. Should stop once we get good snow cover."

Lt. Higgins had led her a considerable distance, far beyond a courtesy jaunt. Should she be concerned? All her life, her father's reputation had ensured her safety among soldiers. But no longer. Sophia touched her pocket where her pistol rested. She ought to conduct herself in a more circumspect manner.

A dreary thought.

"We shall need to turn back soon," she said. "I must return to the Agency before dark."

"I was hoping to show you Fort Randall." A look of disappointment spread over his face. "All right. Let's go up on the ridge, then, before heading back."

Sophia led the way on the plodding mare. The view was more than worth the limited pleasure of the officer's company. From that height, the immense prairie spread to all compass points. Golden-brown grass waved in the westerly wind. Who could see such a vista without acknowledging the presence of a gracious and creative God? She vowed once again to try harder to please Him.

Sophia gave the sun a deliberate glance, then reined the mare eastward.

"Perhaps we can ride again another day." Lt. Higgins tipped his head, leading into his true purpose. "We're having a Christmas ball at the fort. I'd be pleased to escort you."

It was not the most awkward invitation she had received, but it was certainly far from polished.

"I am so sorry, but the Agency is planning a celebration at the church." Or they would be, as soon as Sophia returned. "For the children. You are welcome to attend, you and the entire post."

They rode back along the same path, sending long shadows ahead of them. A hawk spiraled above, searching for supper. Sophia's stomach growled in agreement.

She tightened her knees, leaned forward, and whispered encouragement, but old Pumpkin had no intention of moving any faster than a plod. They arrived at the Agency as the moon rose over the trees.

"Lieutenant, it has been a lovely ride." Sophia gave the mare a pat for effort, then dismounted before the officer could assist her.

"Hope we can go again sometime." He stepped forward as if looking for a more physical expression of gratefulness.

Sophia slapped the reins into his hand. "I do so enjoy riding, but perhaps a livelier mount next time."

"Yeah. You have a good seat. I mean, you ride real good."

"I did my share of falling off as a child. Good evening, Lieutenant." Sophia pulled off her gloves, washed in the basin, then entered the kitchen.

"Where have you been?" James asked.

"We've been worried sick," Henry said, although fretting had evidently not impaired his appetite, as witnessed by the pile of chicken bones on his plate.

Will's brown eyes scanned her head to toe, then he returned to his pie. A thought surprised her, that the ride would have been much more enjoyable in his company.

Nettie moved a full plate from the warming oven to the table. "We saved supper for you. Sit down and tell us about your ride."

"It was inspirational!" Sophia took her place and smiled at them all. "I have the most glorious idea for a Christmas celebration!"

CHAPTER TWENTY-THREE

D id you see the fog rising off the river?" Sophia asked as she
made her entrance for breakfast. "It is quite beautiful."
It was one of the things Will appreciated about
Sophia, her ability to find beauty in the everyday.

The rev, on the other hand, took a darker view. "Nothing good
about this weather." He stomped in, shook the rain off his slicker,
and hung it on a hook near the door.

Sophia fingered the shiny black material. "This sheds water
well. Is it leather?"

Henry shook his head. "Rubberized fabric."

She turned to the agent. "Could we—"

"No chance. They're so expensive, I can't imagine how Henry
could afford one."

The reverend gave a little snort. "Donated by a widow as payment for her husband's funeral."

With a rattle on the roof, the rain changed to sleet.

"School's off." James toasted Sophia with his coffee mug.

"But I told the students we would practice our Christmas performance today."

"Too dangerous." Will glanced out. He'd have to spread ashes
on the path to the outhouse.

Nettie dried her hands on a towel. "Well then, let's unpack
those new boxes."

"I hope they contain useful items this time." Sophia followed her into the front room. James and Henry disappeared into their offices.

Will settled back with a second cup of coffee and listened to the sounds coming from the front room. Every box turned Nettie into a kid at Christmas. He heard a thump as the lid he'd loosened earlier was set on the floor.

"Here's a letter for you," Nettie said. "Oh my. I've never seen the like. It's sized for an adult, but . . ."

"It looks like a frock a child would wear?" Sophia groaned. "That is dear Annabelle, in a nutshell. We shared a suite at the College. She taught English until marrying a congressman. Since we are blessed with her old wardrobe, she must have ordered new."

Nettie muttered, "Four, five different types of lace, chenille ball trim, fringe, tucks and pleats, two dozen bows. All in baby-bottom pink."

In the kitchen, Will suppressed a laugh.

"And soutache trim," Sophia said. "Although it is not quite the same effect without her jewelry." Paper rustled. "Ah. This is useful. A list of senators and congressmen, with addresses."

"Please tell me this isn't the fashion." Fabric rustled.

"Here's another, in butter yellow. How could she teach dressed like an infant ready for christening?"

"Our students were well behaved in the extreme. But our lady principal was sorely vexed, as she had directed the students toward simplicity in dress."

More swishing of cloth. Will considered going to see what the fuss was about, but his coffee had just cooled to the perfect temperature. And after cutting wood all week, he needed to sit a spell.

"Merciful heavens, look at this needlework. A life-sized doll's dress. How will she cope as a legislator's wife?"

"Hosting dinners, navigating the social scene in Washington

as well as New York, managing households in two cities?" Sophia paused. "The dress speaks for itself."

"My word. He should have married you, Sophia!"

Will stopped breathing.

"My thought exactly," Sophia said, her tone light. "Unfortunately, the congressman made other plans."

Will's hands tightened on his cup. That bigwig must be an idiot to pass over Sophia.

Nettie murmured, "You poor dear. Did he break your heart?"

"Certainly not. My heart was never involved. Only my pride, my ambition to be a woman of influence. Which God clearly put to an end by sending me here."

"Oh, I don't know about that. You've had a good influence on your students, and on your former roommate, sending her clothes here. Although these light colors will show dirt." Cloth swished, like a whole collection of petticoats. "Still, you must have been mortified. Did anyone else know you'd set your cap for him?"

"All 370 students, and most of the faculty, teachers, and servants. Everyone counted us a match. I was not alone in my misreading of Montgomery's intentions."

"Sophia, no thought of marriage should enter your head unless your heart is involved. All the way."

"My heart?" Sophia made a short sound, a choked-off laugh.

"Do Russians believe in arranged marriages?"

"Peter the Great put an end to that. Although fathers remain quite involved."

"But your father . . ."

"Being out of the tsar's favor limited my suitors." Her voice sounded sad for a moment, then returned to her usual take-charge briskness. "So. If we disassemble these, perhaps the fabric can be used to make underclothes for my students, do you think?"

Will finished his coffee and slipped out the back door. So she wanted to be a woman of influence? Then she'd hitch her star to James. The agent had aspirations for a job with the Indian Office in Washington. Or she'd choose the army officer—influence and travel.

Anyone but a small-town carpenter.

⁓⁓

Will pulled on long johns and two flannel shirts. Maybe this afternoon it would warm up enough to work on furniture in the warehouse. He sent up a desperate prayer: *Please, God, no more coffins. Especially not for a baby.*

Last week they'd buried Julia's son, Timothy. With the bitter cold and shortage of food, more deaths could be expected. He never got used to it. In fact, the longer he stayed, the more it hurt.

Sophia arrived for breakfast with pink cheeks and a red nose. She scraped a hole in the ice covering the window. "Just a flurry. Will I have many students today?"

"None at all," James said. "Your students don't have coats."

Will set down his fork. The previous teacher had canceled at the first flake and spent the day lounging about the house, smoking cigars and trying to coax him to shirk his job for a card game. "How cold was it in your room?"

"A bit."

"I'll work on the stoves today," Will said.

The Indian Office's theory was that the stoves in the first-floor bedrooms would heat the upstairs rooms. Like the rest of their ideas, it didn't work.

"Hmm." Sophia studied the scene from a different window, almost dancing with excitement. "Well then. If my students will not come to me, I will go to them."

James sprayed coffee over his shirt. "I don't have time to haul you—"

"Are there snowshoes?" she asked.

"What for? Not enough snow to cover the grass." The rev gave her the glare that frightened lesser men. It only made Sophia bolder.

"I'll hunt up a pair," Will said. Best be prepared. Those low gray clouds could dump a foot before night.

Nettie got up from her breakfast. "I always wanted to try snowshoeing."

"Perhaps you could go with me."

Nettie smiled. "I'll bring the yarn, do a knitting lesson. Then let's check on Julia."

Sophia went to bundle up and returned looking like a princess in her fur coat. "I am sorry to overdress, but I have no other."

Nettie wrapped up in a knitted scarf and her wool ulster. She ran a hand down the fur. "Oh, it's as soft as it is beautiful."

"It belonged to my mother."

"Is it warm?" Nettie got Sophia's nod. "Then wear it in her memory and thank God for His provision." They hurried out into the cloud of snow.

⁘

"I wish we had a thermometer," Nettie said. Their breath puffed white as they hurried across the village. "How cold do you suppose it is?"

"Well below freezing," Sophia said. The water in her ewer had turned to a solid block. A layer of ice coated her window, which cut down on the drafts. Frost glazed the walls. She could only imagine how uncomfortable the Poncas must be in their similarly built homes.

"Zlata! Your troika is growing almost as big as you." Sophia unwrapped a scrap of paper holding pieces of pork. All four dogs sat in unison and waited their turn for their treats.

"Will told me you had them trained, but I didn't believe it. Sophia, you're amazing."

"Dogs are easy. Children are more complicated."

"And men," Nettie huffed, "are a lost cause. Although food does help."

The women reached their destination.

"Do we knock or hail?" Sophia wished she had asked Will more about calling customs; his expertise in Ponca culture was unrivaled. A brown dog announced their arrival with all the decorum of a royal butler.

Thomas Jefferson answered the door. It was not much warmer inside. The entire family huddled in blankets around the stove. Were they interrupting? What did the Poncas do during the winter? More questions she should have asked Will.

"Good morning, Mrs.—"

She hesitated. What was this woman's name? If Thomas Jefferson was her son, did that automatically give her the name of Mrs. Jefferson? Or, since her husband was named Walks in the Mud, did that make her Mrs. Walks in the Mud? The woman did not supply another name, so Sophia applied one to her. "Mrs. Jefferson. I am Sophia Makinoff, the teacher. How are you today?"

The woman patted the baby in her lap and replied in Ponca. She did not seem to know any English.

"She says good morning," Thomas said. "And asks if you would like soup."

"No, thank you." They had been warned by Will about Ponca hospitality. Guests must be fed, even if the family did without. "We are not allowed to eat while we teach."

In the absence of chairs, the family sat on woven bulrush mats. Removing only her mittens, Nettie squeezed in next to the mother and began the knitting lesson.

"Where is Martha?" Sophia asked.

"She went to play with Susette." Thomas patted the spot between him and his little brother and she sat.

Walks in the Mud expressed great interest in her coat. The pelts reminded him of the weasels he used to hunt. Sophia told him it was sable, similar to a weasel.

Thomas's little brother had been afraid of her when he visited the school last summer, but today his fear resolved into wide-eyed curiosity. Sophia opened her copy of Townsend's translation of *Aesop's Fables*. Their only lantern shone a tiny circle on the knitting lesson, so she raised the book to the faint light from the window and read the story of the Lion and the Mouse. An appropriate lesson, Sophia thought, of how someone small and weak could nevertheless become a hero to someone powerful and strong.

The father had a story to share too. Using motions and animal sounds, illustrations drawn on the slate, and Thomas's emerging interpretation skill, Walks in the Mud told a cautionary tale about a wolf. It reminded her of the Russian tales of cunning wolves. Wolves were always at the door of those who were hungry.

"Next time," Sophia told Thomas, who had crawled into her lap, "I will bring paper so you can write down your father's story."

The little brother raced into the next room and brought back a piece of wood. Close examination showed it was a toy steamboat with ten pegs as crew. Thomas and his brother counted the pegs while singing, "One little, two little, three little boatmen," to the tune of "Ten Little Indians."

"How clever. Did you make this?" she asked the father.

"Will help me. Will make song."

An excellent teaching aid. She would have to thank Will. She had seen him whittling on several occasions, but, to be certain, she had no idea of his purpose.

Thomas held two pegs in one hand, three in another.

The little one said, "Two and three make five."

Sophia applauded. "Thomas has taught you well. I look forward to having you attend school."

The children brought out other toys their father and Will had made: rattles for the baby, a horse and wagon complete with a leather harness, and a buffalo, deer, wolf, cow, and chicken that fit together like a puzzle. So creative!

Nettie stood and rubbed her fingers. "We should go, so we have time to check on Julia."

Thomas's little brother wiggled out of his father's lap and gave Sophia a big hug.

"Thank you!" Sophia hugged back. Then, much to her surprise, her eyes filled with tears. Unlike many women, she did not yearn for babies. She did not coo over them, or seek them out at church, or make forays into nurseries. But oh, these little arms around her neck, the soft cheek pressed to hers, that delightful smile . . .

Sophia wiped her eyes. The children of this village blessed her so.

"Thank you for letting me visit with your family," Sophia told the parents. One down and two hundred some to go. She hoped winter would not last long enough to complete their visits.

Lazy flakes pirouetted in the air as Sophia and Nettie hurried across the village. Buffalo Woman answered their knock with a solemn nod and they hurried inside.

A faint odor tinged the air. Sophia seized the wall for support and willed the dizziness to pass. She recognized the smell from her father's last days: impending death.

Her stomach mastered, she looked around. Where were the buffalo hides and the pouches of kitchen utensils? The house had been stripped of its accoutrements, leaving just a roll of blankets in the corner. Sophia closed her eyes, seeing her room in St. Petersburg, with its draped and canopied bed, parquet floor, tall windows, and crystal chandeliers. Why did some have so much, and others have nothing?

Buffalo Woman sat on the floor, pulled back the blanket, and unveiled the frail shell of what had been Julia. Her thick, shiny braids and clear complexion had been replaced by grizzled patches of hair and wrinkled-paper skin. All energy and humor were gone from her eyes. And worst of all, her arms had gone from being full of a lively toddler to being empty.

Nettie gasped and sank to the floor beside the widow. Buffalo Woman propped Julia up and put a cup of what appeared to be tea to her mouth. The patient closed her lips and turned her head. Buffalo Woman blinked away tears. She set the cup aside with a shake of her head.

Poor Julia had lost her husband in the Brulé raid in June, soon after Sophia arrived. Then last week Timothy, her only child, had died. Sophia could not be certain, as no doctor attended her, but she suspected malnutrition played a part in the baby's death.

Nettie took a turn supporting Julia. Buffalo Woman held a cedar branch in the fire until it smoked, then passed it over her patient and sang softly, looking ever so much like an orthodox priest waving incense.

Nettie clasped Sophia's hands and whispered, "Dear Jesus, please help our sister Julia. Please comfort her. Please heal her."

Sophia should have brought her prayer book. Why could she not remember the Prayer for the Sick? She had read it constantly when her father was ill. Something about infirmities and asking God to be the physician. *Oh Lord, be the physician unto Thy servant Julia . . . because we have no doctor here.*

Nettie finished praying. They said good-bye and started back to the house. The snow continued, with smaller, more serious flakes now.

"I shall take her some food after lunch," Sophia said. "And firewood. She has none."

But Nettie had cooked the food and Will had cut the wood.

How could Sophia help? "It must be dreadfully cold sleeping on the floor. Do we have extra mattresses at the house? Will brought me one when the roof leaked on my bed."

Nettie held the door open for her. With eyebrows raised, she said, "He gave you his mattress. There are no extras."

How kind of him. Yet, if he had given her his mattress, what had he slept on? Perhaps he might know where to find another. Sophia tromped through the blessedly warm kitchen to the front room and called, "Will?"

"He went up to the warehouse," Henry told her.

The agent stuck his head out of his office. "Can I help you?"

"No, thank you. I am sorry to disturb you." Sophia could see the large building from the kitchen door. And she still had her coat on. "I shall go see if Will can make a bed for Julia."

Nettie glanced up from her place at the stove and nodded. "Too cold for troublemakers."

Too cold and too quiet. St. Petersburg had church bells, skating parties on the river, streets filled with sleighs. This village's quiet spoke of desertion and loneliness, impoverishment so deep all energy must be committed to survival. Sophia hurried, almost running, and slipped into the warehouse. At her entrance, half a dozen men looked up from a table. What had she interrupted?

"Sophia? Did you need something?" Will stood, putting down a well-worn book with numerous scraps marking the pages. Ah, his Bible. Will held a Bible study? Why had she, the missionary, not thought to do so?

"Yes. I am sorry to bother you, but Julia has taken ill. She sleeps on the floor. Perhaps you know of a bed?"

The men smiled. Will donned his coat and grabbed a stack of boards wrapped in canvas. "We were just praying about who'd get this."

"Wonderful." Sophia followed him down the hill. "And Nettie is making soup. I wish I could help Julia too."

"You could sing. With your gusli."

It was not a miracle cure, but what else did she have? Sophia retrieved her instrument from the house, then raced back to Julia's.

Will unrolled long poles connected by a sheet of canvas. He fitted the ends into the headboard and footboard and held them in place with pins as thick as a finger. The frame assembled as quickly as an army cot.

"How clever. Where did you get the long spikes?"

"Those andirons from the last allotment. The canvas is from a tent Fort Randall tried to throw away. Won't support anyone heavy." He lifted the ill woman, blankets and all, and set her on the bed. "Miss Julia's about to float away."

A smile flickered across the woman's face as she settled into her new bed. Susette Primeau, Standing Bear's wife, had replaced Buffalo Woman as caregiver. She propped her patient up with a backrest made from willow rods laced with leather strips.

Sophia unbuttoned her coat and sat on the floor beside her. "Do you have a favorite song?"

Julia gave a tiny shake of her head, too tired to speak.

Susette asked, "Do you know *'Cantique de Noel'*?"

Sophia had not heard the song since she had left France six years ago and suspected it had been much longer for the Ponca women, but the music returned to them all. Will sat beside her and hummed through the French verses, then continued in English, singing "O Holy Night" in a rich baritone that raised the temperature of the room above freezing.

The fierce creases of pain in Julia's face eased and she slept.

Even in Sophia's effort to bless Julia, it was Will who truly made the difference.

CHAPTER TWENTY-FOUR

Sophia looked up from helping Luke Adams with his sums to see Will slipping into the back row. Since early November when the afternoon temperatures barely climbed above freezing, Sophia had invited her escort to wait inside.

She glanced at her pocket watch. It seemed he arrived earlier every day, perhaps guided by dusk rather than time.

Rather than interfering or interrupting like Henry, Will helped in his own quiet way. He said he had not attended many years of school, but she had yet to find an arithmetic problem that stumped him. And his skills in geometry far exceeded hers.

When the lesson ended, Sophia asked, "Who can tell me what happened at the first Christmas?"

"It's when Jesus came!"

"His mother's name was Mary," said Mark Adams, the one with low eyebrows like the Grand Duke Sergei Alexandrovich.

Susette raised her hand. "Jesus' parents did not have a horse, so His mother rode on a donkey. And she had the baby in a stable."

Sophia would have to give Henry credit—the children knew the Christmas story.

"Last year a fat man came to church," Rosalie told them with wide eyes. "He had a red shirt and white hair like a cloud on his face."

Sophia explained, "In some countries he is called Father Christmas or Saint Nicholas." In some countries he brought gifts, but probably not to the Ponca Agency.

"White people brought a tree into church." Luke Adams giggled. "And put popcorn on it with a string."

Sophia exchanged a grin with Will. The students were right, some traditions were silly. Decorating with food must seem especially foolish to hungry children.

Martha Jefferson looked her in the eye for a moment. "And the tree had paper cones with nuts and hard candy."

"And an orange for each of us!" Matthew clapped.

"And Mrs. Nettie made lemonade. It made my mouth go—" Luke sucked his cheeks in.

Ah, that was why Nettie had been saving those cans of lemonade. Sophia noted: *Bring lots of food.*

"What songs did you sing?"

Sophia tuned her gusli and the students reviewed the carols they knew: "O Come, O Come, Emmanuel," "While Shepherds Watched Their Flocks"—sheep again!—"Hark! the Herald Angels Sing," "O Come, All Ye Faithful," and "It Came upon a Midnight Clear." Will's fine baritone added to the choir. A good foundation.

"Now I need an older girl to play Mary, an older boy to be Joseph, and someone to bring their baby from home. A good-natured baby—no fussing."

"We have a new baby." Rosalie bounced, making the bench thud on the floor. "He does not cry too much."

"Wonderful, but please remember to raise your hand." Ah, yes, Elisabeth had been *enceinte* when they climbed the waterfall. "What is your new brother's name?"

This question generated considerable discussion among the siblings. The answer seemed to be either Raccoon or Michael.

"Please ask your—" Was Rosalie's mother Elisabeth, or Mary?

She couldn't remember. "Please ask your parents if your brother can be in our Christmas play."

The students agreed to have Joseph and Marguerite fill the roles. Frank, their best oral reader, would narrate. Matthew, Mark, and Luke became wise men. The rest of the boys would be shepherds. The girls would be angels. At the end of every school day, they would practice.

The students completed their chores—sweeping out the mud took longer than usual—and dressed to walk home. Will helped Rosalie wind her scarf around her head, then the children rushed out, leaving a moment of blessed quiet.

Sophia banked the fire. "Before today I have never understood the importance of Jesus' poverty. The world has only a handful of kings and princes, but millions of poor, who know what it is like to be without money for hotels and horses."

"I like that His earthly father, Joseph, was a carpenter." Will nodded and picked up her gusli. "Could we bring this, go visit Julia again?"

"Yes. It should not stay in a room without heat."

He tucked it under his coat.

Sophia locked the school. "The angels announced Jesus' birth to the shepherds first, before the wise men. That is also important." She increased her pace as their path led them out from the cover of the trees to the windy bank of the river. "I think often of your words of wisdom: ignore the rushing water. With all the needs, how do you keep from drowning? How do you sort through all the requests for help?"

"I just focus on the person in front of me, being Jesus for that person at that moment. Seems like you—" He stopped. "Never mind. None of my business."

Sophia jostled his elbow with hers. "Will. You have been here three years. You share your thoughts without scolding. Please, I would like to hear what you are thinking."

Zlata and her troika trotted out from their den beneath Julia's house. When Sophia finished feeding them, she looked up at Will.

He studied the bluff, limned by the setting sun, then swallowed and scratched his chin. "Well, I'm not sure you really ignore the rushing water. Every evening you're penning a letter to someone asking for help, complaining about conditions here. Jesus didn't write to rich people, asking them to solve His problems."

"Writing letters is wrong?"

He did not speak again until they reached the house. "I don't know. Just seems . . . shouldn't God supply their needs?"

"Perhaps I am to be His instrument of provision."

He shrugged and held the door open for her. "Maybe."

"Sit by the Christmas tree." The rev handed the bucket to Sound of the Water, then hurried up front to light the candles on the cedar. Will had found it in a draw west of here, when they were out cutting firewood. Nettie and Sophia had decked it with strings of popcorn and cranberries, and paper cones of nuts, raisins, and hard candy. Sound of the Water looked in the bucket, then asked Will in Ponca, "What do I do with this?"

On the walk from the agency house, the water inside had steamed, lost all its heat, and was rapidly on its way to becoming a useless chunk of ice.

Will took the bucket since Sound of the Water's winter weather gear was limited to one moth-eaten blanket. "I'll dump it outside and refill it with snow."

The weather—light snow and severe cold—kept the people of Hubdon and Point Village home. Will scanned the pews, mentally matching each group with their house. All of Brown Eagle's family, all of Walks in the Mud's, all of Yellow Horse's . . .

everyone from the agency village made it except Julia, whom they had visited earlier today.

"Merry Christmas," he said to his friends.

James hauled in a basket of oranges.

Sophia, a princess in her fur coat, lined up the students. With a bag of scraps and rags, she had turned the Ponca children into the citizens of the Holy Land. The girls wore halos of crocheted yellow yarn. Three boys had crowns of yellow paper and the rest wore towels on their heads. All shivered and a hefty portion coughed. Good thing Christmas was on a Sunday this year; the people couldn't survive a second church service at this temperature.

Up front Nettie led "It Came upon a Midnight Clear" on the melodeon. Sophia had asked Will to sing "O Holy Night," but the rev didn't allow any songs not in the hymnal.

Henry marched back from the pulpit, his hard shoes echoing on the wood floor. "What is the meaning of this?"

Will stepped forward, ready to bust him across the jaw, Christmas or not.

"Our Christmas pageant." Sophia managed to have a commanding presence even when the rev towered over her and she had to whisper. "The children have worked hard on their presentation."

"But . . ." He scowled at Marguerite, holding her baby brother, and Joseph. "Indians playing the Holy Family?"

"Who played them last year?"

"Mother and I."

Will thought having an elderly woman and her son in the roles confused the congregation. It sure hadn't set well with him.

Sophia made a face like she'd bit into a wormy apple. "The students voted—"

"Indians can't vote!" he hissed.

"The goal of this mission—"

Will stepped between them. "Frank's starting. You'll have to settle this later." Which with Henry would be his "All the good I've tried to do has been undone by your actions" sermon.

Distinguished in a top hat and overcoat with a velvet collar, Frank read the Gospel account of Jesus' birth. Sophia sent Marguerite and Joseph down the aisle. The young girl unwrapped her baby brother. The little one studied the congregation. His lower lip trembled as if he might be working up to a cry. Joseph leaned forward and whispered. The baby reached up and grabbed on to his brother's finger, then relaxed in his sister's arms. Angels took their places. Shepherds arrived, then the kings.

Frank finished the reading, then looked toward the back of the church. Will gave him a thumbs-up. The young man had nailed every word. All their practice after school had paid off.

The congregation stood and sang "O Come, All Ye Faithful." Baby Michael waved in time with the music and gave a no-teeth grin, which got the whole church smiling.

Will had met only one or two Jewish people, but he figured Mary and Joseph looked more like Poncas than blue-eyed Nettie and Henry. And Nazareth and Bethlehem were small, poor towns like this village, places where the Poncas would feel at home.

A lacy handkerchief fluttered. Sophia was crying. Will put his hand on her shoulder. "Henry's wrong. It came out well."

"If I had gone to China, I would have missed all this." She covered his hand and smiled with a Christmas-star sparkle. "Thank you."

Will stepped up on the porch with an armload of firewood. If this cold kept up, he'd have to—

Sophia opened the door. Her cheeks glowed as red as Santa Claus's. "Merry Christmas! How is it outside?"

"Half inch of squeaky snow." Will finished stocking the wood box, then rubbed his nose. "Feels like I breathed in icicles."

"Perhaps we might visit Julia later?"

He nodded. Sophia had said something about China last night. He wanted to ask her what she meant. Nettie called them to the table, where she'd set out oatmeal and sausage.

James passed the coffee. "I bet you're missing some fancy parties in New York."

"Last year was no celebration." Sophia shook her head. "My father worked at West Point—"

"The military academy?" Will asked.

She nodded. "Down the river from the College. He taught cavalry tactics. Last Christmas I spent caring for him in his final illness."

Nettie murmured her condolences.

"So this year is much improved." Sophia toasted the staff with her tea. "It is my joy to celebrate the birth of our Savior with all of you. Your dedication and perseverance are an inspiration."

"Hear, hear!" James lifted his coffee cup.

"Thank you," Henry choked out. He could hardly yell at Sophia after such a compliment.

"We're having a better year too," Will said. "Staff's healthy." Last year they'd passed around the grippe. Will, as the only one not ailing, ended up doing all the work short of preaching.

"Thank the Lord for good health." Sophia turned to Nettie. "Do you need help with the dinner?"

Nettie shook her head. "All it needs is time." She leaned on the table. "Tell us about Christmas in Paris."

Sophia's eyes closed halfway and her face relaxed. "Of course the climate is much more temperate. Church bells ring. Oysters for dinner. The air is fragrant with roasting chestnuts from street vendors and bread from bakeries."

"Paris sounds so nice. Why did you leave?" Nettie asked.

Even her shrug seemed like part of a dance, involving both shoulders and a sway of her head. "Certain members of the Russian community there professed loyalty to the King of Heaven, but obeyed only the tsar. Then war with Prussia broke out. Father declined to participate in the conflict."

"You've had such a sophisticated life. What do you miss most?" Nettie asked. "Balls and dinner parties? Going to the opera and ballet?"

"The heat at Vassar?" Will guessed. "I hear they keep the rooms at sixty-five degrees."

Nettie gave a little snort. "Sixty-five? I can barely get my oven that warm."

James rubbed his mouth. "French wine."

"Not what *you* would miss," the rev growled at James, then lowered his heavy eyebrows at Sophia. "Bathtub. I heard you fussing about having to use the washtub."

"Forgive me. I should not complain. Not when our neighbors lack even that necessity." Her blue eyes focused on something none of them could see. "No, what I miss most is reading. Selecting a book or periodical from the library, settling into my favorite chair by the window or under the lamp. Or in Paris, in a public garden. Many of the joys of Paris are without cost, which was fortunate. We had left much behind, necessitating simple living."

She turned to Will with a smile. "Perhaps God used that challenge to prepare me for His work here."

Another piece of the Sophia-puzzle dropped into place. As his sister-in-law would so delicately put it, Sophia had endured times of reduced circumstances.

"Doesn't get much more simple than this," Henry muttered.

Nettie shot him a warning frown, then asked Sophia, "And how do you celebrate Christmas in Russia?"

"Also ringing church bells, but higher, more musical. So far north, St. Petersburg is blessed with plenty of cold and snow. We have festivals on the river. The Church follows the old calendar, so Christmas is a week later—January 7. We fast on Christmas Eve and attend church twice."

"So you've never had a normal, American Christmas?" the rev asked.

Will noticed Sophia's left eyebrow arch upward in response to Henry's assumption that only American Christmas was "normal," but to her credit, she refused to take the bait. "Sometimes Father and I celebrated with students who could not return home."

"Sounds fun," Will said.

"We tried, but it was quite melancholic, with everyone wishing for family. Certainly I understand. Many years when I was at Smolny, my father could not return for me. It is not a life I would wish for a child."

"We traveled a bit too, depending on where the church sent us." Nettie patted Henry's hand. "But we always had each other."

"Michigan, Wisconsin, Illinois. Always cold and snowing," Henry complained, gaining another kick from his mother. His gloom and doom would earn him a permanent bruise.

"Every year my father and I would go stomping around the hills, looking for the perfect Christmas tree." James refilled his coffee. "It had to be at least ten feet tall to hold all the baubles my sisters made. And it had to topple over at least once during the holidays, preferably during our Christmas party. Horrified my mother."

"Will?" Sophia asked. "Did you have a tree?"

"Trees are pretty scarce in Iowa. But we got stockings with nuts, an orange, hard candy." Like the Poncas got last night.

The years blurred together. He recalled his father bringing home a turkey, his mother serving a gingerbread cake sprinkled with white sugar, Will squeezing between his brother and sister at the table. His family all together. Maybe he hadn't been to Paris, but he'd been blessed in other ways.

Nettie pushed back from the table. "Sophia, while I check the roast, how about you get out your gusli and sing us a few Christmas carols?"

"Speaking of Christmas carols—" Will hoped the good feelings Sophia had sparked would stretch around the table to the Ebenezer Scrooge of books. "I don't suppose we could read Mr. Dickens?"

Henry gulped and tried to find a way to refuse, but Sophia clapped her hands and gasped. "You have a copy of Dickens's *A Christmas Carol*? Oh yes, let us read it!" In her best British accent she quoted, "'He knew how to keep Christmas well.'"

CHAPTER TWENTY-FIVE

Easy. A little less pressure." Will adjusted Spotted Horse's hold on the plane. They had joined three planks with dowels and were smoothing them into a tabletop. The plane peeled off a yellow curl almost as pretty as one of Sophia's.

No. He had to attend to his work. No thinking about Sophia, hoping her hair would escape her pins. Wondering how it would feel—

"Better?" Spotted Horse hadn't finished the table for Christmas. Maybe he'd have it done by New Year's.

"Uh. Yes. You got it."

When she got off the boat, Will had pegged Sophia as high society. But he was wrong. She knew the lingo, had crossed paths with some of its members, had taught their daughters. But she wasn't one of them.

A gust of wind sprayed him in the face with snow, cooling his thoughts. The warehouse needed major roof repairs, but the rafters were too rotted to risk sending anyone up to fix it.

Brown Eagle dashed in and shook the snow off his blanket.

Walks in the Mud pulled benches close to the potbellied stove. "Hurry up. We want to hear Will read."

Spotted Horse put away the tools, and Will opened his Bible to the last chapter of First Corinthians. "'Now concerning the collection for the saints . . . ,'" Will read. "'And when I come, whosoever ye shall approve by your letters . . .'"

Sophia was right. The apostle Paul had written letters to wealthy churches asking them to help the poor in Jerusalem. Just like she had.

Brown Eagle nudged him with his elbow. "Falling asleep?"

"No." Will rubbed his hands over his face and straightened. "Waking up."

"He is thinking about the teacher," Spotted Horse said.

"How do white people marry?" Walks in the Mud asked. "She has no family and you have no horses."

"He could make a herd." Brown Eagle held up one of the toys Will had carved.

Will's face heated. Spotted Horse chuckled and nodded at him. "I do not know why they call *us* redskins."

The off-kilter door rattled, and Henry stuck his head in. The men fell silent.

"We need another coffin."

The rest of the world celebrated the new year, but not the Ponca Agency. Yesterday they buried Julia.

Sophia blew her nose and wiped her eyes. She must not mope about waiting for her heartache to ease. Nettie had lost her closest Ponca friend and assistant. Sophia must attempt to console her. She took her tangle of yarn to the kitchen. "I fear I have misplaced a stitch."

"More than one, I'd say." Nettie's glance slid from the pot she stirred to Sophia's project, but she avoided eye contact. Perhaps the Poncas did not look into each other's eyes to avoid seeing all the pain hovering there.

The older woman sat down at the kitchen table and unraveled hours of work. "Sophia, a sock is too ambitious for a first project. Let's try a scarf."

"Ambition is a stumbling block for me."

Will hauled in two buckets of snow, then he joined them at the table. The pile of shavings on the floor indicated that he, too, had been keeping Nettie company today.

"What are you working on?" Sophia asked him.

He held up a branch with a bend in it. "Making a cane for one of the elders in Hubdon." His knife worked over the bent end, smoothing it into a handle. It seemed so much simpler than knitting, perhaps she might—

Henry shuffled in and rattled the empty coffeepot.

James took up a stance blocking the doorway. "Let us reflect on our accomplishments of the old year and our goals for the new one."

"Let's not." Henry stomped to the far corner of the room.

The agent read from a sheet of lined paper. "'Our tribe has made considerable progress. All wear citizens' clothes and send their children to school. We had an orderly and efficient distribution of the annuity in October. We haven't had an attack by the Brulé since June.'"

"But their clothing is inadequate to keep them warm," Sophia said. "And the annuity was only a fraction of the money owed."

"Yes, and the Poncas should get the credit for their treaty with the Brulé." Will's knife kept its even pace.

The agent reported on acres cultivated, but did not say how little had been harvested, or how many cattle and horses had been lost. His goal for 1877 was for the Poncas to be self-sufficient farmers. He raised an eyebrow at Henry. "Well?"

Henry stared out the back window, arms crossed, shoulders hunched. "Fifty-two sermons, seven baptisms, three marriages, twenty-one funerals." He spat out the words rapidly, as if he had prepared for this interrogation.

"And your goal for the new year?" James taunted.

The reverend's expression was colder than the north wind. "Plod on."

"We shall continue to labor in the fields of the Lord," Nettie said. She reported gardens now grew beside every home. She had taught some of the women canning, although they did not have much to work with.

"Don't forget," Will said, "you fed us, fixed lunches for the students, kept us in clean clothes, and did all the housework." He noted that everyone was out of tepees and into cabins or frame houses, a total of 236 homes. All dirt floors had been replaced by wood. Barns, outbuildings, gristmill, sawmill, church, and school were usable. He had a crew of four who could build homes and furniture. Most of the men knew how to make basic repairs.

Will paused his carving to give the agent a narrow gaze. "For the new year? Depends on if we get any of the supplies I asked for."

"You built the latrine and vestibule for the schoolhouse too," Sophia said. "You provide firewood for our stove."

"And the stoves here too," Nettie added. "And haul water."

"Sophia?"

She pondered the question. What had she accomplished? What good was she?

"Sorry. Should have warned you," Will said to Sophia. Then to James, "Everyone else is used to your New Year's questions. Give Sophia a day or two to think on it."

The agent had no intention of waiting. "You've had consistent attendance of twenty-eight—"

"Twenty-five," she corrected.

"All of them are writing their names and counting to a hundred," Will said. "Frank, Marguerite, and Joseph are in the third reader already."

"Marguerite's in the third reader?" Henry asked. "Maybe she should come work with Mother."

Sophia would not permit him to divert her best student. "Marguerite shows great potential to become a teacher. What an asset she will be to the tribe, an inspiration to her students."

James and Henry stared at her, mouths open.

"It's a good idea," Will said. "Marguerite's got the patience for teaching."

Nettie rolled the yarn into a ball. "If we don't tell the Indian Office she's Ponca—"

"Mother!" Henry could not decide who to scowl at first. He settled on Sophia. "Any goals for this year?" he asked, his tone indicating he expected her answer to be no.

"I have been thinking—"

"Dangerous," Henry muttered.

"—about the students in the other villages. Could we transport them to school, perhaps in a wagon with a cover?"

"Would need runners in winter," Will said.

"True. Or perhaps we could pay families here to board students during the week."

"Pay them with what?" James tapped his pencil against the door frame.

Even in her grief, Nettie found something to celebrate. "Sophia, you've had a successful letter-writing campaign, bringing in clothing and shoes."

James said, "You haven't quit."

"Hey. That's right." Will straightened and set down his knife. "She didn't quit."

"Pardon me?"

"Why God doesn't whack you over your fool heads with lightning bolts, I'll never know." Nettie rapped the table with the knitting needles. "Pay up and be done with it."

James dug a quarter from his pocket and tossed it to Will.

Sophia blinked at the agent. "You bet I would not stay?"

The needles waved dangerously at Henry. "You too. I heard."

"And you? Oh ye of little faith."

Will stacked the coins in the middle of the table.

Sophia turned to Will. "So. You won the bet."

"I'm thinking . . ." The ends of his wide mouth curved up. He added another from his pocket and pushed the quarters to her. "*You* won."

"And I am thinking . . ." Sophia slid the stack toward Henry. "The only place for such ill-gotten gain is the offering plate."

This time even Henry smiled.

Henry shuffled out of James's office around midnight. "Why are you still awake?"

Sophia looked up from the kitchen table. "There is no sense lying down if sleep will not come."

"So this place has finally gotten to you too." He leaned on the door frame. The lantern light showed the despair in his eyes. "It eats away at you, the constant failures, each worse than the last."

"But you have had successes. Seven baptisms, did you say? Fifty-two sermons? Perhaps that is the problem. You have not had any respite from your duties. Do not the clergy attend annual meetings?"

"Not going. Don't want to hear how wonderful everyone else is doing. How they've got all their people baptized, Sunday school's packed, half dozen men of the tribe have become priests and deacons. To see their scorn about my miserable, paltry seven baptisms."

Sophia felt a rush of sympathy for the poor man, bearing such a burden on his shoulders. "God knows your struggles. He does not judge by numbers." Although administrators seemed easily beguiled by quantities.

"Everywhere else we've had success starting churches. In Michigan we had the building up and paid for in less than a year.

In Wisconsin the original congregation grew into two. In Illinois we raised support for three missionaries."

"Three? You, Nettie, and me? I should write and thank them." She pulled out a fresh sheet of stationery. "What is the name of the church?"

"No. They don't want to hear about failure."

"A wise man gave me some good advice," Sophia said. "Ignore the rushing waters."

Henry chose to ignore her instead. He shuffled into his room and slammed the door behind him.

◦⟨≈⟩◦

The blankets sparked in the January-dry air when Will climbed out of bed. Breathing in froze his nose, and breathing out made a white puff. Woolen drawers didn't keep him from shivering. He added a second shirt, pants, another pair of socks, then carried his boots into the kitchen.

What's this? A small bear at the table? No, it's Sophia, wrapped in her fur coat, head on her arms. Driven downstairs by the cold in her room, no doubt. Will had tinkered, patched, and repaired. He'd made bed warmers for Sophia and Nettie from old popcorn makers some church in Connecticut had decided they needed. With her room catching the north wind and her bones carrying less natural insulation, Sophia couldn't sleep through the cold like Nettie.

There was no way to help it—building a fire made noise. The door squeaked, the shovel scraped, the wood thunked . . . and Sophia groaned.

"Sorry."

She pushed the hair off her face and blinked at him. "Do not apologize for making it warmer in here." Her voice came out low and sleepy, firing up thoughts he shouldn't be thinking.

Will lit the lantern, not wanting Henry to find them together in the dark. Letters, appeals for aid, spread across the table. She wrote neatly, of course, with enough flourishes to make the script elegant, but not enough to make it unreadable. And of course, she used fancy words, but not enough to confuse a simple carpenter.

"Dakota League of Massachusetts, Indians' Hope Association of Philadelphia, Providence Indian Aid Association. I didn't know there were so many groups."

"Not to mention the Baltimore Indian Aid Association and the Board of Missions Women's Auxiliary. I hope they are not all discussing the color of napkins to use at their next tea or dithering over bylaws." She stacked the letters. "My ink froze."

Will took the bottle from her and set it on the stove. "I was wrong about your letter writing. The apostle Paul did it too. In First Corinthians, he talks about asking the wealthy churches for aid to the poor."

"Thank you. Few men are strong enough to admit a change of mind." She awarded the compliment like knighthood. "So, you will commence letter writing?"

"Don't know anyone worth the price of a stamp." His insides got all squirmy. "Figure it's one of those situations where some are called to be apostles, others prophets, others teachers." Will had been called to build, that much he was sure of. Everything else he'd leave up to God.

Sophia's blue gaze fastened on his as if she could see straight into his soul. "Perhaps."

Will pushed away from the table to fuss with the coffeepot. Maybe he was hiding again, not wanting to try something new, afraid his lack of schooling would show in his writing. He could put a note for the bishop in his next letter home, since they were already praying for him.

He dampened a clean cloth and turned back to the table. "No

inkblots on your letters, but you got yourself." He nodded at her cheek. Instead of taking the cloth, she tilted her face toward him. Her perfect, porcelain-smooth face.

Will swallowed, pulled up a chair, and touched her. He hoped she didn't notice his hand shook. Maybe she'd chalk it up to the cold. The mark came off with one swipe of the cloth.

Now what? If he sat here much longer, this close, he'd make a fool of himself. He nodded at the letters. "Sorry I can't get more heat upstairs."

"Dear Will." She did that dance with her eyelashes, warming him faster than the stove. "Russians are used to cold. Although I am surprised at the dearth of snow."

She called him *dear*? Did she think of him in a special way, or was she stuck in letter-writing mode? "Other years, we've had more. And more wind."

She stacked the letters. He'd heard of people having a haunted look, but this morning was the first time he'd seen it. Sophia stared at the windows, too frosted to see through. "So many deaths . . ."

The kettle rattled. Will fixed her tea, then his coffee, then came back to the table. "What helps me is knowing Julia's with Walking Together and little Timothy in heaven."

She rolled the teacup between her hands, holding her face over its steam. Will reckoned it was a sign of their friendship, that neither of them felt obliged to fill the air with talk.

Finally she turned to him with a smile, with peace in her eyes. "Thank you. Yes, it does help."

Chapter Twenty-Six

Will heard the kitchen door close and hurried to catch up with Sophia. If he dawdled too much, she'd head out without him, ready to handle any problem with her pistol. He grabbed the stewpot off the stove and followed.

Sophia stood in the yard, bundled in her fur coat, surrounded by the yellow dogs. Was she still sneaking food to them? The pups sat for their treat, then loped off. Sophia turned to him. The morning light through thin clouds made her look even more out of the ordinary, as if she'd escaped from a painting. Lazy snowflakes caught in her hair and sparkled like diamonds. She turned at the scrape of his boots. "Snowshoes are not necessary today, I do not think."

Will shook free of his addlepated musing. "Only a flurry." Since Christmas, the weather had been bitterly cold, allowing the school to open only four days in the last three weeks. Will set the stewpot in the sled, slipped the traces over his shoulders, and headed out. "So, Teacher, what's your plan for today?"

"The students are writing down traditional Ponca stories, how the world was created, where the tribe came from, how they hunted buffalo."

"Hope Henry doesn't find out."

Sophia pressed her lips together and gave a slow blink with her eyebrows raised. She had a whole collection of interesting expressions he didn't see on American women. "I am surprised at how much their creation story resembles the first chapters of Genesis. Do you think God could have spoken to them?"

"That's a question for Henry."

"I am asking your opinion. You know what they believe."

Another compliment from Sophia. Will's swelling chest threatened to burst the buttons off his coat. "All things are possible with God, right? Nothing in the Bible says God didn't talk to them."

A cold gust hit him at the knees, carrying a few more enthusiastic snowflakes.

"And also, I have been thinking—" She seemed to do an awful lot of that. "About accomplishments. I am learning to see God's hand at work. Through changing trains, running aground, the broken stateroom lock, He kept me safe on the journey here. And He kept me safe here through attacks of the Brulé and angry whiskey dealers. The school books the church sent were the ones the students needed. The shoes arrived before the first snow and were enough so every student had a pair. Your sister sent socks."

"I see what you're getting at," Will said. "With the situation so bad here, if anything goes right, it has to be God."

"Exactly. So my goal is to see more clearly what God is doing, so I know better what I am to do."

"Seems like—" He turned to look at her and gasped. A large dark cloud was barreling over the bluff, dumping snow on the village.

They needed shelter. Fast.

Sophia followed his gaze. She must have seen this kind of blizzard in Russia too, because in a heartbeat she turned and pivoted the sled back toward the agency house.

There was no time to think, no time even to pray. The only prayer that came to Will's mind was, *Help, Lord!*

The return trip faced them into the wind, a wind that sucked the breath out of him and peeled the skin off his face. Within a minute or two, blowing snow hid the village, the nearest house, the path.

Jesus, guide us! he thought. They could lose their way, lose each other, wander until they froze to death—which, as fast as the temperature was dropping, might not be long.

He grabbed her elbow. "Sophia!"

Her eyes held a glint of adventure. Surely she knew how dangerous this blizzard was.

With quick, sure motions, she pulled his hat down to his eyebrows and his scarf up over his nose. Then she took the right trace from his arm and slipped it over her shoulders. Ah, yes, now he could keep track of her, and together they pulled faster. She bent and found their footprints, rapidly filling in, and set a fast pace.

The woman was fearless. No whimpering or complaining. Experienced with the toil of winter. God had sent exactly the right person for this job.

A house appeared an arm's length ahead of them.

"Whose is this?" she yelled over the wind.

"Standing Buffalo's." Will recognized the government-issue, knot-filled pine. The knots had popped out, leaving holes that let in drafts and vermin. Standing Buffalo's mud patches gave it a pockmarked appearance. "This way." He steered the sled left. Now Sophia took the brunt of the wind. "Want to switch places?"

"We are almost there."

Will wrapped his arm around her and placed his mittened hand on the side of her face. With this angry weather and the heavy sled, she had to be tired, but still he could feel her energy through their heavy coats. He had to work to keep up with her, to match her pace.

What sort of man would be a match for her? Someone remarkable, that's for certain.

At last the agency house appeared, the only house in the village with a porch.

Will leaned toward where he guessed her ear hid under her scarf and hood. "Go in!"

She turned to slip out of the trace, close enough to kiss.

Kiss? What was he thinking? While he went all soft-headed over the snowflakes on her eyelashes, Sophia hefted the stewpot, which probably weighed as much as she did. Will propped the sled on the porch, then helped her haul the pot inside.

"Lord have mercy!" Nettie said as she hung up their coats and handed them towels. "I woke James up to go look for you."

"Why? With Will as my guide, I had no trouble."

There she went again with her button-busting comments. She wiped Will's face with a gentle touch. "Truth to tell," he said, "I think you were the one leading me."

Sophia's eyes lingered on his mouth as if he had snow stuck to his mustache. He gave his face another scrub. She blinked, then scurried closer to the stove. "Well then, if we are not having school, I might as well write another letter."

James leaned on the doorway. His face drooped, and he breathed unevenly, as if someone had shot his best dog. He crumpled a telegram in his fist. "Too late."

CHAPTER TWENTY-SEVEN

R eady?" Will asked.

Sophia buttoned her coat. "Certainly," she said. The truth was she would never be ready to do what lay before her. But she had no choice.

Nettie shoved her hands into mittens and nodded grimly. The three of them set out for church into a January day too sunny and beautiful for the bad news they brought to the tribe. James and Henry had already left.

"How will they manage?" Sophia asked. "I cannot imagine how difficult this will be. I have never felt the attachment to place that the Poncas have."

"Nor I," Nettie agreed. "The church moved us around. No town holds my heart."

"I don't know where my people are from or where they're buried." Will nodded at the bluff, the Ponca cemetery. "But for the Poncas, this land is their history."

A gust off the river swirled dry snow across the frozen ground.

Nettie shivered. "It's got to be warmer in Indian Territory."

Sophia took the older woman's arm, walking on her west side to block the wind. "Is there any possibility the move will be good for the tribe? Might life be easier for them?"

"So far the Indian Office has had nothing but bad ideas." Will frowned. "If they really want the Poncas to become Americans, shouldn't the choice be theirs? Isn't that what this country is supposed to be about?"

"Good morning, Will, Teacher, Miss Nettie!" Brown Eagle and his family joined them.

Rosalie took Sophia's hand. "Teacher? Are you crying?"

"The wind." Another lie. She wanted to gather Rosalie and all her students, hug them, and vow to keep them safe. Who could she write to? Perhaps the president could reverse Congress's decision.

"Elisabeth still feeling poorly?" Will asked.

Brown Eagle nodded. "With all of us out of the house, I hope she can rest."

Sophia scanned the congregation as they settled in. Standing Buffalo and his family were absent. Who else was ill? Bronchitis, pneumonia, tuberculosis, scrofula, or influenza? Measles, diphtheria, whooping cough, smallpox? It did not matter. In the absence of medical care, illness ravaged all.

"We should pray," she whispered to Will at her side.

"I am."

Henry led the congregation in singing "Savior, Like a Shepherd Lead Us." His sermon's first point was that God's people were mobile. He gave the example of God telling Abraham to move from Ur to the Promised Land.

"The Commissioner of Indian Affairs isn't God," Will muttered to Sophia. "And Indian Territory isn't the Promised Land."

Point two was that the Son of God had no place to call His home. By point three, heaven is our real home, the adults shifted in their seats, exchanging worried glances over their children's heads.

Henry stepped down from the pulpit and attempted to smile. "The Poncas have had terrible times these last few years: illness, raids from hostile Sioux, grasshopper plagues, poor hunting, bad weather. The Great White Father has heard of your plight and provided money for the tribe to move to Indian Territory. The chiefs will meet here Friday to plan the move." He raised his arms for the benediction, but few heard over the clamor.

Brown Eagle and the other men crowded around Will. Henry counted himself the spiritual leader, and James's title was Indian Agent, but the tribe looked to Will for answers.

"What did he say?"

"Move to Indian Territory? Are we not in Indian Territory now? We are Indians and this is our territory."

"We made peace with the Brulé."

"My children are buried here. My parents and grandparents are buried here. I cannot leave."

"My house is built. My land is plowed."

Marguerite slipped her hand into Sophia's. "Will we have school tomorrow?"

"We will have school whenever the weather permits." It would not do to burst into tears. She pretended to open the top of Joseph's head and peer in. "Do you have room for more? What should I teach?"

"The fourth reader!" Joseph suggested.

"Certainly! And mathematics: percentages and interest rates." Sophia prayed God would not allow anyone to cheat these fine people. "And science: how your body works, plants, animals." Whatever she could discover about the flora and fauna of Indian Territory. "History, government, how to write a good letter."

"Music. I would like to learn to read music."

"Me too!" said the students milling about.

Sophia smiled. These people were as resilient as Russians, with half the pathos. She gave in to impulse and hugged Rosalie. "Yes, we shall sing every day."

❧

January thaw brought the temperatures above freezing. Men from Hubdon and Point Village filled the church Friday for the meeting with the inspector from the Office of Indian Affairs.

"You don't have to be here," James told Will. "You have other work."

The rev took Will's side for a change, but not for a good reason. "No sense having Will build anything now."

"He stays." Brown Eagle settled the argument, then switched to Ponca for the rest of his explanation.

"The last council, in 1875," Will interpreted for him, "your interpreter was Ioway and drunk. You did not understand us. We did not understand you. Big mistake."

"Tell him—" Henry pointed at Brown Eagle. "Inspector Kemble brought two interpreters—"

"They are Omaha," Brown Eagle said.

James scowled. "The language is the same."

At least close enough for the Indian Office's purposes. Will leaned toward them and took a deep breath in through his nose. "Are they sober?"

Reverend Hinman, visiting from the Santee Reservation, weighed in on the issue. "Few interpreters are competent in the language of treaties and negotiations."

Inspector Edward C. Kemble, thick of frame and mustache, also had 1875 on his mind. "The Ponca chiefs signed an agreement to move to Indian Territory."

"No, we agreed to live with the Omaha," Standing Bear said.

The interpreters exchanged a look. The government had already shrunk the Omaha tribe's reservation down to a tiny square, then without asking, squeezed the Winnebagos in. Could their land hold a third tribe?

The inspector ignored the discussion and continued in a louder voice. "Last year Congress allocated funds to move the Poncas to Indian Territory."

"Money? *Now* they send money?" White Swan held up his empty hands.

Smoke Maker shook his head. "I do not believe in money until I see it."

Long Runner muttered, "We will never see it."

"We want an accounting of all the tribe's money," Standing Bear said. "Back to the first treaty."

The inspector banged his gavel on the pulpit. "What an insubordinate bunch of malcontents. I thought you said these Indians were well behaved," he muttered to James in an undertone that carried to the back pews.

"Well behaved but not dead." Brown Eagle crossed his arms.

The whole proceeding paused for a spiritual dressing-down by the rev. Henry wrapped up with, "God wants His people to live in peace."

"How can we live in peace when our children are starving?" Standing Bear asked.

Inspector Kemble jumped on that idea. "For the sake of your children, you must move to Indian Territory. You'll be able to plant and harvest. You won't have to work so hard. The Indian Office will pay you for this land and provide what you need: farm equipment, cattle, houses, schools. You will live as American farmers. Other Indians live there—"

"What other Indians? Friends or enemies?" Chicken Hunter asked. "Maybe we do not want to live near them. Maybe they do not want us."

"Kaw, Cherokee, Quapaw, and Osage, who speak a language similar to Ponca. They have agreed to give you some land."

"Some land? Good for hunting or farming?" Big Elk asked. He'd done enough of both to know the difference.

"Are there buffalo?" Black Ghost had been too young to go on the last hunt.

"Is there water? Does it rain and snow?" Buffalo Chip asked.

Henry recited a verse about God giving rain on the good and bad. Will counted the question unanswered. In fact, most questions went without a decent answer.

White Eagle stood. "This land is a gift from God to the Ponca people. We did not sell it. We will not desert it. Here we live. Here we will die and be buried with our ancestors."

Henry scowled. "You must give up this childish ancestor worship and accept the Christian understanding of heaven."

Will couldn't stand it anymore. "The Poncas don't worship their ancestors. They believe those who've gone before will greet them on the other side. Brings to mind how you said your father would meet you at the heavenly gate."

The creases in Henry's forehead deepened to canyons. "Don't you have work to do?"

Inspector Kemble brought out a map. "The Indian Territory is better." The men squeezed in close and frowned at the chicken scratches on the paper.

"No rivers." Big Snake shook his head.

"Where are we?" Buffalo Track asked. "How far away is this Indian Territory?"

The inspector didn't have a US map, but Will knew someone who did. "I'll be right back." He borrowed a horse from Clear Sky Walker and rode to the school.

The students clustered around the map.

"How is the meeting going?" Sophia asked, looking not a bit ruffled by the addition of a dozen children from Point Village and Hubdon.

He gulped. Sophia's beauty always made him lose his thoughts. Probably best to go the Ponca route with her and not look her in the eye. "More asking than answering. Don't suppose I could borrow your map?"

"Of course. I am surprised the inspector did not bring one."

"Afraid of sharing too much knowledge. Kind of the opposite of what you're doing."

"Oh. Thank you." Her cheeks pinked up, making her even prettier than before.

"Thank *you*." He saluted her with the rolled map, then galloped back to church. The inspector didn't look too happy about Will's contribution. And the men weren't happy about the distance.

"How far is it?"

"One finger's width to the Omahas. Eight finger widths to Indian Territory."

"Long way."

"We will not be able to come back."

"That is just to the line. What if the Indian Office puts us down here by Texas?"

"Texas. They have no rain. Plants with needles. Cattle with horns that go out." Crazy Bear stretched his arms wide.

White Eagle said, "I want to see the paper saying we must move to Indian Territory."

"Why? You can't read it." Kemble raised his voice. "Sit down. I have more instructions." He turned to James. "I told you I only wanted to meet with the chiefs."

The Indian Office didn't want chiefs. And they didn't want white farmers. They wanted puppets who would follow instructions and not ask messy questions.

"Order!" James pounded the pulpit and yelled over the hubbub. "Sit down."

"They don't have hereditary chiefs anymore," Henry told Kemble, neglecting to mention the government's role in breaking down that tradition. "Each family head has a say."

"Think of it like Congress," Will told him.

The inspector's jaw clenched. His lower lip jutted out like the prow of a steamboat. "This is nothing like Congress." The inspector's tone said Will spouted foolishness.

If pressed, Will would have to admit he'd never been to Washington City, never seen Congress. But he had seen the city of Omaha's officials in action, throwing chairs and insults with eager abandon. So it seemed to him this Ponca meeting was more than civilized.

"All right." Kemble pointed at the men. "Choose ten of your chiefs or heads of families or whatever you call them. We'll take ten of you to Indian Territory so you can see for yourselves. Then we'll go to the Great White Father to talk it over. If you don't like Indian Territory, you can stay here."

Voices rose, most asking why they would even consider leaving.

"Enough! We're done here." Inspector Kemble snatched up his map, then reached for the US one.

Will caught his arm. "That's not yours."

"I'll put it away, for safekeeping." Meaning no one would ever see it again.

"I return what I borrow." Will tightened his grip, wrinkling the inspector's fancy suit sleeve. "I keep my promises."

Kemble narrowed his eyes. "You're the one stirring up all this trouble."

No sense holding back. Will's job was over when the tribe left. "Much as I'd like to take credit, the Indian Office made its own mess."

Kemble pointed an angry finger at Will's nose. "I'll have you know, thousands of dollars have been spent on these people."

Will took the opportunity to rescue Sophia's map. "Thousands of dollars might have left Washington, but only a few hundred made it here. What's that work out to per acre? Four cents? Two cents?"

"Ridiculous claim. This small tribe never owned all the land from here to the Rockies."

"I will bring the paper to the school," Will told the men in Ponca. "And the map."

Kemble pointed at Will, then asked his interpreter, "What did he say?"

Standing Bear stood. "We will pray about this tonight and give you our decision tomorrow."

Brown Eagle walked out with Will. "When we have a council, everyone has a say. We listen and consider all opinions. We respect each other. But that man thinks his is the only voice."

Over his shoulder Will heard the inspector tell James, "Get rid of the carpenter. The Agency no longer needs him."

Will's gut clenched. He wasn't worried about the job itself. His brother wanted him back. Harrison's last letter said work was piling up, waiting for him.

But . . . how could he leave the people?

And Sophia?

Chapter Twenty-Eight

Sophia helped a little boy from Point Village button his coat. "Where are you going? Where will you find your father?"

John Adams took the child's hand. "I can take him to the church."

Will and Brown Eagle stepped into the school. They drooped with battle fatigue. "Your fathers are coming here. You may as well wait inside."

"The meeting is over?"

"For now." Will hung her map on the front wall. "I have to get back to the agency house now."

"Shall I wait for you here?"

"No, I need your help now. Brown Eagle has my key. He'll lock the school after the children are picked up."

Every afternoon Sophia had been so careful to secure the school and the supplies donated by the churches back east. She studied Brown Eagle's round, strong face. Will trusted him as a brother in Christ. His children were honest. She never lost any of the money she passed around during her lessons. "Thank you," she told the man, then hurried to join Will on the path back to the house.

"The meeting was difficult?"

"Arguing in two languages." He set a brisk pace. "You didn't get off easy either."

"Thirteen extra students attended today. Three needed new English names and five could not remember their names given to them at the Fourth of July. I am embarrassed to say I cannot recall either."

At the village Henry slammed and locked the church door, then marched with James and a third man back to the house.

"The inspector." Will kept his hands in his pockets and his gaze on the slippery path. "I need you to keep him busy in the kitchen. And James and Henry too. I'm going to find that agreement the chiefs signed in '75. James has a copy in his office."

"James will give it to you, will he not? He objects to the removal of the tribe too."

"His loyalties are divided. He wants a career with the Indian Office." He squeezed her elbow. "I have faith in you, Sophia."

Foolish girl that she was, she warmed, head to toe. Will needed her. She could be useful, heroic even. Will dashed for the house. Sophia had just enough time to hang up her coat when the door opened. "Gentlemen." She stepped forward, reaching out to the inspector. "And this must be—"

Henry remembered his manners. "Sophia Makinoff, may I present Inspector Edward Kemble."

"Welcome." She gave him her best smile and a stiff-armed handshake. He responded with that predatory gleam common to men from the tsar to the roustabouts on the steamboat. Sophia would have to take care around this one.

"Miss Makinoff. I've heard about you."

She raised a flirtatious eyebrow at James and Henry. "None of it true, I hope."

"Sophia teaches."

"You are all exhausted," she cooed. "Nettie made tea. Please have a seat and tell me all about it."

"I'd prefer whiskey," James said.

"Of course." Sophia reached for his coat, hoping he did not expect this service to become a habit. "But I simply must know what happened. Perhaps tea and—" She inhaled, trying to discern what Nettie had prepared.

"Oatmeal cookies." Nettie bustled into the kitchen. "Yes, have a seat. Sophia's right. Once you men disappear into James's office for a tot, we'll never find out how the meeting went."

"Perhaps you would prefer coffee, Mr. Kemble?" Sophia held out a chair for him, and the buffoon sat in it. "And where are you from, sir?" Sophia was quite able to perform the social niceties. What she wanted to say was, *What rock of ill manners did you crawl out from?*

"Pennsylvania. Pittsburgh area."

"Oh, Henry and Nettie are from Pennsylvania, are you not?" She got Henry settled, but James headed for his office. Sophia linked arms and swung him around like a country dance. "And James is from—"

"Ohio." He finally stopped resisting and collapsed into his chair.

"The next state over. Remarkable."

With Nettie's help, coffee was served and cookies distributed.

Sophia sat opposite the inspector and leaned forward. For the first time ever, she wished missionaries wore dresses with décolletage. She was not in the habit of flaunting her assets, but at the moment any distraction would help. "So, Inspector, was it a terrible trial, this meeting?"

"No smoking the peace pipe." He sprayed crumbs over the table. "Reports sent to Washington"—he glared at James—"indicated this bunch was docile, almost civilized. But they're putting up quite the fuss about moving to Indian Territory."

"After all you have done to them," Sophia murmured.

The sarcasm eluded him entirely. "Yes, Congress allocated— Well, money's hardly a fit topic for a lady's ears."

"What happens next?" Nettie asked.

"I'll powwow with the chiefs again tomorrow, make them see the light. They've got to understand, the Indian Office can't keep subsidizing them. It will be much more efficient to have them down in Indian Territory, under the agent for the Osage."

Subsidizing? Sophia dug her fingers into her palms. "With your powers of persuasion, I am certain acquiescence is within proximity." *As close as the moon.* "Do you speak Ponca, then?"

"No. I brought two interpreters."

Sophia looked out the window. "Are they coming? Perhaps we should have held tea—"

"Lands, no. They're Indians. One of their own took them in."

"Standing Bear," James said, pressing a knuckle to his forehead. "He's part Omaha. The interpreters are kin to him, I believe."

Henry started to push back his chair, but Nettie passed him another cookie. *Hurry, Will!*

"This is a momentous undertaking." Sophia managed to sound breathless. "How might we assist in the effort?"

James gaped at her from under his fist.

Inspector Kemble warmed to his subject. "Assure them the Great White Father has their interest at heart and will take care of them. They must put their utmost confidence in him, trusting him to fulfill his promises."

Just as he has kept his promises and taken care of them for the past twenty years, Sophia thought, with an irritation unbecoming a missionary. Silently she urged Will to hurry. She could not stomach much more of this nonsense, and if he did not finish soon, she would surely say something she would regret.

But . . .

Maybe that was the answer. Perhaps Kemble would be better occupied by battle than banter. After all, Will had not said to keep him happy; he had told her to keep him busy.

"I am a missionary," she said. "I must speak the truth."

Kemble choked on his self-importance. "My dear woman, I most certainly am not asking you to lie."

"Do you count being destitute, starving, and naked as being well cared for?"

Nettie gasped. Henry groaned. American women were rarely this confrontational. Perhaps, as with Esther, God had brought her here for such a time as this.

Kemble blustered and reddened. "The root of the tribes' problems is the Indians' innate laziness. These children of nature like to run around naked. What do you think they wore when Lewis and Clark found them?"

"Lewis and Clark found very few Poncas, as the tribe had been decimated by smallpox. The rest had gone west to hunt buffalos for food and to fashion into warm clothing. Due to the treaties they can no longer hunt, no longer provide their own food or clothing. The Poncas do not choose to starve and freeze to death."

"Another meddlesome troublemaker." He turned on James. "Why do you tolerate such insubordination?"

"The church sent her," James mumbled into his coffee mug.

Kemble redirected his wrath to the reverend. Henry raised his hands and backed away, a gesture Pontius Pilate undoubtedly used at Jesus' trial.

"Sophia's a fine addition to our staff." Nettie took the cookie plate away from Kemble, her own style of confrontation. "She's an experienced teacher. When school's not in session, she visits her students' homes to continue their education. And she's secured donations of fabric from church groups out east to make up for the shoddy stuff you sent us."

The inspector raised his nose, trying for an imperial pose, but coming across as a simpleton. "We stretch the allotment by giving contracts to the lowest bidder."

Nettie slapped a bolt of cloth in front of him. "You'd wear a suit made from *this*?"

Kemble knew better than to touch the fabric. "Well, obviously the Indian does not have the same needs as a white man."

"No, Indians live in houses made of warped, knot-holed boards." Will leaned in the doorway. "So they need warmer clothes than white men."

"Troublemakers." Kemble pushed back from the table. "It's a good thing this Agency is being disbanded. I'm ready for that whiskey, James."

Nettie scowled at Henry's back as he followed the other two into the office, then she offered Will a cookie. "Maybe you should take Sophia to tomorrow's meeting."

"Maybe I will." He winked.

Crash!

In a single motion, Sophia sat up in bed, pulled the pistol from beneath her pillow, and aimed. *"Arrête ou je tire!"* she shouted. No, that was not right. She was not in France.

"Stop or I will shoot!" Correct.

Moonlight off the snow showed a stout man in the hall. The tinware Sophia had stacked against her bedroom door now lay scattered across the floor.

Nettie barreled from her room, rolling pin raised like a broadsword, fearsome in red flannel gown and mobcap. "What in the name of Job are you doing up here, Kemble?"

Sophia raised the pistol to avoid hitting Nettie.

"I was looking for the bathroom."

"You know good and well we don't have indoor plumbing at the Agency." Nettie prodded him down the steps.

Will met him halfway, lantern raised high. He still wore his flannel shirt and wool pants from the previous day. With lowered eyebrows and raised jaw, he looked nothing like the kind man who helped small children learn their numbers. "You have no business setting one foot on these steps, Kemble."

"That crazy Russian pointed a gun at me!"

Sophia stowed her pistol in the pocket of her dressing gown. "It is my policy for dealing with invaders."

Henry stepped into the front room, tying the belt on his robe. "Did I tell you Miss Makinoff shot a wild turkey through the head? Made a fine Thanksgiving dinner."

"You allow an insane woman to go about armed? The Board of Missions will hear about this."

"The commissioner of Indian Affairs and the secretary of interior will hear about you," Sophia countered.

Will steered the inspector back to James's room. "I'm sure your boss will be interested to know what you've been doing tonight."

"Man can't get any sleep in this asylum." Kemble pushed past. "You're all fired!"

"Sweet dreams, Inspector." Nettie winked at Sophia. "Smart bit of work, setting up a trap."

"I recognize a weasel when I see one."

CHAPTER TWENTY-NINE

Saturday morning Sophia slipped into the pew next to Will. "Did you get any sleep last night?"

"Sleep? What's that?" He blinked and scrubbed his face with his palms. Whiskers outlined his jaw, showing he had not wasted any time on himself. "Jab me with an elbow if I start to snore."

Sophia battled an odd impulse to smooth his wayward curls, to pull his head to her shoulder, to take care of him. "I have taken up serving coffee as a hobby. Shall I bring you a mug?"

Her reference to last evening's subterfuge earned a smile. "Thanks for your help last night. But you'd better stay put if you want to keep your seat."

The men of the tribe squeezed into the pews. Sophia greeted Frank and Joseph, who joined the older boys on the floor.

"I know proper protocol to address members of royal families and heads of state," she whispered. "And how to set a table and plan a menu for any number of occasions. I even know how to occupy a certain inspector. But I do not know how to pray about this. What are you asking God for?"

"For His will to be done. For Him to tell me what He wants me to do." Will frowned. "Are you worried about finding another job?"

"God will provide. He always has." God's provision was not merely the right thing for a missionary to say; it had become a certainty in her heart. "And you?"

"My brother needs me back home."

Oh dear. If Will left, how would she manage? And more importantly, what would the tribe do without him? "When—"

The chiefs filed in, dressed in their traditional clothing, including impressive bear-claw necklaces and fur hats similar to those worn by Cossacks. They marched, slow and dignified, up the aisle. The audience silenced as one.

Inspector Kemble attempted to start the meeting, but the chiefs reached the front and turned to address their people.

Standing Bear spoke first. "We talked to each other. We prayed."

White Swan nodded. "We will go to Indian Territory. We will see if it is a place for our people."

❦

"Who is preaching?" Sophia asked as she and Nettie walked up the frost-covered path to the Church of the Merciful Father. Friday, Henry had left with James, the inspector, interpreter Charlie LeClaire, and ten chiefs for Indian Territory.

"I thought you were," Nettie joked.

"Poor Henry would have an attack of apoplexy." Sophia opened the door. "Please believe me, it is not my intention to try his soul or add to the enormous burden he carries."

"I had so hoped you would suit. He does need a strong woman." Nettie plopped onto the pew with a weary sigh.

Will sat next to Sophia. Brown Eagle's family joined them. Rosalie climbed onto Sophia's lap for a hug. Had this little one lost weight? Had not they all?

Brown Eagle stepped up to the pulpit. "Welcome," he said in Ponca, then English. "Let us worship." With Sophia's accompaniment on the gusli, he led the congregation in singing "Blest Be the Tie That Binds," then a song in Ponca.

"Could you interpret for me?" Sophia whispered to Will.

"We know the Lord watches over us, so we will not worry."

Not worry? When they had nothing but problems? When they might be forced from their homeland? All around Sophia, people raised their hands in worship. Their tribulations would shake anyone's faith. In comparison, Sophia's problems were mere inconveniences. She had always had money, food, and a warm place to sleep, none of which the Poncas had. Yet through all their suffering, they still believed in God, still celebrated His love. They had a faith anyone would do well to emulate.

At the end of the song, Brown Eagle faced the congregation again. "Today our thoughts and prayers are with our friends in Indian Territory. If anyone would like to share, please step forward."

After reciting the Twenty-Third Psalm, Midst of Eagles said, "God is always with us. Maybe this land along the Niobrara has become a valley of death. Maybe God leads us to green pastures."

Walk in the Wind prayed for safe travels for the group and clear vision so they would see if the Indian Territory was good land or not.

Yellow Spotted Buffalo spoke. "I hope for a place without disease, without grasshoppers. I hope for a place where my children will grow strong and my crops too. If that place is Indian Territory . . ." Choked with tears, he sat.

Brown Eagle closed with "Rock of Ages," then another Ponca song. Will sang both in a beautiful deep voice.

Sophia and Nettie linked arms on the return walk. "I am impressed. Those men have great spiritual maturity. Henry must have been tutoring them."

"He tried." Nettie shook her head. "But Will succeeded."

"The Bible study in the warehouse?"

"Yes, but it's more than that." Nettie searched the cloud-streaked sky, as if the answer might be written there. "Maybe because he works with them."

"Have not others worked with them?"

"Not really. The agency farmer lost patience when they didn't understand. He'd do the work himself instead of teaching them. And the blacksmith deflowered so many of their daughters, they wouldn't go within fifty feet of him. The rest didn't stay long enough to get to know anyone."

Nettie climbed the porch steps, her grip on the rail showing how tiring this winter had been for her. "I know it's against the rules, but Will learned the Ponca tongue. He learned their ways. He's able to reach them when no one else can."

Sophia considered the officers who served under her father's command—those who were successful, and those who were disasters.

"Yes," she said. "Will leads, but he does not lord it over them."

Thomas Jefferson stood in the sunbeam and held the globe between fingers positioned at the poles. Wearing Sophia's gloves, Rosalie held a snowball to signify the moon. "The moon is always there. Sometimes the earth's shadow covers part of it. Sometimes it covers all. Yes, Luke?"

"Will we have a moon in Indian Territory?"

"Yes. It will look the same. Yes, Martha?"

"And stars? And the sun?"

"Yes, the Indian Territory has the same sky as here. Now, in the Southern Hemisphere—"

Will stepped inside, his face red with cold. The children turned and read his expression: no news. Sophia finished her lesson and ended the school day.

"You're missing a lot of students." Will banked the fire.

She nodded. "Standing Buffalo's, Yellow Horse's, and Spotted Horse's children are ill. Brown Eagle's children are well, but Elisabeth continues to ail."

"One grandfather was French." He helped her don her coat. "It seems to give them a leg up on staying healthy, fighting off illness."

A profound insight from someone unschooled in biology. "If the rest had warm clothes and enough to eat—"

"Speaking of eating, how come you're not?"

Of course Will would notice. "It is Lent. Russians fast from certain foods." In previous years, she had neglected the discipline. But this season her small portion of meat and cheese went to her students. "And you? What did you do today?"

"Went to Hubdon and patched some leaky roofs. Fixed some doors that were sticking. Listened to a lot of coughing."

Sophia locked the school. "Perhaps the Mission Board should have sent a doctor instead of a teacher."

"We had a doctor who taught in '75, but he didn't stay. No one stayed." Will tipped his head and studied her a moment. One corner of his mouth curved up. "Until you."

The smoke from a hundred wood-burning stoves formed a halo over the agency village. Dim lights glowed in the windows as residents tried to stretch their kerosene.

"Remember in the summer we would reach this spot and the dogs would run out to greet us? But now, no dogs. Do they keep them inside for winter?"

Will looked away. He hesitated so long Sophia wondered if he had not heard her. "I told you not to name them."

Had the people been so desperate—? "Oh no. Not my Zlata, her puppies . . ."

Will grabbed her elbow and nodded at a small boat approaching the shore. "There's Kemble, James, Henry, Charlie LeClaire, Lone Chief, and Little Chief. Where's the rest?" Will clasped her hand and they took off at a run.

⚬⚭⚬

For someone wearing a skirt and all that other female gear, Sophia kept up pretty well. They dashed into the kitchen as the men, the white men, stepped through the front door.

"Where are the rest of the chiefs?" Will asked.

James and Henry exchanged a grim look.

Puffed up like a rooster, Kemble doffed his top hat and dropped his gloves inside. "They would not choose, so we left them."

"You *what*?" Nettie raised her carving knife.

Sophia unbuttoned her coat and put her gusli on the shelf. "You left them? Where?"

"In Indian Territory." The inspector arched an eyebrow.

"With what?" Will grabbed the table's edge to keep from throttling him. "Money, a wagon, coats?"

Behind Kemble, the rev raised both hands, fingers extended. Ten? Ten dollars to bring eight men six hundred miles? Not nearly enough to pay for train tickets, or a horse and wagon.

Kemble shook his head. "They were treated with greatest consideration and kindness, but they refused to cooperate."

"And just how do you expect them to get home?" Nettie asked. "It's winter. Are you trying to kill them off?"

If killing off the Poncas wasn't the Indian Office's plan, Will figured it would be the end result.

"In order to bring Indians to see the situation as white men see it, you must discipline them like children and decide what is best for them." Kemble ran his stubby fingers down his wool waistcoat. "I am giving the wanderers a lesson in respect for the government."

"Respect? You know nothing of respect. Nor compassion or Christian charity." Sophia reached into her pocket. "I am the teacher. I give the lessons around here."

Will gestured with a sideways movement of his chin, so James and Henry would move and give Sophia a clear shot.

"Smells good." Kemble lifted his nose. "What's for supper?"

"Far as I'm concerned, you're eating what the chiefs are eating tonight." Nettie pointed her knife at Kemble's heart.

"And you sleep where the chiefs sleep." The warrior princess motioned with her pistol toward the exit.

Kemble swore and tried to hide behind James. "I told you to get rid of the Russian."

"Don't let the door hit you in the backside on your way out." Nettie jabbed the knife in his direction, close enough to worry him about the safety of other parts of his anatomy.

"Wait a minute." Kemble's face turned purple as he looked for allies. "You can't throw me out. There's no hotel within miles."

"If you're lucky, the guy with the boat's still around. He can row you over to Niobrara."

"No. He left."

"Then you have a long walk ahead of you. Although not as long as the chiefs'."

"I'm an inspector from the Indian Office, an official of the United States government. You can't do this! It's dark!"

"And cold." Sophia closed one eye and aimed for his heart. "If you walk quickly, perhaps you will avoid death."

"But none of the Indians will take me in."

"Can you blame them?" Will asked.

"You will learn a lesson: to walk in another's shoes. Although for the lesson to be properly learned, you should remove your shoes and empty your pockets."

"You can't—" he sputtered.

"Aim lower," Will told Sophia. "A slower death will give him time to reflect on his education."

"And to confess his many sins." Nettie grinned.

"I'll report you, all of you." Kemble pointed at James. "You'll never work for the government again!"

"Don't know why he'd want to." The rev sighed. "Don't shoot. He'll haul you into court on murder charges."

"Murder?" Sophia aimed. "I call it justice. What you did to those men is murder!"

James slumped into his chair. "Unfortunately the courts don't recognize Indians as people, so he'll never be convicted. A government inspector, though—"

"Hold your fire, Sophia. Can't see you going to prison for this scum. Get the door, Henry." Will grabbed Kemble by his collar and the seat of his pants and tossed him out. He closed the door and bolted it, then washed his hands.

The man screamed all manner of curses on them.

"Such appalling language," the rev said. "In front of Christian women."

Sophia looked for a piece of paper. "I should write down his speech for my next letter."

"My hat!" Kemble yelled. "My hat and gloves! I paid good money for those."

"Good money? Like the good money he gave our friends for their trip back." She used the barrel of her pistol to tip the hat so she could read the label. "R. H. Macy, New York. Yes, he is generous to a fault when it comes to his own needs." She called through the door, "I shall save it for Standing Bear when he returns. Thank you for your donation."

Kemble cursed and banged on the windows a few more minutes, then stomped over to the blacksmith's.

Nettie served the stew. "Fortunately the blockhead doesn't remember we have a back door."

Will leaned on the table. "What happened down there?"

"Horrible weather." Henry gulped his coffee. "Land's full of rocks. Poncas didn't recognize any of the plants."

"Neither did I." James pinched the bridge of his nose.

"Nothing had been prepared for them." Henry started eating without asking the blessing. "No houses, no church, no school."

"The Quapaw and Kaw live in earth lodges. They're sick and miserable." James took a bite, then pushed his bowl away. "The Osage and Pawnee said don't come."

"The chiefs were unanimous. They're not moving." Henry cleaned his bowl. "Kemble refused to take them to Washington, refused to give them a pass, refused to bring them back here."

"Thank God you brought home Lone Chief and Little Chief, old as they are and about blind," Will said. "But White Swan's got a few years on him. Big Elk has that cough. And Sitting Bear was limping when they left. None of them's in prime shape."

"What's between here and Indian Territory?" Nettie asked.

James scowled. "Wasteland."

The north wind shook the house and Sophia shivered. "Could we telegraph the railroad, ask them to let the chiefs on the train for free? Could we send a wagon for them?"

"Kemble wired Washington. They'll notify the army." James pushed back from the table and staggered into his office.

"So, if they do not die of starvation or exposure, the army will hunt them down like animals." Sophia picked apart her bread. "What can we do?"

"We can pray." Will turned to Henry.

"After this mess I can't imagine God would want to listen to me." The rev dropped his empty bowl into the dishpan, then followed James.

"We can pray and we will pray." Nettie grabbed Sophia's and Will's hands.

Nettie's hand was almost as work-hardened as his, but Sophia's was soft and—

He was supposed to be praying.

"Dear Jesus, we ask You to watch over and bless White Eagle,

Sitting Bear, Standing Bear, Standing Buffalo, Big Elk, Little Picker, Smoke Maker, and White Swan tonight. Like the people of Israel traveling in the wilderness, provide them with food and clothes that don't wear out. And a warm place to sleep. Keep them safe and bring them home. Amen."

Sophia squeezed his hand before she let go. "You memorized the names of those who went."

Nettie gave him a hug. "My guess is you've been praying for them all this time."

"Perfect weather for a Good Friday service," Nettie muttered to Sophia as they stood to sing "Go to Dark Gethsemane." Dark clouds blocked the sun, leaving only the candles on the altar as light. Thunder added its bass note to the wheeze of the melodeon.

Four weeks ago the ice had broken up on the Missouri. Ten days ago long lines of geese and ducks began their journeys up the river. Trees budded. On the south side of the school, shoots of green poked through the matted brown grass. Spring had returned but not the chiefs.

Where were they? What happened? Should they plan funerals? The chiefs had been chosen to represent the entire tribe, so everyone was related to at least one of the men. All mourned their loss. The entire tribe, children included, seemed to be holding its breath.

Henry read the lectionary, the account of the crucifixion.

In other years Sophia had listened and wondered how the ancients could be so cruel. If she had been there, she would not have betrayed Jesus. She would not have fallen asleep like the disciples, or denied Christ and run away like Peter. She would not have allowed anyone to beat and kill her Lord.

But this year she understood. The Indian Office's treatment of the Poncas approached crucifixion-levels of cruelty. And despite all her efforts, the torment continued.

She glanced around at the congregation, nearly every face as tear-streaked as her own.

She had failed them.

She had failed God.

Will's gaze met Sophia's as he let her into Brown Eagle's house. He shook his head. She hugged the older children and kissed Rosalie and baby Michael, asleep on a trundle bed.

Henry, her escort, took up a post by the door, hands clasped and eyes closed. Since returning from Indian Territory, his fire and brimstone had turned to cold ashes.

In the back room, dim light from an oil lamp showed a narrow bed close to the stove and Elisabeth propped on it. The young mother opened her eyes for a moment, moaned, then coughed. Mary wiped blood from her chin. Elisabeth looked just like Julia in her last days.

Brown Eagle got up from his place near the bed and offered the chair to Sophia. "My wife cannot eat or sleep. Would you make music for her?"

"I am honored."

Will helped her out of her coat.

Sophia sat and tuned her gusli. "Do you have a favorite hymn?"

Brown Eagle sent a worried glance at Henry. Go ahead, Will motioned. The rev wasn't giving anyone guff these days. Brown Eagle sang their blessing song. As far as Will knew, Sophia had only heard it once, a couple months ago when his friend had led the Sunday service, but she followed along well. From the bench in the front room, the children joined in. They sang two more in Ponca, and a couple in English. Then Sophia played a song that must have been a lullaby, because Elisabeth finally slept.

"Thank you," Brown Eagle whispered as they left.

The moon had set, leaving Henry's lantern and the agency house's lamp the only light in the village.

Will said, "Seems too cold to be Easter."

"It seems like a Russian Easter. We meet outside church around eleven for the Paschal Vigil. Then at midnight, the priest opens the doors."

"Outside, in the middle of the night? Isn't it cold?"

"Of course. Often it snows, but we dress for it. Then, after church, in the early hours of the morning, we feast on all those foods we could not eat for Lent."

"Long church service. Anyone fall asleep?"

"While standing? No." Finally he got a smile out of her. "The worship is exceptionally beautiful, so much singing, hundreds of candles, such a celebration . . ." The smile faded. "Not like here."

"Not like here. No feasting, no warm clothes, no candles here."

Henry's arms shot out. The lantern made wild shadows. "What am I supposed to say in the sermon tomorrow? After all the Poncas have gone through, and now the chiefs missing, are they supposed to believe God loves them?"

Sophia turned to him. "I suggested to God that the chiefs return on Palm Sunday, a reenactment of the Triumphal Entry. I would think Easter Sunday would work as well."

Sophia gave God suggestions? Will waited, but she didn't smile and make a joke of it. And Henry didn't call her on it.

"Hope," Will said. "Talk about how God is our hope. They can't hope in the Great White Father, or the Indian Office, or their agent." He nodded at the dark bulk of the agency house. James's snores rattled the windows. "But they have hope in God."

Sophia climbed the porch steps. "I have been reading in the Bible about the many people who suffered and prayed, yet did not receive what they wanted."

"The faith chapter in Hebrews."

Henry set the lantern on the table, then yanked off his hat, leaving his hair as wild as a madman's. "If I tell them the disciples hoped for the overthrow of Romans, the Poncas might think of revolting against the US government."

"Tell them what the disciples got was better than anything they hoped for: Jesus, come back to life, bringing eternal life for us." Will helped Sophia out of her coat again, another chance to almost touch her. "They didn't expect it, didn't know to hope for it, even. The Poncas would get that."

Henry's train of thought derailed. "Where's Mother?"

"This cold, damp weather exacerbated her rheumatism. She went to bed early."

"Nettie would want us to pray about your sermon." Will bowed his head before Henry could stop him. "Dear Jesus, please help Henry find not the right words, not the best words, but Your words. And help us all to hope, to hang on to faith, and to listen to You in these hard times. Thank You. Amen."

"Back to it." Henry stomped into his office.

Bowls of eggs filled the table. Will pulled the lantern closer. The designs made them look more like jewelry than anything coming from a chicken. "Fancy. How'd you do this?"

"I drew the pattern in melted wax, then dipped it in dye made from red onion skins and vinegar."

"Ah, that's what I've been smelling." Each had a different design. "How did you learn this?"

"Not the way I should have." Sophia rolled an egg between her palms. "In Russia, on the eve of Easter, women dye the eggs, forty days' worth from the Lenten fast, passing down the family recipes and the techniques. I asked my mother if I could join her, but she said I was too young. The next week, she was gone."

"How old were you?"

"Eight. Old enough for Smolny, the boarding school, fortunately."

"Too young." Will thought of himself at that age, following his ma and pa around, asking a hundred questions a day. Going to school made him antsy, even though he had Harrison and Charlotte, even though he'd only be gone a few hours, even though he could see his house from the window. Boarding school would have killed him off for certain.

Sophia held her pocket watch up to the lamp. "Midnight. Christ is risen." She handed him the egg. Her smile, a genuine smile, had Will wondering if his prayer had been answered already.

"He is risen indeed. Are you going to break your fast too?" Will asked. She hadn't eaten much all month, and nothing today as far as he knew.

Her shrug wasn't her usual exotic dance of shoulders, but more of a surrender to fatigue. "I wish I could make for you the special Easter foods, *kulich*, the bread, and *paskha*, the cheese."

"Would an egg salad sandwich do?" Will went to the pantry for bread.

"Do we have any mustard left?"

He grabbed the jar. "Sure do."

"Then let us celebrate."

"Such intricate designs." Nettie examined each egg as she set it in the basket. "Sophia, you're an artist."

She shook her head. "You have not seen the Ukrainian eggs. They are the true artists."

James's hands shook as he poured a mug of coffee. "No Easter bonnets and parades today, ladies."

Sophia handed him an egg as red as his eyes. "Christ is risen."

"Indeed." He slumped into his chair. "Don't suppose we have any Hostetter's left."

"Hostetter's?" Sophia asked.

"Hostetter's Stomach Bitters," Nettie explained. "They call it medicine, but it's no cure for a hangover—it's hardly better than the cause." Nettie put a plate of toast on the table. "Try to get some food down."

Henry bustled in and embraced his mother. "Happy Easter. Are you feeling better?"

She nodded. "Thanks to a restorative night's sleep and drier weather. And you?"

"I have a sermon." He patted his pocket, grabbed a slice of toast, and dashed out as Will returned from lighting the church's stove.

"Coldest Easter I've ever seen. Doubt we'll get above freezing today." He loaded the wood box, then took his place at the table.

Sophia gazed at him, flushed with the cold, and felt an almost overwhelming desire to warm him, to press her cheek against his, to hold his hardworking hands. A flush of shame washed over her at these uncontrolled thoughts.

"Point Village and Hubdon will probably stay home." Nettie set out sausage and scrambled eggs, sending James running for the latrine. "There will be plenty of decorated eggs for everyone."

As the congregation hurried into the sanctuary, Sophia and Nettie handed out the Easter eggs. "Christ is risen," Sophia said, with a smile and a prayer.

"He is risen indeed," her friends dutifully replied. Only little Rosalie returned her smile.

As rapidly as the eggs disappeared, Sophia suspected it was a first breakfast for many.

Sophia went up the aisle with her basket. "Christ is risen," she said to White Swan's wife, Mary. The woman stared at the floor as she took an egg, removed the shell, and handed it to her youngest. Therese squeezed it and babbled when the yolk popped out.

Sophia knelt beside the pew and helped the little one find her mouth. Prayers without ceasing had gone up for the chiefs' safe return. Where were they?

"Miss Makinoff," Henry whispered loudly enough to be heard at Fort Randall. "We're ready to get started."

She slipped three extras into Mary's pocket and hurried to her spot between Nettie and Will.

Henry made a valiant effort on the melodeon with "Christ the Lord Is Risen Today" and a sermon pieced together from Will's thoughts. The sun shone through the windows Eloise had washed yesterday. Candlelight glowed on the white altar cloth.

But still the morning's service felt less like a celebration than a funeral.

CHAPTER THIRTY

*I*gnore the rushing water.

Easter Monday Sophia tried to focus on her students as wind whistled through cracks in the walls and pushed clouds across the sun, changing the light in the classroom every few minutes.

"Correct, Rosalie. Sentences begin with capital letters and end with—"

Slates clattered to the floor. Benches scraped. The students rushed to the windows. "Horses! Someone is coming!"

Had their prayers been answered? Sophia glanced at her watch. No holding them back. "Class dismissed!"

The students grabbed their coats and burst out. Sophia followed but did not see anyone on the path.

"Is this an April fool's joke?" Sophia asked, then wondered if the Poncas even knew about that European custom.

"They are coming!" Frank grabbed her hand. "Can I ring the bell?"

The rumble of hooves accompanied by the ululation of many voices finally reached Sophia's ears. "Yes, you may ring the bell."

A group of horsemen followed by what seemed to be most of the residents of Hubdon and Point Village rounded the corner. Deep lines of travel-weariness changed into smiles as the children cheered. But wait . . . five, six, seven. "Someone's missing."

Joseph jogged a few paces with White Eagle, then returned. "Standing Bear stayed at Joe's Village, with the Omaha people, to visit his brother. Where they got horses."

Sophia locked the school and joined the parade into the village. "Thank the Lord. They all survived the ordeal."

And ordeal it had been, Will told them at supper. The chiefs had walked home six hundred miles in winter without food, clothing, or money. When their moccasins had disintegrated, they had left a trail of blood in the snow.

"Kemble said they didn't have to move to Indian Territory if they didn't like it." His expression grim, Will leaned forward, making sure he had the attention of everyone at the table. "He . . . *promised*."

Sophia's heart sank. Promises were never kept.

ᢒᢙ

"The inspector's back," Will told the staff at breakfast.

"Why'd you tell her?" James asked. "Now she'll be pointing her pistol everywhere."

"Perhaps I will load it this week." Sophia's smile held a world of secrets.

Henry choked on his coffee. "You scared Kemble off with an unloaded pistol?"

Sophia peeled a hard-boiled egg. "So why is our precious inspector here?"

Which was exactly the question Standing Bear asked later at the council. "Why are you here? We did not invite you. Go away. Do not return unless you have cash. A lot of cash."

His brother Big Snake towered head and shoulders above everyone. "This is our land," he said. "Here we will stay."

"You chiefs have proved yourselves incapable of acting for the people," Kemble said. "So military force is necessary."

White Eagle stood. "You say you are Christian. You say you love God. Yet you will shoot us, shoot our women and children. The Warm Country is full of sickness. It is better to die here, from soldier's bullets, than to die in the Warm Country. Kill us all. We will die for what is right." He headed to the door. The rest of the tribe followed.

"You *agreed* to relinquish this reservation and take homes in Indian Territory, to let the Great Father make provision for you," Kemble shouted. "No food. No more food allotments until you Indians learn to behave! To respect the agent of the US government!" Kemble stormed out, managed to climb on his horse on the third try, and galloped west.

"Hmm. Does he know the town of Niobrara is the other way?" Brown Eagle asked.

Icy fear sawed through Will's gut. "He's heading to Fort Randall."

All night the mourning song echoed through the village. Sophia tossed and turned . . . and prayed. If the Poncas resisted, would the soldiers shoot unarmed civilians? Gentle elders, women carrying babies, her students? Will had told her of other instances where the army had.

In the misty dawn from her bed, she watched Lone Chief reach the top of the bluff. But before he started his prayer, he turned and ran down the hill, moving faster than a white-haired great-grandfather should have to.

Sophia climbed out of bed and lifted the window, leaning out to see what had caused him to cut short his matins. Whatever it was could not be seen from here. She threw on her clothes—ridiculous fashions, requiring all these foolish layers. Men had it so much easier. Finally dressed, she shoved her feet into boots and raced downstairs.

The view from the front window showed a troop riding into the village, led by Edward Kemble. The inspector pointed to Big Snake's house.

"Wake up!" Sophia raced through the house, pounding on doors. "Soldiers!"

"On a Sunday morning? A sacrilege." Henry tied a robe over his nightshirt and went to the window to scowl. "See if they brought food." The agency pantry was nearly empty.

"Put on your collar! We must stop them from shooting the children!"

Where was Will? He would know—

Will dashed into the kitchen from outside and set an empty stew pot on the stove. He still wore his green shirt from yesterday. Where had he been? Had he not slept? "Stay here. I don't want them arresting you too."

Sophia raced past him. "They cannot arrest me. I have done nothing wrong."

"Neither has Big Snake." Will caught up to her. "And don't show your pistol. You're outgunned."

"Why Big Snake?"

"He's Standing Bear's brother. On his way back from the Omaha Agency, Standing Bear telegraphed President Hayes and told his story to the Sioux City *Journal*. I'm guessing Washington is making noise about whether Kemble can get the job done."

"I will not let them shoot my students. Or their families."

Sophia scanned the troop. The highest-ranking officer was Lt. Higgins. Perhaps she might have some influence. She paused to get her hair in order; then, with a deep breath, she marched up to him. "Good morning, Lieutenant. What brings you here so early?"

"Miss Makinoff." His eyes brightened. "Well, if you aren't a pretty sight this morning."

A pretty sight? Perhaps he did not see well enough to aim. "Would you like to come over to the house for breakfast? Miss Nettie is an excellent cook." Now that she had stopped running, the chill of the damp April morning cut through her.

The lieutenant held his rifle at ready. "I'd surely love to, ma'am, but we're a mite busy this morning. In fact, you'd be safer back at the agency house. I'll visit another day."

Four soldiers emerged, dragging Big Snake in chains. His wife and children followed, crying.

"Please, Lieutenant." Sophia stepped in front of him and grabbed his arm. If she could not stop him from firing, perhaps she could keep him from hitting anyone. "There must be a mistake. Big Snake is a kind man with a placid temperament."

"I'm sorrier than I can say. The Poncas never gave us a bit of trouble." The lieutenant lowered his voice. "I'm supposed to leave a few men here to make sure none of 'em starts plowing and planting. Uh-oh. Here comes the skunk."

Kemble emerged from the house and glared at Sophia. "I arrested Big Snake for defying orders, inciting disturbance, and imperiling the peace of the Agency. The US government cannot allow such insubordination. In fact"—he turned to the officer—"this woman threatened me too. With a gun. Arrest her."

"Miss Makinoff threatened you with a gun? Tell me another whopper." The lieutenant started to laugh, but Kemble's red-faced scowl stopped him. "Inspector, my orders didn't say anything about arresting any women."

Will went to talk to the soldiers. Sophia could count on him to fight with her against this injustice . . . as she had never relied on anyone before.

"Arrest him too!" Kemble screamed. "He threw me into the snow."

The lieutenant's mustache twitched. "Don't have orders about him either."

With Will's persuasion, the soldiers allowed Big Snake a trip to the latrine. Then they hauled the tall man into a wagon and rode south.

"Where are they going?" Sophia asked Will.

"To arrest Standing Bear."

❧

Will entered the school, battling the wind for control of the door. He nodded at the empty benches. "Students went home early?"

The wind had whipped his curls into a coronet. Sophia longed to touch them, to draw him close, to run her fingers through his hair . . .

"We sang, read a story, held a spelling bee. But they are all so distraught. And this wind, pounding the building, and the dark clouds. We felt under attack."

He gave a grim nod.

"We prayed about the council. How did it go?"

"Standing Bear and Big Snake are back from Fort Randall." He cleaned out the stove. The temperature climbed to comfortable in the afternoon, but mornings came with a chill. "Solomon Draper, the editor of the Niobrara *Pioneer*, spoke up for the tribe. He's a lawyer. He asked Kemble to show the paperwork saying the tribe had to move, and when the inspector couldn't come up with it, he called him a liar, thief, and scoundrel, and recommended hanging. Kemble called him meddlesome and refused to let him talk anymore."

"Meddlesome? I like Mr. Draper's style of meddling." She drew her shawl about her shoulders. "Why would Mr. Draper advocate for the Poncas?"

"Niobrara shop owners appreciate the tribe's business. And they're afraid if the Poncas go, the Sioux will move in. The tribe sold off the last of their horses to send Draper to Washington to plead their case."

Oh dear. Long Runner had told her the bloodline of their horses ran back to the Spanish conquistadors. But what else did they have to sell?

Will put a hand on her elbow and turned her toward him. His brown eyes searched hers, as if reaching into her depths. "Sophia, what you said yesterday, about not letting your students get shot. You're not . . . you wouldn't . . ."

He shook his head. A lock of hair fell across his cheek.

To keep from smoothing his curls back into place, Sophia busied her hands with closing the school. "I am named after a martyr. When the tsar took my classmate as his mistress, my father spoke up. He lost his title, his lands, his country. God provided for us. So how can I fail to act?"

"But, Sophia . . ."

"Christians must not be afraid when God asks us to do right, to say what is true. Think of John the Baptist."

"Who got his head chopped off." Will shuddered. "We've still got work to do on this side of heaven. If something happens to you, who will tell the Poncas' story? Who will say what happened here?" He reached toward her face. "Sophia, please—"

A line of wagons creaked along the path. Last evening's thunderstorm had left the road a muddy mess. Will and Sophia moved out of the way.

"Where you going?" Will yelled to James, who drove the lead. Lone Chief sat beside him, his face wet with tears.

"The half-breeds have seen the light." James's sarcastic tone indicated the light they had seen was in Kemble's vicious eyes. "They're heading to Indian Territory."

Sophia studied their faces and found only fear, grief, defeat. "It is like watching a runaway train heading for a broken bridge. What can we do?" She pulled out her handkerchief and wiped her eyes.

Will's broad shoulders shook. "Pray," he said in a choked voice.

"Mr. Dunn!" Joseph ran toward them, gasping, his face pale. "Please come," he gasped. "My father needs you."

"What is wrong? What happened?" Sophia asked.

The boy let out a sob. "Elisabeth."

Chapter Thirty-One

A pack of coyotes howled on the bluff, adding their voices to the cries of pain echoing through the village. Sophia hauled herself out of bed and went to the window. A curtain of yellow-green light rippled across the sky. Aurora borealis on—what day was it? The second of May.

Sophia dressed, then tiptoed downstairs, although how anyone could sleep through the Poncas' mourning wails was beyond her comprehension. Outside, the noise filled her ears. She took a few steps, moving far enough from the house to see the full sweep of the lights, then realized she was not alone.

The aurora's light showed a man with hair waving back from his forehead to curl at his nape. His straight nose tipped down a fraction at the end, balanced by the curve of his chin.

Will.

She took a breath. He turned.

"Where's your coat?" Will opened his arms, beckoning her into the shelter of his blanket.

Sophia glanced back at the house.

He invited her again with a tip of his head. "C'mon. Anyone who looks will only see one."

She stepped into the circle, her back against his broad chest, against his heartbeat. His big hands held the corners of the blanket to her shoulders. His wrist brushed her neck with a gentle rasp of hair. The man was as warm as a coal furnace.

Sophia had never let anyone this close before, not to her body. Nor, if she was honest with herself, to her heart.

Pale-green lights fluttered across the sky like a sheer curtain in a gentle breeze.

"What does it mean?" she whispered. "Could it be a sign?"

"Other than electrical particles dancing?" Will's breath warmed her ear.

Electrical particles seemed to dance through her body too. Her thoughts fluttered like the lights. "Do the Poncas . . . have any beliefs about the aurora?"

"Some believe the Milky Way is a holy path. I've never heard the people talk about the northern lights. Maybe . . ."

"Yes?"

"Maybe God's reminding us He's in charge. Reminding us to look for His work, His beauty." He hummed *Cantique de Noel.* This close to her ear, his music covered the sound of lamenting, his breath warmed her neck. She leaned against him, surrendering to the surge of joy that came with his nearness. He smelled like— well, like himself. With a hint of fresh-cut wood.

"Please sing."

"'A thrill of hope, the weary world rejoices, for yonder breaks a new and glorious morn.'"

Sophia listened to the words, and to the timbre of his voice, with a bittersweet mixture of sadness and longing. *Dear Lord, where is the hope? Where is the new morn for the Poncas? How long, oh Lord?*

"'Oh night divine, oh night divine . . .'"

The aurora faded to a mist, then disappeared altogether. Morning, glorious or not, broke over the Ponca Agency.

"Thank you for watching with me." He opened the blanket to let her back into the house. She found herself reluctant to move away from him, to leave the safety and contentment she felt in his arms.

"Will." Sophia took his hand, but then she could not think of the words, in any language, to express her appreciation for him. Not for this morning alone, but for her entire time with the Poncas. Will had made the year not just endurable, but a season of spiritual growth. In everything she had tried to do here, she could count on Will to work with her, to guide and aid her efforts.

Sophia stretched on tiptoes and kissed his cheek. "Thank you."

"What are you doing up here?" Yellow Spotted Buffalo climbed up the ladder and sat next to Will. "Shines White will not need his roof when we are evicted."

"We are keeping an eye on the village."

And trying not to think about Sophia. How she tucked into his arms with a perfect fit. How she smelled like honey and spices from another country. How she had kissed him. If he had turned his head an inch, he could have caught her lips with his.

Will nailed another wood shingle into place. And they were taking a break from building coffins. Burying Brown Eagle's Elisabeth nearly did them all in.

He caught a flicker of movement on the path and heard the clop of a horse's hooves. In seconds Will shinned down the ladder and headed toward the stable.

James dismounted and ran a hand over his face. All done in. He could pass for a man twice his age. "Kemble assumed charge of the wagon train in Columbus. The roads are near impassable. No shelter, inadequate food. Awful."

A rumble of thunder warned of another storm. Will relieved the horse of his saddle. Yellow Spotted Buffalo took the tools back to the warehouse. The men who had been plowing and planting wheat and corn in hope of answered prayers left the fields.

James hefted his knapsack and trudged toward the house. "I need a drink."

"You need Someone stronger than drink."

James turned on him, his face flushed. "You see God helping these people? Ever? Stopping the Brulé, holding back the grasshoppers, bringing rain on a regular basis?" He shook his head. "Me neither. I'm beginning to think He means for the Poncas to die off, like the passenger pigeon and the buffalo. It'd be a better fate for them than that godforsaken Indian Territory."

Will didn't blame James for his cynicism. He had been praying every day, several times a day. Yet Elisabeth and Julia hadn't been healed. The tools he'd requested hadn't come. And the Indian Office still seemed bent on driving the Poncas from their land. He swallowed. "God's going to work it out," he said.

Soon, Lord. Don't hold back Your hand.

They washed and stepped inside.

Nettie narrowed her eyes. Her jaw was clenched so tight, words hissed through her teeth. "Good afternoon, gentlemen."

Before Will could ask what was wrong, thunder crashed and the storm broke. A voice echoed from the front room. "I'm Inspector Howard. Here to solve your Indian problem."

Chapter Thirty-Two

Will augered a hole in the hay wagon's floor, fit a table leg into the space, and swung his mallet to smash the leg down. Spotted Horse had spent hours smoothing this table's surface. He had measured and sawed the legs with precision.

All for nothing. All that hard work, gone to waste. The furniture he'd taught them to build, torn apart to make wagons for their exodus.

Will hefted the hammer in his hand. He'd rather take a swing at those rats from the Indian Office.

The other legs went into their spots, then he nailed the tabletop to the uprights.

Next came Fast Little Runner's table, oiled and ready to assemble. But it would never be finished. Brown Eagle had built well too. It took all the strength Will had to yank it apart.

He worked his way around, disassembling furniture, patching with scraps, until he had a wagon box as ramshackle as everything else the Indian Office had forced on the Poncas.

He took a step toward the toolbox, then let the auger and mallet drop to the dirt floor. There were no more wagon frames, no more lumber. Nothing more he could do.

Will slogged back to the house through the mud from the

rainiest May ever. He toed off his shoes, yanked off his wet clothes, and fell into bed.

Despite his exhaustion he couldn't sleep. Yesterday's council echoed through his head. Inspector Howard had ordered the tribe to bring their possessions to the agency warehouse, then load up for Indian Territory.

It was over. The Poncas would no longer live where the Niobrara met the Missouri.

Hard as the rain drummed, it didn't block out the people's cries. Will pushed out of bed, dressed, and shuffled into the kitchen. He found Sophia trying to coax the fire to life. "Here. I'll get it."

"You cannot sleep either?" She stared out the window. "I see only rain. No miracle. The reservation closes today. All our friends must leave."

"Looks that way." Will shoveled out the cold ashes. The wood box was near to empty. "See if there's an old newspaper in the front room." He went out for an armload of logs. All that was left was pieces of the Christmas tree. He'd have to cut more so Nettie could cook today. Back inside, he found Sophia reading the paper at the table.

She was blinking back tears.

Will knew the Poncas' story wouldn't merit attention from any newspaper. What else could make her so sad? "What's wrong?"

She shook herself and pushed the paper toward him. "Russia invaded Turkey."

Another country, another war. Will scanned the article. "You weren't thinking about going back, were you? Isn't the same guy in charge, the tsar?"

She faced the window, but Will sensed she was seeing a different scene altogether. Her slender fingers scratched a mosquito bite on the back of her hand. "I had thought to return, yes. But it will not be possible."

Nettie appeared in the doorway, fatigue dragging her steps. She paused and stretched her back. "Sorry, children. I'm late getting going."

"No, we're early." Will coaxed the fire back to life.

Nettie patted Sophia's shoulder. "It's a wonder we haven't run out of tears."

"I signed up with the Mission Board to escape the humiliation of being jilted. I thought if they sent me to China, I could make my way back to Russia. I did not pray about it." She let loose with a sob that nearly tore Will's heart in pieces.

Nettie wrapped an arm around her shoulders. "Yet God used you anyway."

"No. I hoped to do a great work for God, like my father. But nothing I have done here helped. I protested too much, wrote too many letters, instead of tending my own garden, ignoring the rushing water." Sophia pounded her fists on the table. "And now the government is moving the Poncas because I told them conditions here were inhumane."

"No. Congress voted for removal before you got here." Will dusted his palms on his pants, then grabbed her cold hands. "You were right to speak up. I should have done the same when I first got here."

He knew it was true, although this was the first time he'd said it out loud. He'd been too late writing the bishop. He should have been writing letters all along.

Nettie's other arm clasped Will's waist. "Children, I don't believe God is causing this disaster of a fiasco. But I do believe He will make it work out. And I also know, no matter what, He expects His people to be about His business. Sophia Makinoff, you have a school to box up. And Willoughby Dunn, you have wagons to rig and a warehouse to organize. And I have empty bellies to fill."

Nettie bustled around, stirring up breakfast, leaving Will holding Sophia's hands for one glorious moment. She didn't have anywhere to go. Would she go with him?

A rain storm veiled the school in a gray curtain. Sophia locked herself inside to pack. She collected the slates, finding the owl design Matthew Adams had carved into the frame of one. Then the McGuffey Readers—how excited the children had been, marveling over each picture. And the globe. Lone Chief had said that God's hands hold up the earth. She collected the coins, remembering Rosalie studying the pictures on them, Susette puzzling over the trickster dime.

She swallowed down her tears and dropped the money into her pocket. It clinked against her pistol.

As she worked, Sophia prayed again for God's intervention. All her efforts were for naught. Only the Lord could remedy the Poncas' situation.

"Miss Makinoff?" Marguerite knocked at the window, then called to someone on the path. "She is here."

Sophia opened the door to Mary, Buffalo Woman, Susette Primeau, and Moon Hawk. The rain had stopped. "Ladies?"

The women filed inside and closed the door.

Marguerite interpreted for her mother. "You have taught our children. You made music for us. You have given us pretty dresses."

Mary held up a buckskin dress covered with the most elaborate quillwork and beadwork Sophia had ever seen.

"We want you to have the dress made by Julia's mother, when she became the wife of Walking Together."

Sophia had difficulty taking in enough air to respond. "Please, I am unworthy to accept such a beautiful gift."

"No one is left in Julia's family. Her last cousin died in Point Village two weeks ago."

"Perhaps Nettie—"

Mary stretched out the waist, showing it was too narrow for the older woman.

"We gave Nettie a bag decorated with quillwork to keep her needles in," Marguerite said.

"You try on," Moon Hawk said.

"But this is part of your heritage, the history of the Ponca people."

Susette said, "You are part of our story too."

The women helped her out of her bodice, skirt, and petticoats. Her corset provoked universal head shaking and frowns. They finally got her down to her chemise, drawers, and stockings. The gown slipped over her head, soft and light. Sophia breathed in a faint odor of leather and smoke.

Moon Hawk undid Sophia's chignon and braided her hair into two plaits running down her back. Buffalo Woman handed her a pair of moccasins and Marguerite tied them, then pushed her drawers up and out of sight. Mary held up a mirror.

"Oh! The dress is so beautiful. I am sure I do not do it justice as Julia did."

"Hey, Sophia, did you pack your—" Will opened the door, then froze in place, his mouth open.

Sophia stepped back into the room's shadow, feeling exposed without the full armor of undergarments. The dress ended at mid-calf, exposing as much leg as her bathing costume. She shivered in the cool damp, but her face heated with a blush. The women giggled. Moon Hawk murmured in Ponca. Will also turned red. He shook his head as the rest chimed in, concurring with Moon Hawk's suggestion.

One more time Sophia drew on Will's expertise. "The ladies

want me to take Julia's dress, but it is so beautiful. Should it not stay with the Poncas?"

"Ordinarily, yes." He swallowed and continued to stare at her. "But they're trying to find safe places for their valuables. I'm keeping a war bonnet, tomahawk, and leggings. So yes, uh, you should hang on to it. Could you . . ." He motioned with his chin for her to step out of the building.

Moon Hawk and Marguerite dragged her into the light.

Will swallowed. "Yes. That is a, uh, great dress. First rate. Uh, best beadwork I've ever seen."

Sophia rubbed her bare arms. If he stared much longer, she would squirm.

"I'll take your box back to the house," he said. "You can come when you've had a chance to . . . ah, change."

With that, he picked up the supplies and left.

Sophia turned to the women. "I am honored that you entrust me with such a treasure. I shall give it my utmost care. And if the time comes when you would like it back, I will return it."

She gave each of them a hug, then hastened away before she began to cry again. And later that night as she packed the dress into her trunk, she realized she was leaving with infinitely more than she had brought.

". . . two corn plows, three axes, one saw, two bedsteads, two ox yokes, one new cooking stove." Will penciled Standing Bear's name on his possessions, then listed them on the lined paper Sophia had given him.

Inspector Howard strode up to the warehouse, pointed at Will's best friend with his index finger, then jerked his thumb over his shoulder. "Brown Eagle. You go back to the Santee Agency. Get on the boat."

"What?" Will blinked. He'd forgotten Brown Eagle was Santee. Their Agency was in good shape. Brown Eagle's family would have a place to live, a school, a church. "He'll need to pack up his family."

"No. They're Poncas. They can't go with him."

"Nothing in the order says to split up families." Will clenched his fists. He'd be all too happy to have a chance to wipe that smug look off the inspector's face. "They have a passel of little ones. His wife just had a baby." Howard didn't need to know the baby was now six months old and his mother had died. Mary had her hands full with six children.

The inspector called to a pair of infantrymen. "Escort this one to the boat."

"I will help your family," Will promised in Ponca. The Santee Agency was only ten miles away. Maybe his family could escape and find their way east.

A white finger jabbed toward Will's face. "And you. No more Indian gibberish."

Sophia ran up, skirts dragging in the mud, tears rolling down her cheeks. "Will—" She started talking in some foreign language, then corrected herself. "The soldiers are herding the children with bayonets!"

Inspector Howard narrowed his eyes. "The Russian! Kemble warned me about her. When the soldiers come back, I'll have them haul her off too. They'll have a good time searching for her pistol." Howard hurried into the warehouse out of the rain.

Will had to hide Sophia. And . . . bayonets? For this, a tribe that had never raised a hand against the United States?

Sophia, ever her father's daughter, calmed herself enough to report what she had seen. "Four detachments of cavalry from Fort Randall and one of infantry from Fort Sully."

Will explained about Brown Eagle.

"His poor wife. I can help too."

He leaned close so the inspector wouldn't hear. "No, you need to help Nettie make food for their journey. I don't know what Russians call it, but my mother called it bannock."

Nettie could keep Sophia out of trouble.

"Of course." Sophia took one step toward the house, then turned back. "I have envelopes with stamps for my students, so they can write. But I do not know where I shall be."

"Use my address and I'll send them on to you. Fifteenth and Jackson, Omaha, Nebraska."

"Bless you." Sophia rose up on tiptoes. Her soft lips brushed his cheek.

By the time Will's world righted itself, she had reached the agency house. He ran past the locked school to Brown Eagle's and found the boys in the yard.

"The soldiers broke the door this morning." Frank showed him. His jaw clenched as he fought to stop crying. "They took everything."

Joseph pounded his leg with a fist. "A soldier picked up Thomas Jefferson's little brother by his hair."

Will dug his fingers into the door frame. The four-year-old hadn't even started school, hadn't yet been subjected to the rev's haircuts. If Will had a gun, he'd . . .

What? Shoot someone? Start a war? Will took a breath and his vision cleared. Brown Eagle's chairs, lamps, bedsteads, washtub, washboard, stove, and table were gone. How were they supposed to cook without utensils or food?

Mary shivered on a blanket in the corner, holding the baby close. Michael, forced into early weaning by his mother's death, gummed a strip of beef jerky. Rosalie and Susette huddled on either side of her, eyes glassy with fever. A half dozen flour sacks contained what was left of their possessions.

"We will need our furniture when we get to Indian Territory." Marguerite wiped her tears on her sleeve. "The soldiers said they would send it. But I do not think they tell the truth."

Frank and Joseph ran inside. "Soldiers!"

A wagon rattled. "Load up!" commanded a sergeant.

"Sergeant, it's raining. And the lady of the house just had a baby."

"I got my orders." The man turned to talk to the driver of a passing wagon.

Will carried Mary and the baby, then helped the rest climb in. Her blanket would be a soggy mess in no time. He pulled off his canvas duster and draped it over them.

Sophia found the table already piled with brown loaves. "I am so sorry. I am too late to help."

Nettie pulled another tray of what looked like oatmeal scones from the oven. "It won't last long for five hundred people. If I had more time, I'd butcher those roosters who wake us up every morning."

A clergyman peeked into the kitchen. "I thought I heard your voice, Miss Nettie."

"Reverend Hinman." Nettie's mouth stretched into a grim smile. She introduced Sophia to the missionary from the Santee Agency. "I wish I could say 'good morning,' but it isn't. I hope you have a miracle for us."

He shook his head. "Since January, Kemble's been telling Washington the Poncas consented to the move. To relent now, he says, would weaken the government's position in dealing with all Indians. Not to mention what it would do to his career. The Commissioner of Indian Affairs plans to move Spotted Tail's and Red Cloud's bands here by summer. The Yankton and Sioux City businessmen are rooting for Sioux, a bigger market for them."

"If they treated the Poncas fairly, all tribes would want to be treated fairly." Sophia started to help Nettie load the food into pillowcases.

"Miss Makinoff, if Henry and I could have a moment of your time?"

Nettie nodded. "Go on, child."

Sophia followed the minister into the office. Henry glanced up from packing his library. He handed her a letter with a weary smile. "I don't know what you've planned next, if you're returning to the College . . ."

"I have worked so hard to prevent this future for my students, I have not spared much thought for my own."

The letter was from the Reverend Doctor Doherty, the rector of a school for young ladies. *I would be pleased to employ a teacher of Miss Makinoff's caliber at Brownell Hall.* Sophia blinked at Henry. He did not like her, yet he had found employment for her. "How kind of you to look out for me."

"You're a good teacher." The compliment slipped through clenched teeth.

"I'm sorry we didn't have an opening at the Santee School," Reverend Hinman said.

"I have school supplies sent by the churches in New York. Could you use them at the Santee Agency?"

"You can't send them with the Poncas?"

Henry scowled. "They have barely enough wagons for the people."

Reverend Hinman shook his head. "Why not send the tribe by boat or railroad?"

Before Henry could respond, Nettie called from the kitchen. "It's time."

Sophia left the Brownell Hall letter in her room, wrote Will's address on her stamped envelopes, then hurried to join the rest. They dressed in their raincoats, grabbed a full pillowcase in each arm, and tromped through the mud. Mist thickened to a downpour. Thunder rumbled. The calendar said May sixteenth, but pounding rain chilled like early March.

A lightweight wagon slogged up behind them. Sophia recognized Pumpkin from her jaunt with Lieutenant Higgins. The other horse, a sorrel mare, appeared equally unenthusiastic about working.

"Dr. Girard, surgeon from Fort Randall," the trim man introduced himself. "You're welcome to ride along. Although I expect this rig was left over from the Civil War."

Henry muttered, "God answered this prayer, but not—"

"We'd love a ride, Doctor." Nettie accepted his hand up onto the seat. The ministers and Sophia climbed in back.

After an hour of bumping across the reservation, they heard the roar of rushing water. The view from the crest of the hill showed the soldiers had herded the people to the shore of the Niobrara. No one spoke. Most were too exhausted to cry. Sophia heard Thomas Jefferson's high-pitched cough, but could not find him in the crowd. As she handed out the food, Will interpreted for Standing Bear and Lt. Higgins.

"The river is fast," the chief noted.

"All the rain we've been getting."

"The bottom is sand. The horses will not be able to pull the wagons."

"Listen, I've crossed the Missouri plenty of times. Guess I can cross this little stream." The lieutenant gave the command to move.

The soldier taking the lead was swept off his horse. Long Runner and Black Elk jumped into the icy water to rescue him.

With a sigh, the lieutenant gave the order to unload the wagons.

Sophia found Brown Eagle's family huddled on the riverbank.

"Please write to me." She handed Marguerite the envelopes. "I will pray for you every day." Would she ever see them again?

"Thank you, Teacher."

Sophia gave a second look at the canvas duster draped over Brown Eagle's family. It was Will's. She found Moon Hawk huddled with White Buffalo Girl in the next wagon and gave her coat away. Nettie glanced over, nodded, then passed hers to Prairie Flower and little Walk in the Wind. The agency kitchen's oilcloths went to Fast Little Runner and his wife, Eloise, White Eagle's wives and children, and the Jefferson children. White Swan wore Henry's rubberized slicker with dignity.

"You women will catch your death," said Lt. Higgins.

"I have a house and dry clothes to change into." Sophia traced his poncho with her gaze. "Perhaps you would care to make a donation?" He shook his head and rode away.

The Ponca men carried the elderly, sick, and young on their shoulders. The soldiers pulled the wagons across with ropes.

"What a mess." Henry shoved his fists into his pockets.

"No crossing of the Red Sea, that's for certain." Reverend Hinman gave his canvas coat to the elderly Walks with Effort, hoisted the man on his shoulders, and joined the swim.

Finally the entire group reached the far side of the river. Canvas tents rose between the wagons.

"How can they start a fire?" Drying out would be an impossibility. Sophia crossed her arms and shivered. The icy sleet cut through her basque, dragged her skirts in the mud, and weighted her hair until it hung down her back in a lump.

"Half those people should be in a hospital," Dr. Girard muttered as he brought the wagon. "Uh-oh. Someone's trying to escape."

It was Will. Sophia hurried to help him.

Will shook his head. "I'm wet."

"Imagine that." She pulled his arm over her shoulders and walked him to the wagon.

"Inspector wouldn't let me stay. Mary and Brown Eagle's children are part of the Bear Clan. They'll watch out for her."

He wiped his eyes. His gaze took in Sophia, Nettie, and Henry, all soaked and coatless. He wiped his palm down his face and swallowed.

"Greater love hath no man. Thank you."

CHAPTER THIRTY-THREE

Will changed into his driest clothes, then hurried to the kitchen. He pulled a chair up to the stove and sat on it backward, resting his head on his arms. Rain pelted the house. No matter how cold he was, the people were colder.

Sophia came in wearing a dry dress. She, too, pulled a chair close. "These long nights, the crying . . . I wanted it to stop. Now it is too quiet."

Until she started talking. Which he'd gotten used to. Gotten to liking it, as a matter of fact.

Sophia let down her hair and fanned it out near the stove. Even wet it shone so pretty. He should talk to her. But in the chaos he hadn't figured out what to say. Still, he'd better grab this chance. He might not have another. "Sophia?"

Her soft blue eyes met his gaze, then looked over his shoulder as Henry staggered in. The rev gave Sophia's hair an appreciative nod, then growled at the empty coffeepot.

"You are welcome to share my tea." She nodded at the canister on the shelf.

"At least it's hot." He grunted and poured a cup. "No fire in my stove."

"We're out of wood."

His fire-and-brimstone glare should have been enough to heat the room. "You haven't had to build anything since Christmas," he said to Will. "What have you been doing with your time?"

Nettie clumped down the stairs, her hair wrapped in a towel. "Now, Henry. Will's been doing the blacksmith's job, getting the wagons ready. And he's been helping everyone pack."

Sophia came to his defense. "And he has stored equipment in the warehouse, keeping inventory."

Inventory. A fancy word for writing a list of what belonged to who. A list that would never be seen again, now that Inspector Howard had taken it.

"We've got enough to keep the kitchen stove going until morning." Nettie fixed herself a cup of tea. "Sophia, thank you for sharing."

Sophia tipped her head toward the back porch. "Did you hear a noise?" On brisk, light steps, she hurried to the door.

"Be careful." Will pushed his weary carcass upright.

She leaned close to the window. Her left hand shielded her eyes. Her right held her pistol at her shoulder, barrel pointing up. "Oh," she said several times, with a mix of surprise and sadness. She pocketed her gun. "I think . . . it is Zlata!"

Will stood by her as she opened the door. The yellow dog trudged in, her head and tail down. Her eyes blinked in the lamplight as she looked around the circle. She settled her gaze on Sophia. Her tail wagged once, just a little, as if asking permission, then she pushed her nose into Sophia's hand.

Without caring that the floor was muddy and the dog muddier, Sophia sat and pulled the dog into her lap. "Zlata. You are so thin. Where have you been? I have missed you so. And you have missed your people."

Will passed Sophia his last clean handkerchief. The dog's tail started up a regular rhythm.

"Thank you. How foolish of me to cry over a dog, when seven

hundred people—" Sophia looked up at him, her face a battle-ground. "Oh, Will. I cannot take her where I am going."

Henry said, "Will can swim her over to the Poncas in the morning."

"Swim that river again?" Nettie asked. "Absolutely not. He's risking pneumonia as it is."

"Then leave the animal here. Indian dogs are fairly resource-ful. She'll be all right."

Nettie looked over Sophia's shoulder. "She seems like a nice dog. We could take her on the boat. See if we can find a farmer who needs her."

Sophia wouldn't go for either of those ideas. Will reached to pet the dog and a long pink tongue licked his hand. "She's friendly, gentle with children. I'd be glad to take her."

"Oh, Will. Could you? Do you live in a place that allows dogs?"

"Sure." It was his house after all.

"Well then, if you're taking her, she'll need a bath." Nettie brought the washtub and a cake of soap in from the porch. "The good Lord's gifted us with plenty of water. May as well make use of it."

"Drown the fleas while you're at it."

Nettie propped her hands on her hips and gave her own ver-sion of a lightning-bolt scowl. "Henry, go to your room."

Will mixed hot water from the stove with cold from the rain barrel, then he lifted the dog in. She shivered and tried to climb out.

"There, there, Zlata. You will be all right." Sophia rolled up her sleeves, showing smooth white arms.

"She'll shake." Will found a worn string around her neck and cut it off. Tomorrow he'd use some old harness and make a collar and leash. "You'll get wet."

"It will not be the first time today." She soaped up a rag, then cooed to her charge, "Zlata, you are going to live with Will. He will take good care of you."

Will wanted to make that same offer to Sophia: *Come with me, let me take care of you.* But Nettie was standing by with a towel.

"Nice markings," the older woman observed. "Red as a fox down her back and buff on her chest."

"I'm not sure my American mouth can reach around her Russian name," Will said. "Would you mind if she went by Goldie?"

The dog's ears pivoted toward him.

"Goldie?" Sophia rinsed her. "You will answer to Goldie? Yes, I think you like your name. Out of the tub, Goldie."

The dog didn't need any coaxing. Will dumped the muddy water into the yard, trying not to look at the empty village beyond.

"Come along." Sophia called her out to the porch. "Now, shake, Goldie, shake. No, do not lift your paw."

"Someone's worked with her. Someone who spoke English."

"Perhaps she has been on a neighboring farm all this time." Sophia's eyes brightened as the idea kindled. "And perhaps her troika, her puppies, also."

"How're you going to get her to shake the water off?"

"Like this!" Sophia twisted and wiggled, flinging her hair around. The dog watched, head tipped, tongue hanging out. "Zlata, Goldie, shake!"

"I thought I wouldn't smile for a long time." Will hung the tub on the wall. "You do that again, I just might have to laugh."

But she didn't have to because the dog caught on, spraying the porch and everything on it, including Sophia.

"Humph." Sophia put her nose in the air, but he could tell she wasn't really angry. "Come inside then, Goldie, and we shall dry our hair by the stove." Sophia took the towel, then paused to wipe Will's face first. "Never mind what Henry thinks. I know how hard you have worked here. Thank you for all you have done. And for taking Zlata. You must rest now, before you fall over."

He took the other end of the towel and caught the drops on Sophia's cheeks and nose. "See you tomorrow?"

And all the rest of our tomorrows? his heart added.

Sophia smiled. "But of course."

Chapter Thirty-Four

Sophia sat on the agency house porch, watching the sun rise over the Missouri River one last time. Her heart ached to leave this beautiful land. She could not imagine the Poncas' grief at being torn from the only place they had ever called home, with its generations of memories.

A damp breeze gusted from the west, and she tightened her wrap. A dozen mosquito bites clamored for her attention, a reminder she had finished Julia's ointment last month. Her stomach growled, but the pickles Nettie had found for breakfast had not appealed any more than the tin of oysters constituting last night's supper. It did not matter how hungry she was, the Poncas were hungrier.

Behind her the village echoed with soldiers' voices and the crash of houses being dismantled. Similar action was under way at the other two villages. From their camp on the opposite bank of the Niobrara, the Poncas would be able to watch the demolition of Point Village.

Dear Lord . . .

Sophia had learned to pray here, but this morning the words could not surmount her heartache.

Will came around the corner, trailed by Goldie and carrying his toolbox. He set it beside the rest of their luggage—Sophia's trunks, Henry's boxes of books, Nettie's kitchen gear. A steamboat would come for them this morning to ferry them to the railhead at Yankton.

The dog spotted her, bounded onto the porch, and put her head in Sophia's lap. "Hello, sweet Goldie." Somehow the wagging tail and bright eyes eased her heart. She found the itchy spot behind the dog's left ear and gave her a good scratching. The dog leaned into her hand with an expression of bliss on her face. "Did you behave for Will last night?"

"Sure did." Will joined Sophia on the bench. He wore his Sunday clothes, black pants, and vest. He had rolled up the sleeves of his white shirt, revealing his well-muscled forearms. "Someone's been keeping her inside."

Sophia reached for his hand, warm and strong, his calluses evidence of the work he had done. "It must be awful to see the houses torn down. Such a waste. Why do they not save them for the Sioux?"

"The Indian Office is afraid our friends will escape the wagon train if they have a place to come back to." He squeezed her hand and swallowed. "I was reading this morning in Philippians about forgetting what's behind and looking ahead. I'll never forget my Ponca friends, but as for ahead . . ." He turned toward her. "Sophia. I've been building houses in Omaha with my brother. The city is growing. Business is good."

Was he proposing? Oh dear. Had she failed to maintain an appropriate distance? She withdrew her hand. "There are so many things you could do, Will. Have you ever considered a line of work other than carpentry? You have a spiritual depth and compassion exceeding that of many ministers. As easily as you learned the Ponca language, perhaps you could be an interpreter. Or a diplomat. The foreign service."

The hope in his eyes collapsed like a razed house. He looked down, rubbed his palms over the shiny knees of his pants, and swallowed. "Uh. No." Goldie wriggled her nose into his palm. "I'd best find a leash."

Will jumped off the porch, the dog at his heels, and loped around the back of the house.

Nettie pushed through the door and let her valise drop with a thud. "Sophia Makinoff. Have you no sense whatsoever?"

"After this week?" She leaned her aching head against the wall. "None at all."

The older woman planted herself in front of Sophia, hands on her hips. "Will was trying to propose to you."

"Out of pity. He does not know I have a teaching position."

Nettie's gray curls trembled with indignation. "He's desperately in love with you. And you reject him because he's less educated than you? Because he hasn't been to college? Because he doesn't meet your high-and-mighty royal standards for husband material?"

Will loved her. But of course. God commanded his people to love one another, and Will obeyed God. "Perhaps—"

"Willoughby Dunn's ability to build a single house here, much less 236 of them, is nothing short of a miracle." Nettie's eyes blazed. She pounded the porch rail, as fierce a fire-and-brimstone preacher as her son.

The rail fractured with a loud crack. "Look what he had to work with: a broken sawmill, third-rate tools, a limited supply of screws and nails and such. You've seen the shoddy stuff sent for clothing; imagine the same as lumber. None of the Ponca men had ever lived in a wood house, much less knew anything about building. Yet he took them in hand and taught them well. Measuring, calculating square feet and roof angles, leveling, repairs, furniture making. You're a good teacher, but I'd say he's better."

"I know." Sophia had been crying so much lately that tears came easily. "But, Nettie, Will is tied to Omaha, by his family and his business. I have never stayed in one place long."

"Will's a fine man, worth hanging up your traveling shoes for. Doesn't your Bible have the book of Ruth? There's a time to pull up stakes and a time to put down roots."

"I know."

"You *know*?" Nettie took hold of Sophia's shoulders with a little shake. "Then what's holding you back? Are you afraid you won't be a 'woman of influence' married to a small town carpenter? Sophia, influence doesn't come from being married to a big, important man, living in a big, important city. It comes from being in God's will, wherever He puts you, and doing whatever He tells you, no matter how big or small."

Sophia could not speak over the lump in her throat.

Nettie sat next to her and pulled her head into a motherly embrace, complete with reassuring shoulder-patting. "You told me Russian fathers have a say in who their children marry. Well, Mr. Makinoff isn't here, but your heavenly Father is. Look at what He's saying to you, the incredible man He's provided for you. Look at how many times this year Will has partnered with you to work for justice and mercy. You're a woman of words and he's a man of action. What better match could you make?"

"I am so skilled at parrying proposals, I do not know how to accept one." Sophia wiped her face with her hands. "I will never find a more dedicated, noble, compassionate—"

Nettie handed her a handkerchief. "Don't forget handsome. The two of you will make beautiful children."

Her heart managed to break and send hot blood to her face at the same time. "But I promised Reverend Hinman I would go to Brownell Hall."

"Sophia." Nettie burst into a big grin. "Oh, dear child. Does God have a surprise for you!"

Will leaned on the support post of the steamboat and trained his spyglass on Yankton. The frontier town had boomed since he passed through on his way upriver in '73. Frame buildings had been replaced by brick. Houses with cupolas, tall windows, and wide porches dotted the hills. Will itched to get back to work. He could build something interesting, something unique, something more than bare-bones shelter.

No more coffins.

He closed his eyes and prayed the Poncas would find better shelter in their new home in Indian Territory.

The boat let loose its deep whistle. Will put his hands over Goldie's triangular ears. Since he traveled with a dog, he'd stayed with the cargo. Although, being a carpenter, not a preacher or teacher or anyone important, he might have had to stay below anyway.

"Ever see so many white people?" Will asked Goldie as the *Katie P* docked. Swarms of folks clogged the shore, most rigged out to prospect in the Black Hills, but a fair share of German and Scandinavian farmers looking to homestead. Even a few women decorated the crowd.

He hadn't seen Sophia since their conversation on the porch when she'd shot him down as surely as she'd shot that Thanksgiving turkey. He offered up a quick prayer for her safety, wherever she ended up.

Will stowed his spyglass in his knapsack, then eyed their luggage. It should all fit in one wagon. The Granvilles would drop him off for the southbound train, then continue on to the Yankton Sioux Agency, their next assignment. Sophia, he assumed, would be catching some eastbound run, to Chicago, then back to New York, or wherever she would go to break hearts and be a woman of influence.

With an excess of yelling, pointing, and looking him bold in the face, the roustabouts got the baggage loaded into a dray.

A sunburnt man stepped between him and the wagon. He waved a dollar in Will's face and pointed at Goldie.

"No. She's not for sale." What did Sophia say? *"Nein. Nyet. Non."* No sense speaking Ponca; those who knew it were gone.

The man flapped two bills then dug out a silver dollar.

"No." Will tightened his grip on the leash. Bad enough he'd lost Sophia. He had no intention of losing Goldie. Finally the man moved out of the way, cursing him in some harsh language.

A stick carved with the word "Yankton," misspelled, blocked his way. "Gentleman, you look famous carrying—oh, it's you!"

"Reynaud." Will took in the man's neat haircut and crisp clothes. "Business is doing well, I see."

"Very well! Want work? You cut wood, me sell, make money!"

"Sorry. I'm off to Omaha."

"Meet you at the depot!" Henry called. Sophia's and Nettie's bonnets showed in the coach's window.

Will lifted Goldie into the back of the wagon, between the trunks, then hopped up beside her. She did a little dance, as if readying to jump off, so he pulled her close. "Ever been in a wagon before? This one seems sturdy enough. Hope the wagons carrying our friends are holding up."

He gave the dog a thorough scratching around her new collar. She leaned into him, then lay down for the ride. "Goldie, you're good company. You never nag me about getting more schooling."

At the depot even more people clogged the platform beside the waiting train. Will sorted the load. Goldie, wary of the noise, wound her leash around his legs.

"Hard-boiled egg? Sandwich?" a round-faced woman with a basket asked. "Cheese, ham, wurst?"

Goldie seemed interested, so Will bought one of each. If only he could buy sandwiches for all their friends. He fired off a quick prayer that they had something to eat today.

Henry towed a baggage man through the crowd and pointed. "Those two big trunks and the toolbox."

"And there's our Goldie," Nettie cooed, earning a good tail-wagging. "How'd she like her first boat ride?"

"Fine." *Wait a minute.* Where was—

"I'm going to miss you." Nettie grabbed Will in a fierce hug. "Please write, let us know how you're getting on."

"I'll miss you too. Thank you for—" Will grabbed Henry's arm and nodded toward the baggage car. "Those trunks are Sophia's."

"Yeah." The hot sun had sweat running into the rev's beard.

"And the toolbox is mine."

"Uh-huh." Henry handed him his pay envelope and ticket, the paper limp in the mugginess.

"You're putting my stuff and Sophia's on the same train." Will stuffed his money in his pocket and unwrapped the leash from his left leg.

"Sophia's already on board."

"But—" He shook the loop off his right ankle.

The baggage man jerked his thumb toward the passenger car. "On with you. Dakota Southern don't put on airs. People bring hens, goats, the whole barnyard. No one will mind a dog."

The train whistled and a conductor yelled. Goldie leaned into his legs.

"Wait a minute. I'm going to Omaha."

The conductor shooed him like a chicken. "Then you'd best get yourself on board."

"This train's for Omaha?"

"Last one until tomorrow." The conductor stepped up into the passenger car.

"Sophia's going to Omaha?" Will's mind couldn't wrap around the idea. Nebraska, after all, wasn't exactly on the way to New York, Paris, or St. Petersburg.

The engine released a cloud of steam. The train inched forward.

Nettie pushed him toward the passenger car. "Will, go! Sophia's going to be teaching at Brownell Hall. She's going to Omaha."

Will grabbed Goldie and ran.

CHAPTER THIRTY-FIVE

As the Dakota Southern departed Yankton, Sophia turned the pages of her prayer book. Nettie had told her the tribe was in God's hands; worrying indicated a lack of faith. But surely she should keep praying. Which would be an appropriate petition for the Poncas' situation? The prayer for those traveling did not quite apply, and neither did the one for those at war. And, please, Lord, not the one for epidemics and death.

Will would know how to pray for the Poncas. Where was he?

She shifted in her seat as much as a lady was permitted and scanned the rows behind her. A soldier and two men in suits leered at her. No Will.

Brownell Hall was in Omaha, Nettie had said. Sophia would have a chance to repair her friendship with Will. And . . . might there be something more?

Across the aisle a rooster confined in a basket voiced his opinion on the journey. If people could bring chickens and goats into the passenger car, surely the conductor would have no objection to a quiet dog like Goldie. But if Will had not been made to ride with the baggage, where was he?

The train rolled south through the wide valley of the Missouri River. On her left, Iowa farmers plowed and planted, bringing nearly every acre under cultivation. To her right, a scattering of

Nebraska homesteaders worked to tame the grasslands. Infinite shades of green painted the landscape.

Will had quoted the Bible passage about forgetting what was behind and looking forward. What might lie ahead? Was Omaha big enough to have a bookstore or library? A daily newspaper? Perhaps even the *New York Times*?

What she really wanted was a good long soak in a hot bath.

And to see Will again.

Her prayer book offered nothing about accepting a proposal or selecting a husband. Sophia had failed to pray about Montgomery and she had been jilted. She had volunteered for missionary work without praying about it, and her lack of prayer may have cost the Poncas their homeland.

And now she had accepted this job as the Lord's provision, without truly consulting Him.

Sophia closed her eyes. *Oh Lord . . .*

How had Will prayed? *Help me say to Will, not the right words or the best words, but Your words.*

"Next stop, Omaha!" called the conductor.

Sophia blinked and shook her head. The rhythmic clatter and sway of the train, and weeks of insufficient sleep, had her dozing off. She awoke to grass-covered hills rippling toward the setting sun. A multistory building with two spires presided over a narrow outpost of civilization. Warehouses and steamboats lined the riverbanks.

With a blast of the steam whistle, the train crossed the bridge and entered a barn-like depot. Sophia gathered her valise and disembarked into a fierce wind. She worked her way through a crowd of well-dressed and well-fed white people, who showed no compunction about pointing or looking her in the face. They yelled in English, German, and several other languages.

At the baggage car she found Will directing the unloading of her trunks into a dray. She had not seen him since they had boarded the steamboat for Yankton. Goldie spotted her, strained at the leash, and gave a quick bark.

Without looking at her, Will said, "This is my brother, Harrison Dunn. Harrison, Miss Sophia Makinoff."

Sophia had expected a sawdust-covered carpenter like Will, but this man wore a tailored suit with a vest. A gold chain held his pocket watch in place, and a thick coating of Macassar oil did the same for his hair.

"A pleasure to make your acquaintance," she said. She offered her hand, and Harrison shook it.

"Will's told us so much about you. We'll give you a ride."

Instead of handing her into the dray, he guided her to an emerald-green extension-top surrey with a matched set of bays, and assisted her into the rear seat. "And this is my dear wife, Matilda."

"Please call me Tilly." A woman with full cheeks, a pointed nose, and green eyes clasped her hands. She wore a dress in a claret damask that reminded Sophia of a couch she had seen in a Paris hotel. The bow and flounce on the back of her skirt compelled her to sit sideways. "We've missed Will so. And of course I was eager to meet you."

Sophia's stomach twisted into a knot. Was his family expecting a big announcement? "I shall be teaching at Brownell Hall."

"Wonderful. We'll see you often." The feathers on Tilly's hat danced with excitement as she laid three publications in Sophia's lap. "The most recent issues."

"Thank you ever so much. It has been impossible to keep up with the news." Sophia looked down: *Godey's*, *Peterson's*, and *Harper's Bazaar*.

But . . . no *New York Times*?

"When's the last time you went shopping?"

Purchasing a pistol from a drummer undoubtedly did not count as shopping in Tilly's world. "A year ago, before I came out west."

"You'll be teaching Omaha's brightest young ladies from the

best families." She cast a worried glance at Sophia's dress, then smiled and clapped her hands. "A wardrobe update is just what you need to boost your spirits. I'll take you shopping tomorrow morning."

"You are too kind, but truly, I do not need anything." How could she shop, how could she enjoy life, knowing her students and their families were being dragged across the continent against their will?

"Don't worry, dear. Brownell teachers may open accounts with any merchant in town."

"We got paid this morning when we came through Yankton." Will stowed his toolbox and bag behind their seat.

"About time," Tilly huffed.

"No place to spend money up there anyway." He shrugged. "Sophia's been wearing the same seven dresses all year. Five dark-blue, one black, one gray."

"I also have a riding habit."

Tilly patted her hand. "You poor dear."

Sophia shook her head. She was not the poor one. Seven dresses made her wealthy beyond measure, beyond what any Ponca woman owned.

Then Will's words penetrated her consciousness. He had noticed her attire?

Well, she had noticed his as well. The same shirts and pants all year. And Nettie's calicos, she recalled, had to have been from the 1860s. Still, compared to what the Poncas endured, her wardrobe was not a hardship.

"Wearing sackcloth and ashes doesn't do the Poncas any good," Will said, as if he had read her mind. He tapped Sophia's worn boot. "You need new shoes. And a raincoat."

"You need a raincoat too." Sophia raised her voice a little. Did Tilly and Harrison know what a gem Will was? "Will gave his raincoat to one of the Ponca families, inspiring the rest of us to donate also. The weather was awful when they left: freezing rain, sleet."

Tilly choked. "You gave your raincoats to Indians? Don't they wear buckskin?"

"They did until the whites scared away all the game." Will lifted Goldie to the floor of the front seat, then climbed on.

Harrison joined him. "They should buy their own."

Will looked away. "If you had seven dollars to support your family for the year, you wouldn't buy yourself a raincoat either."

"Oh, let's not be sad." Tilly fluttered her hands as if the events of the past year could be waved away like a pesky mosquito. "We'll find another raincoat for you, Will. And some clothes that fit. You've lost weight."

"Not enough food to go around."

Will's comment shocked his sister-in-law into silence for a moment. "So tell me about this dog."

"This is Goldie. She's good with children."

Tilly leaned over the seat. Goldie returned her regard with a hopeful wag of her tail. "But we still have Buddy."

"Goldie's mine," Will said, putting his hand on her neck in a possessive way. "I still have a fence, don't I?"

Harrison nodded, then diverted the conversation into topics of business. While the men talked, Sophia had the opportunity to take a look at the town. Streets were laid out in a grid; she would not lose her way as she had in Paris. Few natural trees grew here, but the residents attempted to rectify the situation with plantings.

Omaha appeared to be the embodiment of the battle between good and evil. A church on one corner, a saloon on the next. A row of tidy houses backed up to a gambling parlor. A street-corner preacher faced a streetwalker.

"We've got a fire department and an alarm system using the

telegraph lines." Harrison pointed out the business district and new gasworks. A scattering of gaslights lit up downtown. But his claims of progress were undermined when they had to detour around a block eroded by an overly enthusiastic creek, and again when he abandoned the morass of a road and struck out across a vacant lot. He pointed out a meat packing plant, a hospital, and a grain elevator.

They headed west on muddy streets, up the hill to a three-story building with a mansard roof and dormer windows. It gleamed with fresh paint, tan with dark-brown shutters and trim. A whitewashed fence surrounded the property. A dozen saplings gave evidence of further efforts to transform the prairie. Brownell Hall appeared well built and well maintained.

Sophia prayed her Ponca students might have such an attractive school building in their new home.

On the lawn several young ladies exercised with Indian clubs. *Indian* clubs? The Poncas did not use them.

An older woman with a braided crown of gray hair descended the steps. "Welcome back to Omaha, Mr. Dunn," she called to Will as he helped the driver unload the dray. "Leave those here. We hardly expect you to tote and carry for us. Mr. Sullivan is on his way."

The woman exited the gate and approached the rig as Harrison handed Sophia down. "Mr. and Mrs. Dunn, I see you've brought us a gift."

"Indeed we have. Mrs. Windsor, may I present Miss Sophia Makinoff. Miss Makinoff, this is Mrs. Windsor, the matron, head of house, lady principal . . . any new titles this week?"

"It's a small school." The woman's erect posture and raised chin dared anyone to question her authority. She narrowed her eyes, taking Sophia's measure. "Welcome to Brownell Hall."

Tilly called from the surrey. "I'll be by about ten tomorrow to take Sophia shopping."

"Certainly, Mrs. Dunn."

The matron took orders from Will's sister-in-law?

Mrs. Windsor steered Sophia through the gate. "You must be exhausted, Miss Makinoff. Let's get you settled."

One moment. She had not thanked Harrison for the ride. Nor thanked Will for seeing her luggage safely to Omaha. Nor apologized. A sharp bark echoed from the surrey. And yes, she wanted to ask how Goldie had tolerated the journey.

But Harrison's rig had already rounded the corner. Sophia swallowed back the tears as a flock of girls, Brownell Hall's students, flew down the steps and across the yard toward her.

There was no reason to cry. Absolutely none.

Omaha was a small town. Surely she would see Will again.

Sometime.

Chapter Thirty-Six

Even though Will knew she'd be only a few blocks away, leaving Sophia hurt worse than he expected. He'd kept his distance the whole trip, out of sight, but close enough to keep her safe from Romeos and pickpockets.

And somehow he'd managed to fall in love even more. He liked how her hair twisted up under her hat. Curls worked themselves loose as the day went on, the way thoughts popped loose from her mouth. The inch of skin above her collar that seemed like just the right place to plant a kiss.

He had it bad.

Will braced on the footboard as they rolled downhill from the school. It was all he could do to keep from jumping out and running back to Sophia. Goldie leaned out, as if she might be thinking the same thing.

Will put a restraining hand on her collar, and she rested her nose on Will's knee. Her big brown eyes asked, "Why'd we leave her?" Will ruffled the fur behind her ears. *We'll see her again, don't worry.*

If his heart could take it.

"So?" Harrison raised an eyebrow.

"She's as pretty as you said." Tilly leaned over the seat. "Did you propose yet?"

"No."

Harrison stopped in front of Will's one-and-a-half-story house. The picket fence had been replaced by wrought iron, its curves echoing the scrolls of the spoon carvings on the gables.

"Good-looking fence." Will climbed out and grabbed his knapsack. Goldie nosed around, exploring her new territory.

"We've sold fourteen of them, with orders for another dozen or so." Harrison handed him the key. "May as well leave your toolbox with me. I'll pick you up at seven."

"I stocked your kitchen with bread, coffee, and eggs. Enough for breakfast."

"Thanks." Will helped his sister-in-law to the front seat. "I'll see you at dinner."

Tilly tapped his nose. "What are you waiting for?"

No use pretending. Will sighed and propped his leg on the surrey's step. "Sophia's a woman of the world. A woman of influence."

"How could she be worldly, as little as she thinks of clothes?"

Will shook his head. "She's lived in New York, Paris, St. Petersburg."

"Petersburg, Virginia?" Harrison asked. Their mother was from the Old Dominion.

"Russia."

Tilly fluttered. "We had a Russian visitor a few years ago. You remember."

"Oh yeah. Went buffalo hunting with Custer," Harrison said.

Will nodded. "Grand Duke Alexei. Sophia knows him. Her father taught him to ride." He looked down at his feet. "She doesn't want a carpenter. She wants somebody important. A congressman, a diplomat, a—" He shrugged. "I don't know."

"Well, Omaha is getting bigger, improving," Harrison said.

Will followed Harrison's frown down the muddy track known as Jackson Street. Mrs. Porter's cow had pulled up her picket line and stretched her neck over the fence to chew on Mrs. Crowell's lilac bush. The wind banged the door of the Hendersons' out-house. Sidewalks hadn't made it out this far; pedestrians walked on clumps of prairie grass growing beside the street.

Improving, maybe. But it was a long way from giving New York any competition, and no chance it would ever be Paris.

Tilly squeezed his hand. "Tell you what I'll do. I'll climb to the top of the high school tower and yell, 'Omaha, behave yourself! We've got a visitor!'"

"Appreciate it." Will grinned and waved good-bye. The rig lurched back up the hill.

Will's gate opened without a squeak. He closed it behind him, then let Goldie loose. Rather than race around, enjoying her freedom, she stayed by his heel.

"Glad to see someone wants my company." He gave her a pat, then headed up the brick walk. "I finished this house in '73, before the panic. It's like a peddler's sample case. Little bit of this and that. Harrison keeps it up to show customers what we can do."

The trim had been painted recently, deepened from the original pastels to royal blue and gold, a nice contrast with the sky-blue clapboard. The lawn had been cut. The windows shone and flowers bloomed in a pot by the door. Goldie's toenails clicked on the tile.

"Double entry doors. Helps keep the weather out. Stained glass transom for natural light."

Ah. Furniture polish and floor wax. Will hadn't smelled those in a good long while. Goldie followed her nose into the parlor.

"Walnut and oak floorboards," Will told her. "Dark and light woods make any pattern you want. Don't miss the crown molding, corner protectors, shutters, bookcases built to fit the house." Tilly had picked out new wallpaper in gold with dark-blue stripes, bordered with matching arches.

"Be sure to appreciate the brass hinges." Will opened the doors to the dining room. Replacement wallpaper, also blue with gold, covered the walls and ceiling. Medallions in the corners and around the light fixture repeated the design. He shook his head. "The crew always threatens to quit after a ceiling job."

A vase of white flowers, like daisies with fat petals, stood on the table. "Carrara marble fireplace serves both rooms. Wainscoting, chair rail."

Her nose led her to the kitchen. "Ah, yes, a priority for the lady of the house." It seemed Goldie would be the only female to live here. "The latest setup recommended by Catharine Beecher. Lots of shelves, hooks for utensils, pump and drain so I don't have to carry water."

Big improvement from the agency house. Firewood was neatly laid in the stove. Tomorrow Will would thank Tilly's housekeeper. Was it still Mrs. O'Reilly?

Will found a heavy yellow stoneware bowl, filled it with water, and set it on the floor.

Goldie took a drink, then dashed upstairs.

"Not pausing to appreciate the walnut-and-oak stairway?" The bed had been made with white sheets. A vase with tall stalks of blue flowers decorated the dresser. He dropped his knapsack on the wide floorboards. "We put pine, painted to look like mahogany, in the family areas. Spent the big bucks on the public rooms."

Goldie turned circles on the rag rug beside the bed, then lay down with a satisfied sigh.

"Welcome home," he told her. She grinned in response, her tongue lolling out. Now if only it were this easy to bring Sophia . . .

He had to make himself stop thinking about her. A breeze fluttered the curtain, allowing a glimpse of Brownell Hall on the hill.

Stop thinking about Sophia? Not a chance.

Chapter Thirty-Seven

The clanging of a bell jerked Sophia into wakefulness.

The Brulé!

No, it was morning at Brownell Hall. Sophia rolled out of the feather bed, its carved dark headboard matching the desk and mirrored bureau. She pulled open the heavy drapes. No one would notice her icon against the elaborate red-and-gold fleur-de-lis wallpaper. Brownell might as well be Versailles, as different as it was from the Ponca Agency. The only thing missing was indoor plumbing.

What would Will think of this building? And what were he and Goldie doing this morning?

Mrs. Windsor had given Sophia a room on the northwest corner of the third floor. Window screens protected her from the onslaught of mosquitoes. Her view included the building with the turrets, which Harrison had told her was the high school. Since the town had attempted to locate the state's seat of government here, the area was called "Capitol Hill." It seemed to mark the end of town.

Somewhere off to the west Lone Chief raised his arms to greet the dawn.

On the streets of Omaha, a horse neighed and draymen called to each other in a language she thought might be Czech. Sparrows swirled past the window in search of a tree to call home.

Down the hall, a door banged and small feet pounded.

"Gracie, you ninny," whined a girl. "What did you do with my hairbrush?"

"You're the ninny. You gave it to Maggie."

Another voice, a little older, warned, "If Mrs. Windsor hears you . . ."

The voices moved down the hall before Sophia could learn what consequences the matron might apply for name-calling.

How silly, to be fussing over a hairbrush, when so many were waking up hungry this morning. How could she love students who were so wrapped up in themselves?

Sophia straightened. She was a professional teacher. Love was not necessary to teach them.

The rich aroma of bacon and pancakes wafted up the steps. Sophia finished her morning prayers with a plea for the Poncas, that they might eat today.

She hurried to dress. The clear light of a city morning showed her frayed cuffs. Mysterious stains dotted her skirt. Shopping, she supposed, had become a necessity. And arranging her hair in a more elaborate style. Sophia wove a braid and pinned it to the back of her head, similar to the matron's.

"Good morning, Miss Makinoff," the students chorused as she followed them down the stairs to the dining hall.

"Miss Makinoff!" A tall woman gasped.

"Kitty Lyman!" Sophia embraced her former student. "What are you doing here?"

A sudden silence in the dining hall indicated Sophia had caused a scene. And undoubtedly revealed the young woman's nickname to the entire school.

"Teaching natural science." Miss Lyman grinned and took her arm. "You must be here to finish the term for Mademoiselle Ross. Let me introduce you."

Miss Tarbell, music, presided over a table of the youngest students. Miss Jacobsen, English, stood in line for eggs. Miss Franklin, history, mediated a dispute among the twelve-year-olds. Mrs. Doherty, drawing and painting, finished her breakfast. Reverend Meeks, languages, and Reverend Doherty, the rector, who taught mental and moral science, lingered over coffee. Again, no tea? These Americans!

"Half of the students went home for the weekend," Kitty told her.

Sophia's head spun. How would she remember all these new faces and names?

"So where have you been?" Kitty asked over breakfast.

"In the Dakota Territory, teaching at the Ponca Agency."

"Oh." The young woman did not move for a long moment, as if the information did not fit in her head. Then she blinked, leaned forward, and dropped her voice. "Well then, you haven't heard about Annabelle Montgomery. She's *enceinte*."

Sophia corrected Kitty's pronunciation. For some unknown reason she always spoke French with a Greek accent. "Annabelle will be an excellent mother."

"You're not . . ." Kitty tipped her head. "Upset?"

"Not at all. I shall write to congratulate her."

And to prove it Sophia consumed a hearty breakfast. Truly, her only embarrassment was that anyone might connect her romantically with Montgomery. Having a baby would keep Annabelle home in New York rather than blundering about Washington, a blessing for the capital city.

Sophia listened to news of the College over breakfast, then Kitty gave her a tour of Brownell Hall, the highlight of which was their thousand-volume library. As at the College, the school ran by bells. After classes a study hour was followed by an hour of physical activity, such as tennis, baseball, or dancing. At six tea was served, which Sophia knew meant supper, not the hot beverage made from plant leaves. Recreation, study, and religious exercises filled the evening until lights out at nine.

After the tour, Sophia returned to her room to unpack, then hurried downstairs in time to meet Tilly. They walked two blocks north and caught the Omaha Horse Railway, a yellow carriage pulled on tracks, down to the business district on Farnam Street.

"Let's start with ready-made. If we can't find the right ensemble for you, we have several wonderful dressmakers in town."

Tilly's boots rapped a rhythm on the wooden sidewalks as she towed Sophia past brick buildings two and three stories tall. The north side of the street teemed with workmen removing rubble.

"We had a conflagration last month. Thanks to the skill of our fire department and the divine providence of a torrential downpour, the city was saved."

"Perhaps Will might be working here?"

"Heavens, no. Didn't he tell you? Harrison has several jobs already lined up for him." Tilly gave her a puzzled look, then changed the subject. "This spring's polonaises are longer, showing merely a line of the underskirt."

Sophia would prefer to discuss Will but could not think how to bring the conversation back to him without raising unwarranted speculation. "What fabric is preferred?" She feigned interest in the answer.

"They're made of thin lawn or organdy over black silk or velvet."

"Black for summer?" Already the morning sun heated the May air to a degree uncomfortable for her bombazine dress.

"Yes, and the new bodices have five seams in back instead of three."

Five seams or three, what did it matter? Unless all the out-of-fashion bodices might be sent to the Poncas.

Sophia paused at a window display of children's shoes, enough to outfit the entire tribe. Should she tell Tilly about the miracle of receiving enough shoes to fit all the students in her school? No. Either she would not believe it or she would not think it sufficient to merit the title of miracle.

Sophia blinked back tears. Tilly patted her hand. "I cannot imagine . . ."

No, she could not. No one could. No one would believe what the Poncas had suffered. Sophia blotted her eyes. "Please forgive me."

"You . . . don't like to shop?" Tilly asked with incredulity.

"I have not thought much about clothes this past year."

Not true. Sophia had spent a lot of time worrying about clothing, although not for herself.

She swallowed and mustered a smile at the well-dressed woman in front of her. "This morning, though, as I was introduced to the other teachers, my wardrobe deficiencies became readily apparent. Tilly, I would be ever so grateful if you would help rectify my situation."

Tilly's eyes brightened and her cheeks pinked. She towed Sophia into Welf and McDonald's and sorted through prêt-à-porter dresses with a frightful amount of shirring, ruching, and pleating. She held up a visiting costume of strawberry satin with black velvet bands. "Will's right about sackcloth and ashes. After the somber shades you've been wearing, perhaps something bright? What colors do you wear best?"

What color did Will like best?

The choices were overwhelming. The most restrained choice was a polonaise in golden brown with a dark-brown underskirt, complete with silk cords, tassels, and fringe. Second best was a violet basque and overskirt with a black walking skirt with draping, pleats, and enormous buttons. Both had a pocket for her pistol.

The dressmaker measured her for suits in light blue, spring green, and medium green.

As if her choices were not equipped with sufficient frills, Will's sister-in-law picked out an assortment of jabots as ruffled as those worn in the Elizabethan era, cut steel ornaments in various shapes, and kid gloves in greenish-blue and deep pink with embroidered flowers. New handkerchiefs, stockings, and petticoats joined the pile.

If only she could have outfitted her students in such splendor. The store's dressmaker agreed to make the necessary alterations to the two ensembles and send them to school that afternoon. The rest would be sent during the week.

"You're so fortunate you're slender," Tilly said as they left the store. "The cuirass bodice is perfect for you."

Will's comment about the lack of food had stopped conversation, so Sophia limited herself to a simple, "Thank you."

"Tilly!" A young woman hailed her outside the music store, moving fast enough to launch the bird on her hat into flight. "Did you hear? They were digging for the new school on Eleventh and Dodge and found two Indian skeletons!"

Tilly attempted to make introductions.

"With relics and scalp rings!" The woman's handkerchief fluttered.

"Who were they?" Sophia asked.

"Who?" The florid woman stepped back. "They were *Indians*."

"Louisa, you'll have to excuse us." Tilly linked arms with Sophia and hurried down the street. "And *you* will have to excuse us. Not everyone will understand your work with the Indians."

Not understanding, and apparently not interested in understanding.

Sophia patted her hand. "I do not want to cause problems for you. Your husband has a business here."

"Bosh," Tilly said. "When Louisa wants her house built, she won't care if we're holding powwows and calling ourselves squaws."

Before Sophia could unscramble Tilly's comment, they passed a gun shop. Perhaps she should replenish her supply of bullets? A trio of rough characters emerged, equipped for mining and carrying new Sharps breech-loaders. Tilly tightened her grip, held her breath, and hurried Sophia past. Perhaps another day.

"Will said you're quite the letter writer." Tilly led her into a bookstore. "Do you need more stationery?"

Newspapers covered the counter of R. & J. Wilbur's. "Russo-Turkish War" blazed from one headline. Without reading any further Sophia followed Tilly down the aisle. Even if the war ended tomorrow, Russia no longer called to her. Will lived here, in this rough crossroads. All her curiosity, all her interest, focused on him. Did she have a future with him?

While Tilly cooed over pastel pages with flowers and ribbons, Sophia debated between plain white and ivory. Should she write any more letters about the Poncas? Had her feeble efforts damaged their cause? Will said they had not. She chose ivory.

"Tilly, my word." A stern-looking woman entered as the clerk waited on them. "You're the first person I've recognized today. Have you ever seen the like?" She nodded toward a large company of German farmers in the street, stocking their wagons for homesteading. "The Metropolitan hired a horde of Chinese, and the Grand Central has a pack of Africans. Omaha has hardly any Americans anymore!"

"How wonderful to see our city growing." Tilly completed her purchase.

The woman sniffed. "You would say that, all those houses your husband built for those Italians."

"So much for good behavior," Tilly muttered as they left the store, skirting a drunk man who snored in a doorway. "Don't worry. I'll introduce you to some good people tomorrow at church."

"Tilly, please do not fret. Omaha is no worse than anywhere else."

A loud *thunk* echoed from an alley. Four dogs raced out, carrying large bones. A man in an apron yelled, "Away with you!"

Ah, an opening. "How did Goldie do last night?"

"I don't know. She stayed with Will. Look, shoes!" Tilly scrutinized the stock of W. B. Loring, Henry Dohle, and S. P. Morse's stores, passing over numerous pairs of perfectly acceptable boots, before finding some she would permit Sophia to try on.

Tilly ushered her into a hat shop, confiding, "Mrs. Atkinson just returned from the east." Apparently this journey gave the milliner permission to bedeck bonnets with ribbons, bows shaped like the Maltese cross, and rosettes in impossible colors. Tilly's friend Fannie arrived. The ladies coerced Sophia into selecting two new hats, neither of which had a wide enough brim to be any protection at all from the sun. Sophia consoled herself with the thought that a few snips of her embroidery scissors would bring these confections back to a tasteful amount of adornment.

Back on the sidewalk Tilly grabbed Sophia's elbow and pulled her into a doorway. A strong west wind swirled dust and debris down the street. At the center of the whirlwind, a pair of boys engaged in fisticuffs. Blood sprayed from the melee.

When no one seemed inclined to intervene, Sophia pulled away from Tilly and said in her most authoritative teacher voice, "Boys! For shame!" A loud clap had no impact upon their brawl. "Stop this immediately! Have you no sense of propriety?"

Somehow the pistol came out of her pocket and pointed overhead. Oh dear. Being arrested for the discharge of a firearm would undoubtedly prove detrimental to her teaching career at Brownell Hall.

"No dessert for you!"

Heads turned and jaws dropped along Farnam Street.

"Dessert?" The two, who appeared twenty years older than their behavior led her to expect, stopped pounding each other and stared. "What kind of dessert?"

A man in a blue uniform raced down from the police head-quarters on Sixteenth Street, blowing his whistle. The officer scowled at the pair, then turned to Sophia. "Did you shoot them?"

"No, sir." Sophia returned her pistol to her pocket.

The men helped each other stand. The one with the thick black hair provided a neckerchief for the other's nasal hemorrhage.

"Madam, in the future, please aim and fire." The officer shook his finger at the pair. "These are *newspaper* editors." He stomped back to his station.

The black-haired one whipped out paper and pencil. "Tom Tibbles, the Omaha *Herald*. And this is what's-his-name from one of the other rags in town. I'm sorry about disrupting your shopping trip. Perhaps I might compensate you with a free month subscription?"

The second editor waved from the dust, where he endeavored to stop bleeding. "Don't give it to him. He's always asking pretty girls for their addresses."

"I should think not. I know his wife, Amelia. Good day, Mr. Tibbles." Tilly recovered from her shock and towed Sophia down the street.

"Mrs. Dunn." He tried to tip his hat, then realized he was not wearing one.

Sophia started to apologize for creating a scene, but Tilly ushered her toward New York Dry Goods. "Look! We even have clothing from New York!"

The signboard over the business opposite read Julius Meyer's Indian Wigwam. Two Indian men in citizens' clothes and braids sat outside. What tribe did they belong to? Had they heard from the Poncas?

Tilly steered her into the dry goods emporium. "Sophia, no. They're not anyone you'd know. They've been hanging around for years."

Perhaps she could ask Will to talk to them. By the time they left the store, the Indians were gone. In their place a barker called out, trying to interest passersby in a faro game.

Tilly opened the door of M. Hellman and Company, Merchant Tailors. "Now let's shop for Will."

Sophia summoned a bit more interest. She found a canvas raincoat similar to the one he had given away. "Perhaps—?"

"Heavens, no. He might be mistaken for a carpenter."

"Will is not a carpenter?"

Tilly picked out an expensive rubberized slicker similar to the one Henry had given White Swan. "Will's a house builder."

CHAPTER THIRTY-EIGHT

"Mr. O'Reilly!" Will jumped down from the surrey. "So good to see you."

"And you also, lad." The older man's face had as many wrinkles as Lone Chief's. He seemed to have shrunk a couple inches since Will left. He set his hoe against the carriage house and grabbed the curb chain on Traveler's harness.

Will shook his free hand. "If you're here, then Mrs. O'Reilly's still in the kitchen."

"That she is. And you'd best get in there quick, lest your nephews eat your share."

A white dog with brown ears galloped in from the vacant lot next door. He circled three times, tail wagging and tongue flapping, before he slowed enough for Will to sink his fingers into the curly fur.

"Buddy! You remember me!" In no time, Will had the dog rolling over for a belly rub. "You'll have to come over and meet Goldie. I hope you'll be friends."

Harrison headed inside and Will followed. "Hey, Mrs. O'Reilly!"

"I thought I heard your stomach rumbling." Fingers strong from kneading bread had no trouble pinching his waist. "Belly button's scraping your backbone. I've got the remedy for you."

"Don't fatten him up too quick," Tilly called from the dining room. "I just bought him new clothes."

"Thanks, sis."

"Uncle Will!" The nephews pounded down the back stairs. They'd grown so much, Will wouldn't have recognized them on the street.

Leo's solid-muscle hug almost landed him on the floor. Lafayette hung back until Will grabbed him. "I've missed you two scamps!"

"Hurry, Uncle Will." Lafayette, the spitting image of Harrison, dragged him to the dining room. "I'm starving."

"You don't know what starving is, I'm glad to say." He sent up a quick prayer for those who were all too familiar with starvation.

Two large brown eyes peeked from behind the parlor organ. Will studied the ceiling. The plasterwork was holding up nicely. "I wonder where my niece is. Last time I saw her, she was wearing a diaper and crying all the time."

"I don't wear a diaper." Josie inched out from hiding.

"But she still cries all the time," Leo said.

"I do not."

Will sat in his place between Harrison and Leo. "She couldn't walk, couldn't sit at the table, couldn't feed herself."

"I can now." The little girl scampered to the table, crawled up on her chair, grabbed a pickle, and bit into it. "See?" Her triumphant smile showed the beauty she would be, breaking hearts as easily as Sophia.

"Mom, Josie's eating before grace," Leo yelled.

Lafayette gave him a see-what-I-have-to-put-up-with scowl.

"Inside voices." Tilly set the roasted chicken on the table and sat.

Harrison took his place at the far end of the table. "Lord, bless this food—"

With Mrs. O'Reilly in the kitchen, not much blessing was needed, so Will took the opportunity to remind God he needed help with Sophia.

"—Amen."

"How did the shopping trip go?" he asked.

"I was never so embarrassed." Tilly shuddered and passed the potatoes. "I'm surprised Miss Makinoff didn't demand to be taken to the depot so she could head back to civilization."

"What happened?"

"Nothing we can talk about at the table." She pressed her lips together.

So much for his hope Sophia would find Omaha quaint and charming. How could he keep her here?

"Uncle Will, after dinner can I show you the train I built in the basement?"

"Can we play baseball, Uncle Will? I have a new bat."

"I want to play too."

Will studied the children, sketching out a plan in his head. "After we finish eating"—he glanced at Tilly—"if it's all right with your mother, I want to introduce you to Goldie. Then tomorrow you get to meet Miss Makinoff."

Lafayette stopped chewing, lowered his fork, and raised an all-too-adult eyebrow at his uncle.

"You're courting two girls?"

Sophia opened the door Sunday morning, expecting to see Tilly, but hoping to find Will. Instead she was greeted by the entire Dunn family. She sought Will's gaze, but he was preoccupied with his nephews.

Harrison introduced his children, Lafayette, Napoleon, and Josephine. Fortunately, Will had warned her, so Sophia kept a firm rein on her facial expression and resisted addressing him as *"mon petit caporal."*

"You can call me Leo." Napoleon's eyes were wide with low brows similar to Will's. "Uncle Will says you like to walk, so we're going to walk you to church!"

"So you don't run off with the wild Indians." Josephine, the youngest, had inherited her mother's pointed nose, giving her an elfin look. She had Will's mouth, a straight slash that curved upward at the corners. At only four years of age she stood a head taller than Rosalie.

Lafayette already showed Will's firm jawline. "Omaha doesn't have any wild Indians, Josie."

The boys sported white three-quarter-length pants with matching jackets trimmed with navy braid. Josephine was dressed in pink ruffles.

Leo bounced, then kicked a clod of dirt. "Uncle Will says you have a pistol. Can we shoot it?"

"Not in town, silly." Lafayette swatted his brother, then narrowed his gaze at Sophia. "Uncle Will says you shot a turkey. With a pistol. In the head."

"I did not wish to spoil the meat." Sophia smiled over their heads. Uncle Will had certainly built her quite the reputation. Will doffed his straw hat. He had visited a barber: hair trimmed around the ears, a clean chin, a neat mustache. Dressed in a lightweight buff linen coat, vest, and slacks, he looked city-elegant. She could take him anywhere—New York, St. Petersburg, even Paris—and he would turn heads.

"Come along, children." Tilly herded them ahead of her, then inspected Sophia. She had used her curling iron for the first time in a year to make three long sausage curls. Sophia hoped the pink gloves went with the violet basque. "Pretty."

"Do you know where I might donate my old clothes? They still have some wear in them."

"Will said you'd ask. The church collects them for the Santee Mission." Will's sister-in-law wore a princess dress in deep rose with a train and pleated hem.

"You have a handsome family," Sophia said, including Will in her assessment.

"Thank you." Tilly took her arm. "So, you're a crack shot."

Perhaps not an appropriate entrée into Omaha society. "At only twenty feet, it was difficult to miss."

Josie scooted between her father and uncle, clasping their hands to swing. "Daddy, may I have a pistol?"

"Certainly not."

"But Miss Makinoff has one."

"Had one. When she lived with the wild Indians. I'm sure she doesn't have it anymore, not since she's moved to the city."

Sophia's hand went instinctively to the weight in her pocket. Had she forgotten how to live in a civilized world?

The balmy air felt as perfect as only a day in May could be. Saplings burst into full leaf. Blue and pink flowers waved in the breeze. Robins stood sentry in the grass, keeping watch for incautious worms.

"We should go up Sixteenth to show her the courthouse and city hall," Harrison said as they reached the bottom of the hill where the street ended. "Seventeenth peters out to a track north of Howard."

"Hasn't rained for a couple days." Will turned west. "We'll be all right."

Seventeenth did indeed become a track that passed by a large barn.

"Might there be a livery in town?"

"Yes, but you need not use it," Tilly said. "You're welcome to ride our horses whenever you'd like."

"The bays? Thank you. They have excellent conformation."

They walked north, past new frame homes with fenced yards and a gothic church Tilly informed her belonged to the German Catholics.

Lafayette slowed to join his mother and Sophia. "Uncle Will says you can teach us French. He says we should learn because we have French names."

Apparently Uncle Will's word carried the weight of authority with his nephews. "*Bien sur.* Of course you should learn French. Will is correct—with French names, people will expect you to speak the language. And, *mais oui*, I would be glad to teach you. When does your school session end?"

Leo kicked a horse apple, earning a reprimand from his mother. "I'm tired of school. I don't want to learn French."

"Don't look a gift horse in the mouth." His father tapped the boy on the head, then turned to Sophia, his face red as a strawberry. "Sorry. Didn't mean to say you're a—"

Sophia laughed. "I have often wished I were a horse. I would be the first one to church."

"But they wouldn't let you inside," Leo observed. "Hey, I want to be a horse too."

They turned at the impressive Presbyterian edifice and entered a modest frame building with clear glass windows. Sophia would have mistaken it for a schoolhouse had it not been for the cross on the roof.

"Our previous church burned down a few years ago." Harrison held the door open. "We're saving up to build a masonry cathedral."

"Perhaps Will might assist with its construction?"

Harrison chuckled. "I'm keeping him far too busy."

Inside, Will ended up on one end of the pew surrounded by nephews. Sophia and Josie held down the other end. Harrison and Tilly sat in the middle. The sanctuary filled with parishioners. Such abundance. Everyone dressed, if not in the most recent fashion, in neat and clean attire, complete with footwear. They all looked well fed, too well in certain cases.

The bishop preached on trusting in the Lord instead of leaning on one's own understanding. All her life Sophia had relied on her own efforts instead of depending on God. Until now.

This situation with the Poncas went beyond all understanding, beyond all her efforts. She had no other choice but to trust God.

Had Will, at the other end of the pew, come to the same conclusion?

After the service an elderly lady with a sweet smile and fierce grasp clasped Sophia's hand. "You must be the missionary we've been praying for. I'm Grandma Bean."

"You prayed for me?" Sophia felt a lump rise in her throat. "I am honored and blessed."

Mrs. Bean and Tilly introduced Sophia to an endless stream of women between fourteen and eighty-five, giving her a chance to thank them for their prayers. Then Harrison brought the bishop to her.

Sophia offered her hand. "Dr. Doherty tells me I have you to thank for my new job."

"Glad to help you out," the bishop said. "Anyone Henry complains about is a friend of mine." His eyes sparkled for only a moment. "I've heard bits and pieces about what happened at the Ponca Agency. Perhaps you could tell me the full story."

"I would be delighted, but Mr. Dunn's brother could provide you with a more comprehensive accounting. He worked at the Agency for nearly four years."

"Why don't you and Mrs. Clarkson join us for dinner?" Harrison asked the bishop, then leaned in to whisper, "We'd like to hear what Will's been doing too."

The bishop gathered his wife and the group marched south.

Their destination was a two-story house with a wide porch across the rabbit field from Brownell Hall. Sophia stood in the entry and gaped at the elegant stairway, the fine woodwork, and Eastlake furnishings as the lady of the house bustled about, preparing for dinner.

"Tilly, forgive me. How may I help?"

"You could set another place on each side of the table." She directed Sophia to the well-stocked sideboard. "And, Lafayette, bring two more chairs from the parlor."

In deference to the heat, the men removed their sack coats. After dinner, consuming enough food to supply the entire tribe, the children raced out to play. A white dog accompanied them, but Goldie did not make an appearance.

The bishop leaned on the table, his thumb and index finger smoothing his thick beard. "On every visit I've made to the Niobrara district, I've wondered why the Santees thrive and the Poncas wither."

"Exactly Sophia's question when she arrived." Will gave her a brief nod without looking at her. Then he told the Poncas' story in simple but effective words, letting the listener draw his or her own conclusion.

So eloquent. What a noble profile. And those hands—

"Sophia?"

She blinked at Will. "Pardon me?"

"I asked if you'd tell the bishop about the school."

"Yes, of course." She faced the man whose visage had turned grimmer with every word of Will's. She started with the 1858 treaty's unfulfilled stipulation of a manual labor school to train their youth in letters, agriculture, mechanical arts, and housewifery, through years of more broken promises, concluding with her feeble efforts.

The bishop rested his chin on his fist. "Will they continue their education in Indian Territory?"

Will shook his head. "There wasn't a school when the chiefs checked it out in January."

The bishop bowed his head and led them in prayer for their friends, then consulted his pocket watch. "Mrs. Clarkson and I will walk you back to school, Miss Makinoff."

Visions of a long tête-à-tête with Will melted like snowflakes in the May heat. "Thank you, but I should stay and help Mrs. Dunn with the dishes."

"Heavens, no. Lafayette did them already," Tilly said.

"I hate to make you go out of your way." She sent a desperate glance in Will's direction, hoping he would make the offer. Did he live here or somewhere close?

"Our house is right next door to Brownell Hall." The bishop's wife linked arms with Sophia. "It's no trouble at all."

CHAPTER THIRTY-NINE

S o, what do you think?" Harrison opened the front door and raised his arms, indicating the unfinished staircase in the reception hall.

"It'll be an adventure getting to the bedrooms," Will teased, then stepped out of range of Harrison's swat. "What are you thinking for banisters and newel post?"

"I'm thinking, 'Thank God Will's home!' The owner's a lawyer for the Union Pacific. He came out here in '54, lived in a soddy down on Tenth and Farnam, then took rooms in Herndon House. He and his wife would be ever so grateful if we can make them a showplace, as in 'spare no expense' and 'we've been waiting a long time for this' grateful. She wants a dark stain, walnut or mahogany to match her piano."

"Which is it: walnut or mahogany?"

Harrison shrugged. He couldn't tell the difference. "She wants a lighted finial and their coat of arms carved into the newel post."

"I'll need a good-sized chunk of pear wood." Will squinted, imagining banisters matched to the columns outside, crown molding, inlaid ceilings, hardwood floors laid on a diagonal, stained glass for the window by the stairs. Best head over to the hotel, take a look at the piano.

The parlor was built with tall ceilings and grand proportions. Mrs. Spare-No-Expense planned on some parties.

Harrison rapped on the window frame. "Storm windows for winter, screens for summer. Opens both top and bottom for improved air circulation. Counter-balance system with iron weights and pulleys holds them in place. Never need to prop them open with sticks."

As Sophia had to do at school.

Will raised the window with one finger and it stayed open. "Much safer." He pointed to the capped pipes extending from the ceiling and several head-high places around the wall. "Gaslights?"

"All the latest." Harrison tapped the grating with his foot. "Coal furnace. Let me show you—" He led Will through the dining room, large enough to seat twenty, and the butler's pantry with its floor-to-ceiling cabinetry, to the kitchen. "Ample windows for light and ventilation. Six-burner cookstove uses wood or coal, has a large water reservoir. Closet for the flour barrel. Pantry. Moulding board for bread. Separate cutting boards for meat and vegetables. Sink. Largest icebox in town. And out back—"

The carriage house had been built first to use as an on-site shop. A shiny new circular saw sat in the middle of the floor. Will opened a toolbox and found gimlets, saws, chisels, block planes, and hammers, each sharp and fitted to its handle without a wobble. Another box held squares, scribes, compasses, yardsticks, folding rulers, levels, all first quality. The next held nails and screws, assorted sizes.

The trim pieces stacked in the corner had been planed true and smoothed to velvet. Not a splinter or knot on any of them. Nothing like the junk he'd been forced to use the past four years. If he'd had all this at the Agency, he could have really built some decent houses.

Good enough to impress Sophia.

Will followed Harrison out. Impress Sophia? Since when had that been his goal? He didn't need to impress Sophia.

But . . . he just might.

Harrison waved his meaty hand in front of Will's face. "Hey, you with me?"

Will grinned. "How soon does Mrs. Spare-No-Expense want to move in?"

☙❧

Sophia awoke before the first bell, dressed, then opened the drapes. Last night's heavy rain had ended, and the morning's sun drew a mist from the ground. A yellow dog bounded across the rabbit field, her ears pointing upward and her tail waving in a joyous curve over her back. *Goldie? Goldie!*

Sophia hurried down three flights of stairs, out the west door, and ran across the yard. A pair of doves startled from the fence with flapping wings and shrill cries. Sophia leaned on a post to catch her breath and scanned the field. No Goldie. After a moment she turned and went inside.

Mrs. Windsor met her at the door. "Miss Makinoff, is everything quite all right?"

Fortunately she had not followed her impulse to yell or climb the fence. "Yes, Matron. I thought I saw—" A dog? How very foolish. Omaha overflowed with canines. "Ah, someone I knew."

"I see." The older woman scanned the empty field, then gave a pointed look to Sophia's dew-drenched hem and her mud-splattered boots.

"If you will please excuse me."

The woman hesitated, undoubtedly pondering the need for a lecture on ladylike behavior. "Of course."

❧

Will heard a thump on the back porch, opened his door, and found Goldie. Her tongue hung out and she panted like she'd run a mile. Mud and seeds caked her paws and belly. "Where have you been? If you were hoping Sophia would give you another bath, you're out of luck."

Her tail wagged and she seemed to grin. He leaned over the rail, eyeballing his lot. The gate was latched and the fence upright. "Did you jump over, crawl under, or wriggle through?"

She looked away.

"Not saying, eh? And not going back inside with those paws." He moved her water bowl outside. "You'll have to stay here. I'll be home after work." The young trees didn't give her much shade, but she could crawl under the porch to stay cool.

He left through the front gate, giving it a good rattle to make sure it latched, then headed up the street toward the Poppletons'. As he turned the corner, he glanced back. Goldie nosed the latch, went through the gate, then pushed it closed. She glanced up, realized he watched, and lowered her head and tail. *Caught.*

"Come along, then." Will patted his leg. Any dog clever enough to open a gate could keep herself out of trouble at a construction site. Goldie galloped to him.

"Just wait until Sophia hears about you." She grinned, and he grinned back.

Will arrived at the work site first and unlocked the carriage house. He sorted through the wood—walnut, not mahogany—measured, and calculated out the angles. Easier to do in the quiet.

Goldie barked a warning and Will stowed his pencil behind his ear. "No one's sneaking up on me with you around."

She wagged her tail in agreement and followed him around front.

"My crew. The tall guy's Kjell, short one's Preben. From Sweden and Denmark." Both had gained weight since Will had left. Or maybe Will's eye had gotten used to thinner people. Which reminded him to say another prayer for his friends.

"Welcome back, boss." Kjell pumped his hand, then nodded at the house awaiting their attention. "Just in time."

Preben bent to pet Goldie. "I see you brought a girl home with you. A fine girl."

Will grinned. If Preben thought Goldie was so fine, he ought to see Sophia. "And we've got a fine job here. Let me show you what I'm thinking." They toured the house, discussing plans for the woodwork, making a list for the lumberyard.

Outside, Goldie growled, then barked furiously. Will jumped down the steps and ran out the back. The dog stood at the carriage house door, her hair on end, ears forward, teeth bared, making him wonder if she had a wolf in her family tree. Inside, backed into a dark corner, shivered a kid.

"What are you doing?" Will asked.

"*Nichts.*" His voice squeaked.

"German." Preben spit on the ground. "He said 'nothing,' but I think he is stealing."

Will figured as much. "C'mon out here." He pulled Goldie out of the way, then motioned for the boy. The kid looked even younger in the sunlight. His clothes were too small and his blond hair looked to have been hacked by a dull knife. Toothpick thin. If he'd been dark instead of fair, he could have been a Ponca.

"*Nichts.*" The kid held his arms open.

Kjell untied the rope from a bundle of lumber. "I'll march him down to the police."

"No *polizei.*" The boy sniffled.

Kjell could be gone half the day if he took the kid to the police.

Will asked, "Do you want to work?" With Preben's reluctant

help, Will negotiated terms. The boy, first name Armin, last name Not Saying, agreed to clean up the lot.

Will gave him work gloves and buckets and wished he had shoes for him. "This." Will picked up a bent nail from the grass and put it in one bucket. "Here. And this." He found a four-inch splinter and pointed to the leeward side of the house, where they could safely burn trash at the end of the day. "Work done—" Will pulled three quarters from his pocket.

The boy nodded and licked his lips. Will figured he'd end up throwing a sandwich into the deal too.

With identical skeptical expressions, Goldie, Preben, and Kjell watched Armin work.

"Has to be done, and I don't want either of you wasting your time. With Goldie here, I'd rather it be cleaned up sooner than later."

The dog settled onto the back porch with a sigh. The men followed Will into the carriage house. Soon their worries about Armin were shelved as they focused on cutting out the trim.

Kjell laid out the pieces on the workbench, then flipped them over and tried again. "Boss, this doesn't go together."

Will consulted his sketched plan, then moved the segments around, forming the archway. "Short, short, long, short, short."

"Ah, now I see."

And maybe that was his whole problem with Sophia—she couldn't see how they went together. So that's what he'd pray about, that God would show her.

"Bonjour, mademoiselles. Je suis Mademoiselle Makinoff, votre nouveau professeur de français," Sophia said to the girls arriving in her classroom. "Please introduce yourself." She nodded at a student in the first row to begin.

The girl's blond hair turned neatly in sausage curls. Her plaid dress and high-top boots showed no sign of wear. And her plump cheeks showed she ate well. *Ignore the rushing water*, Sophia reminded herself. These students needed her full attention.

"My name is Henrietta, but Mademoiselle Ross gave us French names at the beginning of the term. I am called Henriette."

"Of course. Henriette." She would have to tell Will that Ponca students were not the only ones who had their names changed. "So tell me, Henriette, why are you learning French?"

"Because my mother said so."

Sophia smiled. "And we must obey our mothers." Henriette's answer was echoed by the next three students until Grace.

"Graziella?"

Long lashes fluttered over dark eyes. "French is the language of romance," the girl said with a mock swoon, setting off a fit of giggles throughout the room.

"The word *romance* has more than one meaning in regard to French." Sophia handed the chalk to the next girl, who introduced herself as Lettie, now Laetitia. "Please write the word *Romance* with a capital *R*."

Was little Rosalie remembering her capital letters?

When Laetitia lifted her arm to write on the chalkboard, her skirt rose to expose her petticoats. An all-female classroom generated a considerable amount of giggling.

"Thank you," Sophia told the student, then addressed the class. "The Bible tells us to be kind to one another. We will not make fun of or embarrass each other." She crossed her arms. "Besides, what you saw is a blessing. Do you realize how fortunate you are? You are eating well enough to grow out of your clothes. And you have clothes to grow out of. My last class had neither blessing."

The girls blinked at her. Florence, called Florentine, raised her hand. "Who did you teach before?"

"The Ponca Indian tribe."

Several girls gasped. "Wild Indians?"

She thought of the gentle people herded into wagons. "No, they were not wild. They have families like you. They had farms and houses. Many are Christian." She must steer the lesson back to French. "When I first arrived at the Agency, I did not know Ponca, their language. And they knew little English. So which language did we converse in?"

Florentine asked, "French?"

"*Trés bien!* How did the Ponca tribe learn French?" Sophia was met with blank looks. "This is not a test. It is acceptable to guess. Did they vacation in Paris?"

Could there be a bigger contrast in material riches? Although the Poncas' emphasis on good manners and their quiet ways were quite Parisian.

"Are they close to Canada?" asked Margaret, now Margaux.

"It is a good thought." Sophia pulled down the US map, another blessing. "Here is Canada. Until last week, the Poncas lived here, on the Missouri River, on Nebraska's northern border."

Henriette's hand shot up. "Fur traders!"

"*Mais, oui.* The French sent fur traders throughout this area. And who else? Someone who told them about Jesus . . ."

"A missionary?"

"*Oui.*" French Jesuits, to be precise, but best not wade too deep into theological morass on her first day. "And before the US government purchased this area, it belonged to—"

More hands shot up. "France!"

"The Louisiana Purchase!"

"*Trés bien!*" A glance at the clock—each classroom had its own!—showed her the bell was about to ring. Sophia gave a brief explanation of Romance languages. "Tomorrow you will greet me and each other in French. And we will assess your skill levels and determine where to go from here. *Au revoir.*"

As the class filed out, Sophia compiled a mental list of everything she had to tell Will.

What was she doing? This was giggling schoolgirl behavior at its worst. Had she, at this grand age of twenty-nine years, fallen in love?

Surely not. They had simply been through a trial together, and she wanted to share her reflections with him and hear the thoughts from his deep well of spiritual wisdom. As she would with any other member of the agency staff.

Well, not Henry. Definitely not James.

Perhaps with Nettie.

No. She must be honest. She desperately missed Will. But did he miss her as well? Doubtful, after their last conversation.

Sophia bowed her head and asked God to give her the opportunity to repair her friendship with Will. And to show her if, as Nettie thought, they might be more than friends in the future.

A round face circled by ringlets peered in the doorway. Wide blue eyes studied her without blinking. "Is it true? You lived with Indians?"

Time, once again, to ignore the rushing water.

CHAPTER FORTY

Sophia's slippers made no sound on the heavily carpeted hallway. The supporting floor did not issue even the slightest creak. Which is why, even with her mind focused on Will, she easily heard the sound of a child crying.

Moonlight through the windows showed the girl in the fourth bed shaking. "Laetitia?"

"Mademoiselle. I'm so sorry to wake you," the girl whispered. She blinked back the tears. In the moon's dim light, this girl bore a striking resemblance to little Rosalie.

"You did not wake me." Sophia sat on the wool rug near the head of the bed, so they could whisper without disturbing the others. She blotted Laetitia's tears with the corner of the sheet. "Are you still upset about the girls' teasing?"

She bit her lip and nodded. "I know you said to be thankful we're growing, but I don't have any larger clothes."

"Perhaps your—" Sophia stopped. Did the child have a mother? "Perhaps this summer, when you return home . . ."

The tears, rather than subsiding, intensified. "Our house burned down. We lost . . . ev-ev-everything."

Sophia stroked the child's head. "I am so sorry."

"It's foolish of me." Laetitia gulped. "I'm far too old to play with dolls and she was packed away and . . ." The deluge resumed.

"And it was a comfort knowing your doll was home, while you are here. I understand. What did you name her?"

Laetitia's blush could be seen even in the dim light. "Oh, mademoiselle. My silly brother named her, because he liked to pull off her head—"

"Marie-Antoinette?"

The girl nodded.

"Was she beautiful?"

"No. I played with her too much. Her stuffing was coming out of her body in lumps like warts. And I'd cut off her hair when I was little, so she was bald in spots. Mother tried to glue it back on, but it came out uneven."

"And you kissed her so much her cheeks turned brown."

"How did you know? Were you a little girl once? I mean—"

"Well, I was never a little boy. Yes, I had a doll. Her name was Roza, not quite so important a name as yours."

Laetitia looked over her shoulder, toward Sophia's room. "Do you have her still? Can I see her?"

Sophia shook her head. "We had to leave Russia quickly, so Roza was left behind." Even now, thirteen years later, the smells returned to her. The bite of vodka when her father whispered the one word that would compel movement from a vain sixteen-year-old: Siberia. The musty peasant cloak used as her disguise. The choking reek of the fishing boat that had spirited them away from St. Petersburg, past Kronstadt's Forts, to the uncertainty of freedom. And overriding all, in her father's sweat, a smell she would later realize was fear.

"Did you go back for her?" Laetitia whispered.

"No, I am sorry to say, we could not."

"Did you cry?"

"Certainly. Great rivers of tears. My father read to me the story of Job in the Bible. Are you familiar with it? Job lost everything, but all was restored, given back to him. But I thought Job probably missed his first family even when he got a new one. And of course I only wanted Roza."

"What do you think happened to her?"

"Ah, Miss Laetitia. A wonderful question. My father said a new family would move into our house. And their daughter would love Roza."

Laetitia greeted that idea with as much suspicion as the young Sophia had. "Do you think so?"

"No. No one could love Roza like I did. Besides, she looked so dreadful, with her stuffing lumpy like tumors, her hair chopped to bald, her cheeks brown. Who but me would want her?"

"Just like Marie-Antoinette."

"Exactly." Sophia stroked Laetitia's hair. Her mother must be so proud to have such a daughter. "Close your eyes and I will tell you what I think. Perhaps, when we get to heaven, we will find Marie-Antoinette and Roza."

The big eyes popped open again. "Maybe they're already in heaven. Maybe they're playing together. And they have perfect skin again. And perfect hair."

"After all, it is heaven." Sophia raised her hands. "Close your eyes again, sweet Laetitia, and dream of Marie-Antoinette."

"And Roza." Her eyes finally closed. "Did you ever get another doll?"

"No. I received something much better," Sophia said slowly, pacing her words to the child's breathing. "I learned that no matter what happens—losing my doll, leaving friends, moving far away—God is always with me. As He is with you."

As He is with the Poncas . . .

"As close as a prayer." She paused and listened to Laetitia's breathing. "And we know we can trust Him with our future."

Whether or not that future included Will . . .

Laetitia slept.

Sophia returned to her bed, praying she did not dream of little girls without dolls, without shoes, without a home.

She read her evening prayers, then closed her prayer book and poured out her worries for the Poncas. *And as far as what happens with Will . . .* She took a deep breath. *Please let my heart and mind be Yours.*

Perhaps if she needed another bookcase in her classroom—

No, the school was more than adequately equipped, and classroom furniture at Brownell Hall was not Will's responsibility. If Sophia asked him to walk with her after Sunday dinner, Tilly and Harrison's children would insist on accompanying them. If . . .

The congregation rose for the final hymn. Had she missed the entire sermon?

Tilly's friend, the one she had introduced in the milliner's, greeted her. "I'm curious about your time with the Indians," the woman said. "Did you live in a tepee?"

Sophia forced her attention back to the woman. Rather than blame others for their ignorance, she needed to take the opportunity to educate. Certainly this time last year she had no concept of the Ponca Agency.

"No, we lived in a house. As did the Indians. They were taught carpentry by Will."

Sophia nodded toward the man who, as her students would say, looked trig in a well-tailored tan suit and patterned necktie. The man on her mind from the time she awoke to the moment she closed her eyes at night. The man she dreamed about too. He guided his nephews toward the door.

While Sophia had been lost in her reverie, Tilly's friend had departed. Sophia watched the back of Will's head and waited for an opportunity to speak to him. Any opportunity. "Mademoiselle! Mademoiselle!" One of her students, what was her name? May. Manon. She towed an older man toward Sophia. Despite his slender frame he carried himself with a presence of power. The crowd parted.

"*Bonjour*, Manon."

"*Bonjour. Je me presente mon papa*, Judge Dundy. Father, Mademoiselle Makinoff."

Sophia extended her hand. "I am honored."

"You're the talk of the town. May told me you've been working up on the Niobrara, with the Indians."

"Yes, that is true."

"I'd like to hear more about it. Could you come to dinner today?"

Oh, these Americans with their spontaneity. In Europe such a request would require a week's exchange of carefully penned correspondence. *Alors*, if informality was the rule of the day, Sophia would break every rule in Europe's etiquette book in her quest.

She smiled and fluttered her lashes in her most charming way. "I would love to. But, Judge Dundy, if you are truly interested in the Ponca Indians, you might also invite my coworker, Mr. Willoughby Dunn—"

She scanned the crowd as May left to rejoin the group of students walking back to Brownell Hall. Had Will left already? Her heart sank.

The judge patted her hand. "Don't worry, little lady. My wife caught him at the door."

"Splendid!" Sophia excused herself to Tilly, then followed Judge Dundy out. This would work well. After dinner Will would escort her home and she would—

She would what? Pummel him with her list of topics to be discussed? She would certainly frighten him off.

Will stood next to an elegant carriage with a matron in a fashionable ensemble. Time with Will. That was what mattered. Sophia's heart lightened. She floated down the church steps with a smile.

The Dundys drove Will and Sophia down Farnam, a street lined with businesses, to a five-story building, the Grand Central Hotel. And grand it was, complete with gas-lit chandeliers in tall ceilings, archways supported by Corinthian columns, and thick wool carpet patterned with large bouquets. In the lobby they were joined by an imposing couple she had noticed in church. The judge introduced Andrew and Caroline Poppleton.

"Will is building our house," Mrs. Poppleton said with pride.

Sophia would love to see what he could do with the proper lumber, tools, and assistance. "When will it be done?"

"The first of September," Mr. Poppleton said.

"Sooner than that." Will smiled.

Why the hurry? Perhaps he needed the funds so he could move out of his brother's house. But Tilly had implied he did not live with his family. Where, then? Another question for her lengthy list.

The waiter guided them to a table set with crisp white linens and an array of utensils found at elaborate dinner parties in St. Petersburg and Paris. Sophia glanced at Will. Could she signal him to let him know which fork to use? The judge palmed his salad fork and dug in. Will knew better.

Mr. Poppleton gestured with his water glass. "So what happened up there with the Ponca?"

Will started to tell the story, but the lawyer could not resist his impulse to interrogate. Any other man would have broken out in a sweat, but Will handled the questions and his venison dinner with confidence.

Mrs. Dundy asked about her daughter's progress in French. Mrs. Poppleton noted their daughter, Ellen Elizabeth, had graduated from the College last year. Sophia remembered her as a first-rate pitcher for one of the baseball teams. She could often be found studying the specimens donated by a local ornithologist.

When a pastry with new strawberries was served, Mr. Poppleton turned his piercing gaze to Sophia and asked, "How much progress did your students make?"

"I had two in the fourth reader." The dessert soured in her mouth as she tried to explain the challenges of teaching at the agency without sounding defensive. She glanced to Will for reinforcement, but he was deep in conversation with Mrs. Poppleton.

Finally the meal and the interrogation were over. Sophia's heart raced. Her time with Will had arrived.

Mr. Poppleton called for his carriage. "I'd like to see how Mrs. P.'s mansion is coming along, Will."

Omaha was a small town. Will could walk her to school from this house, wherever it was. But no, the judge issued his verdict. "We'll take you back to Brownell Hall, Miss Makinoff. Mrs. Dundy has to make sure May's keeping her room in order. And I'm sure you have plenty of work preparing for the week ahead."

Once again she found herself without Will.

CHAPTER FORTY-ONE

Will felt like a house that had gone too long without paint: dried out, cracked, and faded. He'd spent sunrise to sunset at the Poppletons', overseeing the house's transformation from a bare skeleton to a stately home worthy of a lawyer from America's first transcontinental railroad. Usually he left the actual hammer-pounding to Kjell and Preben, but this time, he'd joined in the work. The sooner they finished, the sooner he could show Sophia. After that, it was up to God.

At night when he returned home, he was totally done in, but despite his exhaustion and Goldie's attentive company, he still missed Sophia. Missed her enough that he spent the entire church service watching her from the corner of his eye. He could see her new shoes and knew when she crossed her feet. He watched her hands as she held the Bible and the prayer book. And when the congregation stood for a hymn, he picked out her clear soprano.

Josephine tugged on Sophia's arm at the end of the service. "We're going on a picnic!"

"Careful, Josie-girl," Harrison warned. "Don't hurt Miss Sophie."

"Tough as an oak," Will said, then realized most women wouldn't take that as a compliment.

Her face turned a pretty shade of pink. "Picnics are ever so much fun, are they not?"

"C'mon, Dunn family. And Miss Sophie." Harrison herded them out. "We're going out to Fort Omaha. General Crook has been appointed Commander of the Department of the Platte for the army, in charge of military operations from the Missouri River west to Montana, Canada to Texas."

"Thank you, dear," Tilly said as Harrison handed her into the surrey. "And of course, he wants the best house, so he asks the best builders."

"Thank you, dear," Sophia echoed when Will helped her up. This elicited a giggle from Josie—and a grin from Will. He could get used to hearing that every day.

He climbed into the front seat with Harrison and Josie. He'd rather sit by Sophia, but Harrison had decreed this arrangement balanced the load. At least Josie fell asleep leaning on him. Sophia and Tilly had to contend with boys, who wiggled, kicked, and threatened to fall out with every lurch of the carriage.

Harrison drove north, keeping up his salesman's patter. He pointed out where he had doubled the size of the Lowes' house with an addition. Mrs. Ruth's vine on the south end of her porch gave her nice shade. The Abrams family had contacted him last week about a carriage house to replace their shed.

Will pointed out a cluster of saplings and abandoned buildings. "Saratoga Springs, where Brownell Hall first opened in 1863. The girls weren't allowed out of the yard for fear of Indian attacks."

The boys made *wo-wo-wo-wo* noises with their hands over their mouths.

Will hushed them. "Never heard any Indians make such a racket."

"Saratoga?" Sophia leaned out to study the area. "As in New York?"

"Yep. A New York land speculator had a town going here, including a hotel with sulphur springs, ferry to Iowa, homes, business, and churches. The hotel closed after the Panic of '57. The church bought it and ran the school here for a couple years."

They bumped along past a dozen farms. The muddy tracks had Will wondering if they'd have been better off on horseback. Sophia would have enjoyed the ride. Ah, that's what he'd do—take her riding.

At last Harrison turned west past hay fields in mid-cutting. "And this is Fort Omaha."

The fort spread up a grass-covered slope. Barracks, stables, and story-and-a-half houses, all painted white, formed a rectangle around a parade ground with a tall flagpole. Lafayette jumped down to open the gate in the wooden fence.

"Apparently attack is no longer a concern," Sophia noted.

"But supplies are." Harrison parked the surrey on the hill overlooking the fort. Will lifted his sleepy niece to the ground, then discovered Lafayette had helped Sophia out already.

The boys, hungry as usual, stretched out a blanket on the grass. Sophia helped Tilly set out cold fried chicken, biscuits, strawberry tarts, and jars of tea.

They ate, then the children raced off to roll down the hill. Harrison unfolded a map and pointed to the empty lot below. "The general's house goes there."

"Not on the hill?" Sophia asked.

Will told her, "A cistern up here will provide water to the house."

Sophia took off her hat so she could look between their shoulders, bringing her cheek close enough to kiss. He would have done it too, except that he didn't want to get slapped in front of his brother.

"This general, he is quite important? He will have distinguished guests?"

Harrison grunted. "Yeah, but the US government doesn't build palaces."

Will turned to her, close enough to admire her perfect skin and the glints of gold in her blue eyes. "This will be the headquarters. A few generals, maybe even the president, will visit."

"He will be expected to entertain, then." She smelled like a flower, like—he took a deep breath—honeysuckle. "Fine homes in New York have a call-bell system. A button under the dining table rings in the kitchen, so the lady of the house can call the servants."

"We could wire that in." Will made a note on his sketchpad.

Sophia glanced at Tilly, who bravely piped up, "You could call the guest room 'The Presidential Chamber.'"

Will smiled at his sister-in-law. "I like that. Harrison should ask you for ideas more often."

Harrison grumbled, "This is a military base. No lacy-messy nonsense."

"The College is lit with gas. So is West Point."

"With the gasworks in the town, we could do that." Will wrote another note.

"You've been to West Point?" Harrison asked, finally showing a two-penny nail's worth of respect.

"Sophia's father worked there in the cavalry. She's been in more forts than we've ever seen." He tapped his pencil on the paper. "I'm thinking coal furnace with coal-burning fireplaces in each room for the worst days."

"We need a strong design," Harrison said, waving his fist. "Masculine. American."

"American, eh? How about a tepee?" Will teased. "Don't get much more American than that."

"Will it be wood frame like these?" Sophia asked.

"No, brick. They're planning to replace these buildings. As funds become available."

Wasteful, Will thought. The government could afford to replace perfectly good buildings but never had funds available for the Poncas. He sent off another prayer for his friends.

Sophia said, "Italianate could look rather fortress-like."

"Italianate? With all those curves, cupolas, and balustrades?" Harrison's face went red. He wasn't used to anyone weighing in on his plans. Tilly pushed another strawberry tart into his hand.

"Like the Steele-Johnson building at Twelfth and Harney. Or the Hamiltons' house. Square off the windows, pediments, and brackets. No decorations on the columns or lintels. Keep costs and maintenance low." Will sketched out a two-story house with a porch. "Tall, narrow windows for light and ventilation. Red brick with white trim."

"What about dark blue?" Tilly suggested.

"Perhaps West Point gray?"

Will studied the drawing. "Keep it simple, could work." He gave them a smile. "Could work well."

"Hey? Hey!" A cavalry officer ran up the hill. "Sophia? Yes, it's you! I'd recognize your hair anywhere."

"It is Lt. Higgins." Sophia retied her hat, put her gloves on, and stood.

The officer had shaved, polished his boots, and put on a new uniform.

Will groaned. "Is he hunting you down?"

"I told you, you should have proposed," Tilly whispered.

The lieutenant reached for Sophia. "What are you doing in Omaha?"

"Teaching." Sophia gave the soldier a stiff-armed handshake, then let go and took a step back. "How are my friends? How far did you travel with them?"

"You mean the Poncas?" He made a great study of tucking his gauntlets under his belt. "We were with them until last week, the first of June, when we hit the Kansas border. It was a relief to get away. It's like they're under a cloud of bad luck."

Will stood on Sophia's uphill side, giving himself the advantage. "What happened?"

"What didn't happen?" He scratched under his neckerchief. "Stormed just about all the time. Several were injured in a tornado. Bunch of them died."

The news hit like a hammer to the gut. "Who?" Will reached for Sophia and she leaned on him. He wasn't sure which one steadied the other. He just knew they needed each other. "Who died?"

Lt. Higgins scuffed the dirt with his boot heel. "Three, four children. Two old women. Another little one. Had to bury them along the trail. Didn't set well with the Poncas, having to leave their family behind. Guess I wouldn't be too fond of it myself, leaving my loved ones in a strange land, no one to tend their graves."

"Do you recall their names? Or perhaps what they looked like?"

"Wet. Muddy, wet messes, all of them." He shook his head. "One good thing. The church in Milford gave such a fine burial to a young woman, making her a dress and a coffin, her father decided to become a Christian. He was one of those we arrested in April. The shorter brother."

"Standing Bear." Will groaned. "Must have been Prairie Flower."

"Say, Sophia, now that I'm posted here—"

Will turned away from Sophia and her social life. Who else? Who else had died? Little Cottonwood had been sick, coughing up a storm. Smoke Maker's mother and White Swan's mother were close to ancient. Yellow Horse's little one, Black Elk and Moon Hawk's pretty little White Buffalo Girl, Brown Eagle and Elisabeth's baby . . .

No, it didn't matter. Whoever it was would be missed. And the tribe would ache with every grave left behind. Will bowed his head.

Sophia's lieutenant stomped off to his horse, whacking his leg with his hat. She climbed back to the top of the hill. Tears wet her cheeks. "You are praying, are you not? Could I join you?"

She was the only one here who knew the Poncas as people, as individuals with families, dreams, quirks. Will opened his hands and she slid hers into his grip. He cleared his throat. "Dear Jesus. Please comfort our friends in their grief. Please be with them, strengthen them, heal them. Send Your sun to dry out the road. Give the agent wisdom—"

Wisdom? He'd been asking for wisdom in Washington for four years. And look where that had gotten them.

Sophia choked back a sob. "Be with all my students. Help them remember their lessons. Provide them with a teacher and school. And good houses like they had on the Niobrara."

Good houses? Since when did Sophia think he'd built good houses?

"Lord, I don't understand." The words clogged in his throat. Sophia squeezed his hands and he added, "We don't understand. The Bible says You'll work this all out for good, but seems like it's going the other direction. Help us—Sophia, me, and everyone in the Ponca tribe—to grab hold of our faith with both hands and hang on tight."

Josie's little body hit him in the back of the knees and he stepped forward. Sophia braced him, keeping him from falling on his face.

Will scooped his niece up and threw her over his shoulder. And just like Rosalie, she burst into giggles.

"What are you doing, Uncle Will?" she asked.

"We're praying."

"Well, say 'Amen' already. I want to fly the kite you made!"

"We will not say 'Amen.'" Sophia wiped her eyes with a lacy hankie. "Because we are not done praying."

CHAPTER FORTY-TWO

The girls filed out of the assembly room after chapel, but Sophia stayed in her seat. In preparation for examinations, the rector had asked the students if they had studied to be approved, the same verse the missionary had used back in New York, the night she had been jilted.

Now here she was again, her thoughts entangled by a man. But unlike Montgomery, Will was intelligent, devoted to serving God, handsome, gentle, good with children, and respectful. And oh, how she felt when he held her in his arms.

Sophia folded her hands and focused on the cross over the altar. *Dear Jesus, I put my relationship with Will, whatever it is, whatever it may become, in Your hands. Please keep a firm grip on it, as I have a tendency to snatch it back. Amen.*

Will watched Sophia and another teacher guide the Brownell Hall girls into the first pew. The duty rotated every week and this Sunday was Sophia's turn.

A fellow about his age, with thick brown hair and a drooping mustache, paused at the Dunns' pew. "Will? I'm John Webster, lawyer here in town. I'd be interested in hearing about your time with the Indians. May I take you out to dinner?"

"Indians? What Indians?" A man with a wild shock of black hair leaned across the aisle. "Are you the guy who worked up at the Ponca Agency?" He shook Will's hand. "Thomas Tibbles, Omaha *Herald*. I'd like to hear about it too."

Webster grinned and leaned a hand on his hip. "If you think I'm buying you dinner, Tom—"

"I recognize you." A third man, older than the first two, nodded at Will. "You were coming when I was going. I'm Charles Birkett, Ponca agent in '73. I'd like to hear what's happened since I left."

The organist pumped out the first hymn.

"After the service, let's head for one of the restaurants downtown," Will said. The men took their seats. He'd have to tell Sophia that what he'd missed out on with letter writing, he was making up for in talking.

Summer's heat beat down on the small building and pushed in through the open windows. The bishop skipped his robe. The male parishioners shed their coats.

In the front row Sophia fluttered her fan. A curl loosened and spiraled down the back of her neck. She reached up and undid the top button of her dress.

Will's mouth went dry.

He closed his eyes and prayed.

Mrs. Windsor expected Brownell Hall's young ladies to conduct themselves as part of a noble Christian family, to live up to the plane of high privilege. Which they had done every day until today.

Sophia turned from the window where warm spring air danced. The breeze did not carry any identifiable fragrance like lilac, but a heady mixture of growing grasses. And the echoes of hammers on wood.

Was it Will? She could imagine his strong fingers around a hammer—

Giggling echoed through the halls. Her older class entered, laughing and jostling one another. Not the expected behavior for examination day.

"Oh, Miss Makinoff, it's so exciting! Carrie's getting married!"

The girl in question turned pink to the roots of her hair and bounced on her toes. She looked too young to *spell* "wife," let alone become a bride. "John asked me last night!"

The other three girls burst into discussions about dresses, flowers, and Niagara Falls.

"Mademoiselles." Sophia's firm tone had them scurrying into their seats. "Congratulations," she said to Carrie, then to the class, "Please, for this hour, bring your minds back to your French examination. You have all worked incredibly hard these past five weeks. I hope your test scores will reflect your effort." She passed out the lined paper, then raised the map to unveil their essay questions.

Jeannette, Marielle, and Manon put their hands to the plow, so to speak. But Caroline managed only to write her name before she drifted off.

Love, Sophia pondered as her heart beat to a distant hammer's rhythm, *was quite a bit of trouble.*

❧

Will followed Goldie up the hill to Harrison's house. His knees ached from laying floors all day. His shoulders were sore from nailing crown molding on ceilings yesterday. His eyes stung from varnish fumes. Stain had settled into the cracks and lines of his hands. Sweat stuck sawdust to his skin. He wanted to go home and soak in a hot bath, but first he had to talk to Harrison about Armin.

Goldie spotted a rabbit and dashed across the vacant lot. The cottontail slipped between the pickets of the Morrisons' fence, then turned to gloat with a twitch of long ears and a flash of a white tail. The dog gave a woof of frustration.

Armin had turned out to be a good worker, but they'd about run out of unskilled jobs for him at the Poppletons'. Maybe Harrison could apprentice him to someone. And find a place for the kid to live.

Goldie had nosed the boy out from under the back porch the second morning. Then, bucking Preben and Kjell's dire predictions of theft, Will had brought a blanket for him and let him sleep in the carriage house. Unless the Poppletons needed a stable boy, Armin would have to move out next week.

Buddy dashed down the drive to meet them. The dogs circled and sniffed, then decided to be friends and romped off around the back side of Harrison's house.

Will left his shoes on the porch, paused to admire a sunset as red as new cherrywood, then went in. Smelled delicious. Mrs. O'Reilly must have tried a new recipe.

Goldie must have smelled it too. Before Will got the door closed, she reappeared and nosed her way inside. Buddy stayed in the yard, on guard, but Goldie went straight for a bite of meat on the floor beside the stove. Then she trailed the smell into the dining room.

"Zlata!" A familiar voice began to coo over her in French.

Sophia was here. A lightning bolt shot through Will, tightening his skin and stopping his heart for a moment. He should have washed up, changed clothes. Well, she'd seen him dirtier than this.

"Does the dog know French?" Lafayette asked.

"Bien sur." She spoke again, her voice climbing the scale as if asking questions. Will thought he heard his name, so he met her at the doorway. She wore one of Tilly's aprons over a new green dress.

Her eyes were bright, her cheeks pink, and a whole passel of curls had escaped her knot. He'd never seen anyone prettier.

"Will! You are in time for dinner."

"*Bonjour, Oncle,*" Leo said.

"It's *bonsoir,* you dolt." Lafayette smirked.

"No name-calling," he said in unison with Sophia. He glanced up, met her gaze, and they shared a smile.

"*Bonsoir, ma petite chienne.*" Josie waved at Goldie, who was sniffing the floor for additional tidbits.

Sophia collected a plate and fork from the sideboard. "*S'il vous plaît,* please, join us. We have plenty."

"Plenty of what?" He lifted the heavy silver cover off the serving dish. *Hmm, something new.*

"They're *crêpes,*" Josie informed him. "Miss Makinoff showed us how to make them for our French lesson."

Leo and Lafayette spouted off a bunch of French words, hopefully having to do with food.

Crêpes turned out to be thin pancakes wrapped around asparagus spears, sliced ham, and cheese. Will took Harrison's chair, the better to watch Sophia, who sat in Tilly's.

"Miss Makinoff says we call them *blini* if we want to learn Russian," Josie told him. "But then we'd have to fill them with caviar, which Miss Makinoff says is fish eggs." Her pointed nose wrinkled.

"As if asparagus isn't bad enough." Leo left the stalks on his plate.

"So where are your parents?" Will asked as he dug in. *Hmm. Not bad.*

"Mom and Dad took the O'Reillys to the hospital."

"What's wrong? Who's sick?"

"Mr. O'Reilly took ill." Sophia's hands shook as she cut Josie's food.

"He grabbed his chest and fell on the ground." Leo clutched his shirt, tipped out of his chair, and rolled under the table. "Ew, *Oncle* Will, your feet stink."

Will poked him with a toe. "You wouldn't smell them if you stayed on your chair where you belong." Had he been this unruly the whole time Sophia was here?

Sophia murmured words in French that had Leo scrambling back into his chair and apologizing. Then she turned to Will. "So, how have you been?"

"Busy." He knew he was staring but he couldn't stop himself. Couldn't she see how great this was, having a family, sitting around the table together? No, she was a princess from a fairy tale, visiting the commoners, him the most common of all. "And you?"

Her eyes sparkled in the light from the chandelier. She gave the children a smile. "We have had wonderful fun. Playing French games, cooking French food, singing French songs."

"With a Russian instrument?" Yes, the gusli rested on the organ.

"*Bien sur.* And Goldie? How is she adapting?"

"Great. Big help at work. When we're sawing, hammering, making a racket, she lets us know when someone's coming."

"*Bon travail, ma petite chienne,*" Sophia said. Goldie wagged her whole body and sidled closer.

"*Oncle* Will." Josie uncovered another dish and said a French word that sounded like *dessert.*

Will found more crêpes wrapped around strawberries. He smiled at Sophia. "And you said you couldn't cook."

She did her pretty shoulder dance.

"Miss Makinoff said she can only cook French food." Leo fidgeted as the platter made its slow way around the table.

"I don't mind. Not a bit." Will cleaned his plate.

"Iced tea?" Sophia asked.

"I'd better have coffee, if there's any." He'd have to stop by the hospital, see how Mr. O'Reilly was doing.

"Il voudrait le café," Lafayette pronounced.

"Oh yeah." Leo waved his knife. *"Je voudrais plus de fraises."*

Sophia turned him down, with words that sounded like *stomachache*. Will thought maybe he could learn French too.

Buddy's bark and the rumble of a wagon had everyone racing out the back door. To Will's relief, Mr. O'Reilly was with them. The older man climbed down and started to unharness the horses.

"I'll get that." Will shoved his feet back into his brogans. "You go rest."

"I'm fit as a fiddle, I tell you." The man patted his chest, but Will noticed it took him two breaths to get the words out.

"Seems like fiddles break easily. Thanks, Lafayette," Will told his nephew as he took Traveler.

"The doctor told you to rest." Harrison unhitched Ajax. "We've got it. And you too, Mrs. O'Reilly."

The woman seemed to have shrunk overnight. She wrung her hands and looked from her husband toward the kitchen. "But supper—"

"The children have been fed." Sophia handed her a covered plate. "I hope you do not mind. We harvested some of your beautiful asparagus."

Mrs. O'Reilly thanked her. Dish in one arm, Mr. O'Reilly under the other, they climbed up to the carriage house apartment.

"You got the children to eat asparagus?" Tilly asked.

"Well, not Leo, of course. But the other two were adventurous." She took off Tilly's apron, a gesture that made Will as hot and dizzy as breathing varnish fumes.

"Hey! I'm adventurous." The little stinker stomped his foot.

Will glanced at Goldie, who watched the hubbub from the back porch. He'd say his good-byes, then they could walk Sophia back to school.

"Come try our crêpes!" Josie pulled her mother's arm. "Miss Makinoff said we did a good job."

"Thank you so much for staying with the children." Tilly embraced Sophia. "I hope they weren't too wild."

"Not at all. They were delightful."

"We're not wild," Leo said. "She's used to Indians."

"Who are much more civilized than you." Will rubbed his knuckles in Leo's hair.

Buddy barked. A man climbed up the drive carrying a lantern. The lights from the house showed Mr. Sullivan, the caretaker at Brownell Hall. "I saw the carriage return, so I've come for Miss Makinoff."

So much for Will's plan. Rotten Omaha. Everyone could see what everyone else was doing.

"You are too kind, Mr. Sullivan. One moment, please. I have a concluding French lesson for my students. Line up, *s'il vous plaît. Gros bisous.*" Sophia clasped Lafayette by the shoulders and kissed his cheeks. The boy's eyes widened and his jaw dropped. *Sorry, kid, I saw her first.*

Then she grabbed Leo by the ears and managed to keep him from squirming away. Josie lifted her face and gave as many kisses as she got. Buddy and Goldie joined the line. With a laugh, Sophia bent to the pups, earning a wet kiss in her ear from Goldie.

Will opened his arms and she stepped into them, bringing her own sweet fragrance. Yes. He had her right where she belonged. "I'm sorry I can't walk you home," he whispered as the first kiss brushed his cheek, making his skin tingle.

At the second kiss, she said, "I have missed you terribly."

She missed him? His blood rushed warm, making his head spin. The third kiss was last, but not nearly enough. "Can you wear your riding skirt to the picnic tomorrow?"

Sophia's eyes glittered. "*Mais, oui!* Oh yes!" Then she hurried off with Mr. Sullivan. "*Bonne nuit!*"

"*Bonne nuit!*" the children called.

Floating a good foot off the ground, Will collected Goldie and they headed home.

Sophia had missed him.

Sophia had been thinking about him.

Sophia agreed to go riding with him tomorrow.

At his gate he stopped. Why had he gone to Harrison's? He couldn't remember to save his life.

But it didn't matter. He'd think of it later.

Right now he had Sophia on his mind.

CHAPTER FORTY-THREE

T hen the player grabs the handkerchief and tries to catch the runner," Will's sister, Charlotte, explained. A school-teacher in Exira, Iowa, she expounded on educational topics like a zealot. She had Will's curly hair, albeit with a touch of silver, and Harrison's full cheeks. "Meanwhile the runner tries to get back to the space left open in the circle."

"Yes, I remember playing a similar game in Russia." Sophia fanned herself. The heat must be affecting her head. Ordinarily she enjoyed talking about teaching, but today she could think only of Will. Where was he? When would he come for her?

The Union Pacific Railroad's brass band performed "Yankee Doodle." A company of soldiers passed, marching with enthusiasm if not precision.

"Mama, Aunt Charlotte, Miss Makinoff!" Leo barreled into them. "Elephants, hippopotamus, tigers, rhinoceros!"

"Where?" Sophia reached for her pistol but did not see any danger.

"On a poster." Lafayette shrugged, the expression on his face shifting between childish excitement and adolescent boredom. "The circus is coming Saturday."

"Can we go, Mama?" Josephine asked. "I have *always* wanted

to see a circus." "Always" being the entire four years of her life. Tilly and Sophia exchanged smiles, trying not to laugh.

"Only well-behaved children may attend the circus," Charlotte answered with a waggle of her finger. "No beggars or whiners."

Sophia hoped she set aside her teacher's voice more easily than Charlotte did.

"Sophia, I distinctly remember pink rosettes on your hat," Tilly said. "You'll have to let the milliner know they've fallen off, so she can attach new ones."

"She may have gone back east," Sophia said, trying not to let the hope seem too obvious.

"Let's go watch the baseball game," Harrison called to the children. They headed downhill to a vacant lot with the ambitious name of Jefferson Square.

"We had a lovely Fourth of July picnic last year," Tilly told Sophia as she stacked the plates. "Perfect weather. The whole town celebrated the centennial. One of the Creighton brothers gave a speech. Was it Edward? No, he's passed. It must have been John. Then the news came about General Custer. We were sick with worry for Will."

"We were never in any danger." With the exception of the Brulé, whiskey traders, and the heartbreak of watching friends suffer. Sophia offered up a silent prayer that the Poncas might be spared further anguish. "The Poncas all love and respect Will."

Charlotte fanned herself with a napkin. "Can the Indian understand the concept of love, of respect?"

Sophia gritted her teeth. Charlotte lived in a state with an Indian name, but had yet to meet an actual live Indian. "Certainly. They are a loving people, especially toward their children. Elders are treated with a great deal of reverence."

Charlotte frowned. "You and Will make them sound like regular people."

"Exactly." Sophia stood to help Tilly shake out the blanket. "Perhaps stronger, better than us. How many white people could have survived years of starvation, attacks, broken promises—"

"Do I hear a rousing Fourth of July speech?" Will sauntered up and grabbed the picnic box. He had rolled up the sleeves of his white shirt, exposing his wrists . . . strong bones, ropy muscles, long fingers. Sophia's heart increased its pace from a walk to a trot. She squeezed the blanket to keep from throwing herself into his arms.

"Tilly, how about I stow this." It was not a question. "Charlotte, I'll borrow Sophia for a while, if you don't mind." He gave Sophia a sidelong glance—a Ponca habit or a touch of nervousness? "We can go riding now, if you don't mind missing a couple of innings."

"Not at all." Finally, an opportunity to be alone with Will. She had been waiting for this for weeks, since they had left the Agency. "I would be pleased to join you."

He whistled. A group of children broke apart, releasing a yellow dog. With a joyful woof Goldie raced around Sophia and Will three times before slowing enough to be petted. Her whole back end wagged.

"She looks wonderful," Sophia told Will as they walked to the surrey. "And so do you."

"We're both eating on a regular basis." Will wedged the basket under the carriage seat, then turned to her and shook his head. "Every meal I think about our friends."

"And pray they have something to eat." Sophia nodded her understanding.

With the crowd watching the baseball game, quiet reigned on this street. She should take the opportunity and speak her mind before they were interrupted—before the children decided to join them, or one of Will's old friends recognized him, or someone else wanted to ask about life among the savages. "I have so much to talk to you about, I do not know where to start."

"I have something to show you first." Evidently Will had made considerable effort planning for this ride. He had unharnessed the horses from the surrey, then saddled and bridled them. He held the stirrup for her. "This is Traveler. The other's Ajax."

She released her skirt and mounted. "I have missed you so much. I have missed you at breakfast and supper, and our walks back and forth to school, and your visits—"

His finger pressed under her chin. "We'll talk. After our ride."

He swung into the saddle with ease. Goldie marched ahead of the horses as if she knew their destination.

Sophia squeezed her knees, encouraging Traveler to catch up so she could see Will's face. But the horse seemed determined to keep his nose by the other's tail. Quite frustrating. Except . . . this was the first time she had seen Will ride. In truth the view was rather entrancing. As with everything else he did, he moved with casual grace. She forced her gaze to Traveler's mane and tried to rein in her thoughts.

Her heart galloped but her horse plodded. Why could she not have a mount like the dapple gray Arabian trotting toward them? The dog behind the mare growled at Goldie. The young rider, resplendent in a crimson habit, whistled and brought the dog to heel. She executed a tight turn away from them, picked up speed, and sailed over a fence. The dog followed.

"Oh. That was Grace, one of my favorite students."

"She has a pet coyote? Now that's a curiosity."

"She has a gift with animals. Yes, my students are interesting, and so are the teachers. But they are not you. I miss your thoughts, your way of looking at life, your understanding of our Christian walk."

"You'll make more friends."

"But none challenge me like you."

"Are you saying you don't like your job?" he asked. "Because

I'm sure Charlotte could find you a one-room schoolhouse somewhere in Iowa."

Perhaps he was angrier than she thought. But no, he held his shoulders in a relaxed manner.

"I must apologize," Sophia said. "When I said you would make a good diplomat, I meant it as a compliment to the most talented man I know. I never meant to disparage your gifts as a carpenter or to imply that you are not skilled as a builder of homes."

"That's why I'm bringing you here." He turned the corner and dismounted, looping the reins through a fence of iron made to look like rail.

She hitched Traveler and hurried to catch up. "Will, it truly does not matter to me what you build, what sort of work you do."

"It matters to me." He paused, his hand on the gate, then started up the brick walk. Goldie raced ahead, investigating a newly planted elm.

As many proposals as she had suffered through, Sophia ought to be able to offer one with a modicum of grace. "After this past year," she stammered, "I would venture to say I know you quite well. Well enough to—"

She stopped. Where was he leading her?

Sophia looked up and her breath caught. A two-and-a-half-story mansion with a tower presided over the street. Cream trim and a gray slate roof complemented the handsome dark-red brick. Paired columns supported a deep porch in the front and a porte cochère on the side. "Whose house is this?"

"Andrew and Caroline Poppleton's."

She gasped again. Perhaps she did not know Will. "You built this?"

"In the six weeks since I've been back? No. I'm doing the finish work with my crew. The family moves in next week."

A gangly boy raced from the carriage house, clicked his heels, and bowed.

Will made the introductions. "I'm hoping to find out why he was wandering around Omaha alone, where his family is."

"Guten Tag," Sophia ventured.

Armin burst forth with a long, chattering explanation.

"He speaks a Frisian dialect." Sophia shook her head. "Perhaps the German Catholic church might have a parishioner who could interpret."

Will unlocked the enormous door with etched glass windows and carvings that mirrored the angles of the porch, then held it open for her.

Sophia stepped into the vestibule. The air smelled of fresh-cut wood tinged with the biting odor of varnish. Armin pointed out all the features with the enthusiasm of a patent medicine peddler. Diagonal strips of walnut flooring, polished to a glassy shine, led the eye to a magnificent stairway. It angled upward, graced by a carved newel post and rail. Paired balusters on each step echoed the paired columns outside. A stained glass window of a garden scene lit the soaring space with sparkles of color. "It is beautiful!"

"I'll get the air moving." Will stepped into the drawing room and opened a window. It glided up silently, without any effort on Will's part, and stayed up. A gentle breeze brushed the chandelier with a faint tinkle of crystals.

Armin tugged on Sophia's elbow, directing her attention to the carvings embellishing the bay window, the moldings decorating the tall ceiling, the elegant marble mantel. A second smaller chandelier hung in the corner, at head-height. "This is unusual."

"Mrs. Poppleton has a Steinway grand piano."

The design came together. "How perfect for all manner of entertaining: dances, musicales, weddings—" Oh dear. She truly did have marriage on her mind.

"The wallpaper crew comes tomorrow."

"Wallpaper will distract from the beauty of the woodwork. It is not necessary with plaster this perfect."

The corner of Will's mouth curved upward. "I'll tell Mario you give him a passing grade."

Armin slid open the pocket doors to the dining room.

"And covering these floors with carpet would be an insult, to say the least."

The dining room boasted another chandelier hung from a raised inlay ceiling, the chair rail Will and Mrs. Poppleton had discussed, and—Sophia stepped on the buzzer in the middle of the floor.

"Mrs. Poppleton liked your idea." Will's boots, shiny and new, echoed on the herringbone pattern of the floor, picking up the pace. Armin toured her through a library lined with bookshelves, a window seat, and shutters, then a butler's pantry with floor-to-ceiling cabinets. The kitchen had more cupboards than Sophia had ever seen, plus an icebox, an enormous stove with warming oven, a sink, and a pantry.

Will nodded at the back stairway. "Upstairs, four bedrooms, a bathroom with hot and cold running water, and a maid's room."

"What is this?" An alcove in the hall might hold a treasured sculpture, except for the wires sprouting from its shelf.

"It's for a new invention the Poppletons saw in Philadelphia at the Centennial Exhibition. A telephone. Sends voices over wires. He'll be able to talk to his office downtown without leaving the house."

"Without having to use a telegraph operator or Morse code? I would like to try such an invention."

"I'm not sure when A. J. will be able to buy one, but he wanted a place for it in his house." Will closed the window, then locked the door behind them.

Armin executed another bow, then returned to the carriage house.

"Will, your workmanship is exquisite. I can see how you must have been so insulted. Please accept my apology."

"Sure."

If he accepted her apology, why would he not look at her?

Goldie met them at the front porch and led them to the horses.

"You are an excellent craftsman. I have never seen such quality. Not even in palaces of St. Petersburg or Paris."

"Thanks." He turned the horse south.

"Are you still angry?"

"No."

"Then where are we going?" And why was he so reserved?

Goldie led them to a street by the railroad depot. A row of identical workers' cottages, each a story and a half, marched parallel to the tracks. "Did you build these too?"

"The lots here cost less." Will dismounted in front of one still under construction. The porch railings and uprights were of standard squared lumber. The house awaited a final coat of paint.

"Will and Goldie!" A stocky man toddled over from the house across the street. A thick bandage wrapped his right hand. "Is no-work day, no?"

"Just showing off." Will introduced her to Gino Vanetti, the man who did the stained glass window at the Poppletons'.

"Magnificent," Sophia told him. "It reminded me of the churches in Europe."

"I make for church in Italy. Work years and years. No money. No house. But I come here, work for Will one year"—he raised a thick finger; the other arm made a grand gesture—"and I get house, all mine! Is miracle!"

"With the profit from Poppletons', we build these." Will's nod encompassed the block. "We keep them affordable by cutting back on trim, using pine for the floors, having apprentices do some of the work."

"Come. See." Mr. Vanetti ushered her into a large room well lit by windows. The plaster here was as smooth as the Poppletons' but unadorned. The kitchen contained a small stove, open shelves, and a sink with a pump.

"Will think of everything." Mr. Vanetti opened the back door with a flourish. A row of conifers along the back fence would grow and muffle the sound of the locomotives.

"The enclosed stairway saves heat." Mr. Vanetti led her up to two bedrooms, each with a window for ventilation and light, then ushered her out the front where Goldie waited.

Sophia thanked the craftsman for the tour, then turned to Will. "You economized by simplifying design and reducing the scale, but kept the quality. This is what you could have built for the Poncas, if you had been provided with the appropriate materials."

"And tools."

"You use your gift to bless others. It is wonderful," Sophia told him as he helped her onto the horse again. "It is a worthy calling, providing houses and jobs for people. It is your ministry."

"No, not a ministry. It's what I do." He stood beside her stirrup and stared past the row of houses, down the hill to the river. "I can build anything from a cottage to a mansion, plain to fancy." He was not boasting so much as stating the facts. He turned toward her and scraped the muck from her boot with his thumbnail. "So, if you ever stop wandering the world, I'd like to build one for you."

Sophia's heart sounded a hollow thud, like a Ponca drum. He would build a house for her? Not for them, together? Would he disregard her proposal as she had spurned his?

But he had showed her what mattered: that he, too, worked for God. He did not write letters or hold salons, but in his own way he made a difference.

"Where—" She stopped, pulled a deeper breath into her lungs, then pushed out one of her questions. "Where are you living now?"

The dog barked, lifting her front paws off the ground.

"All right. We'll show you."

He turned west, toward Brownell Hall, and drew up by a charming cottage, slightly larger than the last one. Sky blue, trimmed in royal blue and gold, it glowed in the summer sun. A well-established maple tree in the front yard showed this was no new construction.

Goldie opened the gate with her nose. This time, instead of waiting on the porch when Will opened the door, she rushed inside. The view through the bay window showed a tidy parlor. A Bible lay open on a pie-crust table.

Will's Bible. Will's house.

"How long—"

"Depends on what you want," he interrupted.

"What I want is . . ."

If he said no, she would lose her best friend.

Sophia removed her gloves and reached for him. After a moment, his warm hands enveloped hers. His pulse hammered strong against her fingertips. She took a breath. "I want . . . to stop wandering and live with you, to make a home with you. As my husband. Here in Omaha. Or wherever you may go." And suddenly she knew the right words, the best words, God's words.

"Will, I love you."

He finally met her gaze. He said not a word, but in the hot flame of his eyes, in the warmth of his smile, he revealed his love. Then, as a man who valued action over words, he leaned forward and kissed her.

And, as a man who showed masterful expertise in the use of his tools, he kissed quite well indeed.

Epilogue

March 29, 1879

A buggy rattled up the driveway, the horse at a dangerous trot. "Whoa!" Will yelled. "Armin, get this rig turned around! *Schnell!* Mrs. Abbott, where's my wife?"

Whatever could be wrong? Sophia picked up Nicholas—the toddler was of an age requiring constant supervision—and hurried down the steps. The little boy's ringlets, so like his father's, tickled her chin.

Will paused at the bottom of the stairs, his color high. His gaze met hers, igniting the glow of desire within her. But her wants would have to wait for whatever had him climbing the steps two at a time.

He met her at the landing. Nicholas yelled, "Dada!" and launched himself from her arms. Will caught the baby, but he did not engage in their usual jiggling play.

"Sophia!" he gasped. "Indians. Fort Omaha. Brought in by the army."

Excitement exploded through her like fireworks. "Anyone we know?"

"Let's go find out." Will pulled her through the house, pausing only to pass Nicholas off to Mrs. Abbott, over the child's very vocal objection. Sophia followed him out the door to the carriage.

"If I change into my riding habit—"

"Not in your condition." He lifted her into the carriage.

"May I go with you?" the German boy asked from his place at their gelding's nose.

Sophia unfolded the lap robe. "As I recall, you have an essay on the American War of Independence to write."

"Another time." Will joined her on the seat and snapped the reins. They raced north, dodging emigrant trains, farm wagons, and the snarl of traffic that clogged Omaha streets these days.

"How long has it been?" Sophia clung to the arm rail with one hand, her husband's leg with the other, and braced her feet against the dashboard.

"Twenty-two months." As usual, he could best her in mathematics. "Not a word. No news. Nothing. Could be someone else. Cheyenne from Fort Robinson, maybe."

She had not had time to put on a hat, and now the wind pulled her hair from its pins. She dared not let go to repair it. Perhaps, at this speed, no one would recognize them. Not that it mattered; the name of Willoughby Dunn earned enough respect in Omaha to weather any breach of etiquette.

"Tepees." The gate stood open. Will did not slow for the turn into the fort. The buggy rose up on one wheel, then thudded down with a bump.

Sophia squinted. Indians, yes. But who—

Will braked in front of the work site for General Crook's house. "I'll help you down," he told Sophia. "Don't jump."

She tossed off the lap robe and scanned the encampment for a familiar face. Before Will could set her on the ground, they were surrounded. Standing Bear and his wife, Susette Primeau. Yellow

Horse. Long Runner. Cries for War. Walks in the Mud. Everyone conversing in Ponca.

"Will!" Brown Eagle grabbed her husband. Mary embraced her.

Sophia stood on tiptoe to see past the adults. "Where—"

"Miss Makinoff! Mr. Dunn!"

Marguerite. Joseph. Frank. Susette.

Sophia hugged her students, feeling bones beneath their clothes. Unlike Harrison and Tilly's three, none of these children had grown an inch. All had lost weight. And where—

A tiny body wiggled between Joseph and Frank. A tiny body with big brown eyes and an even bigger smile. Rosalie! And little Micahel!

They were alive! All of them were alive!

"It's Mrs. Dunn now," Will told them as the children pulled them toward their campfire.

"Without horses or family you figured how to marry." Brown Eagle grinned. Gray streaked his hair and deep wrinkles lined his face. He looked ten years older. Mary had lost several teeth.

Then the sad story poured out: the deaths of White Buffalo Girl, Prairie Flower, and seven others on the march south. Starvation, unending misery, and more death in Indian Territory. Then Bear Shield died. In an attempt to save those remaining, Standing Bear had led twenty-five of his people toward home. Soldiers caught them at the Omaha tribe's reservation and brought them as prisoners to Fort Omaha.

"How can I help?" Sophia wiped her tears and surveyed the camp. "I should have brought food."

"The army is feeding us." Brown Eagle's Mary nodded at the pot simmering over the fire.

"I could collect clothes."

"The Omaha people—" A cough interrupted Susette's words. "—gave us clothes."

"Perhaps I could bring a doctor."

"The post physician is tending our sick."

Will covered Sophia's hand. "We'll keep praying." Then, sensing her exhaustion, he stood. "We'd better get going before it's dark."

With more hugs and promises to return again tomorrow, they walked out of the camp.

Sophia leaned into him as they walked. "I have cried myself dry."

Will wrapped his arm around her. "I'll drive slowly. You can nap on the ride home."

"Quel mélange!" She let out a bone-deep breath. "I am grateful for those who survived, grieving for those who did not, and angry with the Indian Office. To God, I can only ask why."

"Only?" The corner of his mouth twitched. He knew her better than that.

"No. I want to know what He wants me to do. Should I write more letters? Send a telegram to the president? Should I—"

"Just you?"

She flashed him a smile. "We. What should we do?"

They approached the buggy. In the shadows of the general's house, a man in civilian clothes pushed himself to standing. Sophia reached for her pistol.

"I surrender." He raised his arms and stepped into the sunset's last beam.

"General Crook. Thank the Lord it is you." Sophia's heart returned to a normal pace, and she stepped forward to shake his hand. "We departed in such a hurry, I left my pistol behind."

"Being shot wouldn't be the worst thing that's happened today." He nodded toward the encampment. "Washington says I've got to haul them back to Indian Territory. What am I going to do?"

"Would you like a ride home, sir?" Will asked. The general was living near the church until his house was finished. They squeezed into the buggy and headed out. A mile down the road, Will almost dropped the reins. "Hey, I know who—"

At the same time, Sophia said, "I have an idea."

"Tom Tibbles," Will said as Sophia nodded.

"From the newspaper?" General Crook studied the night sky, then straightened. "Drop me off at the *Herald*'s office. And keep praying. Both of you."

May 12, 1879

The lawyers had argued for days, using every six-dollar word in the dictionary. Then the judge let Standing Bear speak. In minutes the chief blew off the sawdust of confusion and made history.

"This hand is not the same color as yours, but if I pierce it, I shall feel pain. The blood that will flow from mine will be the same color as yours. I am a man. The same God made us both."

The chief used the analogy of trying to save his family from rushing floodwaters, a very real fear for those living along the Missouri. A man blocked him. If the man allowed, Standing Bear could continue on toward freedom. If the man refused, he and his family would sink under the flood. "You are that man," he told the judge.

Not an eye in the courtroom was dry when he finished. The judge had returned with the verdict: Indians are people in the eyes of the law.

Goldie's bark announced another arrival. A carriage pulled into the porte cochère. Will started to excuse himself to General Crook, then caught a glimpse of Sophia nearby in the dining room. She smiled at him and glided across the hall to greet the newcomer with a swish of petticoats and brisk steps. In the gaslights her fancy dress looked like bronze.

The fabric was called "brilliantine," she had told him. He figured it must have been named for her. She had her hair done up in curls, like a crown. Every time he looked at her, Will marveled. How did it happen that a carpenter from Iowa had married a member of Russian royalty?

He smiled, imagining Sophia correcting him: nobility, not royalty. No matter. She'd always be the queen of his heart. He thanked God every day, every moment, for the incredible blessing of this woman.

"Congressman Montgomery. How providential that your schedule permitted you to attend the trial."

Will stiffened, then stepped back into the study, close enough to answer any questions the general might have, yet within sight of this Montgomery character. He had to see what sort of fool had passed over Sophia. And make sure the man didn't make an attempt to correct his mistake.

The congressman gave a smile oily enough to rust-proof every tool Will owned. "Sophia, you're looking more beautiful than ever."

Sophia narrowed her eyes. His false charm didn't impress. "It is rather warm this evening. Perhaps you might dispense with formalities as we do in the West."

Montgomery hung his coat and top hat on the hall tree, then tore his gaze away from Sophia to spare the house a glance, probably calculating its worth.

As he gawked, Sophia caught Will's eye and gave him her special smile. *Do not worry*, her expression said. *All my love is yours.* She led the congressman into the dining room, where a cold supper had been set out.

General Crook unrolled the building diagram. "What are you planning for heat?"

"Same as your house." Will pointed out the symbols. "Coal furnace with supplemental stoves."

"Lovely place you have here." The congressman's voice carried over the other guests', a useful tool for giving speeches and shouting down the opposition. "So how did you get involved in this Indian trial?"

"I taught at the Ponca Agency until the tribe was evicted."

"They moved to Indian Territory in '77, correct?"

"'Moved' is too gentle a word for what happened." Clever Sophia had Montgomery stuffing his cheeks so she could fill his ears without interruption. She told him about the nightmare the Poncas had endured the past two years.

"Your wife's good at speechifying," General Crook murmured.

"You should hear her when she really gets her dander up."

Montgomery scavenged the table. "I thought the purpose of the Indian Territory was to preserve them from extinction."

"Since arriving in Indian Territory, one-third of the Poncas have died and the rest are ill."

Nicholas dashed out of the kitchen, chased by Goldie and Buffalo Woman. The smell of food sidetracked the dog into the dining room, where Sophia dealt her a brisk "Sit." Will scooped up his son, who hugged his neck, then settled onto his shoulder. "It is all right. I will hold him," Will told Buffalo Woman in Ponca.

The general glanced up and smiled, then tapped the top corner of the diagram. "Indoor plumbing. You're spoiling my staff."

"Yes, sir." Will nodded. The general worked his officers hard but treated them well.

Sophia continued, "When the Poncas were evicted from their homeland, the Indian Office confiscated their belongings—farming tools, furniture, livestock, and stoves—and promised to send it all to them. No one has seen it since."

"What happened?" Montgomery mumbled around the food in his mouth. "Did the other tribes steal it?"

"The warehouse was empty by the time the Sioux arrived. Perhaps the inspector sold it, or the locals stole it. Either way, the Indian Office must compensate the tribe for this loss."

Will's gaze drifted out the back window where the children were playing ball. Little Susette hit one of Lafayette's pitches into the empty lot behind them. With Armin's help, Joseph and Frank rooted through the tangled prairie grass, looking for the ball. Standing Bear's grandson, Walk in the Wind, ran home, followed by Leo. From the swing under the brush arbor, which Sophia persisted in calling a pergola, Standing Bear's wife and Tilly cheered.

Montgomery muttered about the budget and then, politician that he was, changed the subject to a side issue. "So, this whole mess, the trial, came about because Standing Bear tried to return his son's body to the family cemetery. Was this Bear Shield a student of yours?"

Will held Nicholas close. Now that he was a father, he couldn't imagine how Standing Bear had survived the loss.

"Bear Shield had already learned English," Sophia said. "So no, he was not my student. I did share my library with him, though. An excellent mind. A devastating loss for Standing Bear and the future of the tribe."

Rosalie and Josie tiptoed down the stairs, pretending no one could see them, then scampered into the kitchen with a burst of giggles. Will hoped their next would be a girl.

Montgomery pushed away from the chow, and Sophia herded him into the parlor. "Let me introduce you to those involved."

In the presence of so many greats, one man dominated the parlor. Standing Bear sat in a tall chair opposite the door, his legs propped on a footstool. He wore citizens' clothes with a bear claw necklace.

"There's an Indian in your parlor!" the congressman gasped.

"We are honored to host several distinguished guests this evening," Sophia said. She tilted her head at an angle Will recognized. Montgomery scraped the edge off her patience.

When the chief saw them approach, he started to stand.

"Please rest yourself," Sophia said in Ponca and touched his moccasins. "You have walked far."

The congressman perched on the chair next to Standing Bear and reached down from his self-important pedestal to return the chief's handshake. Standing Bear repeated some of his testimony from the trial, and with great dignity entered a plea for the return of his land.

Susette LaFlesche, called Bright Eyes, a highly educated member of the Omaha tribe, interpreted for them. The young woman had seemed shy when Will first met her, her big round eyes taking it all in, her voice barely above a whisper. But being around Sophia brought out the crusader in her.

"I will give the matter my utmost attention," Montgomery promised.

A muscle twitched in the chief's jaw. It was evident that Montgomery had worn out his welcome.

Sophia saw it too. She guided the congressman to two men talking beside the piano.

"—the most important civil rights trial since the Dred Scott decision," expounded a man with a thick wave of dark hair to a young Indian man in a suit.

Sophia introduced the congressman to Thomas Henry Tibbles, the associate editor of the Omaha *Herald*.

"I read your articles in the New York paper. Good writing," Montgomery said. "Smart move enlisting the churches' support."

"God and the Declaration of Independence say all men are created equal. Let us work to make it so." Mr. Tibbles and Mr. Montgomery exchanged some serious hand pumping. Then Tom nodded at Sophia. "I couldn't have done it without Sophia and Will providing the context, the history of the tribe."

"All I did was tell the truth."

"Newspapermen need more than one source to verify a story. Your help was essential."

"You are too kind," she murmured. She introduced Montgomery to Francis LaFlesche, Susette's brother, who had interpreted for Standing Bear at the trial. The young man asked about job opportunities in Washington. The congressman beat around the bush so fast he made himself dizzy.

Next she introduced the lawyers, Andrew Poppleton and John Webster, and Judge Elmer Dundy. The men traded credentials like poker players laying out their hands. It turned out Poppleton had studied with a New York lawyer Montgomery knew.

"For all the hot air in here," the general muttered to Will, "your house is still remarkably comfortable."

Will grinned and took the opportunity to explain his system to optimize air circulation. *Optimize?* Being married to Sophia sure had expanded his vocabulary.

"How did you meet this young lady?" Montgomery asked the lawyers, pointing to Sophia.

"We go to church together at Trinity," Mr. Webster said.

Mr. Poppleton nodded. "My daughter was in Sophia's French class at the College. And Will built my house. Finer people you've never met."

Judge Dundy toasted Sophia with his cup of punch. "Sophia taught my daughter, May, at Brownell Hall. I'm a trustee there. So when Mr. Tibbles told us the army was holding the Poncas at Fort Omaha, we already had a handle on the situation—background information, you might say."

"I notice Dundy's not admitting he was out hunting when we needed him," the general noted.

"I'm surprised he's not dragging the bear out to show

everyone." Will nodded at the rug, which lay between the fireplace and Sophia's reading chair.

"That's the one?" General Crook studied the pelt. "Not bad."

Montgomery tipped his head like a king giving a favor. "I should meet this Will everyone raves about. Even the driver who brought me up from the hotel bragged about the house Will built for him."

The general murmured, "I'd better take your little fellow; leave your arms free to punch this windbag."

"And of course you must meet General Crook." Sophia led Montgomery into the study and made the introductions.

Nicholas managed to grab the points of the man's beard in each fist.

"General, I am so sorry." Sophia held out her hands. The baby smiled, let go, and reached for his mother. She turned him away from her to save her necklace from his eager grasp.

The general winced and patted his jaw as if trying to reattach his whiskers. "Powerful grip for a little fellow." Then he turned his piercing gaze on Montgomery. "You boys in Congress have sure put my army between a rock and a hard place. Washington always orders the opposite of what I recommend."

Montgomery squirmed. "The electorate has spoken—" The plans caught his eye. "You're building the general a house?"

"His is about done. These drawings are for officers' quarters at the fort."

"We have soldiers doing the work under Will's command. And a few of his Ponca friends, skilled carpenters, have made good use of their time at Fort Omaha." The general looked up, his open hand indicating their house. "As you can see, his work is unrivaled."

"You built this?" Montgomery gave the room a second look, noticing the Ponca design inlaid into the floor and around the fireplace. He gave a low whistle. The guy might be a fool when it came to women, but he seemed to recognize quality woodwork. He twirled his mustache. "Don't suppose you'd be interested in setting up shop in New York?"

Sophia shook her head. "Omaha is home."

The thought had preyed on Will's mind that marrying him had circumscribed Sophia's life, making her world smaller than she might have otherwise chosen. Tonight she put an end to that worry.

"Thanks," Will said, mostly to Sophia. Then he turned to Montgomery. "I've got enough here to keep me busy through the end of the century."

"And what a fine century it will be." Montgomery blinked at the baby who regarded him with solemn wariness. "Ah, another masterpiece."

Sophia kissed the fuzz on the baby's head. "Our son, Nicholas." *We are so blessed.*

The mantel clock chimed the hour. "I must go," the congressman declared to everyone's relief. "I'm on the night train to Chicago."

"Trying one of those new Pullman sleeping cars?" the general asked. "So comfortable, it hardly seems like travel."

Julia's wedding dress, displayed on the long wall beside the stairway, caught the congressman's eye. The gas chandelier brought out the colors in the beading. "A remarkable artifact. A bold choice in decoration."

If he thought it was amazing on the wall, Will thought, he ought to see it on Sophia. Not that Will would ever allow that to happen.

Sophia rolled her lips together, a sure sign her patience had reached its limit. The congressman had passed by tomahawks in the dining room, a war bonnet in the parlor, and a bear claw necklace in the study without noticing. When he leaned on the desk, he'd almost put his hand through Sophia's gusli; Will guessed she'd never played it for him.

She led Montgomery to the hall tree. "Thank you again for your interest in the Poncas' cause."

His interest was minimal at best, since Indians weren't allowed to vote, but Sophia had ways of twisting his arm. "You're welcome," he said with a grunt.

"You have not said how Annabelle and Zelinda are doing."

"The baby is fine." Montgomery's voice echoed off the tile of the vestibule. "You correspond with Annabelle. You know how she is. Not the legislator's wife you would have been, Sophia. You've accomplished so much: freeing the Poncas, teaching, making a home, starting a family."

He shook the baby's hand with a formality that had Will wondering how much time the man spent with his own child. "What crusade will you undertake next? Women's suffrage, the temperance movement, workers' rights?"

"All worthy causes. But the Poncas still need to receive title to their homeland. The Sioux do not want it. No one lives on it now." She put his coat and hat into his hands so he couldn't sneak in a hug. "The only barrier to restoration is the United States government."

Montgomery twitched, bracing for the onslaught of Sophia's persuasion. "I sense the emergence of another letter-writing campaign."

"As God directs."

Will came up behind Sophia, wrapped his arm around her, and rested his palm on her waist. "If she can work it into her schedule."

Realization dawned in Montgomery's eyes. "Congratulations. I wish you the best, both of you."

Sophia watched him go, then turned to Will. "I have a thought." She always did. "When my ambition was to become a woman of influence, I gained nothing. But when I let go of those aspirations and allowed God to lead me, I found fulfillment, and purpose, and"—she smiled at him—"love."

Will leaned down and she rose on tiptoes to meet him. Her willing body melted into his arms. Her lips met his in a perfect fit.

A little boy's hand swatted his cheek.

Ah, yes. They had a young man who needed to be put to bed. A house full of guests. Work to do. A calling to fulfill.

And love.

Always, always love.

READING GROUP GUIDE

1. Sophia signed up for a mission trip with mixed motives. Nettie assures her God can use her anyway. What is your experience with mission trips? What is the "right" motive? How has God used you?

2. What is your impression about missionaries and culture? In what ways does culture entangle the gospel?

3. At times, Sophia feels useless and is concerned her actions have brought disaster to the Ponca people. Have you ever felt that way about your work? What was behind that feeling?

4. On New Year's Day, James asks the staff to list their accomplishments of the previous year and goals for the next. How can we evaluate the effectiveness of a mission? Should we?

5. In the United States, more women than men earn college degrees. As with Sophia, today's woman may marry a man who has less formal education than she does. What challenges will this disparity bring to the relationship?

6. Will tells Sophia to "ignore the rushing waters." What rushing waters in your life must you ignore?

7. Five of the people involved in the trial of Standing Bear were connected to one church. What is the role of the church in government policies and social justice issues?

8. When Sophia sees a problem, she charges in, saying, "Don't worry, God! I'll fix this!" When Will sees a problem, unless it is his area of expertise, he waits to see what God will do. Who is right? Where are you on this spectrum?

AUTHOR'S NOTE

S tanding Bear's speeches are the only documentation of the removal by a member of the Ponca tribe. The lack of other eyewitness accounts is testimony to the depth of tragedy this eviction represents. In the struggle for survival, stories were one of their many losses. Undoubtedly I have made errors in recounting the Poncas' story; please accept my apology.

Government employees, on the other hand, left a substantial paper trail. Whenever possible their words were used in dialogue. I hope you find them offensive. There is no evidence that agent James Lawrence imbibed, only the question of how he coped.

The character of Sophia originated from the discovery that a Russian woman taught at a Ponca school. A woman with the same name, Eugenie Nicolas, taught French at Vassar. Was this the same person?

Will is a tribute to all those unnamed heroes in every ministry who make sure the lights turn on, the furnace heats, and the projector shows the next song. We never spare a thought for them until something breaks.

Through Rushing Water is a work of fiction. If you'd like to know more, I recommend *"I Am a Man": Standing Bear's Journey for Justice* by Joe Starita and *Unspeakable Sadness* by David Wishart.

ACKNOWLEDGMENTS

For research help, I'm grateful to Stanford Taylor of the Ponca Museum, Rebecca White, chairwoman of the Ponca Tribe of Nebraska, Deacon Ellen Ross of Trinity Church, Beverly Otis, president of the Trinity Historical Society, DeVon Coble of Brownell-Talbott School, and Larisa Treskunova, formerly of Russia. Nebraska Novelists went above and beyond for this story, especially Katherine Barnett on the Russian Orthodox Church, Angela Kroeger on coinage, and Jeanne Reames on Native American culture. Any errors are my own.

A standing ovation to Amanda Bostic and the Thomas Nelson team for their expertise and commitment to quality. It's an honor to work with you.

Heartfelt thanks to agent Sandra Bishop for her wise guidance through the publishing maze.

Many thanks to my family, especially Mom for visits to the Douglas County Historical Society and the Smithsonian Anthropological Archives, and George for chauffeuring me around the gorgeous homeland of the Ponca tribe.

And thank you to my readers—your encouragement means more than you'll ever know. I'd love to connect with you through my website, www.CatherineRichmond.com, or Facebook's Fans of Catherine Richmond page, or by mail at Thomas Nelson, P.O. Box 141000, Nashville, TN 37214, Attn: Author Mail. Blessings on your mission!

HUNDREDS OF MILES FROM HOME,
Susannah faces an uncertain future as a mail-order
bride on the untamed Dakota prairie.

THOMAS NELSON
Since 1798

AVAILABLE IN PRINT AND E-BOOK

9781595549259-A

About the Author

Catherine Richmond was focused on her career as an occupational therapist until a special song planted a story idea in her mind. That idea would ultimately become *Spring for Susannah*, her first novel. She is also a founder and moderator of Nebraska Novelists critique group and lives in Nebraska with her husband.